C · U · R · F · E · W

C·U·R·F·E·W

A novel by

 JOSÉ DONOSO

Translated from the Spanish by
ALFRED MACADAM

GROVE PRESS
NEW YORK

Grove Press

841 Broadway

New York, NY 10003

Published simultaneously in Canada

Originally published in Spain by Seix Barral, S.A.,
Barcelona, under the title La Desesperanza.

Library of Congress Cataloging-in-Publication Data

Donoso, José, 1924–
    [Desesperanza. English]
    Curfew: a novel / by José Donoso; translated from the Spanish by
Alfred MacAdam.
    Translation of: La desesperanza.
    I. Title.
PQ8097.D617D4713
863

ISBN 0-8021-3381-9 (pbk.)

Manufactured in the United States of America
Designed by Ronnie Ann Herman
First American paperback edition
10 9 8 7 6 5 4 3 2 1

FOR MY DAUGHTER PILAR

CONTENTS

·I·
EVENING

✦ *M* añungo Vera wondered if Pablo
Neruda had decided to live on the southern slope of San Cristóbal
hill so he could hear the roars of Carlitos, the only lion in the Santiago
zoo. It would be just like Neruda, Mañungo thought; just the kind of
reason he'd give for picking one house over another. It was probably
his way of satisfying some long-forgotten childhood desire, the same
sort of whim that imbued his everyday life with poetry. On the way
to the poet's house, Mañungo couldn't stop thinking about all this,
about Carlitos, and Matilde, unconsciously comparing his grief with
the pleasure of the evenings he'd spent in Paris, when Neruda would
arbitrate between his French translator and don Celedonio Villanueva
as they debated the fine points of the Pléiade edition of Neruda's
works.

Splayed out at the poet's feet, in his study at the Chilean embassy,
was a huge plush lion, useless and luxurious, bought in a Paris toy
store. The apocryphal beast meekly accepted the comb Matilde used
to tease his mane, of the same coppery color as her own. The toy
probably reminded Neruda of his mournful neighbor caged up on
the side of the hill they both called home: his compatriot Carlitos,
born in a broken-down circus in Iquique, son of a sickly Bolivian lion,
itself born in captivity many miles and generations away from its jungle
ancestors. People said comrade Carlitos had barely a tooth in his head,
that he had bad breath, that he suffered from melancholy, and that
his chronic indispositions made him incapable of scaring even the
children, who, their mouths filled with cotton candy, would make fun
of him because he only roared at night or when he was afraid—in
sum, a cowardly old lion. But he was *our* lion, and the nation didn't
have the money to buy another. Pablo and Matilde must have been

awakened more than once out of their nocturnal embraces by those lamentations.

Inside the taxi, Mañungo could hear Carlitos's frayed vocal cords, a cry more appropriate for a stuffed animal than for a real man-eater. The farther the taxi went into the Bellavista neighborhood, the more the roars confirmed the fact that they were drawing close to Pablo and Matilde's house. The neighborhood, in which so many boutiques and little restaurants had recently sprouted, was suffering a corresponding growth in traffic, accompanied by broken stoplights and one-way streets that abruptly switched direction. The confused driver couldn't find the way to Neruda's house.

"Let's ask someone," Mañungo proposed.

The driver was just about to stop beside a legless beggar wearing a hat pulled down over one eye when Mañungo caught sight of an obviously better-informed teenage girl in a miniskirt, sucking a poisonously purple popsicle; he recalled that in Chiloé the purple popsicles were imitation vanilla. Leaning out of the window, he shouted to the girl, "How do we get to Pablo Ne—"

Before he could finish the question, she pointed her purple popsicle toward the hill. "Second right, then take the first turnoff," she said, and immediately went back to sucking her treat.

"Thanks."

Mañungo concluded that she'd replied so promptly because everyone who drove by this afternoon must have asked her how to get to Pablo Neruda's house. The streets were clogged with cars; she was no doubt having fun giving directions to all these outsiders. Besides, Mañungo thought, she'd recognized him. In Paris, until two or three years ago (here it would probably still happen), he was frequently recognized in the street, especially by teenagers and university students. His dialogue with the girl was, of course, too short for her to have identified him—although by his beard and long hair (which, alas, had begun to recede) it was easy to classify him as a vaguely artistic last gasp of a post-hippyism he knew was becoming extinct in Europe. Here the disdainful bourgeois would identify him as a "bohemian" and type him as an inoffensive dealer in handicrafts, an expert in zen or exotic religions, an eater of macrobiotic food, a sexually eclectic marijuana addict. The younger people—and the older ones—did not understand this code of nonconformism, being sensitive only to his affected style of dress as a form of protest. For that very reason, many people in Mañungo Vera's generation went on waving that angry banner. Mañungo wore this uniform not only to be faithful to his own history but also because of his public image: his agent made him dress this way, despite the fact that at the age of thirty-four he thought himself too old for a style he would gladly have toned down.

The girl whom he'd asked for directions had surely identified him as a "type" from his outfit even before she recognized him personally. But as the driver began to follow her instructions, Mañungo couldn't resist the temptation to look back at her through the window. No, he didn't look at her; what he really did was to show her his face so that at least one person would recognize him here in Chile after his thirteen-year absence.

The teenager stood there staring at him. When she took a second look at his mop of unruly hair, his black beard, his diminutive glasses, his front teeth peeking out of his ever so slightly rabbitlike smile—all of this framed in the rear window as if in a poster—how could she not recognize the idol, after all his cassettes, his LPs, his festival appearances, and the juicy stories about him in fan magazines? Her face lit up with disbelief, and she waved enthusiastically to him from the corner, regretting that she hadn't taken advantage of the opportunity to ask him for his autograph. When she was out of sight, he turned around in his seat and heard Carlitos emit a growl of recognition to announce that Mañungo Vera had returned from Paris to attend the wake of Matilde Neruda, which was being held in the house where, in another era, he'd been invited not only to sing but to visit as a friend.

This was by no means the ideal program for his first day back. Of course, he was returning to his country blindly, for no good reason, just when everyday life was being stifled by a brand-new state of siege. But he'd read the announcement of Matilde's death on the way to the Holiday Inn after stepping off the six-o'clock Air France flight. He'd deposited his son at the hotel with their bags, and, despite the boy's whining, continued on in the same cab. Going directly to Neruda's house was the only proper route he could take: the route of gratitude, admiration, and memory. If he hadn't received this painful news on his arrival, news that committed him to an itinerary for the immediate present, what would he have done? Whom would he have seen? Where would he have gone? He imagined himself opening his luggage alone, as he had so many times in the hotels his tours had taken him to, while Jean-Paul turned on the television. Later he would leaf through the newspapers on the chance his eyes would stumble over some familiar name. Finally, he would give in and call his agent, the most depressing alternative he could imagine.

After thirteen years abroad, he had no friends left here. Chileans were terrible letter writers, he the worst of all. But he might have wandered out with Juan Pablo for a walk along Avenida Providencia and managed to recognize someone. . . . His father was down south in Chiloé on the farm. Suppose he called him, demanded he leave Curaco de Vélez, and dragged him to Santiago, promising in return that he and Jean-Paul would come to the island and spend a season with him so he could get to know his French grandson. He could go even further, though the old man wouldn't really understand, and pour his heart out to him straightaway—after all, isn't that what fathers are for? He could show his father all the tangled feelings that had brought him back, so that when they finally embraced, Mañungo could give some kind of shape to his own perplexity.

In point of fact, things would have been much easier if he had told his agent to set up a safety net of press conferences and receptions, ritual protection against this descent into loneliness. But the need to say goodbye to someone who only this morning had become a mere uninhabited body defined for now the cardinal points of his feelings.

A respectful friendship of many years' duration had united him with the Nerudas, his protectors—hadn't they discovered him?—early on in Chile, and later his sponsors in Paris when the poet was ambassador. Mañungo had set several of Neruda's poems to music and sung them. The LP *Songbook for Guerrilla Poets*, a million-copy-seller in France, was in its time the greatest success ever achieved by a Latin American singer in Europe. He'd heard rumors lately that a certain disease was killing Matilde, but he'd preferred to ignore them. Returning by chance on the day of her death and attending her funeral, which the papers had announced for the next day, lent purpose to his trip.

The closer he got to the house on the side of the hill, the more clearly he could hear the roars of the toy lion. Or did he hear it purring in satisfaction, spread out on the rug while Matilde, using the green comb she'd bought just for that purpose, teased its mane until it was as wild as her own? He guessed that, like him, Matilde had only a cursory interest in the discussion between the translator and don Celedonio. With his cigar, his gold-headed cane, and his elegant decades in Paris, don Celedonio was Neruda's preferred companion—not only for visits to secondhand book shops, but to stir up memories of a sparkling Paris gone by, where the two of them had lived alongside Juan Gris, Vicente Huidobro, and Juan Emar. Dazzling chitchat for Mañungo, who had so much to learn, above all the lesson that nostalgia did not have to be melancholy; it could be joyous if, as in the case of these two accomplices, you had lived the past so completely that nothing was left out to regret. Such and such a café no longer existed; dozens of dead cronies could be discussed without euphemisms. Don Celedonio, it was true, suffered the ailments common to someone his age, and Pablo had a gray tinge about him that it was best not to mention. He was often seen visiting certain clinics before breakfast. Neither Matilde's laughter, the generosity of her table, don Celedonio's surrealist jokes, nor the hopes they all held for the policies of the Popular Unity Party or Cuba seemed to presage dangers beyond those typical of our tortured age. For Mañungo, Matilde had been the present made eternal in a song about love and the things of this world: now he was going to face an object that had been that woman, whom many had considered harsh (Mañungo not among them, for he too knew the rigors of peasant life), and who had been able to erect a wall of reserve around the clashing elements that constituted the poet's greatness.

2

*T*he moment had come for Mañungo Vera to turn into something else. But how? He couldn't use the ancient art of witchcraft to become the nocturnal owl that flaps its ominous wings around the shingled belfry, or the serpent that bites the heel of someone fleeing muffled shouts at nightfall, so he'd have to change the circumstances that had made him feel like a stranger to himself. His shape would change, the way the lazy flow of fog changes an island into a mountain, a lake into a sea, a river, or a ship, or turns a rowboat into a cow or a jeep, a fog that finally coagulates in black rain and erases towns and villages for weeks at a time.

Traveling is easy—who knew that better than Mañungo, habitual occupant of first-class seats in jumbo jets that carried him from Rome to Tokyo, from Los Angeles to Amsterdam?—but it alters nothing: four triumphant nights at a Hilton, a Sheraton, or a Holiday Inn are identical to four nights at any other Hilton, Sheraton, or Holiday Inn, no matter where they are. Traveling to be seen and heard means that you neither see nor hear.

The trip he was planning now had been taking shape in his mind for a long time. It was a corollary of his own blurred history, lost in the same fog that drove the magic ship off course, a supplement that would involve painful changes he hoped he could face. All this talk about wanting to be someone else was masochism, pure and simple, Nadja had observed, without understanding that for many Latin Americans today a season in that particular hell is necessary if the sought-for change is to be more than a formal exercise in escapism. But escape from what, after all, since all these years had been a horn of plenty for him, with possibly more to come? It would be easy to let himself be convinced by his agent in Paris, who assured him that it was not too late for him to be a star again, that everything could go back to being just as it was in his best years.

The agent shouldn't have become so hysterical about the trip, because this particular problem was located in regions to which the poor pomaded fop had no access. Mañungo still felt capable of reaching the same heights as when he'd first stepped out onstage to face a huge audience willing to believe anything he said, galvanized by his adrenaline, ignited into a blaze of total certainty, of transcendent love—love that did not exclude masochism. The guerrilla singer was possessed by the potency of his guitar-phallus-machine gun, firing with the strings of his instrument right into the audience, *bang! bang! bang!* After the ovations, girls from Berlin or Paris would drop into his bed like clay pigeons. Using his voice and his gestures, he could still improvise the perfect mask for expressing total potency, even though he found himself changing more and more into that "other" who, despite everything, was himself, recognizable, tactile, dark, with the searing temperature of his slim, febrile body caged up within his sweaty ribs, with the precise rhythm of his vocal cords punctuated by his guitar-phallus-machine gun.

Yes, he was still capable of giving the audience all that. But not the other thing, not what he gave them back then, when he didn't have to fool anyone: then he *was* what he sang, and he would let the students touch his clothes and his beard with all the easy freedom of a young idol of art and revolution. Where was the certainty he had had then, where was the conviction that gave heat to his singing, and that somehow had ended up in smoke? Hadn't it turned into a deception for himself and the audience? Did he have the right, at this stage in his life, to strip off the costume of his notorious cliché, to find out if there was anything left of himself that hadn't been consumed by the mask? Sing now? Sing what? Say what? Suppose the words, the music, and the rhythm of his long agile legs and liquid pelvis meant nothing anymore? Sure, he was a singer and would be all his life, even if he never sang another note. But he was no actor, and that was what his agent wanted him to be, and that's why he wouldn't let Mañungo abandon the stage and demanded he keep his marketable cliché in good working order.

That was the reason for this transformation, which would be different from those that took place onstage precisely because it wouldn't involve acting, but being. What he had really been at one time, he could only pretend to be now. He felt his triumph fading, but he felt no regret, because his conviction had disappeared long before, and that fact left him without the energy necessary to survive. Now—his agent didn't realize it—he wasn't trying to conquer anyone or anything. He was trying to *be*. But be what? An island, a cloud, a mountain, a figure who hides his misty identity by bending over the smoke rising from damp oak logs? To be someone else, to be something else, someone unknown at thirty-four years of age, to decipher that shape dissolved in smoke, to listen to voices more uncertain than his music and his revolution. He yearned to hear the voice of the old woman right there in his apartment on Rue Servandoni, beyond the persistent ringing in his left ear which doctors had diagnosed as tinnitus. If he really concentrated, he thought he could hear the waves breaking on the desolate west coast of the big island. That wheeze, welling up from the sea as if from the throat of a dying old woman, was interpreted by the Chiloé baymen of the other fragmented, protected coast as a sign that change was on the way.

The illusion of change in his country had dissolved, even if his cronies in their seedy exile cafés denied it. It was there he'd become silent when he realized that despair, unfortunately, has no music. Sing what? Did his father in Curaco de Vélez still work his shrunken farm, or had that soil also grown barren with the years, so that now all that could be heard was a whistle in his chest like the old woman's voice, like the voice of the poor plush lion in his final incarnation, that of today, that of defeat, that of death, twelve years after the embassy in Paris, a moth-eaten, forgotten fleabag? Did that lion still exist? Where would they throw what was left of it after Matilde's funeral tomorrow, assuming it was still around the house? Yes, change. A change of scene. A change of time. But mightn't this attempt to clamber aboard the foundering ship of art—this time going in the opposite direction, moving into a world which was nothing more than pure allegory—destroy him?

And Juan Pablo? What would happen to Jean-Paul? Now, during this boring afternoon, weeks after Nadja had come to drop him off—she couldn't tell him for how long, she said; in any case for a long time, perhaps forever. She couldn't tell him where she was going because some terrorist action was involved, and she preferred—for his own good, she said—not to name names. She was sorry this would interfere with his concert schedule, but now it was his turn to take charge of Jean-Paul for the simple reason that it was her turn to live. He'd shouted to his son that if he didn't want a swat in the ass he'd better turn off that damned tape of "Au clair de la lune mon ami Pierrot" he'd been listening to for the millionth time, cloyingly sung by an obviously depraved adult imitating the voice of a child. His irritation cooled after this outburst, and once he'd opened the window onto the Parisian winter, which after all was not so very different from winter in Achao. His voice calmed, and he called his son over to see if he could show him how the two worlds met.

Crouching down behind his son, he hugged him. How small he was! With his bearded face next to the boy's face, fixed in the window through which the western rain poured, he said:

"Écoute."

"Quoi?"

"Tu n'entends rien?"

Juan Pablo made an effort to hear what his father wanted him to hear.

"L'autobus dans la rue d'à côté?" he asked.

"Non. Quelque chose d'autre."

"La musique du café au coin?"

"Non. Quelque chose de plus lointain encore."

After a second, the boy asserted:

"Non. Je n'entends rien."

Having realized not only that he'd been forgiven but that he'd actually won, the boy slipped out of his father's embrace and turned "Au clair de la lune" on again. His mother had told Jean-Paul not to be afraid if his father heard strange sounds. It was an inoffensive illness—although while she was combing her son's hair to bring him over to Rue Servandoni she feared it might be contagious—which mostly afflicted the bourgeoisie and was called neurosis: he should learn that word, because when we know the names of things we don't mix them up, in fact we disarm them. Artists, whose twisted profession was to change the names of things, were neurotics precisely for that reason. Mañungo, his father, was a great artist—she refrained from adding that for her and for people who knew what they were talking about, Mañungo *had been* a great artist, but that because of the softening of his politics he was no longer great—and she told him not to worry if his daddy got to be a bit of a bore.

It was not the ringing in his ear that Mañungo tried to share with Juan Pablo, standing at his window open to the Parisian rain. He closed the window and drew the wool curtains, which even after so many years and at so many miles distance gave off a smell of sheep, grass, Chiloé, his father's wet poncho. In another period of his life, when he was building his career, thinking it permanently ascending, he had had those curtains made in Chile by Nelly Alarcón, when she transformed the Chiloé folk style into a fashion both ubiquitous and exportable. The best fabric, made from the finest wool—that's what he asked for, the best the island could produce. Jean-Paul was incapable of noticing that smell, just as he could not hear the prophecies of the southern Pacific, the zone where the glaciers began and where many races and species were becoming extinct. Did Jean-Paul belong to that endangered race that was unable to hear the voice of the old woman?

Mañungo recognized that his attempt to change might be fatal. It would be like throwing himself into the Rhine, which is what Schumann did when his auditory ghosts drove him insane. Nadja told him all about Schumann when they first spoke about tinnitus on the docks of a frost-covered Hanseatic city after a concert. Or was it just before one of Nadja's harp recitals? Years before, when he'd just arrived from Chile, they were strolling arm in arm one Sunday on Butte de Montmartre among the tourists. He'd made her stand still among the throng and close her eyes while he closed his. Nadja agreed that yes, she too heard what he called the voice of the old woman, and it was like a shout of hope, reassuring them from the other hemisphere that in his poor country the change for which everyone on this side was fighting would soon take place.

That was before his tinnitus began. What he had to do was flee, hide away from all pollution—auditory, human, and political—so he wouldn't go mad with the unbearable screeching in his ear.

Nadja was against running away. When she walked out on Mañungo, after having lived with him on and off for several years, she made a classic scene and insulted him in the cruelest way she could imagine—saying that it was self-evident, not even worth discussing, that no one could hear the waves of the Pacific Ocean breaking like avalanches in the center of Paris. She had lied to him when she was seducing him, yes, that's right, during that stroll in Montmartre, just as she had let him make her pregnant—what a waste of time it was to tell him how sorry she was for that!—so that he would be bound to her, because from the beginning she'd guessed he was governed by primitive instincts like paternity. She had been young and foolish, naive, prepolitical, irresponsible. She had reacted romantically to the situation in Chile and longed to bask in the first blaze of Mañungo's glory among Parisian university students. . . .

The arrogance of 1968 was still alive then, the masses were still galvanized, praise rained down on Mañungo—of course all that had dazzled her, seduced her. Being "in love" was an idea Nadja utterly rejected, comparing it with disorder, classifying it among the neuroses, along with tinnitus. Why, Mañungo wondered, did Nadja have to reject everything? Why reject something that was the truth simply because it wasn't true any longer? He didn't have to deny anything to stop loving Nadja. He hadn't loved her for very long to begin with! But he accepted what once was, and in a rush of nostalgia he relived the abundance of her heavy black hair, so Russian, so thick and heavy and silky. When he'd see her fall asleep next to him after making love, he'd catch a few strands between his thumb and forefinger as if they were pinches of salt, and he would lazily play at counting the hairs in each pinch. How could Nadja refuse to keep memories like that when she had once shown him how aware she was of his entire being by drawing an exact copy of his fingerprints from memory? And how was Juan Pablo going to hear what Mañungo wanted him to hear, standing at the open window above the Luxembourg Gardens? How would he know it was also the Pacific Ocean? They'd studied that remote, broken coastline, but when he'd asked the boy about it, Jean-Paul had confused it once with Alaska and another time with Norway. No, he had no right to demand that the boy hear the same things he'd heard when he was seven years old, in a house with a silvery shingled roof, shining with rain like the scales of a freshly netted mackerel; a human house that creaked and complained and suffered just like a person; animated by old stories, transformed by the semi-darkness into presences that remained just beyond one's individual memory, in the not absolutely mysterious space called the collective memory.

He had no right to demand that the boy hear the voice of the old woman when the gales blew in on the coast of Polynesian Cucao that held its back up against the Pacific. Don Manuel used to hug him next to the kitchen, which seemed to have kept the warmth of his long-dead mother, and then he could hear the voice of the old woman, a wheeze, like the one he'd just heard on Rue Servandoni, harbinger of change. No: Juan Pablo was something else. Alien. It was hard to accept this difference, above all because Mañungo recognized precious little of himself in the boy. At first he'd tried to win him over by singing him songs, but he chose love songs, and love did not seem to touch Juan Pablo. Nadja, through either her discipline or her genes, had placed him beyond the reach of that word. Besides, the songs were in Spanish. And the boy, as if trained by his mother, rejected anything associated with his father—Nadja wasn't evil, only intolerant, ingenuously intolerant of irrational things. If she prejudiced the boy against him, he couldn't accuse her of having done it for revenge, but rather because her ideas were always so definitive, even if they often changed. Jean-Paul bridled at anything that wasn't French. It wasn't strange, then, that his father's most beautiful songs put him out of sorts: he preferred the idiocy of "Au clair de la lune mon ami Pierrot."

He saw the boy next to the stupendous professional sound equipment, the only thing belonging to his father with which he'd been able to feel any kind of connection since coming to Rue Servandoni. That was probably because none of the fathers of his friends in the working-class neighborhood where Nadja lived with Jean-Paul and her new lover had anything like it. Proud of the possession and indifferent to the music: owning things was not a vice Nadja encouraged, but something the poor child had breathed in with the corrupt air of our times.

"*Arrête immédiatement cette musique infernale!*"

"*Pourquoi?*"

"*Parce que je ne veux plus écouter des sottises.*"

"*Je peux mettre les écouteurs.*"

"*Je ne veux pas. Tu vas les abîmer.*"

"*Pourquoi?*"

For no good reason, of course. Because of his malfunctioning inner ear. Because of the stress problem. Because of neurosis. What would he have to go through to make his son understand? In any case, was it necessary that the boy understand everything, the way Nadja—and he in this instant—demanded? Had he, as a boy, understood why strange people arrived at the dock from the Guaitecas Islands, from the Chonos Islands, from all over that fractured geography, purveying unrecognizable fish, skins, and kelp? People whose relationship with the rain, fog, and cold was different from his? The dazzling vice of explanation came later, acquired thanks to Ulda at school and at the university, where everything was reduced to a dialectic redolent of Marxism; and more and more in Europe, where the enslaving mania of explanation demanded that the world be taken apart and put back together again according to different models. Now he proposed to change because no explanation could justify the world that had scarred his inner ear: tinnitus, stress, whatever it was. He just had to transport it all to a faraway place so he could rediscover how to hear shadows brush each other in that huge silence; a place where he could lie down like a dog and lick the wound inflicted on him by having meant something, having understood, and now not meaning or understanding anything.

At times Mañungo was plagued by the anxiety of once again analyzing everything with Nadja. He reviewed recent events. Seven weeks ago, Nadja had disappeared. When she dropped off Juan Pablo she told Mañungo that this was goodbye. She brought all the boy's possessions, even his identification papers, to which Mañungo had paid little attention, putting them into some drawer or other. Now that this trip had become so urgent, he'd have to dig them out. Juan Pablo was not going to be happy with the idea of the trip: he didn't really like going out, even to the Luxembourg Gardens and the *grands magasins*, which every kid seemed to like. He'd rather stay glued to the television set, even when the Parisian springtime announced its glory in the flowers at the traffic circles and the brand-new colors worn by the crowds marching out of the boutiques.

But of course, it was not a question of having Juan Pablo, at his age, "choose"—that terrifying word, revered by Nadja, who, even if she denied it, had never recovered from Sartre. She had made him choose so many times that the poor kid viewed any situation that presented more than one option with horror-stricken eyes. Seeing Jean-Paul protected by the earphones, watching him manipulate the sound system that took up half the wall with its turntables, amplifiers, red, green, and amber lights, made Mañungo wish that Juan Pablo were able to see things as interesting possibilities instead of tyrannical orders from a father sick from indecision. This father who shouts and sets out on trips, and moves him around like an object, just to cover up his weakness by exercising an authority only meant to frighten him.

Despite the distance between him and Jean-Paul, Mañungo felt he had to talk to his son and tell him why he was uneasy. But he was so young: state of siege, censorship, injustice, misery—all that meant nothing to him, and perhaps nothing to Mañungo himself, now. Fine—in order to convince Jean-Paul that the trip was necessary he at least ought to try to charm him with the colorful words he knew he could deploy. Had he ever told him the story about the pious old woman and her parrot?

"*Non.*"

"*C'est très amusant. Écoute.*"

Once upon a time in Chiloé, in a village called Chonchi, there was a pious old woman who lived by herself with a very intelligent parrot she'd taught to say the rosary. She would recite the first part of the Hail Mary, and the parrot would give the response, and that's how they spent their afternoons. One day the parrot flew out the window, and the poor lady almost died of loneliness because she had no one to pray with. But the next year, an enormous flock of parrots darkened the sky over the village. In trees and in the air, they were all repeating the responses of the Hail Mary. As soon as the people of Chonchi heard them, they rushed out into the streets crossing themselves and genuflecting because they thought it was the end of the world. Miracle, miracle! they all shouted.

Mañungo expected his son to smile.

"*Elle était méchante, cette femme,*" commented Jean-Paul.

"*Pourquoi?*"

"*Ça serait stupide que les oiseaux prient.*"

"*Mais c'est une histoire amusante. Tu ne trouves pas?*"

"*Je ne crois pas que ce soit vrai.*"

"*Mais ça ne fait rien. . . .*"

"*Ah, non, si ce n'est pas vrai, c'est une bêtise.*"

How would all this seduce his son, when he wasn't even sure it would seduce him—above and beyond, of course, the intriguing possibility offered by a land that had the obligation of taking him in? How could he demand that the boy be decisive, when even he wasn't sure where his acoustic nightmares could take him, when even they might be nothing more than the sinister musical scales of his own doubts? When he closed the window, the tinnitus turned into a hurricane powerful enough to swallow up the golden-masted ship of art in which he hoped to launch his perplexities toward a safe shore. The noise was so overpowering it blocked out everything but his impulse to throw himself into the river like poor Schumann. The only sure way to eliminate his demons was to eliminate himself, to drown in the slow green waters of the Cipresales River that mirrored the vertigo of the air tangled with the vines of madness; waters in which the tops of the oaks and elms sank, and out of whose lazy current emerged trunks of tortured pewter, bearded with moss and covered with a cancer of lichens and fungus.

*I*n the opinion of those who usually offer their opinion, it isn't a style. Mere snobbery, claim the young people who wear clothes with fancy labels and drink draft beer in the pubs along Providencia. The usual failures and perpetually dissatisfied burnt-out cases confirm it, accusing the growing narcissism of Santiago's Bellavista quarter of being artificial, decadent, an imitation of San Telmo, Soho, Saint-Germain-des-Prés, reduced to Chile's lilliputian scale; a den for long-haired, armchair Leninists and marijuana smokers; an ugly neighborhood devoid of personality. According to some it was the invention of nostalgic aesthetes who were now trying by sheer force of will to turn all this into boutiques, art galleries, cafés, phony antique shops, handcraft stores, and pocket-sized theaters: the same old story, gentrification for tourists who, God willing, will never see it.

Until quite recently, Bellavista looked like a quiet peasant village forgotten in the middle of Santiago, separated from the city by Forestal Park and the Mapocho River, cut off five blocks to the north by the hill with its ancient, rusty funicular railway. A curtained window facing the street, a door, two windows, another door, an alley, an occasional two-story house with a wooden balcony, a railing, or a widow's walk, tile roofs, painted columns, a palm tree standing erect behind a tenement, not particularly venerable trees lining the sidewalks, a domestic neighborhood of corner stores where cats nap on stacks of newspaper used to wrap candy or bread, a neighborhood that up until a short time ago offered no spectacle more exciting than the funeral processions that cross it from the east heading for the cemeteries behind San Cristóbal hill. Five years ago, Bellavista seemed immersed in the anachronistic anorexia of oblivion. The government, at that time, favored a different style, opulent and new, and Santiago was decorated with crystallized structures commanding panoramic views, to house a thousand blond families, a thousand hypothetical stores, a thousand dentists, a thousand masseurs, a thousand unisex barbers, and when that megalomaniac dream suddenly dissolved, the buildings were abandoned on their never-completed avenues, dinosaurs from another paleontological period, discarded from a sinister papier-mâché operetta.

Reacting, in part, to that failure, a certain number of young people who had gone back to wearing long hair and beards began to take serious notice of the pleasant neighborhood of Bellavista: it was cheap, it was downtown, it was old without being oppressively ancient or museumlike. The houses, with their human dimensions, announced the survival of simple pleasures, of life without tension. In the afternoon, one neighborhood lady or another would drag her wicker chair out to the front door and sit waving to lifelong friends, and in the glow of the streetlights girls would play hopscotch in the street.

Some houses were discreetly restored. Stores appeared with modest pretensions about being "different." Young people walked the streets with musical scores and manuscripts under their arms, and long-skirted girls with hennaed hair attended happenings or trysts in tenements that aspired to be the Chilean Bateau-Lavoir, or dined at restaurants a bit more chic and a bit more expensive than their earlier avatars, or were measured for vests in weavers' shops.

Don Celedonio Villanueva, an erstwhile denizen of Montparnasse, used to visit the surrealist painter Camilo Mori and his wife, Maruja, in their studio when Mori was setting it up forty years ago, in the ornate little plaza that resembled a Disneyland interpretation of one of King Ludwig's castles. He declared he'd known for a long time this would be Bellavista's destiny. But don Celedonio always "knew" things beforehand. It was impossible to surprise him with predictions, or news of a political or social nature, or even with the title of a book he'd not read. The neighborhood's destiny seemed complete to him when Pablo Neruda moved into the most secluded house on a tortuously discreet cul-de-sac.

Neruda was a great inventor of geography: Isla Negra, which many suspected would never have existed without him; a Valparaíso that was completely his, which he superimposed onto the real city, erasing all other possible Valparaísos; a Temuco where it rained as it had never rained in Temuco; the violet sunsets of Maruri Street; the yellow mimosas of the Loncoche fields—and you ended up making the boring trip to Loncoche, where of course there were no more mimosas, so *ça ne valait pas vraiment le coup*, thundered don Celedonio. Even this America to which Neruda's marvelous poetry has condemned us is more Nerudian than real—which, by the way, was what made it interesting.

People were destined sooner or later to follow Neruda to Bellavista—an ugly neighborhood, according to don Celedonio. More of Pablo's tricks! He had a talent for picking an object out of a junkman's shop—a flask in the tone of blue which, it turned out, could only be of the period Charles X, a *pétanque* ball which had been curiously deformed by use—and infusing these worthless objects with the lyricism or irony that gave them the uniquely personal stamp of his imagination.

His house in Bellavista was pure fantasy. Constructed on the last possible building site on the steep mountain, uncomfortable, miscellaneous in design, it was a secret at the back of a cul-de-sac, the house Neruda had created for Matilde while she was still his mistress. It was the kind of house where a woman in such a situation allows only the most discreet visits, in order that older loyalties not be offended. Thus came into being La Chascona, the wild woman, which was also Neruda's nickname for Matilde because of her tangled mop of hair. The house radiated her presence in the neighborhood and was the setting both for the poems of Neruda's later years and his great political acts—Neruda the symbol, Neruda the ambassador, Neruda the Nobel laureate—the house, in short, of his glory.

To many, Matilde seemed much too simple and abrupt. But no one found fault with her qualities as astute peacekeeper in the house, with all its culinary and social complexities. In those years, all the big names passed through La Chascona, always a gregarious and festive place. Matilde herself was then a young, desirable woman of peasant background, as juicy as a ripe apricot. She took long, wine-soaked siestas with the poet, and was evidently related to the inspiration Neruda derived from the flesh.

The house is insignificant from the outside, in keeping with the other houses on the dead end. When you open the door, a narrow stone staircase springs up in front of you, and it is as if all the magnificence of the mountain unfolds from the first step, as if that step were a magic entrance for the chosen few. Going up, you reach the patio where the bar and dining room are located, and then, climbing a staircase made of cedar logs, reminiscent of Capri, you reach the living room and the bedroom. Crossing the terraced garden, which

has a view over the tile roofs and belltowers of Bellavista, you enter
Pablo's study, where he wrote his last poems.

The patio, usually cool because it is as dark as a box covered with
rock and ivy, is not a place where people congregate. Nevertheless,
on the day of Matilde's death, as the light faded and the mountain
breeze fluttered the leaves, friends stood on the patio, the log staircase,
and the garden paths, weaving anecdotes about the deceased into their
conversation. But what more was there to say? Matilde had been dying,
stubbornly and proudly alone, for so long! What can be said about
her, except to repeat that her death signaled the end of a world?

When the boys wearing red T-shirts let in don Celedonio, envied
and feared because he knew secrets about Neruda which would never
be revealed unless he chose to do so, a silence fell over the company
as his diminutive figure, wrapped in an old-fashioned, beautifully cut
flannel suit, passed by. An incongruous note: he wore folk-style sandals
and wool socks, even though it was the middle of summer. He returned
greetings courteously, although he really couldn't see more than the
shadow of the people closest to him. He mumbled his thanks to those
who took him by the arm to help him up a stair, or to avoid a bench
whose location he'd known since before his would-be helpers were
born. His voice was nothing more than a reflection of so many things
now withered, of the solemnity of this place which was anything but
solemn. Even though he was not family, Matilde's ever-so-discreet
relatives (realizing they were closer by blood but infinitely distant in
life), like everyone else, acknowledged him as principal mourner.

The frayed edges of his awareness enabled him to surmise what
some of these barely identifiable silhouettes were probably saying:
Fausta Manquileo, her makeup smeared by fatigue, standing under
the ylang-ylang, and that other person, recently returned from exile,
whose name escaped him. So many people of sketchy identity who'd
come to pay their respects! Meanwhile, the grim boys in red T-shirts
were doubtless trying to figure out, every time he appeared, the basis
for the friendship between this leftover aristocrat and poet of cos-
mopolitan pretensions and the man who, for them, could be nothing
other than the symbol of revolution and the voice of the people.

When he reached the living room he knew only too well—the room
he loved, argued over, criticized, admired, enjoyed, the room alive
with stories that animated every single object and piece of furniture
in it—when he reached that living room he saw the intrusive coffin
surrounded by four huge candles ("Real ones," Fausta insisted, "not

electric. With the smell of bees and smoke, just as Pablo would have wanted it"), the old man had the sensation of entering a room different from the one he knew, a room reduced to its material reality, which was barely a shadow of all it suggested.

On the wall, as always (and now perversely hanging at the head of the bier), blazed the portrait of Matilde with two heads, as Diego Rivera had painted her years ago. That portrait, once a joke, now lacked any power to evoke the real Matilde. It had always been a bad Rivera, even if you happened to like Rivera. Today it was just plain ugly.

Everything was ugly in this dead house, because the pair of magicians, whose presence had managed to transubstantiate what was ordinary into poetry, had disappeared. All that remained was a series of inert objects, and among them the inert object that Matilde was now. The room reflected nothing more than the dubious taste Pablo had picked up in Mexico during the thirties—the world of María Asúnsolo and Frida Khalo—the hideous, crude Totonaca style contaminated by the no less hideous style of the Spanish Civil War exiles fused with sentimental memories of Capri. This house, once marvelously complex, was today easy to analyze. It revealed its more modest truth now that it had been abandoned by the twin spirits of poetry and love. Reduced to its elements, it died.

At the foot of the bier, don Celedonio, docile in the face of death, leaned on his cane and bowed his head. Three students and a blonde of astounding equine beauty—she looked a little like the young Virginia Woolf—stood guard around the coffin, charged with the gravity of their task. "Virginia Woolf," whose name was Judit Torre, had greeted him by just barely wrinkling her complicitous eyelids, while he closed his own in response. He didn't know exactly how long he held his eyes closed. When he opened them, his head still bowed, don Celedonio distractedly noticed a wreath of white flowers with a hammer and sickle of red carnations making its bold statement at the foot of the coffin.

"These communists certainly know how to make hay while the sun shines," he said to himself.

Judit, of course, was not wearing a red T-shirt. But after a few minutes, the indefatigable Lisboa—yes, his last name was Lisboa, and he belonged to the "I-was-exiled-so-I'm-better-than-you" crowd; imbued with authority abroad, he now took charge here and organized everything as if it were a gymkhana—tried to tie a red handkerchief on Judit's arm. She refused it without moving a muscle. Don Celedonio closed his eyes again. He felt an annoying burn in his cornea—not even heartfelt tears. Even his grief was now reduced to a matter of form. That was his body's response to his sadness, automatic and prior to his realization that it was Matilde's eternal immobility three feet away from him which stilled the entire house. Then, with a fervor he hadn't experienced since praying in the chapel in his grandmother's house on Huérfanos Street to atone for his first and most illuminating sins, his lips automatically formulated the ancient words: "Holy Mary, Mother of God, blessed art thou among women . . ."

He stopped because he'd forgotten the rest. Even if you weren't a believer, you belonged to a Catholic civilization, to the aromatic penumbra of old rites swarming with things understood but unspoken. He and Pablo and Matilde, even if these punks seeking to change history tried to contradict him, were connected by myriad ties to that ancient prayer. He forgot to search his memory for the rest of the prayer because he was fumbling in his pockets for a handkerchief to dry the tears finally streaming down his cheeks. But soon even that need faded as, overcome with grief, he dropped onto the sofa, a distraught old man, the victim of his own memories, the last survivor of a world that, with the death of Matilde, who was so much younger than he, was coming to an end.

Don Celedonio had no illusions about his own position in that world. He had never been a star, had never gone beyond being a conduit for foreign artistic fashions, a friend of Neruda and other greats in the art world. He was a tremendous conversationalist who knew every anecdote, who had met everyone, and who had read all the books. His own writing, half a dozen *plaquettes*—uninteresting bibliographic rarities nowadays—meant nothing, not even as the poems of a marginal poet or dandy, the kind that had once again become so fashionable. His works were merely the mirror of what had happened in Paris during the twenties, in Spain during the thirties, in New York during the forties, and of the writing and the glories of his close friends.

To cheer him up in his moments of depression, Fausta would tell him that his collection of letters was extremely valuable. But did those to whom he wrote ever bother to save Celedonio Villanueva's letters, or show the care he did when he archived his four hundred or more letters signed by Neruda, or his letters from García Lorca, Diego Rivera, Trotsky, Gerald Brenan, and Anaïs Nin? He knew that in this moment of irremediable melancholy, when the fortunes of his humiliated country were at their lowest, when Matilde had died so obstinately alone that she didn't even want to see him, and he'd hear her voice on the telephone, worn thin by pain, as she asked him to take care of some literary business or other after her death—in this moment, weighing his own worth seemed trivial.

But how could he not ask himself the most anguishing question of all: "Did I really exist only as a reflection in the eyes of those I admired?" What importance could his thoughts on the relative magic of this room have, when it was here that Pablo's wake had been held in 1973, surrounded by a catastrophic mess of windows and books broken by savages, when Matilde's tragic face appeared all over the world? How could one imagine Matilde definitively still in the darkness of her coffin, when it was impossible to forget how boldly her cape had flown before the machine guns wielded by the "forces of order" at the 1977 trials, when the opposition carried out its first protests? It was then that this object which had been that woman shouted, "Arrest me if you dare, kill me, shoot"—and some ignorant captain did in fact arrest her and the news flew around the world.

The pretty Virginia Woolf, this afternoon more Virginia Woolf than the familiar Judit, had been replaced by a boy with Indian features, with no other expression than the square will of his jaw decorated with dark peach fuzz. In the corner of the sofa, don Celedonio fell asleep.

✦ *A*sleep? Perhaps not. Only trans-
posed, suspended in that zone of consciousness where fatigue converts
an old man's refusal to go on living into another kind of lucidity.
Something like a fine net hung just this side of sleep filtered the events
taking place in the room: someone was turning on a light; someone
was opening a shutter closed by the breeze; unidentified people came
and went whispering to each other or stopped in front of him intending to pay their respects, but, realizing he was asleep, moved on.
Then came more flowers to add their fragrance to the aroma of the
candles, a smell of death that penetrated even the sleeping consciousness of the old man, the unmistakable scent of a wake, from the most
glorious to the most humble. It was the fragrance of his own, imminent
funeral, when he'd be locked inside a tightly sealed coffin that nonetheless would let a cold draft from the open windows slip under the
collar of his shirt. His poor neck, its skin roughened by the years, had
become scrawny. Don Celedonio was startled awake by the sudden
darkness produced when someone turned off the lights.

"Who turned off the lights?"

"We did," answered Lisboa from the other side of the coffin.

"Oh, Lisboa. Turn them back on, Lisboa, if you don't mind."

"Right away, don Celedonio. We had to unplug the lamp so we
could remove this table, because there's no way all these people and
all these wreaths are going to fit otherwise."

Supporting himself on his cane, the old man tried to stand up and
smash that idiot Lisboa for daring to change the order of this room
in which something of Pablo and Matilde still survived. But he couldn't
get up. What Lisboa was doing was sordid, robbing the gold teeth of
the dead after a battle—they were vultures, Lisboa and that tiny,
officious woman who worked with him and whose name he couldn't

remember, but who lately, like a bird of ill omen, had flapped around this house, ever since Matilde had begun to falter.

"Turn them back on!" shouted don Celedonio. "Don't change a thing. Who cares about the wreaths? Pile them up. Save the cards—actually, don't bother. No one's going to send thank-you notes. They're all the same anyway."

"Some are very beautiful," offered the tiny woman, with the voice of a . . .

Voice of a what? A bird? No, it wasn't high-pitched enough. A cat? It had no purr in it. A little girl? It lacked ingenuousness. A voice of wool, bland, monotonous, like a ball of yarn unwinding indifferently, her diction so imprecise that her words lost their definition and any meaning they might have had: an odious *criollo* custom, this habit of slurring words, above all for a lover of French precision like himself. But on the other hand, he had to recognize that this woman's tone was not at all bossy—it was even relaxing. Her words hardly mattered. That's why Matilde had kept her around during the final months, since she was certainly incapable of asking nettlesome questions or evoking painful memories in Matilde's mind. Now she was like a vulture, tearing Matilde to pieces. A nightmarish hyena, exaggerated don Celedonio out of literary habit, a bird of ill omen. She belonged to that race of women who officiate at burials and pray for the dead without love or piety, who offer tea and coffee just so they can show they have access to cupboards forbidden to others. These women were neither young nor old (this one had pretty pink legs, observed don Celedonio, solid hams where her skirt outlined them), of the kind that appear at funerals even though they remain unidentifiable, opaque cousins of cousins who acquire a fleeting brilliance only on these occasions, old servants summoned by the smell of death, from who knows what corners of the city.

Who would organize the ceremony for his own departure when it was his turn? Who would make sure the wreaths would fit in his Empire-style library, the only appropriate place for his wake? Who would see to it the cards didn't get lost or the whole sad affair didn't bog down in the intolerable conventionality of his widowed, childless daughter-in-law, whom he saw no more than twice a year because he could never forgive her for her attitude toward Fausta? He knew Fausta would outlive him. Why worry about it, since it was clear that she would take care of everything in her efficient way, since her authority in his life was a historical fact, footnoted in some history of

Chilean literature. Still, he could not restrain a malicious smile when he imagined the open war his death would start between those two inflexible women. Once he was not there to control them, they would shamelessly claim their just deserts.

"Turn on the lights, leave it where it is . . ."

Lisboa withstood the old man's stare for a second, then put the red glass lamp back on the table where it had always been. The lights came on again. All around the guards and among the people who came in to stare at the coffin for an instant, Lisboa and the little woman were busily piling up the wreaths wherever they could find space— on the stairs, in corners, outside the doors. "The afternoon coolness will keep them from withering," murmured the woman, as if it mattered. Fully awake now, don Celedonio was greeting everyone who came in. Someone sat down to chat with him on the sofa. Lisboa and the insignificant little woman were just getting ready to leave. What the devil was her name? Don Celedonio wanted to ask her for something. Servile but not a servant, she had a ridiculous name he couldn't seem to remember.

"Ada Luz . . ." he remembered just in time to say it. "Excuse me for bothering you. Could you do me a favor? If you're going downstairs, could you ask someone to bring me up a cup of coffee? But don't say a word to Fausta. She won't let me drink coffee this late because she says it keeps me up all night . . ."

"Don't say another word, don Celedonio," she exclaimed, overjoyed that the principal mourner had recognized her. "I'll bring it right up myself."

Lisboa moved some wreaths so that Ada Luz could precede him down the Capri-style staircase; he stepped aside to let some guests go up or to let others go down more quickly. Lisboa was grumbling that this was the limit, that the bourgeoisie in this country thought they were entitled to anything they wanted, don Celedonio in this house for instance, because he was supposed to be Neruda's literary executor. Or at least he thought he was. The fact is that Matilde's last will, including the codicils establishing the Pablo Neruda Foundation, had not been read yet. And when the will was probated more than one person might be rudely surprised. Wasn't it only natural that some furniture be moved so that a wake could be held, so that all the guests and wreaths would have room?

"But no, we have to do things the way they want, goddam priest-lovers!" murmured Lisboa.

"But don Celedonio's no priest-lover."

"In that case, who ordered a coffin with a cross on it?"

"That's the way it came from the funeral parlor, and no one bothered to change it."

"What do Pablo Neruda and Matilde have to do with all this religious stuff? Nothing, even though nowadays the Church and the Party are so friendly with each other, a thing I personally don't like. The Party opted for armed struggle against this regime, so the Church should have nothing to do with us. It's a contradiction."

"Don't be so sure they had nothing to do with priests."

"Who?"

"Don Pablo and Miss Matilde."

When they reached the bottom of the stairs, Lisboa took Ada Luz aside so she could explain. Below, in the patio, even though the kids from Communist Youth had orders to keep people out so the wake would not turn into a public demonstration, there was a dense crowd milling around, their silhouettes refracted through the patches of light. There really wasn't much space: this was not some magnate's palace, but the refuge of a nostalgic poet.

On the landing, hidden by the branches, they saw old friends, those who still survived, Neruda's political cronies and fellow poets; while up and down the staircase, their identities half veiled by the evening light, filed the elder statesmen of the old left, leaders of the union movement, which had been deftly destroyed, and university figures who had seen their budgets slashed to nothing. After paying their respects at the coffin, these guests gathered near the bushes, and sat on chairs or on the benches made of pink stone from Pelequén that Pablo would find in the cellars of junk shops—it was impossible in Chile for him to decorate his property with Tiberian marble from Capri. The old-timers would wave to each other, exchange banal memories of the widow, and then quietly leave.

Ada Luz slipped out of the arm Lisboa had wrapped around her waist because this was just not the proper time and place: despite the crowd, the house retained an air of seclusion that pleased her. As she commented on Lisboa's last remark, she held his hand on the banister so he wouldn't feel rejected.

"Miss Matilde was no atheist."

"So she was an agnostic."

"Judging by what she said, not even that."

Lisboa frowned and demanded an explanation.

"Well," began Ada Luz, stammering slightly, "when Miss Matilde came back from Houston the last time and took to bed for good, I brought her two bedjackets she had me knit. One was yellow, very light yellow, almost beige, a real nice shade she chose herself before she left, and the other was aqua. That afternoon she was very depressed, and when I passed her the hand mirror she'd asked for, she started in talking about dying. Her face was so sad . . . I wasn't looking straight into her face because she was talking to me from her reflection in the mirror, and she seemed to be crying. I felt a little odd because we weren't close or anything and to talk about those things with a stranger . . . well, of course, she was so alone . . ."

"What's all this got to do with it?"

"Well, just then while she was looking into the mirror, she told me the strangest thing."

"What?"

"That in Houston she'd asked for last rites."

"Did they give it to her?"

"Yes. And she took communion. Weird, right? I was real confused. Know what else she told me?"

"What?"

"That she'd like to have a mass said at her funeral."

Lisboa turned to face her. "So what's so special about that? It follows the new Party guidelines, although, of course, Matilde wasn't a Party member. It fits in with unifying the opposition. Me, personally, I have to laugh when I think of myself fighting on the same side as the Church, but . . ."

"And then she told me she'd like her mass to be said by one of those revolutionary priests who live in the slums."

"She did? That's a horse of a different color."

"Why?"

"I don't like this mass business at all, or communion either, for that matter. Any priest who says mass at a funeral is just that: a priest saying mass at a funeral. Get it? It doesn't hurt us at all."

"Of course not."

"But a revolutionary priest saying mass for Miss Matilde would be too much of a provocation. If that happened, the opposition would be turning into a resistance movement, and *we* have to be in charge of any resistance, not the priests."

"So what do we do about the mass?"

"Why didn't you tell me before?"

"Because I didn't think it mattered."

He took the hand she'd rested on the banister and smiled at her kindly.

"That's right. It doesn't matter in the slightest. Forget about the whole thing, kid. Have you talked about it with anyone else?"

The threat in his eyes was more effective in silencing her than the hand he'd placed over hers, hers as light and spidery as his was thick. It was a difficult moment, but this was a pleasure not to be passed over—even if it was a little risky: Lisboa was a married man—this little business of finding herself involved with him. In this semidark space, wedged between the shafts of light falling from above or rising from below, she felt the blue energy of Lisboa's eyes grasping her with such force that it made the back of her neck moist with perspiration. Would he come over to her place tonight? He hadn't visited for months! But even if he suggested coming over, she'd have to put him off because she had other business today. She tried to free her hand so she wouldn't give in to her temptation to see him. But it was Lisboa's blue stare and not his hand that held her in place. He softened his eyes and his voice, murmuring: "Better say nothing about it."

"Why?"

"Because people might use what Miss Matilde said for their own purposes and it might work against us."

"Don't include me in your 'us,' Lisboa. We women don't have anything to do with you. Not even with your people. Why should it work against you when everyone knows that the Party and the Church are working together? Judit left the Party when the armed struggle was announced, but that doesn't mean she's quit us too."

"Who can figure Judit out?"

"Nobody, that's for sure."

"And what about the Church? You can't figure them out either. You just can't trust them. The priests are devils who'll take advantage of any situation that suits them. If a revolutionary priest were to say mass for Miss Matilde in the name of all the political parties opposed to the regime, the Church would be counted as foremost among them. That's what they want, to be seen as heading up the struggle, but that's not what the Party wants. We can't allow it because we have to lead the fight ourselves. Understand? So just keep your mouth shut, okay, kid? Don't say anything to anyone, not even to Judit, because who knows what she's gotten herself into."

"I may not understand Judit, Lisboa, but I want you to know once and for all that if it weren't for her, with what she knows, and who she knows, we'd be dead."

"Just don't tell her until after the funeral. Look, she's a good friend of doña Fausta, and who knows what kind of trouble doña Fausta and don Celedonio might make with this mass business. Anyway, there's no time to do anything about it now. When the funeral's over you can publish an article about Miss Matilde's conversion if you want and have all the masses said you like. But for now we don't want to have a mass said by a revolutionary priest with Miss Matilde's body right there in front of everyone."

"Miss Matilde's more than just a body, you know."

"Okay, okay. I meant no offense. Anyway, Adita, believe me and do what I'm asking you. You and your women are so disorganized!"

"And happy to be that way!"

"Anyway, just keep quiet about the mass until the funeral's over. I've had so many arguments with the Party heads about this priest nonsense! I'm sure I'm more correct than they are. I'm asking you for the good of the country and the Party."

"I have nothing to do with your Party, understand? What Miss Matilde told me was just something she said. Now I'm sorry I ever said anything about it to you, because of this mess you're making."

"Once and for all: nothing that Neruda's widow said can ever be 'just something she said.' Every single word she spoke has a political value, even if she was never one of us."

He let go of Ada Luz's hand after giving it a gentle pat, which annoyed her because she felt it was empty of emotion.

"I just don't know . . ." she replied.

"*What* don't you know? Don't be a fool. Come on, they need us downstairs."

5

"◆*L*ook," Lopito said to Judit. "Lisboa descending the staircase."

"Yes," she replied, "but not by Duchamp. By some second-rate Latin American, imitating Duchamp without ever having heard of cubism."

"Uh-oh, Lisboa's got a problem."

"He looks furious!"

They were seated on the low stone wall at the edge of the patio, where groups of people milled around, blocking out what little light remained.

"It's political fury. By their farts shalt thou know them."

"How vulgar you are, Lopito!" hissed Judit, forgetting she'd sworn not to try to reform him years ago. "Look at him now in the kitchen with his guards, as angry as a scoutmaster when one of his boys acts up."

They both yawned as they contemplated this assembly that would never again take place. After silently observing the throng, Lopito said, "You could convince her."

"What are you talking about?"

"What we were talking about before 'Lisboa descending the staircase.'"

"You mean Ada Luz?"

"The room she wants to rent. Right here in Bellavista, Judit, so handy."

"You're crazy, Lopito. Ada Luz is my friend. Do you really think I'd inflict a creature like you on a poor soul like her? You'd never pay the rent and you'd drive her out of her mind. And she's so timid she'd never complain."

"The ideal woman for me! Have you ever heard my wife complain about me? Well, we should record it—on videocassette, of course. So we could get the faces she makes along with her squawking. A week ago she threw me out: three shirts, two pairs of underpants, a vest, and that's it. She kept my books to pay for what she called 'services rendered,' the little whore, as if her services were so good. And she swore she was going to sell them to pay Moira's tuition in March. But she's not going to get that much money out of the deal, because I already sold the best things. Only a few good ones are left. But she has my Rimbaud! I need my Rimbaud!"

"Frankly, I don't understand how she put up with you for these four months. She must be a saint! I couldn't stand you even for a week."

Cigarette smoke filtered through the few remaining greenish teeth that punctuated Lopito's smile, as fixed and archaic as the face on a pre-Columbian idol. His face was covered over by skin that seemed peeled off someone else's, but it was a tight fit, and left the crude red of his gums and the edges of his eyelids exposed. As if to protect himself from Judit's intolerable truths, he ran his hand over his battered forehead down to his jutting jaw, as if drawing a curtain that transformed his smiling grimace into a mask of pain. Were those signs (Judit wondered again on seeing the change she knew so well) scars of some ancestral pain, the residue of brutal experiences accumulated by primitive societies she would never know? were they the thing that had impelled her, despite Lopito's ugliness and grime, to sleep with him when she first went to the university, when both campaigned in the Revolutionary Left Movement? How could she resist him, when he was a window open to forbidden territories?

Lopito, who feared neither abjection nor humiliation nor ridicule—because he had never known anything else—would chase her around the university and even at political rallies, imploring her to make love with him, she so blond, so slender, so intelligent, a woman unattainable even in his wildest dreams, impossible for him even to think of approaching, the transitory goddess of the young revolutionaries that year. What could it matter to him that his comrades laughed at his pretensions? Being a hopeless loser gave him the freedom of not being able to fall any lower.

Judit would give in, but only out of pity—which in any case was all he needed. Shamelessly crying his eyes out, he begged her to let him touch her or to let him see her naked so he could masturbate dreaming of her, that's all he asked, begging access to her body in an outburst of sadness that she understood to be not desire, but a kind of hunger.

Which is why, even though the night they'd spent together was tech-nically a disaster, it nourished Judit on another level. Afterward, all hungers seemed respectable to her, even this hunger that made her its object.

Lopito opened a world of unmitigated pain. It was the first time that she experienced pain firsthand. In those days, Judit was only seventeen; her other adventures had been mere rhetorical exercises compared with Lopito's abyss of awkwardness and desire, to say noth-ing of the stench of that night spent with him. Juan López, the popular Lopito—"If I'd been born with a name like Celedonio, no one would dare call me 'Lopito' "—tolerated by everyone, even to a certain extent loved by everyone, but included by no one.

Nevertheless, an affection in the form of complicity blossomed be-tween Judit and Lopito after that night, even though they no longer fought for the same cause—what cause could Lopito fight for nowa-days, after disgracing himself in every one he'd been involved in? What cause did Judit fight for, now that she was enmeshed in her own guilt? The thing that united them was a long list of public defeats and private failures. Nothing ended between them when Judit went to live with one of the bravest militants of that era, known only as Ramón, who was later tortured to death. Their friendship was sus-pended during the time Judit was living underground. She would occasionally ask him for help, which Lopito could not give because his own scruffy neck was also in danger. Why should they try to reform each other, to be more noble? Why try to be better? Why even make the effort to harmonize their lives with the different kinds of truth they knew could exist simultaneously, when they knew each other so well and things were as they were?

After Lopito's hand covered his face, the peeled-off skin that seemed to cover his own receded somewhat, revealing his blood-red gums. The archaic smile of pain fixed itself once again, not as a festive gesture but as a defense against the atavistic storms of misery. The smoke from the moist cigarette perpetually stuck to his lips curled between his teeth.

"It's her fault this time."

"I don't believe a word of it."

"You're always putting me down. Why do you say it's my fault without even knowing what happened?"

"Your only charm," replied Judit, knowing she was avoiding the truth of his words, "is that you don't need anyone to tell you it's your fault. It's been your fault since you were born. So, tell me, how did it happen this time?"

"I hit the kid."

"You bastard! She's only seven years old! You were drunk."

"Elementary, Watson. But just one little bottle!"

"You get drunk just sniffing booze."

"I can't remember what my buddy Ríos and I were celebrating."

"I don't believe anybody ever drank just one bottle of anything with Ríos."

"It's just that Moira was a pain in the ass that night!"

"What did she do?"

"She wouldn't stop crying."

"Was she sick?"

"No. I was reading *Le Bateau Ivre* out loud, which is the only thing that consoles me when I'm depressed and cold, and since it was the fifth or sixth time in a row I'd read it, and since the kid and Flora couldn't sleep, who knows . . ."

"What time was that?"

"About three in the morning. Ríos and I had been drinking for a long time."

"Frankly, if someone read *Le Bateau Ivre* to me for the sixth time at three in the morning . . ."

"The problem is that Flora is intolerant."

"Don't give me that."

"Okay, maybe 'intolerant' isn't the right word. Anyway, she can't stand Rimbaud. Can you imagine anyone not liking Rimbaud? Unbelievable! And the brat would start crying every time I'd start over. Imagine, the little bitch, a chip off the old block, must have been born with a poetic sensibility, because she would start crying just when I'd start over, as if she could guess what was the beginning and what was the end by following the structure of the poem. And she'd scream so you couldn't stand it, louder each time I started over, the little whore, until I grabbed her and gave her a good beating. Then Flora started hitting me with the heel of her shoe, lucky for me it was a cork heel . . . but look what she did to my face, and you should've heard what the fucking bitch said to me. That I hadn't written a poem in years, which is true, but you don't stop being a poet just because you stop writing. That I'd run away from a hospital for drunks just so I could start drinking again and that she couldn't stand me any more. That the *poètes maudits* were out of fashion, as if that asshole knew what was in fashion. . . . How could I put up with that shit? I socked her, and she threw me out. For about a week now I've been wandering around, sleeping wherever I can, at friends' houses or friends of friends. But you know, not many people can put up with me, because when you get a bad reputation in a gossipy little burg like Santiago, you never get rid of it."

"And after telling me a story like that you expect me to help you get that room in poor Ada Luz's house? She's so scared of everything she locks the door at eight and goes to bed at nine. If you want, you can sleep at my place tonight, but just tonight. I can't help you anymore. I have no maternal instincts, not even for my own daughter. Besides, I've got my own life to lead, and I'm not going to give it up to try to reform you. So one night is all you get."

"I accept your kind offer. Thank you."

"Wait, there's one condition."

"What?"

"You have to take a bath. You stink to high heaven."

"It'll be my pleasure."

"Here's the key."

"Thanks."

"Where are you going to eat?"

"Is that an invitation?"

"I think there might be an egg or two in the refrigerator."

"Can we leave together?"

"I don't know yet. . . ."

6

◆ *O*ver the years Fausta Manquileo
had become a lady who displaced an immense amount of cultural
water in Chile, a haughty *Q.E.2* that navigated with inexplicable ease
through the stormy channels of national politics and literature. True,
she had never been a beauty, but, as the novels of the nineteenth
century would say, "she carried herself like a queen." She never looked
better cast than she did on this evening of mourning, beclouded by
an aura of melancholy, among the leafy shadows that dissolved in the
patio, where her role was to hold court. After publishing seven books
of erratic inspiration, she was mentioned as a real possibility for the
first National Literary Prize that would be given when political con-
ditions in the country changed. The regime, of course, had refused
to hear of it, since she was a communist—something she never was—
or because she was a dissident, which for the government was the
same thing as being a communist. Whenever anyone mentioned the
prize to her, Fausta would declare (not because she was coy but because
she still felt the fervor of having begun as one of his disciples), "Celedonio deserves it more than I."

That wasn't true. She was more independent of international literary
fashion than he was, was gifted with a more impetuous imagination
and more pathos, but she had other traits that kept her from realizing
her full potential. She was lackadaisical, for one, much preferring her
role as local goddess to the solitude of greatness. Because now, at this
time in her life, she recognized that it was the literary life—book
presentations, the skirmishes of friendships and resentments, the ma-
nipulation of the prizes and awards she showered down on her pro-
tégés and those of don Celedonio—more than literature itself that
stimulated her passions.

On a melancholy evening such as this, where the fading light barely allowed one to make out the identity of the mourners gathered in the patio, she carried out her task as administrator of grief admirably. But how could she not acquit herself well in a situation that was such a social event? That was what those who observed her from the windows that opened onto the miniature stage dominated by her important figure were saying. In point of fact, she'd been doing it all her life. She was the only (and pampered) daughter of a radical senator, a potentate in his day, who owned vast estates stolen from the Indians down in Temuco, and whose now-forgotten name immortalized a side street in Santiago.

One summer day when she was twenty years old, she foolishly married the overseer at the plantation and took his Indian name. Ten months later the overseer died, as the author of *Djktrplñ/Poems*, sitting on a bench in the patio, told the lady novelist who wrote *Nests*, adding that her father had probably had him killed—not an unlikely hypothesis given the mores of the southern frontier in those days. It was an episode that don Celedonio regularly recited to great comic effect at the Nerudas' house when new people were at dinner, adorning it with periodic additions that Fausta had the good sense not to deny so that her legend would grow.

During the first year of her widowhood, locked away on her father's estate, from which he refused to allow her to stray and thereby advertise his shame, she wrote her first book: *Window on a Sea of Wheat*. It was an autobiographical novella which the literary critic Alone launched from the pages of the newspaper *El Mercurio*. A very sensitive, very fragile girl, totally unlike Fausta, but very like her at the same time because that was the style in the feminine novel of the period, is mysteriously left a widow and decides to remain alone on her farm to find out if it is true that her father had her husband murdered. It was an original combination of regionalist and detective fiction, according to the sagacious critic, who quoted many of the lively passages from the book published under the pseudonym Fausta Manquileo. Her father soon found out that his daughter, Maria Angélica Rosales, educated by the most prudish nuns in Santiago so she could marry in the most conventional style, was the author of this defamatory book everyone was talking about. A book in which she frivolously—because in the first place Manquileo never meant a fucking thing to Angélica, and in the second place it was just that she was hot to trot that summer, a simple problem she could have taken care of in a more discreet way—and straightforwardly accused him of murder.

"It's the only good thing she ever wrote," one of the Communist Youth boys, who had just read the novella in school, remarked to one of his comrades.

"I think *The Blue Net* is better. It's more earthy, more a part of our world," answered the comrade, pushing his way through the crowd to go downstairs and stand guard on the street.

The late lamented senator passed away shortly thereafter. With a daughter like Angélica, more and more the bohemian, how could he avoid heart attacks? After his decease, Fausta moved to Santiago, dragging along with her a militantly rustic style of life which she set up in an immense and uncomfortable house in a neighborhood just on the edge of fashion. She filled the house with huge pieces of dark furniture in need of repair, with vines and ivy in chipped porcelain planters, with dogs that ambled through the dining room during dinner, and with servants whose only known function was to tell stories about the family or prepare desserts that smelled of childhood: "You remind me of Madame Hanska when she had just left the Ukraine for Neuchâtel with her retinue," said don Celedonio Villanueva, infatuated with Fausta's feudal dimensions.

He made her read Balzac just after he met her with her colorful native servants in Rome. When they returned, they were a couple whose long-standing stability mocked those who prophesied their breakup. In Santiago they opened their house to friends who were "rather unconventional"—just like that, in quotation marks, because, as the lady author of *Nests* commented to the author of *Djktrplñ/Poems*, the very expression seemed to have an out-of-fashion air to it. In any case, since it was getting late and there were so many people, she would rather be on her way, because everyone was too busy to tell her anything about the Neruda Foundation and she had to write her article.

Among those "rather unconventional" friends was, of course, Pablo. According to rumors that still circulated today, even in the funerary patio, the poet had momentarily—he had defined himself as a "successively monogamous" man—lost his head over this home-grown princess whose complexion was just too dark and whose hair was tightly pulled back in a bun on the back of her neck, hair that she regularly dyed jet-black at the first hint of gray until she reached what some dared to estimate as her seventieth year. Some said that during a trip through Italy with his court of friends, which Fausta and Celedonio had joined, Neruda had made love to this fleshy idol from

Quinchamalí with indigo eyelids and ruby lips. Her laugh was so powerful that, according to what don Celedonio declared in his apartment filled with *petits meubles* and eighteenth-century bindings, it could not only burst the traditional *mousseline* champagne glass, but a jug of new wine as well—a very García Márquez–style comment, but, of course, it was so easy to imitate García Márquez and everyone was doing it. How could it be, people wondered even now after so many decades, when they saw her greet her friends or say goodbye to them with a hug or a smile, that a cosmopolite like Celedonio Villanueva could fall in love with a woman as obvious as Fausta, a precursor of our own arts-and-crafts movement, decked out in pectorals of Araucanian silver and wool woven in Chiloé before either of those things became fashionable, and after they were proper for a person her age? She was still wearing her father's vicuña poncho when she and Matilde challenged the regime's forces during the political demonstrations.

Fausta kept up her friendship with Matilde after Pablo's death. She criticized Matilde's rather melodramatic posturing—the high priestess dedicated to tending the flame at the bard's altar of glory—and vainly (Matilde resisted all intrusions) urged her to live her own life. Neither woman was particularly warm or tender, but both were identical in their passions, in their intelligence, and in their courage; they were women with strong appetites, fond of clothes, jokes, and arguing with men bound up in daring exploits, above all when they'd had too much wine. They both marched vociferously in protests, they both signed open letters, hid fugitives, and worked on the Human Rights Commission, as well as the Association of Families of Prisoners and Disappeared, without fearing reprisals. Matilde's work during her final period of health and the beginning of her illness was clear for all to see. She tried to put in order, insofar as that was possible, with the help of don Celedonio and Fausta (especially don Celedonio), the huge number of papers left by the poet: manuscripts, letters, holographs, unfinished texts, a monumental and seemingly endless task. The papers were of inestimable worth and were kept under lock and key in some part of the house on the hillside, the very place where so many friends on the afternoon in question found themselves grouped together. These papers were to form the nucleus of the Pablo Neruda Foundation.

What would happen to it all now? The Nerudas had named no heir but the foundation, and that project seemed bogged down in a legal morass. The estate was too valuable to be left unguarded: those first

editions, holographs, unpublished originals, correspondence, libraries, paintings, leaving aside the fortune in royalties that would provide
the means to maintain the collections. A lot had been said about the
foundation even when Pablo was alive, and he himself had postulated
it as something apolitical.

But it was Matilde, even when she was sick, her hands and voice
trembling, who obsessively labored to give the project form, because
in addition to erecting one more monument to the immortality of the
poet, the foundation would consolidate the material basis for a center
of fermentation in Latin America, a place where young writers in need
of stimulation could find it. Locked in her bedroom redolent of scents
intended to dissipate the smell of her medicines, her indefatigable
index finger dialed number after number on the telephone she kept
beside her bed. Insistent and demanding, her voice broken, she tried
to construct that vast ship whose outlines she could make out through
her fever even though she knew she would never see it sail.

The will, which should have been probated by then, was mysteriously stalled in some bureaucrat's office, whether out of malice or not
no one could say. No one could find out anything about the will or,
for that matter, about the status of the probate procedure. In her final
months, Matilde was in despair, fearing that because of some secret
conspiracy the foundation would never be established. The influential
people mobilized by her grand name got nowhere, mainly because it
was impossible to know how to go about it properly—suppose it were
the caprice of some anonymous minor official whose political zeal
prompted him to see a communist plot in anything associated with
the name Neruda?

Why not? Hadn't he donated his house on Isla Negra to the Party
a long time ago? The house became the property of the ruling Junta
when it confiscated the Party's possessions. But only the house itself,
not its contents: not the antique figureheads that gazed out to sea
from the portulaca-covered hillsides, not the collections of blue crys-
tals, not the opalescent conch shells in the sealed rooms—none of that
was included in the donation. Now, within that building Matilde's
death would close to outsiders, things were left confused, awaiting an
unknown fate, gathering dust and feeding termites until the legal
tangle in which the foundation was caught was unraveled, and the
regime, or whoever it was, approved the project.

Fausta sailed from one group to another, or she went up the stairs
to exchange pleasantries with some illustrious figure next to the coffin,
always trying to lead the conversation toward kind memories of Ma-

tilde instead of premonitions about the destiny of the foundation. The truth is that this affair concerned don Celedonio more than it did Fausta, because as administrator and coordinator of all this Nerudian detritus, his presence—which had never been especially prominent for the public because his talent was of an intimate nature—was going to take on completely new dimensions which his little books never gave him. He'd be rejuvenated. He'd become a power. More powerful than ever before.

That was the absurd temptation Fausta dangled before him to arouse his enthusiasm. At this stage in his life, don Celedonio was not sure if he really cared about all that, because he thought it might be preferable just to fade away calmly and ironically. He took out a cigar but didn't light it. For the moment he preferred simply to breathe in its dry aroma. Later, when the curious had drifted away and the circle of friends had tightened, he'd light it, because a good cigar requires peace of mind to be enjoyed. Miguel Barnet had sent these from Cuba. The messenger who brought them said they were a homage from the official Cuban cultural institution, Casa de las Américas. The truth is that they were not as good as they used to be. But what was? Beginning with Casa de las Américas, which had lost the heady aroma of its first days. He silenced his thoughts when he felt Fausta, dragging her long black dress, which made her look like a combination Araucanian witch and Greek fury, drop his arm and walk toward the entrance at an uncharacteristically brisk pace. He heard her say in an inappropriately peremptory tone: "What's going on here?"

Standing there in the brightly lit stairway that led to the street, one hand resting theatrically on the door frame and her neck bent forward, Fausta possessed such an incontestable authority that all present focused their attention on the incident in which she was now clearly involved. There had been a small altercation, it seemed, which had interrupted the guards' literary chat and ended with a slammed door. Fausta, aware of everything, let nothing pass, because it was simply not proper that such things take place on an afternoon like this: they might be a prelude to disagreeable altercations at tomorrow's funeral. They all had to be very careful.

A few steps below, there were two guards, one visible from the knees up, the other from the chest up. The first looked like a blond choirboy and the second sought to look tough by cultivating a downy beard. The two Communist Youth members were still arguing when Fausta shut them up: "Shhhh! Who was it?"

"Fox."

"Freddy Fox?"

"Right, Federico Fox."

"Where is he?"

"He left."

"Why?"

"Because this jerk wouldn't let him in."

"Are you crazy?"

"Ask him."

"Look, Miss Fausta, Lisboa put us here to screen people and not let anyone from the government in. Who's more from the government than Federico Fox?"

Fausta remained silent for a second and then decided: "We can't let this happen. Show him up."

They opened the door, looked out, and shouted back to Fausta, "He got into a car."

"Run and catch him."

Lisboa, followed by a group spoiling for a fight, came up behind and asked what was going on. Fausta squared off against him. Tonight, she said, she was not going to put up with bad manners, and not letting Federico Fox into Matilde's house was just that. In the Isla Negra house, they could do as they pleased because the Party didn't recognize the legitimacy of the military government, but this house did not belong to the Party but to the foundation. Above all, it was Matilde's house, it was built for her, a human being, not a pawn on the political chessboard, and no one was going to throw a personal friend of the deceased out of her house while her body was still there.

They thought the regime—which they called stupid but which unfortunately did not seem a bit stupid since it had managed to stay in power through thirteen years of lies, violence, and economic disaster—would commit an act of folly of international proportions on the occasion of Matilde's death. It was as if they wanted an attack, as if they wanted a police raid, a murder, here and now, so they could use Matilde's death. She meant nothing to them. Federico Fox might be one of the thugs who helped tie the country up in an irrational ruin, who stole so much money under the benevolent eye of the authorities that people said he was one of those responsible for the hideous collapse of the national economy. But even if that was true, Lisboa should take notice and learn from experience: Freddy Fox was intelligent, that's right, able to make Pablo and Matilde laugh, and they liked him. Pablo was neither a fanatic nor a pious fraud. She looked at him, lowering her voice to continue: "You, on the other hand, Lisboa, if you want to know, you, with your naive conquering spirit, always bored them to tears."

"I've heard people say that don Pablo never allowed Federico Fox to enter his house," answered Lisboa, impenetrable to everything Fausta said about him in her tirade.

"The occasion never arose. Or they arranged things so that it would never arise. But they met from time to time."

"Where?"

"In my house, for one place. They always had lots to talk about. No one in Chile, except Pablo, has a collection of first editions and holograph texts like Federico Fox's." Hearing steps coming up the stairs, she peered down. "Freddy? Come right up. These kids just made a mistake."

"Just one more of the Party's mistakes," Freddy commented.

Federico Fox's entrance caused a tremor to run through the crowd, similar to the tremor that runs through the audience at a melodrama when the villain, sword in hand, suddenly jumps through a window and lands in the middle of a party. A path opened up before him. They followed him with their eyes to watch him greet don Celedonio, who embraced him, and kiss the lady author of *Nests*, on whom he had just conferred a prize the bluestocking would have preferred to overlook. He asked her about a hyperrealist painter and offered financial aid to a trans-avant-garde sculptor. Then, slowly, he walked up the cedar staircase with Fausta on his arm and don Celedonio bringing up the rear.

"To think I've never been in this house!" he commented to Fausta. "I want you to show me the whole thing so I can see the treasures that a communist with aristocratic tastes collected with Moscow gold. I'm sure he left everything to the Party to expiate his guilt for the good life he led at the expense of the proletariat. What a strange house! How the devil do you get from this part to the other without getting soaked when it rains? But let's go up and say a few Hail Marys to the deceased to help her save her soul. We're all going to find ourselves in trouble when we come face to face with that hard-nosed Saint Peter."

"Well, I'm glad to see you include yourself."

"And you too, you sinner."

Physically, Federico Fox wouldn't inspire fear in anyone, although he had something of the oversized weightless character of figures seen floating like balloons in nightmares. Very tall, very fat, very soft: he looked like a model of a huge baby lubricated with fragrant oils, a baby that, when it grew out of its fetal stage, and its features sharpened and it had a bit of hair on its head, might perhaps be a cute little boy. The splendid curve of his double chin formed a continuous arc with his potbelly, which bounced around inside his high-waisted trousers, themselves held up by suspenders. He sucked his lips in a grotesque semblance of an infant at the maternal breast. Unsatisfied, he comforted himself with caring for his meaty pink hands, which constantly caressed his body. He stared greedily but without hunger at too-young women or books he wanted for the collection he'd accumulated in his ancient, ornate adobe town house in the lower end of town, where his children, who resembled him before he became outsized, grew up under the tutelage of overfed priests.

According to don Celedonio, who said he admired him because he looked so much like a Botero, Federico Fox never looked hungrily at anything because unlike other mortals he'd never experienced that honest need. However, he added, his gluttony was such that he could devour everything, because Freddy was nothing but a huge digestive tract, one who would interrupt a directors' board meeting to protest if he was not instantly given something to eat. His cousin, Judit Torre, brought up on the estate next door, explained that there was no reason for anyone to be surprised at Freddy's obscene gluttony: until he was twelve years old, he'd worn a necklace of amber pacifiers around his neck, which the small Freddy, insatiably and repulsively, would suck to console himself for God knew what obscure lack.

Judit hated him, not only because his political position was radically opposed to hers, but because when he was a teenager, utterly rejected by his older female cousins, he'd taken his revenge by dragging his younger cousins into the barn during siesta and fingering the delightful moisture of their panties. He would then threaten them with the horrible punishments the adults would inflict if they uttered a word about these experiments. Ever since then, the innocent smell of haylofts would send her into an asthma attack. She took her revenge through gossip—rare for her, as she so respected the private lives of others that she had the reputation of being distant and cold—so the notorious pacifier necklace that had once hung around the neck of Federico Fox, president of corporations and banks, was known to all. His claims to power were thus severely compromised.

As he climbed the stairs toward the coffin, he felt a chill; he knew that people were talking about him behind his back. The opposition gathered in the patio was wondering if—leaving aside the story of the pacifiers and some other peccadilloes that were revealed when Freddy came to prominence—he had been named finance minister, when it was said his holding office could turn into a major embarrassment for the regime. Just when rumors about his candidacy had begun to circulate, Freddy had decided to go on an extended vacation as a way of turning down the position and getting out of range of any scandal before it touched him publicly. He was famous as a collector, not only of manuscripts and books but of companies, factories, properties, half-finished buildings, and anything that was wounded, dying, or broken. He would always be ready to buy whenever corporations declared their inability to pay their debts, or the owners of tapestries and carved, gilded archangels announced their bankruptcy.

He crossed himself before the coffin, then dropped down next to don Celedonio on the sofa, all the while commenting on how unattractive he found this renowned residence. His inquisitive eyes seemed to put a price tag on everything, as if they themselves possessed the power to turn over a bowl and check the name of its manufacturer, or to finger a piece of fabric and tell its quality. They found nothing of any worth. Everything was common, ugly. There was nothing to be done: refinement is not something you pick up along the way even if you happen to be a genius like Neruda, because it is something different from culture, something enigmatic, a gift you get in the cradle that comes with the blood in your veins. And Neruda, frankly, never knew what he was doing, neither in politics nor in matters of taste. What a lot of junk! What in the world could people mean when they talked about this house in awestruck tones?

"Of course, of course," replied don Celedonio. "The best things here are the books and manuscripts. And the letters, although I haven't been through all of them. And not counting Neruda's own manuscripts, which haven't been opened yet."

"All holographs?"

"Most."

"What's going to become of all this, Celedonio, for God's sake? What a burden! Who's going to get the first editions, the letters from Rimbaud's sister, a treasure in themselves, the first edition of Whitman annotated by Whitman, the *Sentimental Education* dedicated by Flaubert to George Sand . . . not to mention the folio Shakespeare?"

"Well, the idea is that the foundation will protect these things so they are not scattered. Poor Matilde was so worried."

"I hope the foundation takes care that everything doesn't end up

in Moscow." And with a sweeping gesture of his ecclesiastical hand—
so violent that don Celedonio feared his tiny pink fingernails were
going to fly off the tips of his fingers—Federico changed the subject
abruptly: "They tell me that poor Matilde, when she finally stopped
wanting to talk to people, even on the telephone—I would call from
time to time to see how she was getting along . . ."

"And to offer to buy the collections. I heard you left her notes. Even
prices."

"Why not, Celedonio? They say the foundation is tied up and hasn't
a hope of getting off the ground because the government suspects the
communists are involved in it. It might take years, and the foundation
could turn into one of those eternal processes that get bogged down
in the bureaucracy and never get resolved, the way they do in some
Dickens novel or other. In the meantime, the valuable things that are
subject of all this litigation start to disappear until finally nothing's
left. That's what's going to happen with Neruda's things, and you
communists will be to blame—don't try to deny that you were one
once, when it was so common and everyone was a communist, even
dear old Nancy Cunard . . ."

Don Celedonio felt he was suffocating. Not only because to some
extent he realized that part of what Freddy was saying was true, but
because the banker's breath flowed over him, reeking of the laborious
digestion of pâtés, seafood, and sauces. Leaning on his stick, he stood
up. Federico followed, pestering him with his chatter all the way downstairs to the patio. He declared that Neruda had donated an incredibly
valuable collection of books to the library of the University of Chile
and that almost all of it had disappeared. What was left was under
lock and key, but in any case hundreds of important books were
missing, and no one was taking care of those that remained, no
one catalogued them, arranged them, or even dusted them. And
there were hundreds of other volumes scattered in neighborhood
libraries or in institutions incapable of appreciating their value.
How could Chileans go on being so uncivilized? Was it true that
the things Neruda had were really of such legendary quality? He
doubted it because Pablo, great artist that he was, tended to make
up tales.

"Would you like to see the collection?" asked don Celedonio, suddenly gathering spirit.

"It would be my pleasure."

"Promise you won't ask the price of everything?"

"How tedious you are! Frankly, you're getting just like those low-brow friends of yours."

"And you're getting just like those shameful people you call *your* friends. I'm very upset because of Matilde's death, Freddy, and disgusted by everyone who tries to use her for his own advantage. I suppose I'm old and tired, and the idea that I'm going to have to take charge of the foundation is just too much for me . . ."

They continued down the stairs. In the half-light of the staircase, Federico Fox stopped his friend. He rested his huge, practical man's hand on don Celedonio's frail, minor poet's shoulder, and haltingly—more as a tactic than out of real feeling—said: "Wait . . ."

"What is it?"

"For a long time now I've been meaning to ask you something. This seems like the best moment. Is it true what people say, that you have a handwritten text by Trotsky?"

"I have four."

"Four!"

"Four letters he wrote to me, when I lived in Cuernavaca and he was in Coyoacán."

"Of course. That period when people were saying that Neruda was mixed up with Siqueiros and the Stalinist mafia in the Trotsky assassination, and that to reward him for his action the Party raised him to his later prominence."

"Don't be an ass, Freddy. How can you go on saying these stupid things about one of the few people of genius this miserable country has ever produced? By the by, I have four letters from Trotsky, to say nothing of some others from García Lorca, Anaís Nin, and Henry Miller . . ."

"God in heaven! They're worth a fortune!"

"Want to buy them all?"

Don Celedonio did not hear Freddy's answer. It was the first time he'd ever thought about parting with his collection, the only thing that continued to give him life. Today he saw clearly that he would soon die: the party was over. But a Celedonio Villanueva Foundation would be an absurdity, because in a very short time no one would remember his name. Then Fausta would die, and then not even these bits and pieces of him would remain. Why not scatter it all right now, effect his own *sparaqmos* so that he'd at least know where the pieces of his body would end up without waiting for hyenas like Ada Luz and Lisboa to do it? To sell something that, like these letters, he felt formed part of his being meant that, modestly, something of him was worth something. Yes, the ancient Phoenician sound of clinking coins would assure it as they fell from the pudgy hand of Federico Fox into his own.

Even after his death and the disposal of his things, something of him would still interest people, or, better, perhaps give them pleasure. Diligent scholars from the United States would scrutinize those letters in order to add a footnote, an enlightening comment, a gloss that would illuminate the figure of some great artist with the light that emanated from him, a minor one. Curious academics would visit the Fox collection—the boxes arranged in cases with bronze moldings in air-conditioned rooms in the National Library, the name of the beneficent donor ornamenting in gold the entryway to the hall, and his own name, Celedonio Villaneuva, reduced to a series of entries in the card catalogue to certify the origin of the documents and to identify the person to whom the letters had been sent—looking for hints and suggestions, never for really important information.

It was sad to think about oneself like that. But today everything was sad: melancholy, melanoma, melanism, melanite, melon, melody. *Melos*: a Greek root for song, but doña María Moliner said *Melas*, black. Melanoma: black, death, although the distinguished lexicographer never mentioned this disease. But . . . was that what had killed Matilde? Who knows, because after all any other word, "carcinoma," for example, kills just as efficiently. Perhaps doña María Moliner left out melanoma because any cancer is nothing more than a derivation from sadness: melancholy . . . , mela . . . , black. Sadness. But not fear, because today for the first time it seemed to him more horrible than death to have lived in the company of the great without having been asked to be anything more than a spectator at their banquet.

Yes, everything was black, except the radiant and rubicund Federico Fox. Even after they'd reached the patio he went on proposing that don Celedonio sell his soul—for a good price, of course—to this gluttonous collector who desired to add God knows how many more pacifiers to that slimy collar he'd never outgrown. Freddy took him by the elbow, gesticulating persuasively, superior to all present because of his impunity. The crowd seemed upset by his presence, someone was making him grotesque signals from the other side of the shadows; but of course, with the prospect of perhaps consummating a convenient transaction with don Celedonio, he could only concentrate his lust on him. A few moments later, however, Freddy stopped, the sentence he was pronouncing frozen in his mouth, his arm immobile in the air.

Don Celedonio also stopped, following Freddy's gaze as it penetrated the clots of darkness on the opposite end of the patio: Lopito was waving to the banker. Flicking away his saliva-drenched cigarette, he stood up next to Judit, and, stifling a laugh, advanced along the avenue of people which opened in front of Freddy. With his thumbs hooked in his belt, panting as if it were hard for him to make his way, caricaturing the rolling gait of a gunslinger in the West facing down his enemy in a duel, Lopito, with a sinister wink, approached Freddy Fox. The crowd began to laugh as they understood that Lopito was alluding to the financier when he stuck his fingers into his toothless, demonically infantile mouth and sucked them, moaning with pleasure. Judit Torre followed close behind, and her presence seemed to sanction Lopito's antics.

"Lopito!" shouted don Celedonio.

Lopito moved closer and closer to Freddy, who stood stock-still amid those staring eyes that trapped him, that kept him from obeying his impulse to run out of the house, because who knew what this lunatic might do next. Impossible to understand Judit's friendship with this criminal, this terrorist who should be exiled! You simply never stop being a member of the Revolutionary Left Movement. It was he who'd gotten Judit involved with Marxism! He had to get out! But how could he do it with that monster coming closer and closer, sucking his fingers in front of everyone, and with Judit right behind him?

How delightful the Torre girls had been! On those dusty estates in Colchagua, dressed in organdy and speaking French with Mademoiselle during the siesta, doing petit-point while sitting in white wicker chairs on the lawn. They were always laughed at by the little snotnoses from the local ranches who fell off horses, got impetigo, swam in drainage ditches, and had to have their heads shaved because of lice. But not the young Torre ladies: while the other children were wasting time hanging around, they were doing petit-point under the chestnut trees with Mademoiselle.

"Freddy! My old buddy!" exclaimed Lopito through his vinegary breath. "Ah, just the sight of you brings back so many memories of our youth! And the law school—what a paradise it was. Rather too quickly lost in my case, of course!"

He certainly had lost it quickly! After four months they had expelled him for stealing money from the student union. Everybody has a skeleton in his closet, but Lopito had more than his share. When Freddy felt Lopito's wine-soaked breath wafting over him, his heart froze. He couldn't face him, so he turned away and started to make for the door as quickly as he could. Lopito chased after him, trying to catch him before he got out of this damned commie dump. He drooled over his fingers as if they were pacifiers, laughing himself sick in front of the crowd.

Next to the precipice of the stone stairway, Freddy knew he was trapped. Lopito grabbed him from behind by the vents of his jacket. Freddy pulled to liberate his beautiful glen plaid Hermenegildo Zegna jacket from his enemy's filthy hands, but he lost his balance and fell down the stairs, smashing his knee on the edge of a step and tearing his trousers. Standing at the head of the stairs, Lopito laughed, showing his ruby-red gums, his green teeth, and giving off smoke like an incense burner. The sarcastic demon asked Freddy with feigned sweetness why he was running away when all he, Lopito, wanted was to talk about old times when they were students together, when all Judit wanted was to evoke the golden era of childhood innocence they'd shared.

Judit, despite the expression of repugnance on her face as she watched her cousin fall, went down to help him up. It was a reflex action that contradicted all her principles, because when people like Freddy Fox fall, it's important to let them bleed. Fausta appeared, scolded Lopito for causing an uproar, and brought Freddy to the kitchen. She doused his knee with peroxide and bandaged it. She also closed the tear in his trousers with a safety pin so he could exit with a minimum of dignity from Matilde's house, so his chauffeur wouldn't laugh at him as they probably were doing upstairs.

7

♦ *U*nbearable, Lopito was just unbearable. And where had he ever found liquor around here? Ever since he'd arrived, he'd been nosing into everything and bothering everyone, even Federico Fox. Could it be that without her knowing it he'd gone poking around in the kitchen and found a bottle? But Lopito, of course, was always drunk, even if he'd had nothing to drink, and besides, that wheeze of his could scare anybody—it always sounded like the poor guy was either going to explode or stop breathing altogether, thought Ada Luz as she mulled over the possibility of renting him a room at her place. No, the way he snored she'd never get to sleep. After Federico Fox had departed, he went right back to pestering her, Adita this, Adita that. Luckily there was so much to do down in the patio that it was easy to get rid of him. But now that there were fewer and fewer people, he seemed to be warming to the subject of the room again and started chasing her, until finally Ada Luz fled to the kitchen, crossing the patio with Lopito hot on her heels.

Fortunately, Lopito was unexpectedly interrupted when a stranger arrived. He was very tall, very thin, with a fine leather satchel slung over one shoulder and a mane of hair cascading down to his back. Ada Luz took him to be a foreign hippy because of some indefinable something in his bearing, but she was shocked at Lopito's enthusiasm when she saw him throw himself into the stranger's arms, shout, and make a row while all the rest crowded around to slap him on the back and embrace him—especially the girls.

"He can't be anything that special," Ada Luz managed to think.

Taking advantage of Lopito's outburst, she slipped through the kitchen door and closed it behind her. Her throat was dry: what she wanted was a glass of water. Since they'd posted Ema at the door and the other girls were fooling around God knew where, she was all alone in the kitchen. In the darkness she felt her way around the furniture, and, careful not to make any noise, went to the cabinet where the ordinary glasses were stored. It was better not to turn on the lights. She wanted to rest a bit, wanted not to hear Miss Fausta ordering her around, wanted not to hear don Celedonio ask her for things while pretending not to, wanted not to have Lisboa making sure she said nothing about poor Miss Matilde's mass, wanted not to have that scummy Lopito on her tail. He might figure that she was fussing around in the kitchen, and the idea of finding herself locked up with Lopito and having to hear his labored breathing close up gave her goose bumps. Of course she got goose bumps ever so easily: fear, unhappiness, pleasure, surprise, practically anything made her skin crawl, especially just above her thighs and on her plump forearms.

She still found it difficult to tell the difference between those sensations and what Father Anselmo used to call lust when she was a kid. But with Lopito there was no lust! That nosy body had been in Miss Matilde's house since three in the afternoon, when everyone knows a visit to a wake should be short, and now it must be almost nine in the evening. Always a pain, Lopito, and a joker, even though it was hard to tell when he was joking and when he was serious. Standing next to the sink and sipping her glass of water in the darkness, Ada Luz reflected on the fact that she never knew how to take him.

It was urgent she speak with Judit to confirm the message don César had brought her earlier, when he'd come rolling by the house on the skateboard that replaced his legs. She had to tell Judit the details about the meeting now, because it was set for tonight: a blue Mercedes, in Las Hortensias, after midnight. But it had been impossible to get Judit alone, because Lopito was always hanging around. Ada Luz had to find a way to tell Judit she and Aury would meet her at Ada Luz's house tonight. When Lopito first ran into Ada Luz, he'd said, "Hi, baby." Lopito calling her baby . . . ! That was the limit! And that line about, "Baby, all I want is to move in with you and make you happy, you'll see what a sweet guy I am." The idea of being in Lopito's arms made her sick to her stomach. The feeling only went away when she thought about Lisboa, so neat and clean, with his well-groomed hair, his little gray beard, and his blue eyes because his parents were Spaniards. Bossy, sure he was bossy, and he only came over once in a while because he really loved his Belgian wife. She was just putting her empty glass down when the kitchen light went on.

"Miss Ada Luz! What are you doing here in the dark?" asked Ema.

"And you? Weren't you told to keep an eye on the boys at the front door?"

"That's right, but ever since this Mañungo came, and everybody went crazy and forgot Miss Matilde, the boys said they'd take over the door again. Can I get you something? How about a cup of tea? You look a little tired."

"No thanks. I'm just going to sit right here for a while."

"Well, I'm going to fix myself one, because I'm worn out."

Ema began moving about in her natural habitat with the economy of gesture of a person at home in her world, fixing her cup of tea, muttering that she too was worn out, so many people all day long, and now the wake was sure to go on behind closed doors from the start of curfew at midnight all the way to the end, at six in the morning! Really too much! Ada Luz held a fresh glass of water in her hands, resting it in her lap, not drinking it.

"What are you thinking about?" asked Ema.

"I'm hiding out from Lopito here."

"Why hide from him? Just scream at him. He's chickenhearted! I've seen Miss Matilde give him a talking to and the tears started rolling down his cheeks—just like a woman. If he bothers you, just yell at him and he'll run for the hills."

"He wants to rent a room from me."

"You just tell him no because he's broke and you need a steady income."

"You're right, but I just don't know. It's as if Judit, as if everyone, including me, were afraid of him, were afraid of destroying him, I think, because you can't tell me Lopito's not someone to be afraid of, unless it's only because he's so ugly . . ."

"He's scary."

"And he kept telling me, 'I swear, Adita, I'll be as neat as a nun.' What's he know about nuns, huh? 'I swear I'll help out with every-thing,' he went on, 'cleaning the house, sweeping, shopping, and I'll take care of the kitchen. I'll even help with the knitting business.' Like a jerk I asked him, 'How will you do that, Lopito?' He told me he'd sit next to me on a little stool holding a skein of yarn the way he did for his grandmother when he was a kid in the country, so I could make it into a ball from my easy chair in front of him, and we'd chat about all kinds of things, and he'd tell me all his problems as he moved his hands like this, around and around with his arms spread out, so I could make a good tight ball . . ."

Watching Ada Luz move her arms slowly and rhythmically in front of her, holding up an imaginary skein and imitating Lopito's expression, Ema couldn't hold back a giggle, just imagining the monster in such a domestic setting. They were both still laughing when Fausta came in. She was going to make herself a cup of coffee, but as soon as she saw the cook, she asked her to do it. Things were getting a bit out of hand because Mañungo Vera had turned up, she said. People were going crazy. It just didn't seem right, celebrating on a night like this!

The three women soon went back to the image of Lopito helping Ada Luz with the yarn, or crocheting, wearing a pleated apron, ironing . . . until finally Fausta broke into one of her famous horselaughs that made the glasses shake as she drained the last drop from her cup. It was too comic to imagine Lopito involved in serious women's talk, worried about which stitch to use, or if Flaca was going to want three or four vests in the same style for her boutique. When Fausta finished her coffee, she took a sip of water from Ada Luz's glass so she wouldn't have to get up again. Lopito was the least of her problems: she'd have to get ready for an exhausting night, because of Mañungo Vera's arrival. She hoped to God he wouldn't stay long, because then everyone would stick around on through curfew just to gape at him. Why didn't Ada Luz go home and go to sleep and come early tomorrow, they'd really need her then . . . ? And Ema, why didn't she go to bed? Her back must be breaking with all the work she'd had to do. Ema walked to the patio door and peeked out.

"Okay. But before I leave," she said, "I want to take a look and see if this famous Mañungo is such a big deal."

♦ "Well, well, *le roi est mort. Vive le roi!*
Is that the way it's going to be?" Standing on the cedar stairway, Lisboa
observed the uproar caused by the idol's arrival. A phony idol, of
course, made of plaster or papier-mâché, pure appearance, a com-
mercial product created by the European mass media for an audience
that was bored and wanted to consume revolution and protest, ma-
terials with which Latin America could fertilize the worn-out developed world, just as it had once fertilized it with guano. Phony, that's
what Mañungo was: empty. And yet, Lisboa jealously feared that the
enthusiasm of these people incapable of telling the difference between
the real thing and a fraud could put Mañungo on Pablo's throne.
They simply wouldn't stop to compare the quality of the one with the
other.

In a second, Mañungo had turned the wake upside down. It was as
if a spotlight had suddenly flashed on the scene of quiet dignity and
turned it into a party. Everyone flocked around to say hello to Mañungo and to touch Mañungo, as if he were Saint Mañungo and could
answer their every prayer. Oh yes, he was supposed to look like a man
of the people dressed like that, but his black beard, blue jeans, and
work shirt did just the opposite. It was the uniform worn by people
like Mañungo, and it only made them look different from both the
bourgeoisie and the workers. Which meant they were nowhere, that
their possibilities for changing this corrupt society were practically nil.

Which is not to say that Mañungo was unattractive. Not at all: he
had a terrific combination of luminosity and timidity, even if the timidity was phony. What did he have to be timid about? His pockets were
bulging with gold, and women were at his beck and call. That furtive
way he walked into the patio, even though the guards had gone crazy
when they saw him and abandoned their posts to announce his ar-

rival—that was phony too. Now all he had to do was flash that smile
of his. How could anyone believe that Mañungo Vera thought he
could slip in here unnoticed after being away for twelve years, when
his uniform, his pale skin, and his tiny gold-rimmed glasses were all
sacred relics for these kids? Could anybody actually believe that Mañungo didn't want to be noticed? No. Lisboa could not accept this
kind of insincerity.

After ten minutes, decorum was restored in the patio. The high
spirits of the first moments abated and the earlier, muted quality of
the house returned. People came down from the room where Matilde's
remains were on view to experience firsthand this national phenomenon: the only man aside from Neruda, people said, who had ever
managed to get international attention focused on our country. But
did it mean anything much in the long run? Wasn't it, Lisboa insisted
to himself, a dangerous exaggeration?

He couldn't deny that like everyone else, he had suffered disillu-
sionment when Mañungo officially refused to enter the Communist
Youth because he couldn't, as he said then, *be* anything before he *did*
something that would define him. And he still hadn't done a thing.
When he came to Santiago from the University of Concepción, he
was nothing but a ragged bard with a guitar on his back, nothing but
a hopeful music teacher sidetracked by literature and philosophy courses
until the Party put him on the right track. He made his first public
appearances in clubs frequented by the kids from the Communist
Youth, the very people who not only fed and housed him but were
also his first fans. But when the time came to declare his loyalty once
and for all, Mañungo said no to the Party: "I'm pro-Cuba, pro–Popular
Unity, pro-revolution, but I'm too confused. For now, all I want is to
be the owner of my own doubts so I can work them out for myself.
Besides, for the time being at least, I can only be an artist if I reject
all labels. I have to get to know things—myself especially—travel, read,
meet new people, and study before I declare my loyalty and choose.
Is that petit-bourgeois individualism? Maybe. I'm sorry I have to go
that route, but it's the only way I can work things out for myself. I
share all the hopes of my generation, but I'm still not ready to lock
myself up inside a single way of thinking. Maybe later on . . ."

But there was no "later on" for Mañungo Vera. He went off to
Europe and cashed in on the word "revolution." He never really took
part in it the way the real exiles did—those who were scattered by the
shock waves of defeat after September 11, 1973. Mañungo never knew
anything about persecution and death except what he heard in anx-

iety-ridden café debates in exotic capitals, where he and people like him poured over the Chilean newspapers and *Le Monde* every day in order to reconstruct a sad simulacrum of their native land out of nostalgia and solidarity. With that alcohol-inspired warmth, they managed to give their individual stories a meaning and intensity that at least helped them to survive.

Mañungo became a cliché, the most revolutionary of revolutionaries. He sold revolution even though he had no experience of what it was. How could anyone deny that Mañungo Vera used the Party to make his own career, when it was thanks to an invitation from the Party that he left Chile for a festival in San Francisco, a year before September 11? He sang with Joan Baez on that trip, and all the papers in the remote Chile that was about to change reported his exploits. It was the heroic Vietnam era, with T-shirts stamped with Che Guevara's face, with hippies whose hair hung down to their waist, with boys and girls who smoked dope and made love indiscriminately in parks while Mañungo transformed himself into the super-hippy, an export product, a model that showed the seemingly infinite possibilities of that image.

After 1973, he was warned not to come back because it was dangerous, above all for him because of the way he'd misrepresented the new Chile with the songs he sang abroad. The authorities were marking anyone who might be termed a communist for extermination. He should wait awhile before coming back. It was easy for him to wait, since he was invited to pro-Chile festivals in Havana, Milan, Berlin, and Paris, where he finally decided to live. In the meantime, Neruda exonerated him of any wrongdoing, until even he returned to Chile to die of sadness.

For six or seven years Mañungo Vera's star was on the rise all over Europe: another Neruda, declared the young people who were incapable of telling good from bad when it came to the soul of the martyr-land. Time passed, and Chile lost its allure because the TV generation needs action—bullets and blood—and if they don't get it, they get bored and try something else. Nicaragua had become more exciting, while Chile, with a firmly entrenched dictator and a tangle of internal squabbles that only experts in politics could elucidate, went out of style, like Stroessner in Paraguay. The public lost interest in Chile and Mañungo Vera, and the Party didn't finance him as it did other musicians because, after all, Mañungo had never been a Party member. So what did the Party owe him?

Lisboa recalled that he, ten years older than Mañungo, was one of the first to champion Mañungo when he came north from Concepción, his head still stuffed with a jumble of Chiloé myths, which, he had to admit, Mañungo used in his music in an extremely attractive way. For that reason, for what he had been, it was so difficult to forgive him now. He'd admired Mañungo too much at the beginning. He'd believed in him too fervently. He felt that Mañungo's defection, or his incompetence insofar as genuine commitment was concerned, was like a personal betrayal of his hope that Mañungo, like all great artists, would be an instrument for saving the world. Even before Mañungo's trip to San Francisco they'd stopped speaking. And in Europe, during Lisboa's exile in a capital not so very far from Paris, they'd never tried to see each other.

One had only to look at Mañungo down there in the patio: a puppet, devoid of passion, no more than a hanger for the famous uniform worn by those who attended the wretched concerts of the Intillimani and Quilapayún folk groups, where empty shadows like Mañungo labored under the illusion that all they had to do was sing at a carnival and wear their old costumes in order to have their revolution. They had no idea that revolution meant work, a slow, hidden sacrifice inside and outside the country that only rarely appeared on the international front pages. Only large-scale narcissists like Mañungo, who had become more a name or a trademark than a person, remained on exhibition after the Chilean cause went out of fashion.

Was Mañungo aware of his tragic error? Would he do something about it? No: all you had to do was to look at him now, showing off like some high-priced luxury item in front of everyone while pretending he didn't want to, down there with all the people and the subdued light in Matilde's patio. From on high, among the plants, Lisboa felt the urge to shout, "Mañungo doesn't matter anymore! Don't be fooled by him! He's a failure because he can't commit himself. Now he's come to take refuge in Chile because nobody wants him in Europe. His music doesn't move the masses anymore because the people know it's false. Don't believe him, he's come to feed on our struggle and our sacrifice, to become a star again without giving us anything. Open your eyes! Mañungo Vera doesn't matter anymore."

Besides, his arrival had no importance in comparison with the nonsense—enormously important, but nonsense all the same—that Ada Luz had told him half an hour earlier about Matilde's desire to have mass said at her funeral. By focusing his attention on that problem, he could temporarily block out his rage about Mañungo. The mere thought that Pablo Neruda's widow had gone to confession in Houston was enough to drive him mad.

From his observation post on the log staircase, Lisboa saw Ada Luz go into the kitchen. He was just about to follow her in and scare her into keeping quiet when he saw Fausta Manquileo enter. They must have had a full-scale discussion of the subject, because they'd been in there for ten minutes, a witches' council about the mass, whose political implications would undermine all the Party's projects for tomorrow's funeral. It wasn't impossible that in another minute Fausta would come running out to tell all of Santiago about Matilde's sudden conversion to Catholicism. Fully aware of the political implications, she'd confer with ecclesiastical dignitaries and organize a mass pronounced by some revolutionary priest, thus depriving the Party of its leadership role.

Lisboa was convinced that the funeral should be the first political demonstration by the left in a Chile under state of siege, a direct challenge to the regime; it would finally lay the foundation for an active resistance—not a passive dissidence—which the Party should lead because it was prepared to do so. In the cemetery, whatever they might shout (and Lisboa would make sure there'd be no lack of slogans), the police would do nothing. In the presence of the names of Pablo and Matilde, they'd have no choice but to look the other way. After all, what kind of international repercussions would result from a repression complete with bombs, even if they were only tear-gas bombs, inside the cemetery during the burial of the widow of a Nobel laureate? Lisboa stiffened with excitement at the very thought, even though he knew that it was, unfortunately, impossible.

Don Celedonio and Mañungo hugged each other down below: Mañungo stretched out like a spider, don Celedonio compressed into his dark suit, his eyes overshadowed by his bushy brows. Enthralled in veneration of the idol! Don Celedonio, who was supposed to be so critical! They didn't get to talk much because Fausta strolled casually out of the kitchen, seemingly by chance, with no urgent mission to carry out: Ada Luz must have kept her mouth shut. After a brief appearance, she accompanied the old man as he said his farewells. He was worn out. Fausta convinced him that she was capable of taking charge, while Ada Luz, who also had to go, would accompany him in a taxi. Fausta left him with Ada Luz, who offered him her arm, and walking down the street they disappeared.

Even this did not satisfy Lisboa. Judging by how calm they both were, it was clear that Fausta and Ada Luz hadn't discussed the subject which had him so concerned. It could be that Ada Luz would talk to don Celedonio about it in the taxi, and he was just as powerful as Fausta, just as likely to push for a mass tomorrow. But Celedonio was stumbling as he left—hardly the gait of a man aroused by a dramatic turn of events. Still, he'd have another little talk with Ada Luz, to make sure she'd kept quiet and denied everything. He decided to leave soon so that he would find Ada Luz at home, alone.

Fausta had taken Mañungo's arm and they had begun to walk slowly up the stairs, followed by a group of people. For a second, Lisboa considered the possibility of giving into an old, sentimental impulse and walking over to embrace Mañungo with the same effusiveness as don Celedonio. But he resisted the idea and shrank back into his corner. They passed by without seeing him, which is exactly what he wanted.

Nevertheless, he was not going to miss the tragicomedy that was about to be performed: how many lies, embellished by her histrionics, would Fausta tell Mañungo instead of presenting him with the hard facts of the national tragedy? Lisboa, as anonymously as possible, joined the end of the procession. When he saw that two boys and two girls in red T-shirts were standing guard around the coffin, he congratulated himself for the human profundity that discipline signified. The effusion, the enthusiasm, the tear in the eye, the curiosity all last as long as a snowball in hell, he told himself. On the other hand, this docility in the face of certain norms of conduct, when employed as the sober strategy of an authority that wishes to lead the people to a certain goal, lasts longer. Lisboa remained behind in the group while Fausta, alone with Mañungo, advanced to the foot of the coffin, almost touching it, at least coming as close as the enormous floral wreath would allow.

9

◆ *M*añungo lowered his head, overwhelmed by the black coffin. Through the open window he heard the roar, no, the whimper of the miserable lion in the zoo. Or could it be the lament of the plush lion, because he'd lost his mistress and was calling her from another box where he'd been stored in mothballs? What could have become of that toy lion of . . . yes, thirteen years ago? Where was it, what was left of it? What moths—anonymous as were all moths, dead for hundreds or thousands of moth generations—could have devoured it out of their futile need to reproduce? But was it the plush lion weeping so copiously or was it the voice of the old woman, growling from the beaches of Cucao, calling him to the island so he'd visit Ulda, who taught him to sing, and who would no longer be young, and his father before it was too late, to walk again on that land which even if he inherited it would never be his because he didn't want it?

Or was it the waves breaking on the rocks of Isla Negra he was hearing, that first time the Nerudas invited him to spend a weekend? Matilde, with her mane of leonine hair and her light blue bathing suit, walked down to the beach on a luminous morning, dove into the sea, and was instantly lifted within a transparent, amber-green wave. She was a dragonfly, a fish, a bird, a mermaid flying and swimming in memory now, but who then brutally awakened Mañungo's senses to the warm, salty smell of the Pacific, to the light and the immensity, and above all to the abandon of the beautiful body of a mature woman delightedly swimming. As he gazed at her, he wondered if he would ever be able to love a woman the way Matilde was loved and sung by the poet. He felt sure he himself would never love another woman as he loved this one, now. Mañungo's love lasted as long as the waves of that morning, but the friendship remained.

Or was it Matilde's hoarse laughter Mañungo was hearing as he stood before the black box, from when she sat in the drawing room of the embassy mansion on Avenue de la Motte-Picquet, combing the mane of the plush lion? It wasn't her laughter he heard, standing next to the white chrysanthemum wreath, but a tinnitus too great for him to conquer. He felt it now for the first time since boarding the plane at Orly, a groan that came from within the casket and tore at his throat so he would never sing again. No one should sing now that Matilde was dead.

To dispel the terror that his throat might really be maimed, Mañungo emitted a growl—did those standing just behind him hear it?— which was a complaint translated into the silence of barely visible tears, hidden under his hand, because the memory of that morning at the beach was his alone, and could not be shared. This was the end.

The story ended right here. Was it to participate in tragedies like this that he'd returned to Chile? A little over a year ago, Matilde had been in Paris. She had stayed for a few days in a magnificent hotel in the center of town in order to take care of the publication, at long last, of Pablo's complete works in the Pléiade, which had been delayed because of some problems with the footnotes. Mañungo, as if he guessed that this would be his last chance to see her, and in spite of the fact that he knew she was bored by children, called her to ask permission to bring Juan Pablo along because he wanted him to meet her. She agreed.

In the taxi, Mañungo explained to the boy that he was going to meet a queen. In his country, in Chile, there were no queens and there had never been any, as there had been in France and in fairy tales, but the person who was the queen of the people like himself in Chile was this lady he was about to meet. He'd better behave. It would be a short visit, but Mañungo was worried because Jean-Paul was Nadja's son and therefore resistant to authority. Matilde, however, was never harsh when the occasion called for charm, and she certainly wasn't going to endanger her image for a trivial thing like this visit. As they pulled up at the hotel, the boy saw that the building was flying banners in the sun.

"*Ce sont des drapeaux chiliens?*"

"*Comment? Tu ne connais pas le drapeau chilien?*"

"*Oui. Mais si la dame était vraiment reine, on aurait ôté tous les autres drapeaux et on aurait mis seulement des drapeaux chiliens.*"

During that pleasant meeting, he now realized, Matilde already knew she was doomed. Juan Pablo had behaved so well that the queen gave no sign of impatience during the eighteen minutes they chatted. Jean-Paul behaves this way, Mañungo said to himself then, above all because he thinks the poet's widow is beautiful and luxurious, like the hotel and the service. What was to be done about it? he had anxiously asked Nadja on earlier occasions when he'd noted the same tendency in the boy. Where had he picked up those tastes? Or were they innate? Jean-Paul was easily seduced by beautiful people and sumptuous places and objects. In any case, he was sure that Matilde's image was imprinted on the child's mind, even if it was only because he *was* seduced. When he would remember this visit in years to come, Jean-Paul could say that his father had enabled him to participate in the final moments of a period in history.

Mañungo discreetly brushed his tears with his hand. A camera flash instantly returned him to reality, not on the beach at Isla Negra, not in a grand Parisian hotel, but at the foot of a box that held Matilde's remains: she smiled at him from the wall, two-headed and disheveled. At his feet lay the wreath of white and red flowers: he'd been photographed next to that offering. Who? The CIA or the KGB? It was all the same: antagonistic but parallel powers. If that photo went around the world via satellite—four or five years back, when he was at his peak, that's what would have happened—his agent would get furious. Now it just didn't matter. He could protest . . . no, it was too much trouble to protest about something that, even if it wasn't completely innocent, was meaningless unless he kept on singing, roaring like a lion or like that ocean wave in which Matilde's image was frozen.

♦ *A*s he came downstairs, Mañungo
realized he'd been standing in front of the coffin longer than he'd
thought. Remembering? Thinking? Or perhaps, without consciously
doing it and in his secular, haphazard way, praying? Because when
he returned he found an air of fatigue in the patio, fatigue at least in
comparison to what he'd felt before going upstairs. The crowd had
begun to thin, leaving the space occupied by the shadows of intimate
friends, to whom it never occurred to do something other than stay
with Matilde until the last possible minute, and by a detachment from
the Communist Youth, who had to stay there until they were relieved.

At the bottom of the stairs, Mañungo was surrounded by young
people: questions, autographs, would he sing? what was Paris like?
why had he come back when they were in a state of siege and when
there was a midnight curfew? did he belong to any party? did he have
a girlfriend? He wasn't a member of their generation—they were just
barely adolescents who had been nurtured by the tortuous underground of the dictatorship years—and he realized it with horror when
he had to answer a young girl's question: "How does it feel to be living
under a dictatorship?" This was his first day in such a situation, and
it made him totally different from everyone around him.

Despite all that, the youths around him felt that Mañungo was their
spokesman, that he embodied their longing for the mythical Golden
Age of the Popular Union Party. Theirs was an enthusiasm with no
strictures, an enthusiasm for pure acceleration, speed, which they
knew only in the form of a bewitching legend to which they hungered
to return. And for this reason, they unconsciously imitated Mañungo
Vera's style, or at least the style of Mañungo the protest singer and
guerrilla. The other style, the new one—the one whose nervous, frantic hands snatched material from The Police or the ecology movement,

things foreign to his heart and personal experience, things that blurred his unique profile as a singer and made him indistinguishable from any other second-rate showman—this other Mañungo maintained his prestige in Chile simply by carrying the torch of what in these parts passed for "modern."

When one of the boys suggested calling a television station to announce the news of his arrival and to ask that a camera crew be sent, Mañungo said, "I don't think it's such a good idea."

"Why not? You could be on tonight's news."

"I'm not allowed to appear on TV. The Chilean censor doesn't love me."

"He doesn't love this house either."

"That's for sure."

Despite this, the boy insisted on calling in the sensational news. Just when the station answered his call, Fausta grabbed the telephone out of his hands and shouted into the receiver that she didn't understand what was going on because no one bothered to tell her anything, but that she was not going to allow this house to be used as a stage on a day of mourning. If they wanted to talk to Mañungo, they could interview him at his hotel. She hung up without mentioning the name of his hotel.

In the group around the singer, a young woman with paper and pencil at the ready peppered him with questions for an interview in her paper, a scoop that would boost her career. "Do you believe that armed struggle would be effective against this regime?" "No, because the regime has all the weapons, and violence for violence's sake is a symptom of despair." "Do you have a girlfriend?" "Lots, and I'm faithful to all of them." "What's your solution for the country's current political problems?" "I don't know yet. I don't think anything I might suggest would matter very much. I've been away for too long to know firsthand what's been going on here." "Have you taken part in the active resistance outside the country?" "Yes, to a point: you've heard me sing." "Why 'to a point'?" "Because at this point in time I'm not sure of anything." "Don't you have any convictions at all?" "Only the most basic ones." "Are you a coward?" "I don't think so. I'm brave enough to have doubts and to hesitate and I don't think that's going to destroy me." "Do you think you'll ever take a stand?" "Could be. Give me some time to see things and to think. If I had stayed in Chile, I might know for sure what to be and I would have joined some specific program that would lead me to take a stand, but when you're far away, you can only show your sympathies, admire people, encourage them, help, and keep the faith . . ." "What do you believe in?" Mañungo laughed: "I don't know yet. When I sing here, I'll know."

The interview was shorter than the reporter had hoped it would be, because Mañungo refused to take a firm stand on the issues. His answers were neither polemical nor combative, which was the only truly journalistic aspect to any interview. She put away her paper and pencil thinking that perhaps it would be better to write a story about Matilde's wake than to publish the interview. She could refer to Mañungo and quote some of his less tentative answers to prove he was actually there and that she had spoken with him. In any case, she asked herself as she and the other curious onlookers were being ushered out by Fausta: "Is *this* Mañungo Vera?" Talking in this overly refined and overly sensible style? Uninformed, with no firm position, refusing to attack headfirst? Was this the idol? Where was his burning commitment, the commitment that had stirred them all in his old records? Where was his enthusiasm, his promise of a Golden Age in the future that would be like the Golden Age of the past? Where was his courage, his will, the struggle, where was his strength?

These were the questions the blond choirboy was asking his friend with the scraggly beard, the one with whom he had earlier disagreed about the value of Fausta Manquileo's writing. Mañungo was soft, he was saying, decadent, petit-bourgeois, a delusion. His partner told him to take it easy, despite the fact that he agreed, especially about the delusion.

"He's a traitor!" exclaimed the choirboy, his voice hoarse with rage.

"I don't know if he's a traitor. A coward, yes, of course."

"A traitor. All that doubt is nothing but a prelude to betrayal. This is no time to be worrying about absolute truths. What we should be worrying about is strategy, injustice, hunger . . ."

"What do you know about hunger? Your father's a doctor and you live in a house with a garden and dogs in the best part of town."

"You think you're better because you live in a slum?"

The two friends were about to come to blows when Fausta pushed through the group that had gathered around them to quiet them down. Lopito had finally convinced Mañungo that now, since only a few people remained, he should sing a song in memory of Matilde. After all, wasn't it a custom of ours, a very Chilean, very peasant custom, to sing about glory and holiness at a wake, something ancient and full of dignity?

Everyone felt the strumming, barely insinuated in the night, of the musician exploring the identity of a guitar that wasn't his. The young people eagerly sat in a semicircle around Mañungo; the rest found seats on the benches, the stone divider wall, under the trees. Their shadows became still and several silhouettes appeared at the head of the stairs. Lisboa stood listening at the window. Wasn't it disrespectful to sing now and abandon the casket? He had argued with Fausta. Everyone knew that Matilde had been a singer when she was young. The guitar picked up Matilde's extremely personal style in music, her own intransferable style, which was not Neruda's. Her individuality stood out so that everyone could understand that she was a person in her own right and not the poet's handmaiden. Lopito whispered into Judit's ear that he bet not even Mañungo, despite all his years in Europe, could sing "Ich grolle nicht," for example.

The blond choirboy approached Mañungo and suggested something—in an overly challenging way, Judit judged from behind the persimmon tree where she was sitting—that made Mañungo hesitate. Just when the choirboy was insisting, whispering to him again, Mañungo began to sing. That mellow, almost tactile baritone he'd had all his life and through all his struggles (Lisboa thought exultantly, as he identified the melody Mañungo had decided to sing), now, twelve years later, had an iron catch in it, a powerful, painful, and personal claw, that drowned Mañungo but flooded his voice with an emotion that wasn't only sentiment but power, anger, and thirst for justice:

> "I shall walk the streets again
> Of a Santiago bathed in blood
> And in a beautiful plaza now free
> I shall stop to weep for the dead."

In a flash, physically, Judit felt Mañungo's voice like a painful stab, definitive proof of the singer's power. Never before had she felt this immediacy, this ability to move his audience so naturally. Perhaps it was because voices now held the key of life and death for her as they never had before. Judit had often heard Mañungo's songs at meetings with younger people, but she never bought his records. She was not overly fond of popular music in general. A personal limitation, of course, but what could she do, when her tastes ran to Schubert and Schumann?

These lyrics, in a certain sense, alluded to Judit's biography because they alluded to the biography of an entire generation. Not that Judit thought herself a typical member of her generation, even if she recognized her affiliation with it. Perhaps it was not so much the words themselves as their interplay with the network of halftones which seemed to carry all the answers Mañungo had not given the stupid reporter, who hadn't asked him a single question about music. Mañungo was strong because he was a limited being, extremely strong for that reason and in spite of the rumors of his recent failures, strong even if he broke, strong because he was breaking, strong even if he were shattered into a thousand pieces. Would it be possible to speak with him? In any case, she preferred to remain in the shadows, and besides, Ada Luz was waiting for her at her house. Mañungo went on:

"I'll return from the blazing desert
And I'll come down to the forests and lakes
And on a beautiful hill in Santiago
I shall stop to weep for the dead.

"I measure all who helped me, all who hurt me,
those who love our country free,
I shall fire the first shots,
Then the songs and books will return
Those burned by murdering hands . . ."

The patio filled with Pablo Milanés's lyrics, with the sadness of the house, the sadness of everything, and Fausta, who at the beginning had fought it, now ran to Mañungo, shocked, despite everything, that he would dare to sing a song like that here. But Lisboa, a sentinel on his staircase vantage point, who had slowly but surely come down the stairs to approach his idol, knew that this was the real Mañungo. He had misjudged him: his having dared to sing "Santiago Bathed in Blood" here, tonight, was restoring Lisboa's respect for Mañungo. Then, with the words "murdering hands," the words that were like a banner in the song, Mañungo's voice faded and the guitar fell silent.

In the group that surrounded him, Fausta stood up, dragged her dramatic robes across the open space to the singer, who had fallen silent at a signal from her, and passed through the group of young people sitting on the floor. She bent over to whisper into Mañungo's ear, explaining something to him with emphatic gestures which Mañungo seemed to understand and respect. With Fausta standing next to him, he strummed a few chords, changed tone and rhythm, and she went back to her corner in the semidarkness. After the unfinished song, Mañungo sang verses by Neruda dedicated to Matilde, with all the music of the poet:

> "You come from the destitute houses of the south,
> From regions made hard by cold and earthquakes,
> That gave us the lesson of life from clay
> Even when their gods collapsed into death."

When Mañungo had finished the first stanza, the blond choirboy and his friend stood up so that everyone could see them cross the semicircle in front of the singer, who neither looked at them nor stopped. They went down the stone stairs and walked out of the house, slamming the door behind them. Lisboa followed them while Mañungo went on singing, and only he, standing in the doorway to listen, could understand the insults they shouted from the sidewalk:

"Coward!"

"Whore!"

"Traitor!"

"I shall fire the first shots/Then the songs and books will return/ Those burned by murdering hands," the two boys sang in the street.

Lisboa would have liked the people inside to hear those shouts. But the music drowned out the indignation of the two who had walked out. It was Fausta's fault. *"Nous serons modérés quand nous serons vainqueurs,"* the Party teacher had often said in their exile study group in Brussels. This was no time for moderation. It was going to be a struggle to the death, because this ferocious woman and people like her, who had the undeserved power to silence the truth, were preparing a frontal attack inspired by the death of Matilde, and in doing so were creating a confrontation between two ways of living and thinking. They, the moderates, were the real enemy, the real murderers, to whom there was no response except the blood that scared them so much. Mañungo went on:

> "You are a little mare of black clay,
> Of dark pitch, love, clay poppy,
> An evening dove that flew along roads,
> Following the tears of our poor childhood."

Mañungo's song, insipid despite Neruda's verses, rising from the patio, ended leaving no trace but the ashes of self-absorption. In the tiny space between stanzas, which the singer seemed to extend voluntarily, Lisboa would have liked to hear the kids down on the street shouting, "coward, faggot, traitor," as they had been a few minutes before, so that everyone could hear them, so that the brief silence Mañungo "artistically" produced around himself would fill with the hostility of reality.

All of which did not mean that Lisboa was insensitive to this song that left its melancholy concentrated in the patio. On the contrary: he too shared those sentiments. But the difference, the determining difference, was that those feelings would only receive their maximum energy if they were inscribed within an inexorable, rigid plan, the people's plan, far from poetry, the plan of an "It Will Fall/ It Will Fall/ The People United/ Can Never Be Defeated." This is what he wanted to hear tomorrow in the cemetery, over the speeches and lamentations; he wanted it to stir up and galvanize the masses, ideally to move them to action right during the burial ceremony. Mañungo finished:

"Girl, you've kept your poor girl's heart
your poor girl's feet accustomed to the stones,
your mouth that hasn't always tasted bread or sweets.

"You are from the poor south, land of my soul:
In her heaven, your mother goes on washing clothes
Alongside my mother. That's why I chose you, comrade."

*L*opito told Mañungo that the telephone was in the dining room, as if Mañungo hadn't known it all his life. Lopito then added that he'd keep him company while he called. Mañungo turned on the light, so different from the brilliance of other times. The Nerudian ghosts, the echoes of the people who had occupied those generous chairs and drunk and eaten at that table, were no longer present in the household objects, now too insignificant to house such illustrious spirits.

He saw the telephone on top of the bistro side table and slipped into the space between the table and the bench pushed up against the wall. All the while, Lopito spoke to him, a cigarette dangling from his lip. People might have held Lopito in some regard, but there was no getting around the fact that he was truly repulsive. What would Mañungo have done with him if he'd turned up in Paris, for example, demanding the comradeship of other times, demanding he be introduced to girls, to friends—the obligatory comradeship of student days revived, the disorder, the carousing that was no longer part of Mañungo's life? What would Nadja have said, she who was always at war with all forms of chaos? He dialed the number of the Holiday Inn and asked to speak with his own room.

"Jean-Paul?" he asked.

"Jean-Paul . . . !" laughed Lopito, coughing, choking on cigarette smoke. "Jesus!"

"*Comment vas-tu? C'est bien, la télé au Chili? C'est* Dallas? *Mais tu as déjà vu ça. Il n'y a pas d'autre chose à voir? Ah . . . C'est vrai. . . .*" He says he'd rather watch *Dallas* because he's already seen it in Paris, so he can understand what they're saying in Spanish, not as if it were something new. *Tu n'as besoin de rien? Tu as bien bouffé? Bien, Jean-*

Paul. J'accroche tout de suite pour que tu puisses voir Dallas. *Je voulais seulement savoir si tu étais bien."*

"A quelle heure tu vas rentrer, papa?"

"Je ne sais pas."

"Ne viens pas trop tard."

"Mais si tu es en train de t'amuser . . ."

"Mais je n'aime pas être seul."

"Je rentre dans une heure environ. Je suis avec de très bons amis que je ne voyais pas depuis douze ans."

"Une heure c'est trop, papa."

"Alors, trois quarts d'heure."

"Non, une demi-heure. Quand Dallas *finira."*

"Ça va. A bientôt, Jean-Paul. Jean-Paul . . . Jean-Paul . . . He hung up, the little bastard. He orders me to get back right away, but since he's having a good time watching *Dallas* he doesn't even say goodbye."

"Terrible," commented Lopito. "Children should be well behaved and bid their daddies an affectionate goodnight."

Lopito coughed again, staring seriously at Mañungo. So seriously that it was impossible to miss the mockery of it. Mañungo stood up in the narrow space between the bench and the table, his face near Lopito's mask, which gave off smoke like an archaic clay pot that was only allusively anthropomorphic. When Lopito stopped coughing he said, "But Mañungo, my dear fellow . . . !"

"What?"

"That's the limit, what you're doing . . ."

"What am I doing?"

"That you have to talk to your kid in French! Jesus!"

"He barely knows any Spanish. His mother's French. He's always lived with her. I've tried to get him to learn Spanish, but in school and in the neighborhood . . . impossible. Besides, just now, with the tensions of the trip driving him nuts, I'd rather not pressure him about it."

"Well I'll be damned! You've turned into the model father, Mañungo! It's a pleasure to listen to you! You've got a well-mannered kid, who knows he should say goodbye properly to his dad because his dad provides for him, who speaks fluent French, and who might get a bit neurotic because of tension. Would you like me to recommend a good therapist who could take him in hand while he's here? What would you like: Gestalt, Lacan, or a terrifying disciple of Melanie Klein? This may be the armpit of the world, but we've heard of all these things. Don't think we're so ignorant."

Mañungo stared at him fixedly, and Lopito did not avert his eyes. Without speaking, Mañungo moved away from where he was standing and hung up the telephone behind Lopito, who didn't budge. An instant later, Lopito said in a slow, deep voice, "You've changed, Mañungo."

"How could I not change?" he asked vehemently. "How could I not change after twelve years outside the country, a failed marriage, and a kid to take care of, with the success I had and don't have much of anymore, and the travel, and all that Europe had to offer me? Did you think I'd be the same as I was in the university fifteen years ago?"

"That was the great Mañungo Vera."

"Can't this year's model be great, just because he's different?"

"Let's go have a drink together. Then we'll see."

"I don't feel like taking an exam."

Lopito draped his arm affectionately around his friend's neck. "No one's going to make you take an exam, old buddy. All of us here love and admire you. What kind of exam could we give you, man, when we're all nothing but a bunch of assholes dying of envy because we've never traveled farther than Quilicura? Don't be afraid."

"I'm not afraid. Twelve years away from here have taught me not be afraid of anything."

"Sure! Twelve years of the good life can give you the strength to take anything!"

Mañungo was about to punch Lopito, but when he saw how swollen his face already was from so many beatings he held back. That would be a bad start. What would happen next? Why should he stand for this bum's aggressiveness? Because they were friends thirteen years ago, when they both were different people? He should have foreseen this: Lopito was pure resentment. A filthy slob—okay, that's what he'd always been, but in those days everybody was more or less filthy. Unbearable, stupid, awkward, a hick, a failure . . . no, not a failure, no, he held back, biting his tongue, trying to swallow that last, unpronounceable word, trying not even to think it, but he did not manage to hold his tongue in time to avoid disdaining him for being a failure.

It was forbidden to disdain failures. His own successes taught him that all success contains an all too important quotient of luck, because having enough psychological health to not fall into the infinite temptations of self-destruction is the most gratuitous gift of all, and to ride the crest of fortune's wave is pure chance. So it is forbidden to disdain the failures who did not have the gift of that strength, forbidden to disdain the weak of any kind, the vulnerable, those who wished but who couldn't make it, who drowned in their own self-pity and nostalgia for what they dreamed of doing and never did.

The anger Lopito felt toward Mañungo was the anger of the failure. Yes, indeed, and why not? How well Mañungo knew that anger, but how hard it was to accept it, and how difficult it was to defend against without hurting that person. Ah, Lopito's life! In Paris he'd heard of Lopito's descent from drink to drink, from debt to debt down to hell, those macabre chronicles that never fail to reach even as far as Europe. In this moment Mañungo was feeling disgustingly guilty for disdaining Lopito because his life was a failure, and because Mañungo was stronger than he. Worse, Mañungo hated Lopito for making him feel guilt at being a success in his own lifetime. Perhaps now his own moment had come for the self-destruction that others live before they begin.

He knew that exclusive club only too well, above all from when he was with his less-fortunate compatriots in Europe. That's why he'd become reclusive and avoided them as much as he could, until he'd finally lost sight of them. They whispered that Mañungo Vera thought he was a potentate. He doesn't deal with the likes of us, we're just nobodies, he belongs to the jet set, he wants nothing to do with us, not even to have a drink with us. In more recent times, as he became more and more vulnerable because of his perplexity, which, it was said, had made him weak, he didn't include his compatriots among the people he saw socially. He was left isolated, bereft of any contact with his country, and alone he would look for news about Chile in *Le Monde*, pensively drinking coffee in a place where no one knew him.

"I have to be on my way," he said to Lopito. "Tonight I can't go out for a drink. Besides, I don't drink much these days. I have to go see my kid. He's very young and he's all alone. He's probably afraid."

They were leaving the dining room. Only a few people were left in the patio, because the curfew, although still far off, had appeared on the night's horizon. On a bench, Fausta Manquileo was talking to a blond woman whose back was the part of her they saw, and whose face was hidden behind her fair hair: she was too thin to be the vision that could console Mañungo.

"What are you talking about?" Lopito insisted. "When people have received you with the love you've seen here, despite how sad we are for obvious reasons, how can you think of playing mommy to your little boy? Let him take care of himself. Or call up the hotel. What hotel are you staying in?"

"The Holiday Inn."

"I might have guessed! If you're in the Holiday Inn, where you pay for the very air you breathe, they can find you a baby-sitter to take care of the kid if he's as neurotic as you say."

"I never said he was neurotic."

"Okay, okay. Don't be a pain in the ass, I didn't mean anything. I just feel like knocking back a few bottles of wine with you, man, so you can tell me everything. Christ, do we have things to tell each other!"

"But I promised the kid . . ."

"Don't give me that shit. Look, buddy, I know some French. I'm not as ignorant as you think, so I know you told the kid you'd be back in half an hour. So if it takes you an hour, nothing's going to happen to him, and we have a drink in the bar on the corner. How about it?"

The woman whose long hair hid her
face from Mañungo was Judit Torre, who was commenting on Mañungo's presence to Fausta Manquileo. She was sitting with her elbow
resting on her knee and holding her chin in her hand to pay close
attention to her friend. Her body, with its fine bones, complemented
her angular face, and blended with her jeans and black shirt to make
a gaunt but harmonious whole, while Fausta sat with her arms stretched
out on the back of the bench and her large silver pendant galloping
over her bosom. They were criticizing Mañungo's imprudence in
choosing his first song.

In contrast to Fausta, Judit was as light as a feather, and showed
exactly the right combination of details, a minute harmony of calcu-
lation and design. The features of her extraordinary skull—don Celedonio declared that in a few millennia, when paleontologists dug up
her jawbone, they could use it to reconstruct a perfect specimen of a
woman from the Latin American privileged classes—might have seemed
harsh if it weren't for the fact that her eyes, eyebrows, eyelashes, and
blond mane were just a few shades too light for her beauty, a defect
she might easily have remedied, but which did not seem to bother
her. Her hair no longer had the vitality of early youth, and mixed in
with the blond were the first strands of gray, which she was too proud
to disguise with rinses.

At this time of night, with the lights turned down for farewells and
mourning, those gray hairs were invisible. Fausta, always generous
with her admiration, thought Judit looked like a Noguchi from one
of his good periods because of her finely modeled features, a splendid
creature who in some undefinable way was beginning to dry out without every having flowered, despite having more than enough sap to

do it. Neruda, who had liked her, would have preferred her more earthy and accessible. And Celedonio, when he still had a festive vocation, would have wanted her to be more lighthearted. But Judit was intelligent, ironic when she was in a good mood, too ironic for people not to be a bit afraid of her. On the other hand, she was a great reciter of the anecdotes she had stored up in her memory, which was as long as a granny's.

People said she was presumptuous because of her zeal in protecting her private life—for example, who knew how she had gone from the Party to the Revolutionary Left Movement? And after abandoning that group, what was she into now? What trace was left in her life of her heroic comrade Ramón, whose real name turned out to be Hilario Vilaró, and about whom Judit never spoke and whom no one ever dared mention in her presence? And her incredible friendship with Lopito? And her daughter, Marilú? Why did Judit allow Marilú to live with Ramón's parents? Evil tongues said that Judit Torre was a has-been because she played at being mysterious, the original for "The Sphinx Without a Secret."

Besides, that strange sect it was rumored she belonged to, related to magic or some esoteric philosophy—not surprising she had turned to it after her youthful flirtation with political extremism—was no sect at all. All you had to do was chat with that dumb friend of hers, that Ada Luz, to see that it couldn't be anything interesting. And if Judit sometimes kept company with Ada Luz and her women friends, it was simply to watch television like any neighborhood woman, and to knit, which was something for which Ada Luz really did have a magic touch.

Judit was not very feminine, they concluded, because where for most normal women reality never became real until they discussed it with another woman, she never gossiped with anyone. Yes, Fausta would have liked a more open Judit after all they'd been through together, a Judit she might reach by other means than pure intelligence. Matilde would say when speaking warmly of Judit that Judit was aggressive, cruel, with a disturbing way of bending over backward, as if she wanted to protect the person she was speaking with from the edge of her repressed criticism. And yet, her public behavior had a beguiling surface, as soft as sheepskin. She was a good questioner as well, and a passionate listener, a thing rarely found among women who still have desires but no steady male companion, and tend to deafen everyone by talking about themselves as if to justify their slightly pathetic existences.

"You didn't know him before, even if he does belong to your generation!"

"No . . ."

"It isn't that Mañungo has declined, but he certainly has changed. Naturally, he's still as attractive as ever. That warmth he projects, the way his voice suddenly breaks with emotion . . . it makes you want to hug him. He still sings beautifully, no matter what that fool Lisboa says! The thing is that he used to preach in his songs, which is what they love, because they're like the Jesuits. Now he's different, as if his own vulnerability doesn't matter to him, and if you don't mind my being crude about it, honey, I just *love* vulnerable men . . ."

It was a matter of changing fashions, Judit said to herself. Fausta's tastes corresponded to a certain historical moment as far as men were concerned, just as they would in clothes: the hard but vulnerable men of the post-existentialist period in the Camus-Bogart-Belmondo style, the man who at the end of an art movie flips up the collar of his raincoat and with a classic gesture stops to light up a cigarette. Then he walks off down a rainy street without looking back at the Piaf or Juliette Greco who stays behind, sighing for him at the window. . . . That's what Fausta liked—or thought she liked, because for forty years she'd been faithful to a man of exactly the opposite style—and it filled her with an ambiguous nostalgia.

No one would say that Mañungo belonged to the Camus-Bogart-Belmondo school. He was of a different generation, a different continent. But there was a "retro" touch in the way he kept his leather bag slung over his shoulder, even if the heroes Fausta loved never used leather bags. They were all, as Fausta would say, men with "style"— something poor Ramón never had, because to be an active revolutionary presupposed an aesthetic blindness that only became a style when he gave himself over to the struggle. Exciting enough, of course. But of such moral density that it left a blank space where the aesthetic should have been, a space that Judit—she confessed it only to her pillow—thought would have to be filled in order for her to be really in love, if in fact that highly advertised state actually existed. She admired Ramón madly, the way you can only admire someone who risks his life every single day. Ramón excited her. Ramón inspired her and taught her. But because of her unconfessable hint of frivolity, her aestheticism—she only dared recognize it now, after so many years—she never really loved him, although the mark he made on her was as important as the kind supposedly left by true love.

"In those days, Mañungo was not as interesting as he is now. He was just good-looking," Fausta continued. "Handsome. With a certain Indian or exotic ingredient. And his long legs and long arms and his marvelous hands, and the way he grasped the guitar around the waist as if it were a woman . . . We all felt a bit like guitars then, let me tell you, even the old bags like me, who poured into the clubs to see and hear him. They said he had no address. He lived with the women who were his one-night stands or with friends, and his only property aside from his music books and his guitar was his sleeping bag, which he always carried with him. They said he was in the Revolutionary Left. One of the dangerous ones, the kind who risk their lives and plant bombs. You can imagine the havoc he created in the hormones of the revolutionary girls back then! When he came he made the Caleuche, the Pincoya, and the Imbunche popular—we all talked about our national folklore in those days—and made Chiloé handcrafts into a fashion. The kids shouted themselves hoarse in the clubs cheering his revolutionary songs. Casa de las Américas invited him to Cuba, and the Communist Party to a youth festival in Warsaw, although I don't know how because the Revolutionary Left Movement was outside the Popular Unity movement and they hated the communists. But in those days, remember, everything seemed to have such a total coherence that chaos and enthusiasm were all part of a single spirit, despite the fights and differences of opinion—a single project of which Mañungo was a part. But Mañungo was never meant to be a militant. He was an egomaniac, like all great artists. Later, when he was in Europe, we found out that even though he was supposed to be in the Revolutionary Left Movement he was never actually in it and had never planted any bombs. No one will ever forgive him for staying outside of Chile. He was never officially a political exile, and only stayed out of the country to further his career. I'd love it if you'd say hello to him. Should I introduce you?"

"No, darling. Why bother? I have to go. It's late. Besides, I don't like stars and I don't ever want to be a groupie."

"You're right. Pablo always said, 'That Judit is a real mystery, so charming when she tells stories. I wish she'd come out more often. She's like a museum piece, that girl, because she believes in the importance of private life and that's out of fashion.' Look. Here comes Mañungo. Now you can't escape."

Mañungo was surrounded by friends and was just coming downstairs after saying farewell to Matilde's casket. The introduction was superficial, complicated by the throng of people taking their leave, and inconsequential—so much so that Judit was able to slip unnoticed to the rear of the crowd. Mañungo was kissing Fausta's cheek, arranging to see her the next day at the cemetery, and then again as soon as they could—Fausta was going to have a lot of trouble with the foundation business, which stank of government intrigue—they'd eat together with anyone he'd care to have her invite.

Judit, realizing that Lopito was hurrying toward the group, managed to slip away before he came. Without anyone's noticing, she walked out of the house, pressing her purse under her elbow, as if to make her silhouette even slimmer, more nearly invisible.

13

*J*udit looked at her watch. Nine-thirty. Auristela said they should be there at nine so she would have time to comb her hair and make her up and then go home—home was in a slum on the other side of the world. At night even the people who lived there were afraid to enter, because now there were not only muggings, but flaming barricades and riots in the streets—the first encroachment of the slums on middle-class neighborhoods. These events were never reported in the papers. Afraid of all that, as were all the other women in the group, Aury sometimes slept at Ada Luz's house, which was near the hairdresser's where she worked. But she hadn't slept there much recently, because Ada Luz was involved in a romance and Aury preferred to be discreet. Judit, on the other hand, was always there because she had to know everything. Tonight, nevertheless, her curiosity about Mañungo's arrival was stronger than her tyrannical commitment to the women, and she was late. She had to run to make it.

Bellavista was calm. The morning's death had already been digested, metabolized, and forgotten—as would any other death even before the funeral obliterated the remains. The steep hill spread its light pine scent over the blessed coolness of the summer night. It was as if a door had opened on the noxious suffocation of the day. Against the vertiginous flank of the hill rested the funicular railway Judit loved because it reminded her of the Eiffel Tower. The ocelots, the ibis, the cockatoos, the huge, redoubtable pachyderms slept out their life sentences in the zoo.

Some citizens were peacefully returning to their houses along the city streets, and through the curtains (which ones were real lace, Judit asked herself, and which mere affectation and "revival"? impossible to tell, although the phonies were probably nicer than the real ones) she saw families sitting on plastic chairs at dining-room tables or in incongruous "American-style" kitchens, furnished at ruinous cost, all of which established a melancholy dinnertime atmosphere that was barely mitigated by television. There was little traffic now; some kids were still kicking a ball around under the streetlights. In the bars and restaurants customers were eating Barros Jarpas and Barros Lucos: what was the difference between them? Judit was confused by these names, the names of friends of her grandfather which had been given to sandwiches for men. On the other hand, hot pork barbecue sand-wiches, accompanied by tall glasses of foamy, golden beer seemed so contemporary because they were unisex. There weren't many people enjoying these modest delights. There was no money around for su-perfluous expenses, and it was better to sit down to the family bowl of lentils.

Ada Luz was waiting for her at the house, which looked like a caricature of what was fashionable in Bellavista—light wood, straw, umbrella stands, plants, but also plastic flowers wrapped in cellophane to protect them from any hypothetical dust, and an oilcloth tablecloth with Betty Boop printed on it in three colors. Betty Boop! An effort at nostalgia? Despite everything, Ada Luz's house was permeated by a thick air of intimacy, of uterine protection, of affectionate, feminine warmth, all soft and secret, with lots of embroidered cushions and useless doilies, the edges of things covered over, the feet of tables and chairs skirted over. Baskets lined with bright cretonne, which hid the nobility of the willow, overflowed with colored yarn which Ada Luz would knit or turn over to the women who helped her, whom she helped in turn by giving them work while Judit contributed by getting her orders from people she knew who owned boutiques in Providencia.

Judit was annoyed by so much sticky femininity. But it was impos-sible not to realize that hers was an intellectual, affected annoyance, because after fifteen minutes in Ada Luz's cozy house, in the rear part of a tenement, free from the noise of the street, her aesthetic—really a snobbish and puritanical resistance, which she fought to dissimu-late—was overwhelmed by this atmosphere. So much so that some-times she came by just to sink into Ada Luz's cushions, so they could both watch some stupid television program—the Oscars or the Miss Universe pageant for example—when she felt her demons were pur-suing her overzealously.

Ada Luz breathed a sigh of relief when she opened the door. Thank God it wasn't Lisboa: she'd noticed something threatening in him when she left Miss Matilde's house arm in arm with don Celedonio, she explained, something like a sign that later on—now—he would come to see her.

"Has he ever come without setting a time first?"

"Sure he has, Ju. But you know he's married and can only come when he can break away."

"In love with him?"

"No. Maybe, I don't know . . ."

"Don't think I like the idea that he can come here as he pleases."

"How about a cup of tea?"

"Wonderful."

"Some cookies?"

"What kind? Oh, yes, please. Looks like I've got a long night ahead of me."

"Could be."

"And this afternoon over at Matilde's was murder."

What would Judit, such an atheist, think about the famous mass? When Miss Matilde had confided her secret, she'd wanted to tell Judit at once. And today, as she prepared the tea on the camp stove, she felt the same impulse. But she was ashamed that she always had to tell everything to Judit. Things like this, for example. It made her important. If she kept quiet, on the other hand, the story, which only she knew, would vanish without a trace, and that would be the best thing for everybody.

As she waited for the water to boil, Ada Luz congratulated herself on having gotten Lisboa upset because of her gossipy information about the mass for Miss Matilde. It meant she had him in her clutches, instead of the other way around. If he turned up tonight, she wouldn't let him in. If she did let him in, she'd trick him by telling him she'd already spoken about the matter with don Celedonio, and that to-morrow there would be an article about it in the newspapers, and that the cardinal was going to say a graveside mass. Then Lisboa would start calling people by the thousands without realizing he'd be spreading the news he wanted to hush up.

"What a riot!" she muttered as she put the cookies on a plate.

"What's a riot?"

"Nothing, nothing at all."

Judit felt the swelling wave of irritation Ada Luz frequently caused in her: Ada Luz, whose personality was so anemic, as dim as the electric lights after some act of sabotage. Again she found Ada Luz dumb—even offensive—but for that very reason she was useful: she was incapable of measuring the effect of her actions. Judit shut her eyes to reject the guilt she felt concerning a friend with whom she'd spent time in hell, a fact that was enough to unite them. She could not allow her own arrogance to betray her by fixing the blame on the nearest person, when others deserved it more. Her hatred had to be self-contained, had to be her certainty ever since that man with the nasal voice and the moist hands had her locked up: insults, barking, groans, masculine laughter, obscenities, and among the voices of the women she recognized the ones belonging to those who had spent three days imprisoned together in a stinking little space: Ada Luz, Senta, Domitila, Aury, Beatriz, a group to which the man with the nasal voice and the soft, sweaty hands kept her from being a part because she was the only one who did not suffer the entire martyrdom. Her hatred could not center on a specific person and became a kind of vague narcissism that took the place as much of true hate as of true love.

Ada Luz handed her the cup and the plate of cookies, along with an irritating triangular napkin unnecessarily decorated with harsh zigzags. As Ada Luz was sitting down next to her to knit a lavender vest, Judit asked, "Why are you afraid of Lisboa?"

"Because he's always butting in."

"Don't lie, that's not the reason."

Ada Luz, sole proprietor of her secret, did not feel the slightest inclination to let herself be manipulated by anyone, not even by the admirable Judit Torre.

"It's that Lisboa promised to help me arrange for Daniel to come to Chile so I could see my grandson."

"What power does Lisboa have? None. You know that as well as I do. He's a minor god in the Party, with no influence, who's only in charge of certain sectors of the Youth. You can stop fooling yourself: Daniel is not going to come, even if someone tells you not to give up hope. You might as well face up to it. He isn't going to come, not because he can't, but because he doesn't have the money to travel all the way from Canada. It's tough up there and he's got a great house and he married a *gringa* and he teaches Marxism at the University of Saskatchewan, where he's highly thought of. What do you think he's going to do around here, where the philosophers are taxi drivers because they're out of work? Up there he's got his *gringo* son and his *gringa* wife. She's right to get annoyed at the idea of leaving her house and spending thousands of dollars to visit this shithole and see a woman who frankly doesn't matter one bit to her . . ."

Ada Luz was crying as she knit, "How cold you can be, Judit!"

"It's just that all this stuff wears me out."

"I wonder how you'd like it if I were as cold to you as you are with other people."

Judit glanced at her. Did this woman know of her deception? Was she out of compassion merely pretending that Judit, blindfolded, naked, had suffered the same torture the others had, that she was one of the victims and for that reason her vengeance would be the vengeance of all of them?

"I'm saving money to go see him."

"That sounds like a more realistic idea."

"Sure it does! Realistic, huh? Your family is rich, so saving money sounds easy to you! What about me, with things being the way they are? I'm afraid they'll investigate me if I ask for an exit visa. I must be in their book, and then they won't leave me in peace, me or any of us. Besides, maybe my son and his wife are ashamed to see me. I don't speak English or anything."

A piece of Judit's cookie fell on the floor. She accidentally stepped on it, but with a pair of precise movements picked it up and wiped away the crumbs. Judit had been changing over the course of her sterile years, thought Ada Luz, leaving little more than her precise way of moving and speaking, while the brightness of her blue eyes faded and grew colder, as if she had them fixed on an advancing glacier that would eventually crush her. Someone knocked at the door, and Ada Luz froze.

"Lisboa . . . !"

"But we're waiting for Auristela!"

"Of course—you're right."

Ada Luz opened the door for a smiling little woman, highly made up and coquettish despite her age, wearing high heels and a complicated hairdo—copied, Judit calculated, from one of Carita's sophisticated cuts that had probably appeared in a Chilean magazine. Her bust and calves were on display, as was her backside, and she carried herself with the self-confidence of a woman who knows that the men on street corners will turn around to admire her generous charms, well deserving of gross compliments: Auristela might lack for everything, even food, which she'd gone without on more than one occasion, but she'd never lack for that God-given abundance. Judit objectively reflected that no one ever whistled at her on the street, although some had admired her stylized proportions in more perverse ways: long legs, blond mane, a certain way of walking, of revealing the intimacy of her bare earlobes caressed by her hair.

"Hot and skinny!" the nasal voice she'd searched for ever since had

shouted. For a second his sweaty hand had rested on her knee, then
he'd removed it without carrying out his implicit promise to make her
his victim.

For her group of women, Judit's beauty—ridiculously exaggerated,
she thought, because they didn't know better—was a fact, even though
her melancholy was beginning to wear it out. And her elegance, independent of her modest wardrobe, stimulated their fantasies, which
bestowed on her the ability to accomplish supernatural acts of seduction. She was the perfect instrument to carry out the plan for
revenge—which involved submission, even murder—that her own intelligence had created, and that had so dazzled her comrades that they
willingly became part of it. One more act to destabilize what urgently
had to fall, since they all felt that the violence which they were approaching slowly but surely was nothing more than the incarnation of
the despair the current state of affairs was pushing them to. Therefore,
it was not only acceptable but necessary. Narcissism? A need for heroic
action, which despite her discretion and abnegation she was obscurely
seeking for herself? Could be. But what more could they contribute,
after all, poor, ignorant women, not brave, with no money, with nothing but the admiration that sometimes made Judit uncomfortable? Who
but Judit could take this vengeance when she was the only person they
knew made of heroic material? Aury carried a huge coffee-colored bag
on her arm, out of which a patchwork Raggedy Andy smiled.

"Aury!"

"Adita! Ju!"

They kissed each other on the cheek. Aury sat down on the sofa
next to Judit while Ada Luz went to the kitchen to make more tea
and bring more cookies. She left the door open so she wouldn't miss
a word of the fascinating chat the other two were immersed in: makeup,
hairdos, shampoo, hair coloring. Aury suggested for Judit a highly
novel style with a very modern cut. How lucky it was she'd washed
her hair—it was just perfect! She began to take tubes and small devices
for creating instant hairdos out of her bag. Judit ruled out any exotic
styles. She'd used the same style all her life. Actually all Auristela
would have to do would be to curve the ends in a little, over her ears,
so that her hair would flow slack and heavy, the way it always did.
The hairdresser was disappointed. She looked at her watch.

"In that case," she said, "we'll have more than enough time. It's a
quarter to ten. Did Adita tell you that you have to be there at twelve
because don César's message says a blue Mercedes in Las Hortensias
at the corner of Los Leones after twelve?"

"Was that confirmed?"

"All confirmed."

"Who confirmed it?"

"We talk about miracles, dearie, but we don't mention the saints who work them. But you can rest easy. Your man will be in that Mercedes."

"Our man."

"Our man."

She was like a gypsy reading a fortune: "Your man will come, he'll have a black mustache and green eyes. He will be your destiny." Nevertheless, sitting in the chair in front of the mirror while Auristela combed her hair, and Ada Luz, a cookie crumb stuck to her upper lip, counted the stitches on her lavender vest, Judit felt that the rest of the night would be like a horror movie, that events would only exist in two dimensions in the mirror of repetition. How many times had "her man" been promised her? She'd gone out looking for him, waiting on line at the bank, sitting back to back in the Haiti Café, where everything was haste and coffee smell; two rows in front of him in a movie theater; walking down a certain street at a certain time; and it was never "her man." It was never hers because she had no man, so who could this promised man be?

She was the only one in the group who had none. For that reason her hatred had to consume itself without a concrete image, in pure, sad speculation. Your man, Auristela had said to her, not knowing that Judit had no man. The other women whose screams she had heard in prison didn't know it either. She could distinguish their voices, one from the other: Ada Luz, Senta, Domitila, Beatriz—all their voices, but not hers. She had waited for the man who would make her scream like the others, but he had only put his hand on her knee. The nasal voice of that man exempted her, and filled her with guilt because of the lie she maintained for fear her friends would exclude her.

The others had their men. Cruelty and humiliation were defined in the materiality of an executioner with individual features, one for each woman. She on the other hand was exempted. How did they know, how did don César know that the man who exempted her would be in the blue Mercedes after twelve, when not even she knew who that man was? As if she were reading Judit's mind, Aury, as she removed the rollers from her hair, explained:

"Ricardo Farías. He was in charge of the center during the time we were there. He's going to play canasta tonight with some friends, but

only until twelve because he doesn't like to violate the curfew. They
say he really goes by the book. And his wife and family are on summer
vacation, so he'll probably go home alone.

"Can it really be the same person?"

"Don César's contact says it is. In any case, dearie, only you will be
able to tell for sure. Only you can identify him."

"You think so . . . ?"

She was asking the stupid questions her fear suggested to her. She
knew the information about the man in the blue Mercedes had been
gathered in the bowels of a Santiago without light, where people knew
things they did not suspect were dangerous because danger was the
natural element of their lives, as was terror, being persecuted by the
police, by their brothers, by their children, in abject attics and clan-
destine bars, in neighborhoods where the people were in solidarity
with all those who opposed the authorities: a mute chorus of voices
carrying secrets transmitted by hatred through a rapid network of
contacts interrelated by a common need for revenge, an impulse devoid of ideology. An hour after the information was generated, amid
rot, sickness, and rags, it was sent along a chain of outraged persons
each to each until, near the lighted zones of the surface, the ball
bearings of the little skate wheels could be heard, and don César gave
the information to Auristela, and Aury gave it to Judit: your man will
be in that blue Mercedes. After midnight he would turn toward Las
Hortensias (on the corner of Los Leones) so she could identify him—
but how could she if he was nothing more than a nasal voice, a sweaty
hand?—and take her revenge. The way things were, she would get
no justice unless she took it herself. The man must not recognize her.
And how would he, after twelve years? They had never seen each
other. During the interrogations her eyes were sealed with adhesive
tape and covered with a blindfold, and then her head was enclosed
in a hood, her naked back shivering up against the wall: waiting for
him. How could that man have seen her? Why did he choose her?

"My little skinny's hot to trot!"

Perhaps a fugitive vision before they covered her face remained
bright in his imagination and he ordered the skinny one to be left for
him—he was the boss, after all. In any case, now, so many years later,
that he not recognize her was the work of time and the art of Auristela,
who was making her up as she had never made herself up. It was
meant to distance her as much as possible from the prisoner who had
arrived dressed in jeans and an olive-green shirt, and whom Fausta
and don Celedonio had taken away a week later, bruised, in rags, and

with bloody hands. Aury put the finishing touches on her extravagant makeup while Ada Luz laid out, with the kind of care usually reserved for a wedding dress, a shirtwaist dress made of light silk that she took out of Aury's bag, along with high-heeled shoes and an evening bag.

When she said that she was ready, Judit put on the dress with no trace of vanity. The other two women, laughing and arguing with her as if with a little girl, pulling her this way and that, arranged it on her body; the folds became flattering when they fell over her hips, which, even though slender, filled out the dress and animated it. They buttoned up the front, leaving the three bottom buttons undone so her knees would peek through. Judit could not avoid the pleasure of feeling her hair flowing around her ears and eyes, and the titillation of the silk as it defined her body.

"You look great!" exclaimed Ada Luz, joining her hands in a gesture of admiration. She sat down again to knit while Auristela put the final touches on Judit's makeup.

"Finished," said the professional.

"It's late," murmured Judit. "I'm going now. I want to get a little air and get there on time."

"Be careful. Don't let them catch you walking around there, they're good at things like that," warned Aury.

"I don't think you have to worry, it's a good neighborhood," said Ada Luz. "Come on, girls."

They followed her into the bedroom. From her night table, a modest, scratched and stained Art Deco, with only the stubs of its Bakelite pulls left, Ada Luz extracted two bundles wrapped in flowered handkerchiefs. She unwrapped the first: six bullets, which she placed on the glass top of the night table. She sat down on the blue chenille bedspread, from where a Spanish doll perched on a pillow stared at her. Only the lamp on the night table was lit. The faces of Judit and Auristela floated in the semidarkness, above the space on which Ada Luz was concentrating. She removed the thick elastic holding the other flowered handkerchief: a pistol. Ada Luz took out the clip and loaded one bullet after another, bending over to pick up one that fell on the floor. Then she skillfully pushed the clip into the pistol. She put on the safety and handed the weapon to Judit; Aury watched Judit put it into her bag.

"The safety's on," said Ada Luz. "Don't take it off until you're ready to fire."

"I doubt I'll use it."

"In case you have to defend yourself, I mean."

So what was the revenge she was going to take, then? Seduce him, give herself to him so that finally that part of her fantasy could be realized? No. Ada Luz was dumb, but not naive. As she explained that this was the pistol found on Daniel, the reason why he had to go into exile, Judit felt, first, that what Ada Luz was saying was not true, and, second, that she was giving her the pistol in the hope that she would use it for something other than self-defense in the streets of Santiago during curfew. Judit said, "I've never had to use one before."

"Maybe this will be the first time."

"I don't know. Anyway, it all depends on what happens. I don't know what I want and I won't know until I see him."

"With the curfew, the cops are like wolves."

"Okay," said Judit, "I'm taking off. I don't know why, but I just can't breathe in here."

Of course she couldn't breathe in this room, with the Spanish doll staring at her out of the mystery of her plastic mantilla; she felt something was taking shape here that no one talked about, something that was pushing her toward an action that she would never, even in her days as a militant, have dared to undertake. Surreptitiously, maliciously, these ignorant, powerless women were convincing her, without seeming to do so, by talking about other things while the perverse atmosphere wrapped itself around her, indirectly alluding to a single culmination. Why not, after all? Wasn't it what she wanted too?

Ada Luz went back to her knitting. She was counting rosewood-colored stitches. The crumb had fallen off her lip. Finally! Judit sighed. That crumb had been driving her mad. She remembered the precise moment when it fell off: it was while Ada Luz was putting the fourth bullet into the clip. They accompanied Judit to the door.

"Let's have a look," said Aury before opening it.

And Judit, who knew the pantomime both women were expecting, caricatured the hollow cheeks of a model, one arm stretched out, her hand leaning on the doorframe, the other holding the purse to her waist, one knee sticking out of the open skirt at an exaggerated but extremely elegant angle.

"You look like you stepped right out of *Vogue!*" They both laughed.

"If he doesn't fall for you, he's a jerk," said Ada Luz.

"Don't bother me with all that love crap!" Judit also laughed. "I'm bored! But if he does fall in love with me, then I'll kill him for sure."

It was the first time anyone had said the word, and it was Judit who said it.

14

♦ *I*'m not hungry," said Lopito when
Mañungo Vera suggested he eat something with his second bottle of
red wine. "I'm never hungry."

"That explains why you're so skinny."

"You're not exactly a fatted calf."

"My agent doesn't allow me to get fat. For professional reasons."

"How can you stand them telling you what to eat?"

"Even the women I sleep with."

"At least that doesn't make you fat."

"Only *they* get fat."

"When they decide it's okay."

"You're telling me!"

In the tavern named after Pope Pius IX, they sat on high stools
next to the bar that ran along the wall and ended as a *Bierstübe*.
Mañungo had ordered a nostalgic barbecued pork sandwich to com-
memorate the eternal hunger of the provincial student, which was
never satisfied by the meager monthly check from Chiloé that lasted
exactly one week. After he'd been dreaming about it for twelve years
abroad, the sandwich tasted awful. Lopito, an enthusiastic cultivator
of nostalgia, asked for the same thing, but only took one bite, leaving
a pile of chewed bread, sauerkraut, tomato sauce, and mustard to
color his plate. Mañungo asked for a tall, cool, fresh glass of beer,
which he drank with pleasure because the summer heat seemed to be
sealed up inside the airless bar.

Lopito asked for another bottle of red wine, Mañungo insisting he
order the best. By the time he was halfway through this second bottle,
his thick tongue was stumbling over what remained of his thought
processes. He told salacious anecdotes with his usual style: he was
sharp, perverse, well informed about everything that went on in the

city. But for the past fifteen minutes, Mañungo had begun to notice that Lopito's wit had become charged with ill will, and since it was hard for him to come up with the right words when he needed them, he seemed to be throwing blind punches all around him.

Until now things have been fine, thought Mañungo; my affection for Lopito is solid and I'll see him again because I like being with him, even though nothing matters to him except what's happened here in these past years, local events and new people on the scene, people whose names I don't even know.

Had he come back to Chile to pick up with people like Lopito? It would be better to take off before everything fell apart totally. Juan Pablo was waiting for him at the hotel. He should have been there half an hour ago.

"I have to be going," he said, looking at his Rolex.

Lopito's eyes narrowed into slits. His grime-stained hands (or was it sickness?) trembled as he brought his glass to his mouth, emptied it, and smacked his lips. He exclaimed, "Yeah! Right! I forgot about Jean-Paul."

"May I have the check, please?" Mañungo asked the waiter, refusing to note the sarcastic tone with which Lopito pronounced his son's French name. It might be smart not to see Lopito for a few days, until he'd settled in; later he could enjoy his friend in prudent doses.

"Forget it, I'm paying," demanded Lopito. "Where do you get off, Mañungo? I'm the host here in Chile and I'm inviting you. In Paris, you pay."

"But you just told me you didn't have a cent."

"Isn't it true," Lopito asked the waiter, "that I have credit here?"

"I'll go ask the manager, sir."

"Don't be a pain in the ass, Lopito, let me pay and we'll leave. Juan Pablo's been waiting for a while now."

"Don't lie to me about going to your son."

"What do you mean, lie? You heard me talk to him on the phone."

"You're going because I bore you. Waiter, bring another bottle."

"Don't drink any more now, Lopito. Let's go. You don't bore me, but I might get bored in a little while."

"What's that, a threat?"

"You don't have to take it that way."

"No. I know, buddy. You're a good guy! Everybody's got something good to say about you. I'm shit. Take off! Why waste your time with a bum like me?"

Mañungo was getting ready to leave when he heard Lopito continue:
". . . with a shitty failure like me?"

It was as if Lopito, fumbling around in his drunkenness, had guessed
his friend's most vulnerable point. He pronounced the obscenity: failure. Mañungo asked for another glass of beer. He couldn't walk out
now. The word "failure" tied him to the barstool and to Lopito. He
couldn't deny he hated Lopito for being filthy and abject and self-
destructive and a failure, but he hated himself even more for being
incapable of overlooking all that and clinging to the memories of their
struggle and the youthful friendship they'd shared, overcoming his
repulsion for Lopito's ruin. He was unable to use those memories to
convince himself he was right to hate Lopito, that he had the right to
hate him, because Lopito made him feel desperately and unjustly
guilty for not liking him. And because he decided that this feeling
should not define his attitude toward Lopito, he took a long drink
from his glass while Lopito began to pass out next to his disgusting
plate, which the waiter grabbed just before it fell off the bar.

"May I take it away, sir?"

Mañungo nodded. Sitting at their tables, the other customers recognized Lopito as a regular. They looked at him with the condescen-
sion usually reserved for the inoffensive drunks who turn up in bars
during the afternoon. Lopito woke up, angry about the disappearance
of his plate.

"I didn't tell you to take it away."

"Would you like another?"

"No. I want mine back."

"I'm sorry, sir, but we've already thrown it into the garbage."

"You throw good food in the garbage here? I've heard everything
now. Now you see why this country's in the shape it's in. Are you
crazy? With so many people dying of hunger you throw food away.
Of course, the ones who went to Europe to suffer have no idea of the
misery we've been through here. Lots of little ditties about protest,
tra-la-la, tra-la-la, lots of committed novels, lots of incendiary magazines, lots of poetry recitals, lots of concerts, but, buddy, we stayed here
to resist and to be humiliated and to be hungry. They shit on us and
persecuted us and laughed at us and fucked us over while people like
you had a good time with scholarships and danced and screwed your
brains out with chicks we don't even dare to dream about around here."

"What front did you fight on, Lopito?" Mañungo shouted, standing
up again. "The wine front?"

"Shhhh, don't shout like that, man! You might upset the patients in this leprosarium. Wine might be a front when there's no other."

As if to reinforce that conviction, Lopito downed another glass, which made him even gloomier and turned his face dark red. The people sitting closest to the bar had stopped talking in order to hear their dialogue.

"And the people who had to go because they were being persecuted," asked Mañungo, getting ready to pay and leave, "the ones who had to risk phony passports or take cortisone so they'd swell up and not be recognized, the ones who didn't have the kind of luck at their work that I did, did they also dance and screw all day?"

Lopito stood up, smiling, shining, and patted his friend's shoulder with seraphic affability.

"Luck? But Mañungo, buddy, don't be so modest! What does luck have to do with it? You know very well it was more than luck. Your success came from talent and hard work . . . it was your genius, yes, yes, let me say it, man, you are one of the elect. No, I love you too much to let you talk about luck. You bring yourself down to my level. Just look at me. I'm just shit, and I would have been shit here or anywhere else. Not even the best luck in the world would have saved me. Remember when I published my book?"

"How could I forget? Those poems were like a bible for our generation."

"Thanks for the compliment, old man. Sure, a bible that lasted six months and then was never mentioned again. It stopped there. Now you can't even find a single copy. 'Love is so short and oblivion is so long,' Neruda said. Or was it a tango? You never know with Neruda. Anyway, the Popular Unity did an incredibly poor job of publishing my little book, like everything else they did, because their criterion was that the people don't need anything better. Well, it was a shitty government but it was *our* government, and my poor little book fell apart the first time you read it, and the pages blew away in the first breeze, and that was all she wrote. I should say all *I* wrote, because I could never write another. I haven't written a line for ten years. Not one, buddy, not a single one! My hands start shaking, I get dizzy, I lose my pen, I get incredibly thirsty, I fight with my wife or I screw her even though I don't want to so I don't have to write, and later I blame her for being a whore who's always hot and won't let me write. Anything but writing, which is the worst torture in the world. Except for not writing. I've been in this hell for ten years. It's because of this regime, my well-intentioned friends tell me, although I must say I have fewer and fewer well-intentioned friends. And of course it's all a lie because around here people blame the government for everything, even though it's true it *is* to blame for everything. But it's not the government's fault I'm shit. When I think that during the economic boom I worked and earned good money! You should have seen the clothes I wore. I looked like a prince, and I even paid the first installment to the dentist to fix up my teeth. But he started to pull them out because I had some pretty rotten ones and then I didn't go back because I was afraid of the injections he'd give me in my gums, and I lost that money, which was a lot, and then more, and then the advertising agency where I worked went bankrupt and I was fired and then I was thrown out of the Party, and then I was thrown out everywhere for being a drunk and because I didn't go to meetings, and now I'm in trouble with my second wife, you don't know her. Ugly, my wife. But in winter, when it's cold, she's good to hug up against. And dumb. She doesn't even like Rimbaud."

"I never knew your first wife."

"No, right. You didn't miss anything. Actually I don't even know if I had a first wife. Or if this one is the first. I've married some and not others. I don't keep accounts and it doesn't seem to matter to them, because neither I nor they are what you'd call a good deal. But it's curious that they all reach the same conclusion."

"Which is . . . ?"

"That I'm a disgrace to society and to the Party."

"To what party?"

"How can you ask what party? You think that in this day and age anyone knows anything about parties? There are no more political parties, buddy. This is the disgrace, that they can't agree on anything, or at least that's what they say is a shame because for the time being I've sort of retired from the political scene. All of us have retired from the political scene, even though we keep telling ourselves that the people united will never be defeated when for more than ten years they've had us more defeated than I can imagine, Mañungo. This is total defeat. We're fucked. And we can't even lift a finger. A bomb here, another there, but they don't do anything, like swearing by nonviolent protest or violent protest, or the opposition, or the people united, et cetera. They broke our backs, Mañungo. That's what happened."

"So what's left?"

Lopito silently drank the last, long sip. "Friends like you. And wine."

"Thanks. But I don't think I'm strong enough to compete with wine to justify the defeat of my entire generation."

". . . good, old friends in whose presence I sometimes feel like a filthy rat, like an ant, a slimy worm. Listen, pal, I gave you a lot of shit tonight. I give all my friends shit, and that's why no one wants anything to do with me. Mañungo, buddy, I want to beg your pardon for being a pain in the ass, yes I was, yes I was, don't deny it, and you're bored, and you want to go, because you, Mañungo, are one of the great ones in this world, one of the ones who've made it, and you deserve a prize. Right here, in front of all these fossils looking at us with their mouths open, I'm going to kiss your feet."

Before an incredulous Mañungo or anyone else could stop him, Lopito had slipped off the stool and gone down on his knees to kiss Mañungo's feet. Mañungo stood up in a rage, turning his back on Lopito.

"I can't stand any more," he shouted. "I'm going. I'm getting out of Chile."

But Lopito collapsed, and Mañungo, helped by a waiter who whispered a consolation, got him to his feet. The waiter begged Mañungo to take Lopito home.

"I don't even know where he lives."

He stared at the door in desolation, hoping that someone would open it so that at least a breath of cool air would come in to replace the bar's boiling atmosphere. As he fixed his eyes on the front window of the bar, he suddenly recognized a face that sprang from the most remote past, a face now mature, very different, but which was the face of Judit Torre, despite the makeup and the years that had fixed the individuality of her features. She walked in with a gust of fresh air that alleviated the sweltering heat, hurrying toward them because even from outside she had been able to see that it was Lopito collapsing, repeating one of the habitual adventures of his existence. Had she come in to save him? She brushed some of the dust off Lopito's jacket while the waiter and Mañungo tried to hold him up.

"Judit!" Mañungo exclaimed, trying to get Lopito to move.

"Help me. I'll take him to my place. It's only around the corner."

"Don't you even say hello to Mañungo?" asked Lopito, extremely concerned with the protocol of this second meeting.

"Hi! What a drag Lopito is!"

They sat him on the stool again. Lopito raised his arms toward Judit in a theatrical gesture of admiration.

"*Vissi d'arte!* Most beautiful of the beautiful! The Virginia Woolf of the social and political picaresque world of Chile, although much more beautiful than that frigid bitch! Let's toast Judit! Waiter, another bottle. You look like a juicy piece tonight, skinny! Isn't she a tasty morsel . . . ?"

The waiter glanced at Judit and Mañungo before bringing Lopito the bottle. Judit told him to bring it: after a few more drinks, Lopito would sleep until tomorrow without bothering anyone with his drunken weeping, which might be the next phase. It would be better for him to get totally plastered as quickly as possible.

"And what would you like, my pet?" said Lopito gallantly.

"You know I have forbidden you to call me pet."

"Because you could hear barking in the cell next door? Those were police dogs barking, not sweet little pet poochies like you."

"Would you shut up?"

"What's he talking about?"

"I have no idea," replied Judit.

"How elegant you are!" Lopito went on. "Would you like to eat something? Waiter, the menu. Only the best for Miss Judit Torre, a very refined lady, because in her life she has only known the best, lobster pâté with truffles, canary tongues, shark fins, all those things Mañungo ate every day in Europe but that we only know from reading the novels we used to read when we had enough libido to read novels with pâté and champagne, and not bullshit dictators and revolutions and hunger and Latin American misery which have broken my balls and I can't stand them anymore . . ."

"I think I'll have a little glass of what you're having," said Judit. "You have another and then we'll be on our way."

"No, no. Order something, Ju. Go on. Whatever you want. Don't you see that this millionaire, this member of the jet set, is paying just so he can humiliate his ragged countrymen? See how he takes out his worn but exquisite wallet? Let me see that. Are these the new traveler's checks? I never saw them before. Are you crazy—you're gonna pay with dollars? Look how fat that wallet is. Order something, Judit . . ."

"Let's go, Lopito, you're a mess," Judit said.

Mañungo paid and begged pardon for his friend's behavior with an affable gesture. The manager said it didn't matter, because they knew Lopito quite well. He was okay, and they were used to him. Mañungo could no longer hear his voice or that of the others, because the only thing he could hear was the whirr of his neurosis in his left ear, as if a cassette louder than all the lions in all the zoos were embedded in his skull forever because Lopito existed. But this wasn't the right moment to be thinking about his neurosis.

Judit had draped one of Lopito's arms over her shoulder and Mañungo did the same; they dragged Lopito out of the bar. The fresh air straightened Lopito out as if he were a balloon suddenly inflated. They walked toward Judit's house and put Lopito to bed in a maid's room. Mañungo accidentally touched Judit's fingers, which were cold. As if not a single day had passed since they were in class together! Somehow ashamed, though for what reason he couldn't say, he couldn't look her in the eye, so he had to study her obliquely.

Judit's little house was sober, deliberately poor, but with that nobility Judit had always possessed. The table was pine, but of the most beautiful old washed pine, scrubbed, veined, polished. The curtains were of plain cotton, lightly starched so that they hung a bit stiffly and broke where they reached the floor: I was born Mies van der Rohe and I'll die Mies van der Rohe, what can I do? I just don't understand postmodernism, she would say to Lopito when he teased her about the lack of humor in her good taste and her intolerance of ornament, superfluity, kitsch.

As he put Lopito to bed, Mañungo realized Lopito was crying, and wheezing as if it pained him to breathe. His shortness of breath was like a tempest, and his lips moved around searching for air while Judit, seemingly expert in these matters—how many men had she put to bed like this? Who were they? What relations did she have with them?—loosened his belt so that nothing bad would happen to him, bloated as he was with wine.

"What's he saying?" asked Mañungo.

"I don't know. Nothing of interest. He hasn't said anything worth hearing for years."

While Judit turned out the lights, Mañungo listened to Lopito's repeated litany of sadness: "I'm dying and no one cares . . . my stomach hurts . . . sick . . . gastric ulcer, the kind bums get, the ones that turn into cancer, not a duodenal ulcer like a decent person, someone neurotic and sensitive, the way it should be, all because of this shitty country, and I'm going to die without seeing my daughter . . ."

"Don't give me that crap," Judit interrupted him. "That's the story I can't stand. You don't give a shit about your daughter."

"You don't give a shit about yours either."

"No. But I don't tell myself soap-opera stories about maternal love. I let her live happily with her grandparents, who adore her."

"Who'd you marry?" asked Mañungo from the other side of the bed, in the shadow, covering Lopito's false cadaver, lying between them, with the sheet.

"I didn't. His name was Ramón."

"A lie," murmured Lopito. "His name was Hilario Vilaró, not, of course, as good a political name as Ramón, a kind of popular hero who was tortured to death. You should make up a song about him, Mañungo. It might make people less angry with you. Because here, let me tell you, no one loves you."

You don't love me, thought Mañungo. Or maybe no one. The pain I feel hearing you say it might be justified. Why should anyone love me?

But as he tried to convince himself that this envy was normal, he twisted the knife in his guts and made the blood flow. Maybe he should go back to Paris instantly, once again be a man free of his own history.

"And your daughter?" he asked Judit.

"Poor Ju isn't very maternal," Lopito interrupted again, his syllables blurred by sleep.

"Shut up and go to sleep, Lopito. Of course I'm not maternal. If I were, I'd stay here taking care of you tonight, but I have more interesting plans. Besides, you have more lives than a cat. Nothing's going to happen to you. In five more minutes you'll be asleep."

Lopito was snoring before Judit finished talking. In the greenish light that came in from the street his mask on the sheet was horrifying: his coarse black hair was so thin that his whitish scalp showed through; his eyes had bags under them; his teeth were mere stumps; the shadow of filth clung to his neck; and there was his head on the impeccable linen pillowcase in Judit Torre's perfectly self-sufficient apartment.

"I have to go. Do you have a telephone?"

"Yes."

He called the Holiday Inn. After watching television, Juan Pablo had called room service to ask for a Coca-Cola, even though Nadja had forbidden Coca-Colas after seven because they keep children up all night. Five minutes before he'd called, the woman in charge of Mañungo's floor had reported that the boy was sleeping like an angel. He shouldn't worry, he was told. The woman had taken a liking to the boy who didn't speak Spanish and was going to stay with him. Juan Pablo had left him a message: he should wake him up when he came back, no matter what time it was. The buzz in his left ear stopped as soon as Lopito fell asleep. Now it was only the roar of the Cucao waves. Who knew when he'd get to see them?

"Shall we be on our way?" said Judit, leaving her keys on the night table. "How old is he?"

"Jean-Paul? Seven. Nothing matters to you, right?"

"Not much. But a lot of things matter to you, and I'm polite."

"Let's go."

They walked along Purísima toward the river, commenting on how strange it was to be walking through this Santiago which was so familiar but so far off in time, like Judit herself. He never would have recognized her!

"I'm so old I'm eternal. How come you didn't recognize me at Matilde's house this afternoon?"

"Were you there?"

Judit laughed at his surprise. Her face, above all when she laughed, had the precision of a skull: pure architecture that suggested death behind life, a reminder that the disturbing geometrical harmony in Judit's features would be what it was always destined to be, and the perishable joy of her beauty was nothing more than a heartrending light, the marvelous spark of a brief mutation in a hydrocarbon chain that transcends the matter of which we are made.

"You smile like a mummy in the anthropological museum," Mañungo used to say to her.

"Yesterday you told me I smiled like a pirate flag," Judit answered him, liking him to say those things to her as compliments even though they didn't seem to be. Now he looked at her: she was more attractive than ever, and he told her so.

"It's because I'm dressed to the nines. Real silk."

"Yes, I noticed."

"How did you know?"

"Well, over there you get used to those things."

"Sure, with the actresses you were dating."

"My agent made me do it, so I could be photographed. On every date I was chased by paparazzi."

"I've got a date tonight."

"When?"

"Right now."

"A date? Not an appointment?"

"At this hour of the night, a lady only has dates, never appointments."

"True."

"Or do you think I'm too old for a date?"

"Not at all. I didn't recognize you at Matilde's because I remembered your hair being darker. Are you tinting it? Tell me the truth."

"Are you crazy? Never. I was almost an albino when I was a kid."

"And you never used makeup like this, and you always wore jeans."

"Jeans and an olive-green shirt."

"The way we all dressed. And sandals."

"Not like what you have on now. Gucci?"

"Gucci."

"Of course. But from the good Gucci, on Via Condotti, not these déclassé third-world Guccis."

"Gucci from Via Condotti. How could I recognize you with all that makeup?"

"Not because I'm twelve years older and I haven't had my face plastered over the newspapers of the world like you, so that my friends could follow the slow evolution of my physical deterioration, to say nothing of my political evolution."

"Let's not talk about physical deterioration."

"No. Let's not."

"Or political deterioration."

"Okay. Not yet. But I warn you that if we go on together for ten more minutes we'll end up talking only about that. That's the way it is here. The dictatorship has imposed politics on us as the only respectable theme in conversation, and we repress all other themes, blocking out the horizon with our political obsessions, unable to let any other idea take root."

They reached the filthy river and crossed the iron bridge, which had been bedecked with balustrades, flower stands, and ivy by the diligent magistrates of the regime. They stopped for an instant to look at the mountains illuminated by a mysterious light that made them seem snow-covered in the middle of summer. A volcano, opined Judit. The moon, he suggested. And they walked on toward Forestal Park. Emotion had gripped Mañungo like a delightful illness from which he decided never to recover, as they walked under the plane trees in the legendary park of the youthful Nicanor Parra and Pablo Neruda. The park had belonged to another generation before Mañungo's, at a time when they were young and began to write or paint or sing, but that generation now used bifocals, suffered strokes, and lisped a bit because of their humiliating false teeth. A long block over toward the left was Plaza Italia. They walked in silence. On the dark benches behind the bushes, couples were joined in old-fashioned park kisses,

and along the avenue cars were moving toward the better neighborhoods. During the silence, Mañungo listened to the blame-casting
whirr in his ear, reminding him that instead of speaking to Judit he
was mute.

"So. I'll say goodbye here," she said when they'd reached the German Fountain.

"Okay. Goodbye. But listen . . ."

"What?"

"May I call you one of these days? We might go out. We have a lot
to talk about . . ."

"You certainly haven't made much of this opportunity."

"Could it be that emotion has, as they say, overwhelmed me?"

"Or perhaps we have nothing to say to each other?"

"That's cruel!"

"No, Mañungo!" she said, coming close to him and caressing his
beard, while he lightly put his arms around her waist. "I like it this
way, shorter, less hairy. I was joking. I'd love to see you again. But
we can't go out. You're too much of a celeb, and everyone will talk
because they'll recognize you. Come and eat at my house one of these
days. Take my number."

They sat down under a lamp near the German Fountain, without
even noticing the rhetorical composition of water and bronze that
spouted jets of spray with the false power of optimism. A light haze
of pulverized water refreshed their faces as they wrote down their
telephone numbers. When they'd put away their address books, a dog
came up to them, sniffing a lost trail. Judit could not repress an involuntary movement toward Mañungo, a hint that she wanted him to
protect her.

"Don't you like dogs?"

"No."

"I thought your father raised boxers."

"That's why I don't like them. Shall we go?"

"Why are you afraid?"

"Let's walk a little together."

"I thought you were in a hurry to get to your date."

"I can skip it or get there late. It doesn't matter. I have time. Let's
go."

"Where?"

"What difference does it make?"

·II·

NIGHT

*C*aleutún, metamorphosis; *che*, people. In the old language, now forgotten, like the names of the gods and the volcanos, *caleutún-che*, which means "transformed or changed people," may well be the origin of the word *Caleuche*. As a boy, Mañungo would stand on the sweet, green coasts of the archipelago and stare at the storm-heralding fog, dreaming of the lights on the "ship of art," the *Caleuche*, which was manned by a crew of wizards who would take him away and transform him into someone else. Artist and wizard were synonyms for the island people of Chiloé, for whom the term meant those who practiced seduction, revenge, and metamorphosis.

Now that Mañungo had returned to Chile, had the wizards changed him back into himself? Was he also this man? Or was this street redolent with honeysuckle and jasmine only a mirage experienced by someone he hadn't yet become?

He was not perplexed simply because he was with Judit or because, after walking a few blocks south, they fell into step with each other, their conversation adapting to the echo of their footsteps in a night that might lead them anywhere. Rather, it was more like the confusion he'd felt standing at his window on Rue Servandoni, his anxiety at trying to superimpose the leaden clouds of Achao on the sky of Paris. Here it was the green vigor of these streets, a vigor fertilized by the dew—a place where leaves rot under magnolia branches, where dogs howl from wet lawns behind iron fences, where drops of spray hang from the hedges, and the ylang-ylang hugs the length of the street until the extravagance of its scent displaces the smell of the hot, recently hosed-down sidewalk. All this took hold of his emotions, preventing him from summoning up his nostalgia so he could reconstruct Paris for Judit, as she was asking him to do. Or at least that's what he wanted to believe she was asking, rather than for the details of his life, the part of it that was not blared out in the media. He thought she wanted to know, for example, what he thought he might do once time had pushed Matilde from center stage, what he'd be then, how, where, and transformed into whom.

Walking from the Costanera to Providencia, taking refuge under the old trees along the streets lined with pompous mansions, Mañungo was unable to use Paris as a way to avoid revealing too much about himself. Instead, he reeled off a census of places enhanced by their prestigious names, trying not to remember the hands that had hidden in his own during nocturnal walks after lovemaking—a time when he particularly liked to stroll, from Rue Servandoni to Rue Monsieur-le-Prince and Rue de Seine. At first he lived it all completely, scarcely believing that his enthusiasm could make him forget what had happened in his country. They lived here, they live here, I'm living here until I decide otherwise, along Rue de Seine under Sartre's window—he may even be writing up there now, behind that closed shutter where you can see a little light shining through.

The truth is that even if people believed the opposite—and back when he had to sacrifice everything to his politicized image, he preferred not to explain this insignificant fraud—he had not named his son Juan Pablo after Neruda, but after Sartre. As a university student, he'd stayed up night after night reading Sartre in his boardinghouse, so absorbed that he didn't hear the rats coming up from the river to gnaw at the shingles on the roof. Marx, yes, he'd read the necessary dose. He leaned more toward Bakunin and Lenin. But most of all, he read Sartre, with his questioning of the changing certainties of youth, the residue of which Mañungo had almost forgotten because of the alienating effect of his career. Sartre, with whose words he had fertilized the Chiloé dirt from which he'd sprung.

On the other hand, who the hell was this Mr. Thayer-Ojeda, whose name honored this street darkened by so many interlocked branches? Who could Thayer-Ojeda be? Perhaps an honest minister in some remote government, maybe no more than a pompous, white-whiskered judge now forgotten by everyone except those who liked to stroll at night, illuminated by the car that turns the corner and then abandons the silhouettes of Mañungo and Judit to the foliage of these elms heavy with sleeping birds. How could Mr. Thayer-Ojeda help resolve Mañungo's confusion?

This was another Mañungo. He was not the same man who watched it rain on Rue Servandoni, the tempest of tinnitus torturing his ears, hearing instead the rain on the houses built over the water, where his mother had died in a tidal wave shortly after giving birth. These days, there were barely enough of those houses over the water to illustrate the postcards his father would send him every year from Chiloé. But since the past is not usually one's own experience, but rather experience refracted through the memory of others, Mañungo relived through the memory of don Manuel his mother's cadaver, glowing with lampreys and crowned with algae and kelp, and the way they pulled it out of the cove the night after the disaster.

That was when a town with plank catwalks under which the moon swelled the tides stood on posts driven into the silt at the foot of the Castro hills. There were stores that sold what people needed, products brought over in launches to the doors of the shops by the natives who had caught, salted, hunted, or gathered them, then dried, cured, or roasted them in the aromatic blue smoke of their patios. In that village of weathered shingles, which he had never known because it had disappeared in the fire after the tidal wave, Mañungo began; he was finished long before they turned the corner of Calle Hernando de Aguirre, where they were blinded by the headlights of a car that stopped and went dark. Judit halted. She pulled Mañungo into the shadows and huddled close to him. They felt like reflections of the real couple getting out of the car, like figures fleetingly suggested by smoke. Judit's hand fumbled in her bag even though the car was neither a Mercedes nor blue; it wasn't twelve yet; this street was not Las Hortensias. When the two passengers disappeared into the house, Judit closed her bag and said, "Let's go."

She slung her bag over her shoulder, and they set out again. Where are we going? Mañungo asked himself. He sensed a purpose in Judit's step, although it might be nothing more than a desire to get lost. The fire had left only a fringe of shacks on poles over water—he told her, making an effort not to talk about Paris—and one store, don Basilio's. The fire hadn't touched it, people said, because don Basilio, who served several wizards, had given his beautiful daughter to the *Caleuche*, and that ship of art, whose white sails and golden masts went on shining in the island people's imaginations, would make her immortal as a reward for participating in their festivities.

The singer embarked on that ship along with the other wizards, with Pablo and Matilde as principal passengers, to say nothing of many other illustrious figureheads. Mañungo made music for visiting Bul-

garian poets or Cuban actresses, or to celebrate an election victory or
to welcome senators returning from a meeting in Budapest, while
splendid women in low-cut gowns whirled wildly through rigadoons.
Fausta danced in the *Caleuche* despite her years, a highly colored
figurehead, eager to share in the party because anyone who dances
there never gets old.

A survivor deeply rooted in reality, she now busied herself collecting
Nerudian detritus: Mañungo had heard don Celedonio talking about
it in the patio at the wake. He knew about the obstacles facing the
Pablo Neruda Foundation. Many Chileans stuck in Paris cafés talking
sorrowfully—because of their respect for the bard, because they chose
to repudiate the regime, because they themselves would benefit—of
their disgust with the idea that the project could get bogged down in
a sordid political vendetta. Nevertheless, in the sad, committed buzz
of the exiles, who neither pardon nor forget, but who know that the
cards they're talking about are being dealt at tables quite different
from the ones in their garrulous cafés, Mañungo found at least a few
elements with which to make an identity. Anger, for one, and nostalgia,
and the impossibility of forgiving. These formed a shared vocabulary,
a temporary lingua franca.

This scanty identity, the product of the rage that inflamed his reason
each time new abuses were revealed, helped him not to lose track of
himself while he constructed a new identity out of elements different
from the stares of others. Thus he did not have to remain stupidly
mute next to a woman who expected more from him than his shadow
on the iron fence palings and bushes they passed. From a high, lighted
window they heard a radio playing, and a block later someone was
singing the same song as he watered a lawn—a sad song, as sad as all
things destined to be sung for a single summer. How hard it was, in
a situation like this, to assume either the anguished group identity of
those in foreign cafés or the identity of the passenger on the ship of
art, which, floating up from the depths of a collective memory, still
dazzled his own.

The only truth was the dubious present of his stroll along this
shadowed street, named after a gentlemen Judit remembered as having been secretary of the Conservative Party when her own grandfather was vice-president. Before crossing to the opposite corner, where
a streetlight counterfeited yellow blossoms on a bush they fell silent,
staring from the edge of the sidewalk, trying to peer into the shadows,
where a figure was moving around among the acanthus plants. A

child. A strange gnome in the vegetation. Perhaps it was a hunchback, yes, he seemed deformed. Judit did not take her eyes off the figure.

"What are you staring at?" whispered Mañungo.

"Nothing."

"Who is it?"

"I don't know."

They heard the sound of roller-skate wheels on the pavement, deafening in the silence, and then the dwarf came forward, sliding along, short and muffled, pulling a wagon full of newspapers and boxes up to the group of garbage bags at the next house. As he dug through them under the trees, a dog barked insanely behind the iron fence. But the dwarf scavenger paid no attention, went on with his work, and then slid away on his deafening skates. The dog quieted down behind the hedge that his frantic run was stripping of leaves. The scavenger skated on to the next pile of trash bags. An automobile crossed the intersection, stopping for a second because it didn't have the right of way, and bathed the figure in light. Neither a dwarf nor a child: a sinister being, amputated below the waist, mounted on a skateboard, an amputee with a scarf wrapped around his neck and a fedora pulled down over one eye. The car passed by. The garbage picker went his way, checking bags and looking nervously from one side to the other, as if afraid he'd be caught in the act.

"Is that against the law too?" Mañungo asked.

"No, but this block must not be his territory. He must be on edge because the ones who own this street will probably kick his ass for him."

"And who decides who gets which street?"

"They do it among themselves, I suppose. They follow their own laws—certain poor neighborhoods get certain rich neighborhoods, I think, or it's done among buddies. They say there are cases where people pay to pick through the garbage in good neighborhoods. But they guard their territory jealously. See how nervous he is? Don César should not be on this block. His territory is one block up. What a pig! Wait a minute, stay here. I have to talk to him."

Judit crossed the street to say hello to the amputee, who had dragged his wagon to the corner exactly opposite them. She shook hands with him, and this bothered Mañungo. Wasn't there a menace in all this? Didn't people say that with so much unemployment the city had become dangerous, and that people would murder you for a crust of bread or a few pesos? No, he calmed down. For a cripple like that, all you could feel was pity. But the time of night was starting to make him uncomfortable: it was eleven, Mañungo saw by his watch, one hour before curfew, when everyone, victims of the artificial schedule imposed on them, began to scurry around to take refuge in the first available hole.

How did Judit know this monster? Why did she shake hands with him? Why did there seem to exist between them a bond that went beyond charity? Mañungo waited for her, keeping his eyes open for the dangers he assumed were concealed nearby. But what dangers? What was there to fear from this grotesque figure that ended in what looked like a platter on a skate? Had his Europeanization become so complete that he was afraid of Judit's contact with that fragment of a man, who looked, with his jaunty hat, his elegant mustache, and his rags, like the caricature of a pimp? Judit was carrying his black plastic bag, which she threw over her shoulder as she listened to what seemed to be the amputee's advice.

When he reached the curb on the other side of the street, the cripple, with an admirably dexterous motion, took his skateboard out from under his body, put it on the sidewalk, and with an economic, precise push with both hands, sprang up onto the platter. Propelling himself with one hand on the ground and making a racket with his skate wheels behind Judit, he advanced toward the block where he had the right to scavenge. No, this was not some nobody. He deserved more than pity, Mañungo reflected, watching Judit give him back his bag and say goodbye.

"Who was that?" asked Mañungo, listening to the fading sound of the skate wheels.

"A friend."

A friend, nothing else. Mind your own business. Don't ask. Don't touch me because things can only go so far and then I slam the door in your face. No intimacy. No sharing secrets. Who was that? A friend. But that friend was don César, a horrible outgrowth of this urban night mutilated by the curfew. Who did you become, Judit Torre, after our first year of university? Who, to choose such grotesque friends? Mind your own business. Leave me alone. It's my affair, you say. In those vehement times, she'd identified herself with a dynamic element in the Communist Youth, which embodied her confused desire to be put in order from the outside because she couldn't do it from within. She followed all the commandments: you had to be optimistic and gregarious, and enthusiastic; disdain the exquisite, intellectual bourgeoisie; reject psychologizing, Europeanist, aestheticist depressions; venerate great drinkers, eaters, and lovers to serve as a mirror and stimulus to the working class and thus prepare for the advent of the revolution.

That's where he had left her: the most submissive militant, she, Judit Torre, the most attractively arrogant girl Mañungo had ever met. Nevertheless, at night, in his arms, her marvelous jaw rigid and her too-clear eyes red with stupid tears, she confessed she didn't know what she was doing. Split in two? four? or sixteen? She gave him only the scrap of her body, which she did not succeed in relating to herself, leaving Mañungo outside the tangle of her feminine failure. Wasn't that what her revolutionaries denounced as a decadent bourgeois problem?

When Mañungo left for San Francisco to sing in the concert Joan Baez had organized in support of North Vietnam, Judit was at the University of Antofagasta, agitating for the election of aldermen before the general election. Mañungo received the invitation without warning, as an urgent request; they had no time to say goodbye, or discuss a future they might or might not share. She declared she was not ready to disrupt a collective project, the Antofagasta plan, for sentimental matters they could resolve over the telephone.

Later Mañungo wrote to her from abroad. She did not answer. He wrote again, more insistently, when he found out she'd left the Communist Party to join a group whose crazy revolutionary activism was typical of the youth of her generation. He asked her to explain how, for what purpose, why, since her reasons might help him get beyond his own rejection of patterns. She did not answer this letter either, and for twelve years Mañungo did not know who Judit Torre was.

As they walked under the trees, Judit periodically pointed out the silhouettes of boys emerging from the corners of the night, mute shadows, ancient ghosts, a bearded elder, all bent over garbage bags or pulling wagons or pedaling fantastic bicycles or improvised tricycles that quickly vanished in the vegetation or were pierced like pictures in a slideshow by the headlights of passing cars. The helter-skelter movement of these scavengers increased, their vehicles became more fantastic, their faces more deformed, their rags more ragged, and their loads more and more like huge pies piled high with booty as the curfew hour approached and the streets emptied.

The scavengers would soon stampede in order to avoid the patrols that would chase them away. This was the "green ghetto" of the privileged classes, she explained, as if Mañungo didn't remember; a neighborhood that was emotionally charged with whispers, but was, at the same time, besieged by slums a hundred times larger and more hostile, a world that grew outward, threatening to extinguish all this self-absorbed greenery.

The tattered humanity rummaging in the garbage was merely the silent advance guard that nightly entered this bastion to reclaim the spoils that, for the time being, were its part of the banquet. Shadows torn from fear and guilt, bent figures dragging phantasmagorical strollers, coughing, worn out, spitting blood, astride bicycles with side-cars, old people tugging platforms mounted on different-sized wheels discarded from other vehicles, children pushing carts, disappeared furtively around corners or blended with an immobile tree trunk or dissolved in an alley, while Judit and Mañungo, hand in hand, passed street after street kept awake by the fragrant breeze.

Angry dogs occasionally barked from behind the palings.

"Shut up, Czar!" shouted Judit to a Doberman growling itself hoarse.

"Do you know him?"

"No."

"Why did you call him Czar, then?"

"So many of these dogs are named Czar! They're vicious."

"This one might be nice if he weren't so spooked by the darkness."

Judit approached the fence. The dog, gone berserk from smelling a female, barked as he ran around the well-watered garden. *Czar! Czar!* Judit taunted him, moving even closer, dangling her handbag before the animal's nose from the other side of the fence that separated her from his bloody rage and the heat of his breath, her hand just a few inches from his impotent jaws. Mañungo was about to say: Careful, Judit, he could tear off your hand with one bite, look at the power of those jaws, the shining teeth . . . But his warning would be useless. No matter how strong the beast might be he still couldn't knock down the iron fence and sink his teeth into Judit's throat. Hateful and mocking, she swung her handbag, singing him lullabies, whispering to him, almost touching his nose as he snorted and writhed. She laughed at him and his rage, tantalized him; torture turned into play.

Mañungo felt that Judit took danger as the raw material for play. He feared for her, particularly since this imbalance afflicted him as well, and for the first time that night, he felt not unlike the dog, wanting Judit. He needed to make love to her, as he had needed to long ago, but now with a certain sadness because they were all so broken—above all this woman, who was condemned even by the games she played. Czar jumped, howled, beside himself with fury. Mañungo took Judit by the elbow to pull her away, but she refused to budge. Only when he spun her around by force could he see that her face was wet with tears.

"Judit!" he exclaimed, genuinely shocked, and then he embraced her.

She allowed herself to be embraced, kissed, and touched, sobbing, and then she embraced and kissed in turn, seeking Mañungo's lips the way someone in pain seeks an anesthetic, not the way someone seeks love. The animal, a few inches from their tangled bodies, mocked them by growling, jumping, and biting the air. Czar! Czar! His name echoed off the walls, voices ordering him to attack: a woman's scream. Which of the five women was it, while, naked and hooded in her cell, she waited for the torturer who never came? *Czar!* urged the voices, and the well-trained dog jumped on one of them, Judit explained to Mañungo as she stared at the pavement distorted by her tears, but no one knew on which of the five: they never talked about it. It's as if they wanted to share the pain and dilute it by not resolving that mystery. The barking mixes with the laughter and masculine bravado cheering Czar's triumph, pure brutality, words of terror echoing empty because of the absence of eroticism, sexuality supplanted by the fear that finally they are coming for her by order of the man with the nasal voice who exempted her. Hours immobile in the cold. Naked. Blind inside the hood. The wet, cold, greasy wall stuck to her back. The gag suffocates her. She's waiting for Czar. On the other side of the walls, the men treat the dog as an equal, congratulating him for his prowess as a don Juan. *Czar!* First faint, then gone completely, Czar's barking remains fenced off, part of the block they leave behind.

*W*as this simply another chapter in the wretched history of our times? His own personal history, which had managed to darken for him the familiar image of the *Caleuche* with its golden masts, and transform it into something else? *Ca*: other; *calén*: to be other; *caleún*: to transform oneself into another being or another thing—so suggests an etymological enthusiast in order to demonstrate that the magic of the island people is not powerless to effect metamorphoses. And it's true, because even when he had lost all hope of being carried to immortality, the ship of art in exile would surface from time to time in Mañungo's dreams, transformed into a cruel, piratical *Caleuche*, its crew made up of foreigners with Mongolian eyes carrying everyone off, not to the beautiful city promised by legend, but herding them like animals to slaughter. Galley slaves under the black sails, their limbs twisted by charms that kept them from escaping: Fausta groaning in her vomit-stained clothes, don Celedonio chained to his oar, Judit, dying after having been raped by the crew, Pablo and Matilde rotting with plague in a corner, Nadja groaning from hunger and Jean-Paul from fear under the glitter in the sails, Lopito trembling in the cold of the ship as it crossed through a hurricane with colossal waves, the spines of the white volcanoes reddening the sky with their lava, and from the islands the natives calling to be taken away because they don't know that these days, when the *Caleuche* is out, it only carries its passengers to death.

Mañungo told Judit about his frozen nightmare with its squalls and darkness in the southern seas as they wandered in the sleeping street under the acacias. Along the avenue that crossed their street, they saw a bus go by with all its lights on: slow, empty, majestic, abandoned by its phantom crew and its passengers. Its brief passage beached it in a bank of leafy shadows, where it seemed to submerge. What if they were to run to catch that bus of art, proposed Mañungo, to take a trip through the city in this urban *Caleuche* that drifted with no one at the wheel?

"Okay, let's go." Judit smiled at him.

Taking her by the hand, Mañungo made her run across the street with her eyes closed because an automatic sprinkler on one of the lawns had soaked both of them. On the other side of the mist, rejuvenated, Judit's wet silk dress clinging to her body, they laughed as they dried each other's face, clothes, and Mañungo's tiny glasses with their hands, with the wet dress itself, it didn't matter, they only wanted to touch each other, laugh, kiss, drink each other in, transformed, refreshed, trembling because the cool night had become cold. She shuddered as she let Mañungo put his arm around her waist again. To go on walking she took refuge in Mañungo's body, as if that were the most natural place to be to hear him sing the *Vocalise* in a very low voice. Judit laughed, also in a very low voice, congratulating him because he sang Rachmaninoff Latin American style, she said, with anti-imperialist content and everything—perhaps because it was a song without words. Despite the irony, Mañungo understood that it was his voice and not a chill that made Judit shiver. He whispered that he was happy to see his voice could move her.

"Your tone is richer," she commented. "I love dark voices, the way yours has become, thick, like a black voice. It sounds as if it's matured . . . as if you could sing Richard Strauss or Mahler."

"Now you're asking too much! I never sing those things."

"A pity."

"You never used to be so sensitive to music."

"Or to voices."

"To voices but not to music?"

"To music too. But when you've had your eyes sealed up, voices become the entire universe and acquire traits as individual as the features on a face. Have you ever seen those 'composite portraits' the police use to identify criminals? They're made up out of oral information. They turn out to be quite accurate. I could recognize someone by means of an oral composite portrait—not of his looks, but of his voice. Not beautiful, not hoarse, not thick, a man's voice, rather high-pitched, very Chilean, halting, and full of fake gentleness despite his brutality. A wounded voice. That voice didn't dare come close to me. With the other men and women it was an authoritarian voice, obscene, get 'er moving, get the gag out of her mouth so she can scream and set Czar on her, get going, asshole, no, wait, put the muzzle on Czar and get him out of here, he's hungry and I don't want him to bite the skinny one because I want to enjoy her the way she is, nice and white. His tone was an insult. But when he talked to me, when no one else could hear—because as you say I've gotten very sensitive to such things—I felt as if that unique voice lost its edges and shed something . . . something like a skin . . ."

"What are you talking about, Judit, for God's sake?"

She came back to herself suddenly, as if she had emerged from darkness into light: "Of the usual thing. I haven't talked about anything else for years. Just like everyone else in this country. I've forgotten how to talk about subjects other than injustice, lack of freedom, misery, or violence. I feel guilty if I talk about other things, and my intellect has reduced its scope to keeping up to date about these topics. I'd like to talk about music, for example. But in my heart I'm afraid it would be frivolous."

They crossed the intersections arm in arm, without raising their eyes from the pavement. There were no more cars and the sidewalks were empty except for the odd scavenger. Mañungo told Judit that Lopito had loaded him with guilt that afternoon, making him feel that he'd obtained his success at the cost of the suffering of those who stayed behind. And in part it was true, and that's what led him to failure. Yes, failure. He begged Judit to pardon him for shocking her tender Marxist-Leninist heart by confessing he'd had to undergo psychoanalysis for three years—"What else could I do if right in the middle of a concert I stiffened up, lost my voice, and they had to give me a shot right there in front of forty thousand people and carry me off the stage on a stretcher?"—in order to be able to face defeat and recognize that people weren't talking about the decline of his popularity out of envy, but because it was a fact. The cliché, once the passion that sustained it weakened, refused to go on working.

So Mañungo the monolith, Mañungo the good revolutionary boy, Mañungo the symbol, cheated his public at concerts by publicly showing them that he was not the person they wanted him to be. . . . Hysteria? Yes, hysteria. How shameful! And in public! his indignant agent had bellowed at him. And right then and there he began to stop being a symbol because according to the newspaper articles on the "Mañungo Vera case," the singer was suffering "serious psychological problems" in addition to an "ideological crisis," things a symbol should not and cannot suffer.

Mañungo refused to speak. He gave no interviews, although Nadja, with total discretion it must be said, stood in for him. No, he wasn't drinking excessively; money had nothing to do with it; a love affair, no; no drugs beyond the ones everybody used socially; no, he doesn't want to talk. His answers were of little interest, and after a week the reporters stopped paying him any attention, to the despair of his agent, who was trying to capitalize on the negative situation.

The truth was that after all these years, Mañungo, with his protest, his bam, bam, bam, had nothing new to say; his fervor was even hard for him to believe. It collapsed in front of forty thousand witnesses, and there was no going back: forty thousand pairs of eyes defining him from the audience, demanding that his faith in the revolution go on dominating all his experience just as it had twelve years back, that his enthusiasm remain at the same level as always, that as always his rabbit teeth peek out cutely between his beard and his mustache, that his hairline not recede, that he remain identical to himself, the image fixed outside and inside.

But if outwardly he could go on being the sought-after cliché, inwardly the entire structure had been falling apart. His silence, sometimes still talked about in the media, was interpreted in many different ways in exile cafés. None of the interpretations was favorable, but none was so conclusive that it made audiences abandon Mañungo for good. When he tried to begin touring again, he didn't find the suit of his public image hanging in the closet. So he had to sing naked because he could find no other clothes to fit, and he choked because he was ashamed that forty thousand pairs of eyes would see him naked and that forty thousand pairs of ears would hear his voice. He fled, and here he was walking with Judit under the rustling plane trees.

Enthusiasm for the Chilean cause, meanwhile, had shifted to other causes: Central America especially, because in Chile the mass murders that made front-page news had ceased, to be replaced by this long, slow pauperization, this chaos, this fear that was not a Massacre of the Innocents to keep the attention of the outside world, this agony that was too deep to move the audience. To be serious for them meant singing about revolution and politics, to romanticize revolution and politics, to live on revolution and politics, to think about revolution and politics, immersed in the collective tragedy, banishing and cursing any hint of modest personal problems.

He, Mañungo, just couldn't take any more. He wanted to be a private person, something, according to what he'd heard, that really had ex-

isted once, even if it seemed extinct nowadays. Pleasure, fun, sex had
no value, not only because they were obscene but because they were
reactionary. The only thing that mattered was the adrenaline of raging
protest. Everybody had become puritan, esteemed only the litanies of
collective pain because anything else was weakness. Hesitation was
disdained by certain young people who were incapable of accepting
hesitation as a sign of complexity, which might also have some value.
No, he wanted to sing about other things now.

"It'll be hard to do," murmured Judit.

"Why?"

"There's no space left for personal problems."

"But how do you live?"

"We don't live. We survive. And just barely, if you're lucky enough
not to be hit by a 'terrorist bullet' or killed in a 'minor incident.' Gags,
among their other accomplishments, have radicalized the people.
They're in a combative mood and feel they have to go all the way
because they have very little to lose."

After a short laugh, Mañungo went on: "A weakling. That's what
they called me. Most of all because I'd undergone psychoanalysis and
didn't attend those optimistic-and-hopeful-despite-everything meetings, and I gave up my guitar. I wanted my right to lie down and die
if I chose to. And my popularity began to wane when word got around
that the regime was not prohibiting me from returning to Chile, because I'd never taken things to their limit. My songs were always bland,
people discovered—a bit late in the day—and my attacks on the regime
had never been brave or direct: Mañungo Vera was a bourgeois in-
dividualist who had disguised himself as a guerrilla for ten years and
fooled them with his disguise. What was I trying to do, they asked,
pass for a martyr?"

On the corner, where the chlorophyll had cleaned up all traces of
daytime pollution and scattered the stars in the only piece of sky left
visible through the branches, Judit and Mañungo stopped to kiss,
letting a hasty car pass by. What would become of those kisses? Where
would the two of them end up after this peace enriched by their two
bodies touching? It didn't matter, Mañungo said to himself. Now he
felt impelled to tell Judit everything, get it out and look at it once and
for all, and perhaps understand it.

". . . it was as if I'd missed the most painful part of the history of
my generation. I was tied up in my obsession with that history I hadn't
lived, which made me feel mutilated and incomplete. I think that's

why I came back, to see if I can find those mutilated pieces or regenerate them like a lizard regenerating its tail. I'd like to reenter the history of my generation so I can sing again, but not sing like a high-priced doll. Coming back to a Chile under state of siege is to take part in the madness of this second coup d'état, since I didn't live through the first."

"Are you saying that by coming back you expiate some sin?"

"That's it."

"You're a romantic idiot! What sin do you have to expiate?"

"I suppose my disgust at having to sing only about political protest and collective experience. Those things are burned into me, but they're not the only ones. I can't get rid of them, but I hate them. I'm ambivalent. I'm drowning because I can't find anything to hang on to. I've dedicated so many years to discussing only revolution and protest that I'm disconnected from other sources. I'm always dreaming about enchanted ships, mermaids, flying dwarfs, children with their eyes, ears, mouths, and asses all sewn up, most of all about that strange Chiloé equation of the wizard and the artist, a thing I'd like to sing about. But how?"

"Just do it!"

Mañungo laughed again. "I've only been back for a few hours. First I walk into an ideological hornets' nest for singing and then for *not* singing 'Santiago Bathed in Blood.' Now I see we still haven't managed to free ourselves from the slavery of this eternal discussion. Didn't you say no one can talk about anything else? Now you see what I mean."

Judit had dissociated herself from the conversation. It was as if she were incapable of taking any interest in abstractions, even though the adventures involved in surviving a night like this one linked her with the wandering figures who appeared among the trees and disappeared loaded with treasures found in garbage. As they turned a corner and entered a street covered over by branches, Judit waved at the last scavenger, who was pulling along a cart loaded with boxes and stacks of newspapers, mounted on three different-sized bicycle wheels. It was a boy, walking barefoot so that, in case of emergency, he could run off at top speed, Judit explained. She stopped him. "Darío! Why are you in such a hurry? You still have time."

"Miss Judit! What are you doing here?"

"You've seen me here lots of times."

"Don César didn't tell you anything?"

"About what?"

"Pa's got to talk to you right away. All that stuff about the blue Mercedes don César told you is a lie. It's a Volvo."

"Where?"

"I don't know. But Pa knows."

"Where are you going to meet tonight?"

"A new place you don't know. Follow me. It's right around here, but it's getting late."

The boy balanced his cart so he could go more quickly, and went ahead pulling his load. Far behind, Mañungo and Judit walked along the wooded street without catching up to him. In front of a gateway, on the sidewalk, Darío spotted a box half hidden in the bushes. Unable to resist taking it along, he plunged into the bushes to grab this last prize of the night. Two black shapes jumped him; a knife blade flashed, there were shouts, and one of the men held the boy from behind while the other one transferred the miserable loot from the boy's cart to his own.

"Don César!" shouted Judit.

Judit was about to jump onto the other man, the one who was holding Darío, in order to save the boy. Mañungo had to hold her back to keep her from risking a knife thrust. She was crying and shouting at him to let her go, kicking him in the shins with her pointed shoes and stabbing with her high heels, biting and scratching him, the deafening roar of don César's skateboard in their ears while he completed his hijacking operation against Darío, he should let her go, what did he know, fool, he should let go of her arm because she couldn't move, I don't want you to hold me, I don't want anyone to touch me, I don't want anyone to touch skinny, he says, seeing her struggle in the arms of the goon holding her, don't touch her, I don't want anyone to touch this skinny one I've been looking at since she came. I've reserved her for myself. Leave her to me! Judit the untouchable. The untouched. Why didn't you let them touch me, I would have shouted if I weren't still trying to get loose. Why didn't you let me go through the same things the other women went through? Why this privilege of being reserved for the boss, excused by that nasal voice I never heard again, except perhaps an hour before Fausta and Celedonio put me on the plane to Caracas?

Mañungo's voice tries to calm me down, but I twist around and kick in his embrace to save the kid from the thug who's holding him while don César unloads his cart. The nasal voice, the warm, moist hand.

He didn't save the others. They had to go through hell, all except me: don't touch skinny! You locked me in alone with you in the cell. This skinny's ready! My little skinny's good and hot! We're sitting face to face because your assistant dragged me in his arms, naked, with no physical sensations of the kind I'm feeling now, struggling in the arms of Mañungo, whose hard body I inventory as he presses it against me.

He put his hand on my bare knee to initiate what you could call our relationship. He took it off, as if he'd been burned. Shout! Do what I say and shout. Shout as if I were fucking you and you didn't want me to! Shout more, more! I waited for his hand to touch me again, my skin waited to be caressed by that viscous, tepid hand that never went further although the nasal voice whispered, Shout more, as if you were enjoying yourself, as if you wanted more, as if I were hurting you but you wanted more, and I shout my lungs out howling like a bitch because I'm reaching a shameful pleasure I'd never felt before, not even with Ramón. Shout, shout, he repeated, and I call for help because his whisper threatens me if I don't shout, and I shout with terror at myself, because in this totally unerotic situation I shout my shame at my pleasure while in the other cells my friends are howling like me, but because of tortures different from the torture of being exempted from torture. I shouted in order to keep a humiliating secret that should not be our complicity, but my shout was also because of a first-time pleasure that betrayed me and separated me from the other women. I didn't shout because of the tragedy of the other women. I didn't take part in the feast of that majestic collective form, from which the soft hand excluded me in order to satisfy God knows what fantasies, this impotent monster who demanded I shout with greater and greater conviction without knowing that my shouts of terror and pleasure were real.

Mañungo's arms hold me back. I bite and shout for fear they'll hit Darío. Were you always impotent? Or do you see something in me that freezes you, something you fear? Looking at me in the patio without my seeing you, you said to yourself, That skinny one is the best, the boss's prize, and I'm the boss. Filthy, beaten, naked, even then I drag along the mantle of privilege. The moment you put your hand on my knee something must have defined me as a symbol of a world you honored because your embarrassment produced in you a dizziness of insecurity, and it was your poor individual history, your complex humanity confronting your appetites, that left you impotent, shocked, even more vulnerable and more afraid than I if your underlings suspected your inability and figured out your fraud. I wonder where and how you had seen me. From what filthy window did you hear my educated voice, in what patio or corridor did you sense my manners to be different from the manners of the women you know, since you could have discerned nothing of all that from my nakedness and under my hood? They say I move like a thoroughbred horse, that I toss my heavy blond hair around like an Afghan hound: all the commonplaces that describe the abstraction of my origin. You perceived all that because, poor guy, you may be sensitive. You don't know one pays a price for being that way. Maybe you heard me talking with my friends, spying on me from behind the walls that have eyes and ears, making up fantasies about me that, in the moment of truth, you couldn't bring to life. That's why you never touched me again. You respected me without daring to commit the sacrilege of becoming my owner, the sacrilege Mañungo is committing now as he slaps me for being hysterical so I'll stop whining and calm down, so he can help the boy who's crying because they stole his booty. Sensitive, the bastard with the nasal voice. His sensitivity tore away my right to hatred and revenge. I don't have a rapist even though everyone thinks I have one, and that's what I'm looking for. I have no torturer.

17

When don César and his accomplice disappeared, taking the spoils of their hijacking with them, Judit sat down on the curb to console Darío, who was crying about his lost treasure with Judit's arm around his neck. Mañungo was surprised by that almost tender gesture because he thought Judit was only capable of other kinds of relationships, the kind linking her with Czar's fury, for example. Now, however, it was as if through Darío she had plunged into the very intestines of the condemned city; as if the kid, wailing like an undernourished rat, were synonymous with the clamor of the whole population. Judit, no doubt, could take on large-scale commitments, but she was incapable of something as elemental as letting her heart be touched: it was certainly not tenderness, he thought, but solidarity that made her put her arm around Darío's neck. The contact lasted only an instant. The flow of energy ceased when Judit took her arm away and each one went back to being isolated within his own projects for the night.

"We have to go," urged Darío, standing up.

"Where?"

"You can't believe an old crook like don César. Let's go where my dad is."

"All right. Let's go."

"What time is it, mister?"

"Twenty-five after eleven."

Judit shook her dress where she'd been sitting down. "Then I don't have time to go and talk to your father. I'm going straight to Las Hortensias. Curfew's in half an hour."

Darío took hold of her dress to keep her from making that mistake. "Didn't you hear me? It isn't there, it isn't a Mercedes. That's don César's lies."

"Why would don César lie to me when he's been my friend for so many years?"

"He's nobody's friend! He doesn't want to be seen with you because people say the cops are looking for you again."

Judit laughed. "I don't think they're looking for me, but ever since they arrested me in don César's house years ago, they keep an eye on me. What's new in all that for him, since he's my best informer?"

"Better than my dad, who's a contact for Lisboa?"

"What do you know about Lisboa?"

"Nothing. That he's the boss, that's all. And he helps us. Let's go, Miss Judit. Let's go where my pa is. He knows everything."

The boy took his wagon. He didn't have to balance it because, empty, it was light. He took off running down the street in the direction opposite to the one don César had taken. Judit slipped off her high heels to run after the boy. When she skidded on some leftover food spilled out of a plastic bag clawed open by a cat, she took Mañungo's hand to follow Darío. They went down narrow, tree-covered streets, along avenues lighted by mercury vapor lamps that suffused every-thing with a tenuous fog, grainy and slightly orange. A few remaining cars sped by to find refuge before curfew became a legal fact, while the scavenger dashing in the opposite direction didn't even look at them. The throb of a helicopter flying over a far-off slum was part of the threat that also declared its presence in the form of distant police-car or ambulance sirens, beyond the plazas from which secret streets branched off, each garden suspended in its own silence, each house lost in the depth of its shade trees where some music or a laugh faded— there was as yet no law against laughing in a garden.

Halfway down one of the most silent streets, Darío slowed his pace. Mañungo and Judit slowed down behind him. It was twenty-five min-utes before twelve. The mansions in this neighborhood had fences whose palings were hung on the inside with sheet metal to make them impenetrable to curious eyes or menacing hands. Darío stopped in front of a fence that doubtless protected the luxurious privacy of a garden, of a family, of a way of life. He put his hand through a hidden hole in the sheet metal near the lock. As he opened the gate, the hinges squeaked. Darío signaled them to follow him.

There was no house: an empty lot with the remains of a pool from which the tiles had been ripped, the ruins of a grape arbor, a terrace and a balustrade, the outline of a foundation and holes from the old basements, invaded now by the shoots of sycamore trees, young agaves, and scrub oak. Many houses in this neighborhood, ornamented with columns, stairways, and decorative vases that were incongruous with today's life-styles, had been bought by builders who demolished them to build apartment houses which covered the old gardens. The empty lots on which, finally, nothing was built remained stuck in the darkness between the few surviving mansions and the illuminated towers.

The people who entered mixed in with the cypresses, yews, and thuyas whose spontaneous growth blurred their elegant, artificial silhouettes. A pyramid-shaped box tree moved: a man stepped forward. Two other bushes, unidentifiable behind the man, also lost their decorative distinctiveness by silently moving their bodies, which were stuffed into cast-off overcoats that camouflaged poverty better than they protected their wearers from the cold night.

"Pa!" shouted Darío.

"Miss Judit," one of the bushes greeted her.

"Lucky you made it! There's almost no time left. And you . . . ? What happened to you? Do you think I got you this wagon so you could take walks with it?"

He was just about to slap his son when Darío, whimpering before he was hit, explained don César's hijacking.

"Darío says the story about the blue Mercedes and Las Hortensias is a lie," said Judit.

"Sure it's a lie."

"Why has don César got it in for me?"

"People say he's turned into a stool pigeon."

"No. We know each other too well. I was living in his house when I was arrested, and he's the brother of Aury's disappeared brother-in-law. He may steal, but he's not a traitor. Not him, his nine kids, or his second wife."

"Why did he change the message he sent you by Aury, then? Aren't you afraid it's a trap?"

"And suppose it's Lisboa who set the trap?"

Darío's father took a step back and hesitated for a full minute before recovering his calm. "But don César set it up for you just after curfew, and that's dangerous. With what don César knows, it would be easy for them to catch you tonight."

Judit looked at Mañungo, hoping he would help her decide whom to believe, which plan to follow. Mañungo put his arm around her among the neatly trimmed bushes of the Luxembourg Gardens, where he used to take Jean-Paul to feed the pigeons on the exasperating days it was his turn to take care of him. Don't keep him cooped up on Rue Servandoni, Nadja warned him; the kid needed fresh air and she rarely had time to take him for walks. Take him to the Bois or to Vincennes, because at night I hear him cough. But recently, especially now, when Mañungo had dejectedly turned down several contracts that had excited his agent, he didn't have the energy to argue with Jean-Paul's insistence on staying home on Rue Servandoni to play with the sound equipment.

Would he turn out to be a musician too? Or an electronics expert, like all kids? Or was it simply the boy's wish to be alone to figure out who he was and to be free from Nadja's and his pressures? Nadja's body, Mañungo remembered, filled his embrace more completely than this too-fragile woman's body. What did all this mean? Why was this figure disguised in the large overcoat telling Judit that she shouldn't believe the story about the blue Mercedes after twelve, that instead she should believe what he was saying about a green Volvo on Lota Street at the corner of Suecia, and that Lisboa was the source of the information and he was the voice of the Party? What was her connection with this marginal life, with its informers, contacts, arrests, false passports? Did Judit say that a passport she talked about was false, or had he added that part out of his own imagination, because it fit in with this atmosphere of intrigue? Or had Judit deliberately dragged him into this situation to use him? Use him and help herself, implicate him and defend herself? Was there anything spontaneous or free in her, then, or was it all part of a plan? Looking at his watch, Mañungo realized that it was very near the time that meant danger: it was twenty minutes to twelve, and from now on it was all going to be running, half-baked explanations—because there was no time for analysis and picking or choosing meeting times or making deals before saving their skin. Darío's father implored Judit to hurry up. She shouldn't believe don César, an anarchist capable of betraying anybody; she should believe *him*. She should make her way to Lota at the corner of Suecia at twelve sharp to take the revenge she'd promised herself for so long.

"Do you have what you need?" asked Darío's father.

Judit put her hand in her bag and then stretched out her arm, which ended in something shining that Mañungo at first could not see clearly. As soon as he did, he leapt at Judit to take it away from her: it was one thing to play with a dog behind a fence, but another thing entirely to walk around with a pistol in her handbag. You're crazy! he shouted.

How many people do you want to involve in your craziness? The black bushes pulled him off Judit, who dropped the pistol. When they had them separated, Judit retrieved the weapon and put it back in her bag.

"Take off!" Darío's father said to Judit. "We'll handle this guy. Go to Suecia. Friends will be there ready to help you."

Judit didn't move as they urged her on.

"Hurry up."

"The meeting is for twelve sharp."

But she turned to Mañungo. "You have to accept me as I am."

"You're out of your mind!"

After an instant, Judit asked him, "Do you want to come with me?"

"Yes."

"Let him go."

She pulled him toward the gate and opened it. They ran toward Calle Carlos Antúnez, where, they found a taxi to take them to Las Hortensias. It was ten minutes before twelve.

18

◆ What "a blue Mercedes after twelve" really meant was a blue Mercedes at any moment during the curfew and a wait that could last until dawn, while the armored cars silently patrolled the empty streets like cockroaches. Without warning, anywhere on the urban landscape, the howl of a siren would erupt and then die away, leaving the whir of the helicopters as the only sign of life.

"After midnight": don César's message, brought by Aury, who hated Lisboa's sectarianism and was planning to break up his idyll with Ada Luz, both because she considered it dangerous for their group and because she wanted to damage his prestige. Don César, her respected relative, whose sons were just beginning to make a name for themselves as guerrillas in the outlying slums, was the best vehicle for tearing down Lisboa and seeing to it he left poor Ada Luz in peace. Don César knew his skateboard and his cocked hat were so eye-catching that he rarely left his own neighborhood, where until now even the authorities barely dared to penetrate; but questions, emissaries, contacts, and orders from his superiors, which he distributed by dispersing his sons with messages throughout the city, all managed to reach him. He only left his zone at night to scavenge. People gathered at the windows of their shacks when they heard him rolling down the street.

A thief, of course. Don César had always been a thief. But not a traitor. Judit thought his information seemed more plausible than "Lota at the corner of Suecia at twelve sharp."

The "sharp" part seemed too rigid and too much in Lisboa's style to be the truth, in comparison with don César's information, which took chance and waiting into account. The informant had recommended caution, and Judit concluded that since everything was happening within the curfew, whoever was driving the blue Mercedes must have some kind of pull with the authorities. After all, after twelve you had to drive not only under twenty-five miles per hour and with the car's interior lights on—otherwise the police could open fire on you legally—but carrying a pass issued only to influential people.

They had waited almost half an hour. They first hid in the darkest gate of Las Hortensias—not at the number indicated by don César but at another, near the corner of Los Leones, so they could spot the Mercedes as soon as it appeared. They remained leaning against each other under the honeysuckle, using the base of the fence as a bench. Mañungo caressed the back of Judit's neck, which was warm from her hair, and slipped his arm around her shoulders to bring her closer. He put his hand down her dress and plucked at her nipple as if it were a guitar string. It was docile but unresponsive; her whole body was so involved in something else that it did not vibrate under the flutter of his fingers, so expert in producing music.

"How long do we wait?" Mañungo whispered in her ear.

"I don't know."

"Can't we go to your place?"

"It would be hard because of all the patrols," answered Judit, thinking that Lopito's snores would be filling her house. "We'll have to hide out here until the all-clear sounds."

"What?" Mañungo felt he had a right to complain; after all, here he was squiring around a woman with a gun in her bag.

"Let's sit on the grass," suggested Judit.

Farther along Las Hortensias, at some distance from the corner, they stretched out on the grass along the darkened sidewalk, hidden by the acanthus plants. Judit smoked and rested her head against Mañungo's leg. Alert to the slightest noises, to every nocturnal episode, she could determine no distances, identify no sounds, around them. Was that a shot or a twig breaking? The rustle of leaves or a far-off cry? They were all echoes of legal crimes, at this time of night free of witnesses, when victims could be tossed onto sidewalks, explained Judit to Mañungo as he lit up another cigarette for her. In any case, the time for waiting seemed to have passed, because all that remained was the lethargy that follows disenchantment. The blue Mercedes was not going to appear, and they had no idea how to reconstruct the fragments of this night scattered among the violet branches of the plum trees.

Mañungo's sex felt Judit's head pressing down on his trousers. He let it rest there, enjoying the expectancy of lengthened erotic time, proximity making them both anxious to be enfolded in the advent of pleasure. They spoke of disparate things: despite the fact that they had so much to say to each other they could pursue no topic. Their respective centers were too far away from words. Any false movement, the slightest error of the senses, would destroy their desired inter-weaving, which was growing more and more urgent.

Judit, after blowing out a mouthful of smoke, turned her head toward him to tell him something unimportant, which she never got around to saying. Her real reason for turning was to cover his sex and caress it ever so slightly with her hair. It drove him mad, but he didn't move a muscle. He didn't move, because Judit, in turning her head, had twisted around so that her tobacco-laden breath would burn through his trousers as she talked. She stayed that way, talking to him, burning him for a while, until neither of them could stand it any longer. Then, after taking one last drag on her cigarette, she threw it away. She arranged her hair with the same hand, touching his erect penis as she did so. Then, quite deliberately, she exhaled the final mouthful of hot smoke onto him. She opened his fly, allowing her blond mane to cover and caress his erection. Barely moving to one side, she tossed her hair back and took his sex in her mouth. Mañungo groaned deeply; his entire body was groaning. He tried to caress her as she devoured him, but she stopped him: "Let me."

She began to suck it again, now more slowly. Protected from the wind by the acanthus plants, with Judit lost between his legs, refusing to allow him to share that pleasure half of which at least belonged to him, his hands flat on the grass, holding his body at an angle, Mañungo let himself be used; he found that all he could do was divide his attention between his fear that some passerby would spot them from the intersection, and his own excitement about the greediness of that mouth and the moist caress of her rough tongue and silky throat. A car stopped on the corner. Mañungo, flattening out in case they opened fire, managed to roll with Judit under the acanthus.

"Don't take it away from me," Judit begged amid the danger, and she took covetous control of his penis again, unconcerned that the car's searchlight might pick her out as it swept the block.

"Careful," he whispered.

Mañungo's entire body vibrated in harmony with the invisible heli-copters that filled the night, the voice of the old woman howled with the waves of Cucao, the point of his tinnitus scratched the glass just before shattering it, a drum, the beat of a thousand drums pounding out the wet secret of Judit's mouth while the car's searchlight swept through the crenated leathery leaves of the acanthus, his heart and the helicopter pulsing within and without them, the light stopping on them without revealing that in that instant the wave flooded Judit's mouth. Even though she rejected his caress, Mañungo fleetingly recovered the word "love," which Nadja had once erased from his vocabulary. The car turned off its inquisitorial searchlight and left, leaving both of them splayed out on the grass.

When Judit could finally move, sliding from Mañungo's legs up into his arms, which folded around her, he knew he no longer loved her: this tenderness he was feeling now was very different from the vertigo that, despite their refusals, had made them equals a moment ago. Compared with that flight, the present moment of this embrace was a nullity.

"Wait until when . . . ?" he repeated, picking up a much earlier dialogue, moved by Judit's disorientation as she sought the two halves of a fractured pleasure in order to reconnect them, as if it were still possible, when in fact it had been too late for who knew how long.

Wait until when? Did he really have to ask that question? Her answer would be generic, identical to all of Judit's answers, which invariably led to the same words: underground, run away, arrest. And rape too, perhaps? The tragic cliché could be an explanation for this Judit huddled in his arms, looking for a truce because she had become unable to fight with yesterday's certainties; above all now, with Matilde resting in a black box on the southern slope of the hill while only Carlitos held a wake for her, walking back and forth behind the bars of his cage.

If she started playing around with him, could Judit make the lion rage the way she made the dog rage with her handbag, the way she made him rage with her tongue? He'd like to see the beast break through the bars and attack her. Because Mañungo, lying under the acanthus, didn't think he was a bastard when he felt a shudder of pleasure at the idea of Judit's being raped. Was it her destiny? All he had to do was look at her and feel her blond mane mixed with his black beard to remember that she'd tried lots of ways to destroy herself. For that reason—and to expiate ancestral sins that weren't even her own—she'd made love with Lopito.

It had been compassion, certainly. But more than anything it had been curiosity, to see if she had the strength to go through with it, then bragging about her triumph in class as if she'd won a medal in some contest. Lopito and his friends guided her through all the cataclysms of the times, as she enthusiastically went from pit to pit, seeking absolution, until finally her comrades held up a gas station and the photo of Judit Torre—*Debutante Turns Criminal*—was on all the front pages and the television for days on end.

"That thing about the gas station was not true," she whispered in Mañungo's ear. "Accusations like that were always being thrown around in order to vilify the left and convince people that we were a danger to everyone. Anyway, the robbery charge got the political police off my back, since I was a political prisoner at the time, and I was handed over to the regular justice system for being a thief. In the public jail I was a little better off because you don't disappear from there: the law says that within five days you either indict a prisoner or you let him go. Fausta and Celedonio got me out. It had to be quick. So they never talked to my family because they wouldn't have done anything but hesitate about legalities and we would have lost time."

"How would you lose time?"

"Well, Mommy, poor thing, had died. She was scared to death of me."

"Who wouldn't be? Poor lady."

The story of Judit's relationship with her mother had preceded her arrival at the university. When Judit was fourteen, she had had fair hair and braces on her teeth. One day, she took off her braces in front of her mother, who reproached her for doing it and warned her that if she didn't put them right back on, she would never have the perfect teeth all the members of the Fox family had. Judit, dressed in her blue school uniform, with knee-high socks, stared her mother in the eye and tossed the braces into a corner of her bedroom. She didn't, she announced, want the teeth of the Fox family, because they were the ugliest teeth in the world. She went on to say that she hated everyone in the family, beginning with her mother, and didn't want to look like her in any way. She was going to be as different as possible from her and her older sisters, and she was informing her mother that she had no real authority over her because her mother was stupid, ignorant, a coward, devoid of imagination, uninteresting, and she was warning her not to try to dominate her because she'd never succeed. She would run her life as she saw fit. To show her, she grabbed a pair of pinking shears out of a sewing basket and without taking her eyes off her mother, she stood in front of the three oval mirrors of her gray lacquer Louis XVI vanity table, which reflected her face and her mother's, and cut off her hair, leaving just a white stubble, which became her trademark during her early militant years.

Her mother didn't say a word. She let her go on because as dumb as she might have been she realized that she'd lost her daughter. At dinner, neither her parents nor her sisters commented on her appearance, they simply went on eating their soup as the maid changed the plates. When dessert was served, Judit announced that since she had received the best grades in her class in all subjects and that since she had a gift for study, she wanted to take advantage of her talents in a high school where they might be of use, so she had transferred from the nuns' school where her mother had been educated to a public school in a neighborhood that seemed shockingly proletarian to the family.

"At least let the chauffeur drop you off in the morning!" begged her mother.

"Shut up, stupid!" hissed her father, as Judit left her chair, silently and haughtily, and, without asking permission, walked out of the dining room, disgusted by that abject scene, which her family would have judged vulgar if it had been acted out by other players.

Mañungo participated in the sequel to that incident. In the political pressure cookers the high schools were at the end of the Frei era, the children, once innocent and now radicalized, didn't study because they lived and argued politics. Judit was dragged into that first juvenile madness by her math teacher, whom she was dating, and who made her join the Communist Youth. The exaltation of demonstrations, cell meetings, indoctrination, ideological controversy, totally eclipsed Euclid.

In their house on Calle Málaga, her parents suspected that Judit was "involved" in something, but they never dared ask her about it. When she left high school, Judit was so dedicated to the Communist Youth that she followed their order to study economics at the university because the Party needed economists, not because she'd ever shown any inclination for the subject. It hardly mattered, because she was so totally involved in agitation and polemics that she never took a test or cracked a book: life was taking place elsewhere. She started coming home late. Her family accepted the idea that as a university student she had a different routine and got used to not seeing her, but no one knew who her friends were, although her older sisters told some nasty tales to her mother, saying they'd seen their crazy sister raising a ruckus downtown, shouting like a lunatic while she painted obscenities on a wall and some indecent, bearded types fought with the police. "One of these days . . ." her sisters predicted at the beginning, but they soon stopped because they got married and lost interest in Judit.

Her mother took to her bed definitively, victim of nameless ailments, in the depth of the biggest and darkest bedroom in the house, where she made up her world out of bills and sewing under the high stucco ceilings that slowly crumbled away. Since she saw little of Judit around the house, because of what everyone politely referred to as her "studies," no one even suspected she wasn't living there but with a well-known singer somewhere in a "bohemian" neighborhood. When the singer went to the United States, Judit moved in with her old math teacher, who had just left the Communist Party to join the terrifying Revolutionary Left Movement, which was recruiting heavily among the young people and establishing new modes of behavior. Now there was no question of ever coming to an accommodation with her family. One fine day, she came home to pick up her belongings and to try to make peace and explain things. However, even the cook asked her if she was insane and didn't believe a thing she said. Her father was down at the stock exchange at the time because things there had gone to hell, and her mother had a maid tell Judit she couldn't speak to her because she wasn't feeling well, that it would be better if she spoke to her tomorrow, after class.

A car stopped on the corner. Judit put out her cigarette so no one would see its glow. This block was heavily patrolled, which meant that some V.I.P. must live around here. So she was right about Las Hortensias and the blue Mercedes! A minute later, when the car pulled away, Judit said they couldn't stay there any longer because even though there was small chance that the Mercedes would come, if it did, they could never stop it from where they were.

"Stop it?" exclaimed Mañungo. "What is this, a gangster movie?"

"Practically. That's what Santiago's all about."

"Are you going to kill the guy in the car?"

"I don't know. I want to hear his voice so I can know if he's the man I've been looking for. Then we'll see how I feel."

"You're out of your mind! You've been talking about voices all night. How are you going to hear somebody's voice if he's inside a Mercedes-Benz? Come on, give me the gun."

"I've got a plan. You're going to help. You're the bait."

She didn't go into details. They stood up and brushed their clothes. When they sat down again on the base of the fence, Judit unbuttoned her dress at the bottom, crossed her legs, and revealed her fine knee and part of her thigh. Mañungo cupped his hand around a breast that trembled under the caress of the silk: Come on, he pleaded, let's forget this absurd, fanatical project, and find some way of getting back home. Judit didn't answer. Don César's message was that she should wait for the Mercedes "after twelve," so she couldn't give up now.

"Ramón had already disappeared when Luz was born," she was saying to Mañungo as they sat down on the fence.

"How old is she?"

"Let's see. I'm talking now about two years after the coup, eleven, twelve—I get mixed up with the months."

"She's older than Jean-Paul."

"She lives with Ramón's parents."

"Not with you?"

"No. I don't see her much because it upsets me. She doesn't love me, just as I didn't love my mother. She says everything I do is wrong. She thinks I'm an old nut, a details freak, she calls me, because I always call her Luz, which is her real name, instead of Marilú, her nickname. All she's interested in is clothes from Fiorucci and things like that. Ramón's family is poor, so in a certain sense her excitement over that stuff is justifiable. But she isn't dumb and maybe she'll forget that shit."

"And what does Ramón say?"

"He was killed. He'd been missing for a few months. Then one day his name came out in the paper in a list: 'Argentine Police Exterminate Chilean Infiltrators Like Rats,' implying that these members of the RLM, the ones on the list, had secretly fled to Argentina, where they ran into some cops who gunned them down. But we found out. They weren't killed there. Ramón was never in Argentina. They killed him here, and his body disappeared."

Mañungo froze listening to her matter-of-fact answer. It was a concrete truth with which she seemed to have no further connection. She didn't even seem to demand recognition or respect for her grief. Her husband, or comrade, in any case the father of her daughter, had been killed just as the husbands and comrades of so many people she knew. During the eleven months that Ramón had been missing, they'd only seen each other once, at night, in a vacant lot, where he arranged to meet her by means of don César's henchmen. They made love right then and there. He told her not to ask anything about what he and his friends were doing so her ignorance would protect her. The product of that meeting was Luz, two months after Ramón's death.

To erase these memories, Judit smiled, and spoke to him about the jubilant days of the Popular Unity, the rejuvenation, the daring, the vitality. She lived with Ramón then, when everyone seemed happy, in a clean little slum house, working as a union leader in a furniture factory in Maipú. She never went to class. She never gave much of a damn about all that, of course, and spent her time going to demonstrations, because political militancy was the most interesting possibility open to young people in those years. They became deluded because they thought they were changing history. She organized protests, marches, and strikes, until finally, under her leadership, her union took over the factory and began to produce furniture on their own.

Judit, who still had some charm and was good-looking despite her jeans and her olive green shirt ("Had your hair grown in by then?" "Yes, it was about the same length it is now, not the way it was when we first met"), would meet with the authorities at the various ministries, pestering the "comrade minister" until she got new benefits for her union, which was one of the best-managed at the time. Judit was very happy, very satisfied in those days. Nothing mattered to her, not even the fact that the functionaries of the Popular Unity who dealt with her demands and her union comrades were all a bit suspicious of her and laughed at her behind her back because no matter how she might try to hide it she would always be a "lady." Even in the way she did her job she revealed the signs of privilege. Her comrades did not bother to hide the fact that they thought it was silly for her to give up her comfort and security to dedicate herself to the fight for an abstract idea like social justice.

"When they killed Ramón I had to go underground, because the police were chasing me down to tell them where the others were. Comrades were disappearing every day, and every day we'd hear hideous rumors about torture. My parents, I think just so they could go on living, gave me up for dead, and it was Fausta who brought my daughter to Ramón's parents, good people even though they fill her head with stupid ideas. They live in a small place over behind the stadium. I ran from house to house, from slum to slum, always one jump ahead of the cops, who raided quite a few of the places where I'd been hiding, except a few secret ones, where I couldn't stay too long or they'd be discovered. During the time I lived underground, I gradually lost contact with the people in my party, until I was completely isolated from the few left with whom I'd shared myths, danger, faith, adventure, hunger, and bed. I lost sight of them and was left so alone I couldn't stand it. The regime had taken us apart, there was no center left, nothing to begin rebuilding with.

"I'd known don César for ages. He was called 'the dogger,' because when he was a kid in the Lota coal mines he'd jump aboard the coal trains while they were moving and throw 'dogs' down to his buddies who were running next to the train, which slowed down as it went uphill. 'Dogs' were the big pieces of coal they'd later sell for good money. Well, one day don César slipped and the train cut his legs off. That never stopped him from being a skirt chaser, and even though he was miserably poor, he managed to get a cute girl twenty years younger to fall in love with him and bear him nine children. One of his daughters and three of his sons died or disappeared. The hatred he and his sons have for the regime is comparable only to their hatred for the Party, and that's why he works politically for himself without being responsible to anyone. Why not, when violence is the only answer for those of us who have no hope? At night I hear his skateboard near my house. He doesn't go out much by day, and I only see him at dusk, winter or summer, muffled up in his scarf with his hat pulled over one eye as if he wanted to hide, though of course that only makes him more visible. When I hear him coming I understand he's got a message for me or a plan to present. He won't allow me to stay out of the struggle after I've fought so much, because it's our fight, it belongs to each one of us, and our mission is to spread chaos. In my underground days, living with people like don César in his miserable den, sharing a pallet on the floor with his sons—once or twice one of them was my lover, but that meant nothing—or on the floor in other houses, I'd stay three or four days before running to another slum so the cops would lose my trail. Those were the times of terror.

"People who thought like don César, and that's why I believe his story about the blue Mercedes, were willing to help in every way, and they gave me a place to stay and a bowl of soup as long as I kept my voice down and kept my hatred to myself. They formed a very effective network of spies, whose hatred gave them the strength to survive, dissimulate, and support others, risking everything in the process.

"Sometimes, when I couldn't stand the scum and the hunger that were killing me, I would use those same contacts to meet with Fausta and Celedonio on the outskirts of the city or on some corner in a slum so they could pick me up in a car and nurse me back to humanity for a few days. They never asked me anything, despite the risk they ran in hiding me. They were militants on the other extreme of the left, more like the center, really, tolerable for the regime, and the police never bothered them, although they did keep them under surveillance. Frei's government, which Fausta hated, had expropriated a lot of her land during their reform. And what Frei didn't take dwindled after Allende's executive orders. Fausta didn't hate Allende, probably because she had dinner with him so often with Pablo and Matilde.

"The regime was not suspicious of Fausta because she was known to be still rich, even though she marched in the first row during the demonstrations in support of the left. When I stayed with them, she and Celedonio would beg me to accept some money and get out of Chile, which had become hell for people like me, who had a right to our ideas no matter what they happened to be. I knew I could never get out of Chile because I was on record as being in the RLM. I was convinced my name was on those damned lists they kept at the airports, although I had no proof of it. To leave, you needed, besides the passport I didn't have, a certificate that proved you hadn't been in any political 'trouble,' which of course I could never get.

"Fausta urged me to stay in their house. It was horrible to see me so thin, with my eyes wandering like a madwoman's, full of impetigo, and ticks, and flea bites. No, I would say, without getting them to understand, I have to have the same fate as my comrades, I have to go on wandering from house to house, from night to night, hungry, with impetigo so none of my hatred for the killers of my comrades and of Ramón—whom I never loved, but with whom I shared a political complicity which was sometimes more than love—would ever abate. I can't stay cozy in your warm lap as you say I should, Fausta, because it would only make me feel guiltier about those who don't have the same chance. Besides, I shouldn't compromise you and Celedonio. You belong to another generation, another world, and this macabre fascination we have with dangerous ideas and death belongs exclusively to our generation. Why? Fausta wept without understanding. What do you have to feel guilty about, honey, what horror are you expiating? Haven't you suffered enough? I left without answering her because Fausta is a romantic woman, very simple, I'd even say glandular, and it's useless to try to involve her. When I left, I assured her that I'd emerge from my darkness every so often to stay with them for a few days when I couldn't take it anymore.

"One day, Celedonio happened to run into my father in the library of the Union Club. They didn't say hello, but their hands reached simultaneously for *Time*. My father snatched at the magazine with such an arrogant, I-own-the-world attitude that Celedonio automatically withdrew his hand, leaving *Time* to my father. Humiliated because of that defeat, he telephoned Fausta to pick him up: he felt so old and so weak that he didn't want to be there another second. He told Fausta he had to see me, to find out if an explanation from me could make him understand my need to destroy, and not remain, as he had until now, within the logic of moderation.

"I had given them a contact for reaching don César, a relative of Ada Luz—I didn't meet her until later in jail, where my women's group formed—a guy who worked as a waiter in a clam bar down at the Central Market. By digging through the city like moles, they managed to get me the message, that at such and such an hour a gray Citroën would pick me up on a certain corner of Avenida Brazil. I kept the date because in those desolate days I was ready to drop from hunger and despair, and I needed to feel loved and protected, and to hear music, an appetite, as you know better than I, Mañungo, more powerful than hunger.

"Fausta had meat for me, I remember, a steak, vulgar because it was so big, almost Argentine, and eggs, yes, lots of reconstructive protein, and an excellent red wine. After I finished eating—I'll never forget it!—we withdrew, obedient to the attentive silence, to Celedonio's library, with its famous dark green walls, its Empire furniture, and its French magazines piled up in corners. I realized Celedonio was getting ready to ask me something. He hadn't yet formulated his question, and kept digressing into other less important matters, it seemed to me, so he wouldn't have to start. What he didn't or couldn't say was more important than what he was managing to say.

"I could hear the city outside rolling by, ignorant of us, and the rain, in which I felt the need to immerse myself and which seemed to be calling to me. But there in the study, under the old light, I realized that Celedonio's lack of resolution was nothing more than the way he expressed luxury. We were listening to Claudio Arrau playing Schumann's *Papillons*—both Celedonio and I love Schumann, Mañungo, just like you—and for an instant I was charmed by having so much silence, so much time to listen and feel pleasure, that I feared my hatred might evaporate. But when *Papillons* was over, I recovered my rage: I had to forget its heart-rending subtlety. My road had to be rougher, and I had to wander on it forever. This kind of commitment excluded my right to Schumann's beautiful complexities. Celedonio nodded off on the sofa. Fausta was knitting something violet to keep me warm even though I begged her not to because a color like that would make me stand out like a target in the leaden poverty of the slums.

"Later we went to bed. I couldn't rest in my bed. I had no right to be there. As the hours passed, I got angrier and angrier until I was angry at Fausta, Schumann, and Celedonio, all of whom were accomplices, all of whom were covering up injustice and our enemies.

After Celedonio turned out the light, when I could hear Fausta snoring—she'd drunk a bottle of red wine reminiscing about how she'd ride over her lands down south with her father—I got up and after stupidly stealing all the money Fausta had in her bag, I ran away. Not through the door, but breaking a window like a thief, an enemy, because that's how I wanted to be and so it had to be. It was necessary that they hate me for things like that, to cut off my return to them and to Schumann, things I had to forget if I didn't want them to undermine my convictions.

"It was true it was stealing in name only, because Fausta always offered me all the money I could need to hide out in a mountain village, for example, and then to flee to Argentina on horseback, the way Neruda did when Gabriel González Videla was president. I rejected all her offers because I had another destiny, which was rooted in danger, revenge, and justice. Besides—I saw it clearly the moment I poked around in Fausta's bag looking for money—the most important thing was not to accept money as a gift, because that would make me their accomplice. Because they were moderates they were the real corruptors, the real guilty parties. I shouldn't even accept the idea that Fausta could 'give' me money, because 'her' money actually belonged as much to me, to us, as it did to them, and I had the right to take as much as I wanted. Why should I ask her for it or thank her for it? What I had to do was steal it, insult, wound, and disappear. I headed for the slum called Lo Hermida, where the men who arrested me were hiding in don César's house. I already told you about how it was in jail along with the five women I met there . . . I heard their screams through the walls . . . Aury, Senta, Ada Luz, Beatriz, Domitila . . . they think I'm their equal but I'm not, but they mustn't know that I'm not equal to them because they'll say, Why? Why you, when you're not one of us?"

20

✦ *F*or many years the idea of awarding the National Literary Prize to Fausta Manquileo had inspired a recurrent, impassioned controversy in Chile. During Frei's regime, her Araucanian name made her a candidate among the demagogues, but when time came to award the prize it was invariably given to writers who, it was said, deserved to get it before she did. During the Popular Unity years, she was rejected for being reactionary: she didn't participate in the revolution and was still the owner of considerable acreage down south, while among the comrades there were lots of writers of slender means and ardent loyalty who needed the prize money to survive. After 1973, she was accused, like so many moderates, of being a communist (because every moderate was a potential communist), and she was again denied the prize, which was given to writers closer to power.

Despite all that, Fausta Manquileo was one of the most prestigious names in Chilean literature, although literature no longer had much weight in Chilean life. Fausta was the last of yesterday's giants, from a time when knowledge of our country's lore and the commemoration of that noble subject constituted the great theme of our narrative tradition. With Fausta the dimensions of our literary forefathers shrank a bit, true enough, but what could you do about that?—it was a sign of the times. The regime liked the idea that Fausta hadn't published anything for over a decade, so even though she'd been a friend of the Nerudas and had a substantial role in political protests, her first, innocent novel, *Window on a Sea of Wheat*, was still suitable for use in the public secondary schools; besides, those naive Yankees, when it came time for a loan, might think twice if the government was accused of censoring the book. Her later novels popped up from time to time in used-book stores, but were never republished.

Santiago was essentially a small town, according to don Celedonio

Villanueva, so that no matter how things changed, traditional family, school, neighborhood, even summer-house relationships remained in place; they were hard currency that in times of stress could be translated into influence. Everybody "knew" Fausta and Celedonio: their unmistakable silhouettes, ill matched but always together on the streets of Santiago and at embassy receptions, physically augmented their literary prestige, which, honestly speaking, had no new merits to rest on.

So that the prestige she enjoyed not be linked with Judit's and endanger her further, Fausta did not publicly charge Judit with that stupid theft. Ingrate! False friend! That was her first reaction, although the robbery itself was of little importance. She'd often offered Judit double, triple, ten times the amount she had stolen, and been turned down every time. Why do this now, and in such a sordid way? Fausta, who loved few people, counted crazy Judit Torre among her favorites, so how could this betrayal of her friendship not hurt her?

Don Celedonio, a subtler theoretician than Fausta, made her reflect while he shaved and gave her an objective analysis of the crisis of Judit's generation. The great novelist spent the rest of her morning in bed, bathed in her own tears—her newspaper, her clothes, her breakfast tray all in a pile—swearing that she would use all her power to extricate poor Judit from the tragic circuit in which she was wasting away.

During the following eight days they were unable to make contact with Judit. The communication system seemed to have broken down, the messengers swallowed up by the earth; all addresses, numbers, and names seemed mistaken because suddenly no one seemed to know anybody. Where was she? What the devil was going on? Then, on the ninth day, Judit's picture appeared in the paper: *Well-known Radical and High-Society Figure Arrested as Common Criminal*. They grabbed the paper away from each other to read the story. Judit Torre had been arrested the night before with several members of the proscribed RLM when they tried to hold up a gas station in Pudahuel. Three of the assailants were shot, one fatally. Being listed as a member of the RLM meant she'd be taken to one of the sinister detention centers for political prisoners, where, using brutal techniques they'd learned in Panama and Brazil, the interrogators would force the prisoners to confess their crimes and tell where their leaders were hiding. Those who went through this process usually died or went insane. Often they simply disappeared. In any case, they were rarely the same afterward.

Common criminals, on the other hand, were taken to the public jail, where the regular criminal justice system took charge of them. It was a fact of life during that era, when these distinctions were made clear in every household as a kind of preventive knowledge about the dangerous contamination young people were subject to, that common criminals could not be held for more than five days unless they were indicted. If the evidence was proven to be insubstantial, the person detained was set free and given a certificate of good conduct that stated "no police record." If the case was strong, on the other hand, then the suspect could be charged and held in jail until the trial. Although the jail had an ominous reputation for being filthy, a hotbed of vice, drug traffic, prostitution, and malnutrition, and had no sanitary facilities or heat, it was not feared as much as the detention centers for political prisoners, because the torturers' notorious talents did not reach the public jail.

Fausta and Celedonio got dressed as quickly as possible and went straight to the women's section of the jail. The authorities brought Judit out, battered, stammering, and incoherent, her blue eyes so pale and devoid of expression that they seemed to have fled her face. She was thin from suffering; her body was covered with cuts and bruises, her hands and nails bloody from tortures that Fausta preferred not to imagine. They'd brought her to the jail the night before, she said, after curfew, when the city was silent and atrocities could be committed with discretion. There wasn't even a murmur in the uptown streets, which she guessed she was crossing even though she was sealed up inside the police van with five other "radicals," who knew nothing of the neighborhood's charms—yes, yes, it was the upper part of town, her own neighborhood. Nothing in the world could compare with the fragrance of a summer night on those streets, she'd thought as she recognized it with the heartbreak of someone living it for the last time on the way to the gallows; nothing in the world smelled like freshly watered roses, and the cascades of honeysuckle, and the piles of freshly mown grass the gardeners would carry away the next day. Now, just before her death, she realized inside the van that it was impossible to confuse a summer night uptown with any night anywhere else in the world. Judit explained that she herself had no idea why they'd brought them here. They'd first been held somewhere else for three days, and later they were brought to another center so they could regain some strength before being delivered to the public jail.

"The first place was terrible. They arrested me when I left your place the night I stole the money. I was in the second center for five days."

"Eight days in all," said don Celedonio, drying his sweating brow. "Listen, Ju, listen to me . . ."

She didn't answer.

"Judit," Celedonio raised his voice.

"What?"

"They didn't arrest you yesterday morning then?"

"No. Eight days ago. Yesterday morning I was locked up in the second center."

When they unfolded the newspaper so that Judit could read the headline, she seemed to revive. There wasn't one iota of truth in it. All lies. She'd never heard those names or seen those faces. At the time the paper said the robbery took place, she was locked up in a cell with her five companions. She had witnesses to prove it. Any one of her five friends could testify she was telling the truth.

"If they brought you here last night, we have time to get you out before they . . . they do something to you," said don Celedonio.

"No," said Judit; later she recognized this as the first moment, when she could no longer resist the necessity to make up her lie. "In the first center, right at the start, that's where they already did the worst."

"Poor baby!" exclaimed Fausta. "You'll tell me all about it later. What we've got to do now is get you out. You mustn't stay here."

Judit held on to Fausta. "Don't let them send me back to the detention center! Please, don't let them do it!"

Some people rotted away for years in the leper colony called the public jail, emerging prematurely aged and addicted after serving incalculable sentences while awaiting trial. As bad as it was, that situation was infinitely better than the political prisons. What the hell was going on with Judit? Was the newspaper printing phony dates and events just to muddle things up? They would have to establish as soon as possible whether Judit was a political prisoner or a common criminal. The authorities had made the mistake—not exactly an innocent one—of accusing her of having committed a crime, when it could be proven that she was already locked up elsewhere. But if they did prove that the newspaper article was phony and that Judit was not a common criminal, then the center for political prisoners would get her back for sure and she'd be held incommunicado, and not even a lawyer could get to her. Even if they could reach her, they would never succeed in extracting her from the tangle the authorities had woven around her.

Fausta and Celedonio followed the police wagon in their car right to the courthouse, a respectable old mansion in the lower end of town, made of adobe gussied up with pretentious *fin-de-siècle* decorations; its moldings were falling down, its paint peeling; a mob of people, relatives of the defendants, nervously whispered at the doors. Judit and the other prisoners were led from the police wagon and locked up inside the building, awaiting their turn before the judge. Fausta and Celedonio, their nerves about to short-circuit despite their fatigue, walked up the sagging stairs, then down, passed through littered patios, and sat down on one of the empty benches to wait for a handcuffed Judit to be called. They saw prisoners returning from these interviews, being locked up again by the police amid the clanking of keys and bolts, anxiety written on every face because of the intolerable slowness. Groups of men smoked and chatted in hushed tones at the door of the courthouse, looking up at the sky, commenting on the smog, listening to the bells of Gratitud Nacional and San Lázaro churches. No one gave Fausta and Celedonio a straight answer to any of their questions. The best was: "Your turn will come when the judge calls you."

They'd already considered every eventuality for Judit; to do it again would provoke a simultaneous nervous breakdown in both of them. The first alternative was that the press's error about Judit's heist would be cleared up, and she would be returned to the political police—this was their greatest fear, and the most likely scenario. The second alternative was that, despite the proof, she would be declared a common criminal and locked up forever in the pestilent jail. The third was that her case would be thrown out and she'd be set free, no questions asked—or answered, which seemed to be the way the justice system worked these days—and that Fausta and Celedonio would simply take her home. And then what? What could they do with Judit once she was free? Let her go back to running from place to place, with the regime's eye fixed on her every move?

"She has to get out of Chile right away," declared Fausta for the millionth time.

"She can't," answered Celedonio, also for the millionth time that morning, certain about his logic although uncertain about its effectiveness. "She has no passport and no certificate, and her name must be on the blacklist at the airport."

Fausta combed her hair, stood up, and said, "Well, let's just find out."

It was precisely at that moment, thought Fausta afterward, that things started to speed up in an insane fashion, like a movie gone out of control. They drove to the Venezuelan embassy, where the ambassador graciously accepted don Celedonio's pardon for not smoking a cigar with him; when he learned what the problem was, he became serious and excused himself to make some telephone calls. After twenty minutes, during which the world seemed to have stopped spinning on its axis, the ambassador returned and announced that Judit's name was not on the blacklist at any Chilean airport, but that they were not to ask how he found out—it had been a very special favor done for them by someone who admired them both very much.

In addition to providing them with that vital information, he gave them a paper which would equip the lady in question with a visa to enter Venezuela. Fausta and Celedonio ran out with the paper in their hands to speak with Judit's father—but he was in the United States on business. Next they spoke to a highly trusted lawyer, who said but of course, they were to wait for him at noon in the courthouse. When he learned who the prisoner was, however, her photo having appeared that morning in all the newspapers, her name ringing out of every radio news report, he said that, well, after thinking the matter over, he had too much to do and since these things take so long, it wouldn't matter if he didn't get to the court until four o'clock.

Fearful that Judit's case would be called during their absence—"Why?" asked the lawyer. "What good will it do for you to be there? Just calm down!"—don Celedonio and Fausta ran to the nearest bar to drink a whiskey, because if they didn't they'd die, and then went back to the court just in time to see a handcuffed Judit led in to make her statement. They followed her to a hall where there was an incessant clatter of typewriters, but were not allowed to enter. They could make out Judit's silhouette diffused in the frosted glass of the door, which was blocked by a policeman.

Whenever the door opened, the relatives of the prisoners inside flocked to see. Peering through the heads, Fausta and Celedonio could discern Judit, her head bowed, humbled, speaking, it seemed, slowly and monotonously, standing in front of the clerk's desk as he typed out her answers. Where the devil was the damned lawyer? Why would he come down when it wasn't even noon and he'd told them to expect him at four? Should they call another lawyer? Which one? Where? How could they leave the poor thing alone, so filthy, ragged, and weak? Celedonio told Fausta to calm down and pushed his way through the crowd the policeman was trying to keep at bay: they shouldn't get worked up, there was no hurry, these trials took days, ages—or at

least, those five days the judge had in which to decide whether to try
the defendant or throw the case out seemed like an age. So the lawyer
had more than enough time if he got there at four, and they, after
the judges left and the prisoners were sent back to their cells to spend
the night, would have all the time they'd need to call those important
people they said they knew. They should wait, like everyone else.
Fausta and Celedonio collapsed onto a bench, she fanning herself with
a newspaper and fanning Celedonio in the process, who was suffocating because of the rotten cigarettes everyone seemed to be smoking.
He repeated over and over, "That her name is not on the blacklist is
something. Don't you think so? Of course it might be just that they
haven't yet added the names from last night. Will this makeshift visa
the ambassador gave us be any good?"

"And what about the other certificate?" asked Fausta.

"The judge will give us that one here."

"That's the certificate for police problems. But what about the certificate that covers political things?"

Don Celedonio shrugged his shoulders by way of answering. Who
could know a thing like that? Who knew anything in this hell of a
country? He closed his eyes and leaned back against the wall. Only
then did he whisper in a low voice, with a sigh, "I don't know."

"What about the passport?"

"I don't know, I tell you, I just don't know."

From their typewriters, the severe, overworked clerks would glance
up at the group of people gathered outside peering in at them through
the door. The clerks would shout for them to quiet down. The police
took away the prisoners who'd exhausted their defense and locked the
doors. At twelve-fifteen, Fausta and Celedonio were required to appear in the tiny office of the judge, where Judit was waiting for them.
The judge informed them that the charges against Judit would be
dropped.

"May I take her, then?" asked Fausta.

The judge, looking at her over the top of the sheaf of papers he
held straight up in front of him, said unfortunately no: the prisoner
Torre Fox, despite her high-powered name, would have to go back
to the public jail so that from there the authorities from the political
section could take charge of her. That was where she belonged, even
if those gentlemen had put responsibility for her on the ordinary
courts. The matter, as far as he was concerned, was closed—there was
no doubt that it was an ill-intentioned mistake made by some journalist.

But there were certain ambiguities in the case that suggested the civil court could never come to an agreement on the matter with the political authorities. Who knew who was going to end up dead in this unfortunate episode. . . . He had no choice but to wash his hands of the affair and return Judit Torre Fox to the political police. Fausta smelled defeat. She took Judit's handcuffed hands. The judge handed her a paper, asking, "Sign here please, ma'am."

Out of the corner of her eye, signing she didn't know what or why, Fausta observed the judge, calculating how many minutes, or rather seconds, she had left to save Judit, although she didn't know how. How could she convince this delicate boy with gold-rimmed glasses, two crystal fishbowls in which his enormous and timid black eyes swam? He was thin, but had the beginnings of the potbelly of the young groom whose wife dominates him through his stomach. When Fausta handed back the paper, the judge stared at it, deciphering the signature.

"What does this say?" he asked without raising his eyes.

"Fausta Manquileo."

The boy dropped the paper on the desk and allowed his timid eyes to float to the surface of their respective bowls; he stared Fausta in the eye. Suddenly ceremonious, he stood up: "I can't believe it!" he exclaimed boldly, approaching Fausta and shaking her hand.

He'd completely forgotten Judit, her case, and don Celedonio. He didn't hear the clatter of the typewriters, the bustle around him, or the voices in the next hall. He was telling the writer that he'd read *Window on a Sea of Wheat* in high school, like everyone else, and his enthusiasm had been so great that not only had he chosen for a wife a cousin who looked like Nélida, the heroine, but he'd even ransacked the secondhand bookstores on Calle San Diego to find her other books— he thought he had her complete works. She couldn't imagine what an honor it was for him to meet her, how happy it made him . . . ! He begged Fausta to sit down for a moment in front of him. Yes, they had plenty of time, the others could wait. With Fausta's help he reviewed her every title, the publication date of every edition. He also wrote, he confessed: those black fish did not move, but remained close to the glass edge of their bowls, attentive to the reaction of his illustrious guest.

"In a profession like this," commented the budding judge,"I see human-interest stories every single day, so I have no lack of themes for my literary endeavors."

He'd so like to show his work to someone who understood these things, because he lived in a professional world that was, well, flat, distanced from spiritual things, and his colleagues might laugh at him if they were to find out . . . Yes? Was it possible? What a great honor, that she would give him her opinion! Of course, she'd be delighted, answered Fausta, seeing the time running out without being able to stop it, without being able to flee with poor Judit, whom she felt shivering next to her from something other than cold. In fact, added Fausta, she would even give him a certain little volume of erotic poems published in a limited edition, oh, quite some time back, when she was young, naturally, and those things . . . And if he wanted, she would be glad to sign all her works in his collection. Thank you, thank you! The judge declared it was absolutely urgent that the National Literary Prize be given to Fausta Manquileo, since that honor had lost much of its prestige, having been given for purely political reasons, just as so many things in the recent past had destroyed the moral structure of the nation.

They chatted for almost half an hour. From time to time secretaries would leave documents that began to pile up on a corner of the desk, or a clerk would walk in to remind the judge that a line of people was waiting for him to finish with this case. Furious, the judge ordered his door to be closed and went on with his delightful literary disquisition, which he was addressing to such an illustrious personage while the illustrious personage felt her world crumbling around her. Tomorrow she would bring him the *plaquette*, a truly rare item, Fausta assured him. And if tomorrow he would do her the favor of bringing her his writing, she could look it over and give him her opinion.

"Besides," added Fausta, drying her perspiration, stuttering because she knew she was exaggerating everything, overacting, offering too much, pressing too hard, so hard that the judge was sure to catch on, "besides, I have friends in several publishing companies, so if I can possibly help you there, I'd be delighted. Of course, it all depends on whether your work deserves it, because you understand I can't compromise my professional reputation recommending just anything . . ."

Of course! He took that for granted! It would never occur to him to ask a person as important as she to risk her reputation on some piece of junk. It would be like asking him to sign something in whose merits he didn't believe, and that was impossible. For example, in the case of Miss Judit Torre, he just had to send her back to the political police in order to show those gentlemen that they were incompetent, liars, and that he, as a representative of the ordinary justice system, didn't believe a word they said.

"You don't believe the stickup story?" asked don Celedonio, walking toward the desk.

"Of course not. Neither the stickup story nor many other things."

With Fausta standing by in shock, don Celedonio launched into a diatribe against the political police, accusing them of being too cozy with those corrupt journalists who published whatever came into their heads, mucking everything up and sullying sound traditional institutions. Did the judge actually believe that the error made in the case of Judit Torre Fox was really an error? Wasn't it actually an agreement, a sinister intrigue carried out by those two institutions—both of which were of dubious character, to say the least—in order to corrupt and complicate ordinary justice, which was a noble tradition in our country? Was it not also the case that if all this business was a lie created by the political police working in unison with venal journalists, then it must also be the case that the political police could not claim her, but that she had to be discharged by regular justice?

Fausta, the judge who signed more and more triplicate forms under the hallucinogenic effect of the presence of his favorite writer, and even Judit, who seemed to revive because of don Celedonio's discourse, kept a stupefied silence. They seemed to watch, as one watches a passing troop of horsemen, the irrefutable order of the minor poet's arguments, deployed in military style. He finished in a cutting tone:

"Judit Torre Fox must be set free right now! These internal struggles between the forces that should maintain order in our country and instead are undermining it will be what finally overturns the security of the state, not terrorism or the left, which as we all know has been decimated. This is shameful! It makes me fear for the future of my country! Your honor, if the business of the political police is none of your affair, if you've dropped all charges against Judit Torre, and if you've signed the certificate declaring the charges to be null and void and Miss Torre Fox to be a citizen in good standing with the regular police, it seems to me logical for you to set her free. What more do you want from her? Do the political police want to go on abusing their authority and have the blame put on you, who are innocent? Do they want stinking, nosy journalists to butt in where they don't belong and invent new, even more absurd ways of making fools of you? No! No! It cannot be allowed! If the political police feel you are afraid of them, they will go on obstructing and degrading the very institution you represent."

Fausta couldn't believe it. It was all so brilliant but also so fragile. One false move, one word too many or too few, and it would all fall apart and land them all—not only Judit, but them as well—in jail. She brought the meeting to a close as quickly as possible, with her best smile: "Tomorrow, then, with your manuscripts?"

The judge put his seal on the papers. Then, without saying a word, he rang a bell. A jailer appeared, to whom the judge signaled to remove the handcuffs from the prisoner. Fausta never stopped talking—who knows what she said?—just to fill the air, so the judge wouldn't think, because she, of course, could not believe what she was seeing with her own eyes. She realized that if they didn't get Judit out of the court-house right then and there, taking advantage of the charm they'd worked on the two black fish peering out from their bowls without seeing a thing, she would be lost forever.

The virtues of poetic prose, its false values, the second-rate writers who think they are first-rate, Neruda's house on Isla Negra, the vanity of the poets in this country who think themselves more important than the prose writers, publications, scholarships—these were some of the myriad subjects Fausta's nervous frenzy spun out during the minute it took to remove Judit's handcuffs (something she pretended not to see) and to sign the last documents. Finally, Judit raised her eyes, charged with a tiny spark of amusement at the novel with which Fausta was bombarding the judge's astonished ears, a novel in which Fausta used the skeleton of Judit's biography as a framework for a moving story of innocence, which certainly had nothing to do with Judit Torre. The judge handed over the documents, the sentence, and the certificate, to Miss Judit Torre Fox.

"Tomorrow then?" the magistrate asked Fausta, walking around his desk to squeeze that distinguished hand just one last time.

"At about this time?"

Don Celedonio remained in the background with Judit, because he understood that the major role had now reverted to Fausta; only she, with her regal air, was capable of negotiating a triumphal exit.

"Yes, at this time tomorrow, if it's convenient for you."

"I'd be delighted. Don't forget your manuscripts, now."

"I wouldn't dream of it."

"Thanks for everything."

"No, thank *you*. For me, it's been an unexpected honor."

"And for me a genuine pleasure. Till tomorrow. Shall we be on our way then, Ju?"

Fausta had to clench her fists and twist her toes inside her stiletto-heeled shoes to overcome her impulse to run out of the court before the police grabbed Judit again. Both women took long but decorous strides through the stuffy corridors, followed by don Celedonio, who could barely keep up, limping along with his cane. Thank God, thank the merciful God of those who don't believe in Him, murmured Fausta as they emerged and headed for their car, parked a block away. Thank the God of atheists like herself, who had heard their prayers, as He had whenever she'd invoked Him when she was on the verge of giving up, thank Celedonio, whose gift of gab really had some use.

Fausta drove, Celedonio sat next to her, and Judit, with what seemed the shadow of a smile, was in the backseat. They opened the windows on both sides so the air would blow on her, refreshing her face and her hair, which was stuck to her head with grime. She began to laugh nervously as she recited the names of the churches and public buildings they passed, as if to confirm that after all she'd gone through, things were still in their place.

What to do now? That was what Fausta and Celedonio discussed in front, although Judit paid no attention and stared at the streets. What to do? What had they achieved by getting Judit out? She was free, but her freedom might be momentary because the political police would hunt her down and them as well as accessories unless they could figure out what to do with her. They had the police certificate, true enough. But not the political certificate. Her name, at least as of two hours ago, was not on the airport blacklist. Who knew if it was there now?

Don Celedonio gave Judit money, which she might need. At Padahuel Airport it would be easy to get a ticket to Caracas and enter with the diplomatic visa supplied by the ambassador. They drove around downtown, through the traffic jams and fumes, discussing the next step. Judit said she had a friend who could get her a forged passport. No, none of that! It was too risky, and besides, it would take days, and she had to leave right away! Just to be on the safe side, why not take some photos?

They parked and found a kiosk where they could get instant photos. Ten desperate minutes later, they had a series of photos of Judit—disheveled, thin, bruised, and recognizably Judit Torre. They got back into the car and went over the false-passport idea again, rejecting it because it would take too much time and Judit had to leave Chile on the next flight. There was a Swissair flight at four—while the women were in the kiosk getting the photographs, Celedonio had inquired at the tourist agency—an Air France flight at five, a Pan Am flight at five-thirty: the Swissair flight at four. But what about the passport? How could they get one? They were talking nonsense because with no passport it was all just talk.

"And clothes," said Fausta. "You can't travel looking like that."

"Are you crazy? Clothes at a time like this?" shouted Celedonio.

Judit was pitiful: a ragged, stained skirt that was falling off because she'd lost so much weight; a blouse missing buttons, with one sleeve torn open. Fausta and Celedonio got into an argument, trading accusations of frivolity and cowardice, an argument in which it was easy to see that what they were arguing about had nothing to do with their mutual insults, and that they were only using those words to ventilate old quarrels. Or perhaps they argued because they feared for their lives, as did everyone else in Chile, which always seemed on the point of foundering, sinking, and disappearing with all of them aboard.

"Twenty minutes to two," read Judit out loud as they passed the university clock tower. "Government offices close at two."

"So what?"

"Exactly," explained don Celedonio to reconcile everyone. "Judit's right. The only things we have that are solid are the police certificate and the knowledge that Judit's name is not on the blacklist. We have to go to the passport office to get the passport."

"You're out of your head!" shouted Fausta.

"No, let's go there," insisted Judit, with the authority of a person who has made a decision about her own life. Fausta immediately drove toward Calle General Mackenna and the passport office.

They were silent for the rest of the trip. They reached the door of the passport office at ten minutes before two. The last people to be taken care of were leaving, self-satisfied, with their documents in hand or safely put away. A guard stopped Celedonio: "It's closing time."

Don Celedonio lied as serenely as he could, saying he hadn't come to request a passport but to pick up a document that was waiting for him. As he wasted two minutes convincing the guard, he saw in the large hall ten employees behind their desks, putting their papers in order and getting ready to leave. How much longer than ten minutes would they have to wait to prepare the passport? The policeman looked at Judit, who lowered her eyes as if by doing so she hoped to hide her identity.

"Go on in."

The three stood on the threshold of the hall, in front of the row of tables, from which the employees contemplated them while covering over their typewriters. It was as if they were trying to choose which of those ten employees would decide Judit's fate. Judit chose at random, walking toward a man who had his desk close to the center of the line of employees, not because he seemed more important or more understanding, but simply by chance. He was a corpulent man with fat olive-toned cheeks, heavy eyelids, and a thin, well-trimmed mustache that was too small for his face and body. He hadn't shaved that morning. Like the others, he had taken off his jacket and hung it on the back of his chair; his white shirt was gray from use, the fabric worn thin by washing, revealing his hairy chest underneath. Above his head, near the domelike ceiling, there was a large clock that showed six minutes before two. They approached, don Celedonio next to Judit, Fausta just behind.

"What do you want?" asked the man with a slightly nasal voice, as if he had a summer cold, the kind that put you in a bad mood.

"A passport for this child."

"It's almost two. There's no time."

"It's six before two," don Celedonio pointed out as politely as possible.

The nasal-voiced man stared at Judit. Did he recognize her from her photos in the morning papers? Maybe he hadn't had time to read the papers. But something began to work in his face, in the depths of his moist, silken eyes with their thick lashes, shipwrecked in that vulgar face, as if they alone had remained beautiful and caressing precisely to immobilize Judit with their tenderness. The man who'd exempted her in the cell, the one with the nasal voice, he had to have eyes like these. His pudgy hands shuffled, straightened, and messed up the pile of papers on his desk as if that vacuous activity were unrelated to what was happening in the depth of his eyes. Were his hands warm, soft, and moist? Had he recognized her? At the desk behind his, another employee stood up, slowly putting on his jacket: don Celedonio noticed the discolored fabric in its armpits. At another desk, another employee was putting papers in a drawer he then slammed, the noise echoing in the hall. Behind their desks, two employees chatted, offered each other cigarettes and lit them.

"The photos?"

While don Celedonio was taking the photos out of his wallet, the man with the nasal voice scrutinized Judit from his typewriter. Judit withstood his stare. Either he recognized her from the newspapers, or he remembered her despite her hood and he was the man—yes, yes, he was the one, he had to be, and he was going to exempt her again!—or he simply didn't recognize her. Now he was examining the photos, a second more than was necessary, almost as if he were choosing one as a souvenir. Then, raising his head again, he asked, "Police certificate?"

Fausta handed it over. From the other tables, the employees looked on without saying a word. Who were these men who slyly examined her in order to keep her from running away because they recognized her? The All-merciful hesitated behind his typewriter, not having decided whether he'd pardon her again. His voice was nasal, like that of all rapists, and his hands were smooth: Judit longed to feel that comforting hand on her knee. The other employees covered their old Underwoods with terrible, cracked oilcloth covers, as black as coffins, like old Singer sewing machines, like outmoded pay phones. But not the All-merciful with the nasal voice. He looked at the certificate as if this were the first one he'd ever seen in his life, as if he didn't see them ten, twenty, or fifty times a day, every day of his poor, routine existence. He examined the certificate: no problems with the police. But nothing about her political problems. He raised his glassy eyes. Did he drink?

"Listen," he said, talking to his colleague at the next desk.

"What?"

"Is this thing okay?" He leaned over to show the police certificate. The other looked at it for a second and said, "I guess so."

"Sure it is," butted in a man who had just put on his jacket and was straightening his tie in front of a tiny mirror near a door. He hadn't looked at the certificate, he hadn't even seemed to notice them when they walked in, so how could he know what kind of document it was? Nevertheless, he saw, because everything had become terrifying and transparent. The man with the nasal voice opened a drawer and took out a fresh passport. He asked Judit's name, date of birth, place of birth, without giving the slightest hint that he already knew all that information from the morning papers. A silence fell over the entire hall, and all the other employees stood motionless, transparent, waiting.

"Married?"

"Yes."

"Got the marriage certificate?"

"No."

"Ah, well then I can't . . ."

From another desk an exasperated voice said softly, but drowning in that softness a shout of despair, "Come on, Medina. Get a move on. How long are we going to be waiting here?"

Then Medina said, writing, "So we'll put down single."

Was this some kind of plan? Judit asked herself. Were these all people from the left who had managed to infiltrate the passports section and, knowing who she was, were helping her get out of the country so she wouldn't be killed? Were they employees from the Popular Unity days who had kept their jobs to feed their families despite the humiliation of having to put up with so much, or were they getting even by helping one of their own to escape? Or was it that the ten employees had perceived in her what the All-merciful with the nasal voice had perceived in her when she'd terrified him with her nakedness in the cell and he didn't dare claim her privileged body, leaving only the memory of a warm, moist hand on her knee?

Medina finally held her hand to take her fingerprints: it was not *his* hand. It was muscular and dry. He was not the man with the nasal voice. Later, without letting her wash her hands, he said, "Sign here."

The pen slipped from Judit's martyred fingers. Medina bent over, picked it up, and wiped off the ink from the fingerprinting. He handed it to her.

"Thanks."

"Now the boss has to sign," said Medina, getting up. "Wait a minute."

Fausta stepped forward. "Please, could you hurry things a little?"

"Lady, we're doing you a favor. We don't know if the boss is going to want to sign anything now. He may have left already."

"Tell him I'm Fausta Manquileo."

The employee who was in a hurry looked at her insolently, as if trying to dig an identity out of her messy makeup: "And just who is Fausta Manquileo?"

Fausta kept quiet and stepped back.

"Hurry up, Medina," they whispered from various desks.

"The boss's gone, Medina, he took off," said one who hadn't spoken before. "I'll sign. Who's going to notice?"

Medina brought him the passport. Almost all the others had stood up, contemplating the scene in silence. One said, "That'll be two thousand pesos. Want me to make out the receipt, Medina? Just to speed things up is all. It's three minutes after two."

"Yeah, please, Lorca."

Lorca wrote. The others watched, straightened the handkerchiefs in their jacket pockets, combed their hair, stretched their shirt cuffs, and finished putting away their work. Medina went back to his desk with the passport, waving it in the air as if to dry the ink.

"Here you are," he said, handing it to Judit after inserting it in the machine that put on the official seal, a hard, implacable device, as a torture apparatus should be.

"And the police certificate?" asked don Celedonio.

"Oh yes," said Medina, folding it up and returning it.

"Thanks," said don Celedonio to Medina.

"Thanks," added Fausta.

Assuming Judit would add her own "Thanks," Medina did not say "You're welcome." But Judit said nothing because his hand was not *the* hand, his voice not *the* voice. The group in the passports room stared at them in silence as they left at four minutes after two. Fausta first, leaning on Judit's arm because she could not believe it all and was feeling very old with all this nonsense, and very tired, and fearing she'd faint. Don Celedonio brought up the rear. To celebrate, he lit up a comforting cigar as they walked down the stairs of the documents office. They got into the car and drove straight to Pudahuel Airport. All the horror was left behind. And at three-thirty, Judit boarded a Swissair jumbo jet for Caracas, with no baggage, bruised, hungry because the fear that she would be recognized or that her name would be on the list kept her from eating anything in the airport restaurant.

*S*tretched out among the acanthus plants, exhausted by the story, Mañungo and Judit fell asleep in each other's arms. The night had grown extremely calm, uninterrupted by passersby or stray dogs—even the stars seemed permanently fixed in their paths. After midnight the lights in the buildings beyond the lawns went out one after another, until only the buildings themselves were left standing guard under the liquid sky. Fear had cleansed the streets of all those who did not belong on them. They all went silently back to their lairs to invent stratagems for destroying the privileges enjoyed by those who lived in this neighborhood. The story Judit told belonged to the fear that cut through the outraged city from end to end, that made it feel decapitated, impotent, with no voice, with no pulse other than the beat of the helicopter rotors that earlier had made the night shake, but that could no longer be heard. On the sidewalk, in their pale clothes, their arms around each other, hidden by plants that were so strong they looked carnivorous, Judit and Mañungo resembled inhabitants of a strange universe which barely needed the flow of love and sleep.

A Mercedes appeared on the corner. It slowed down and passed under the shadow of the plum trees, moving forward noiselessly because, given the hour, it would be better not to wake the neighborhood dogs. The car's interior light was on. The man driving had a huge, Mexican-style mustache; next to him sat a movie-star-type blonde, and on the rear seat was a small, nervous dog with mutilated ears and a pointy muzzle, a miniature Doberman: cruelty reduced to its essence. The Mercedes stopped at 2788 Las Hortensias, then turned in to the driveway. It touched the gate affectionately with its nose, as if it were an animal sniffing for recognition. The man got out to open the gate. The dog followed him, walking a little farther to sniff the familiar urine that had yellowed the bases of the pilasters on both sides of the entrance. It was raising its leg to urinate when the man got back into the Mercedes and drove through the gate. A minute later, the blonde appeared, carrying a flashlight and yawning, and the man came out to the street to call the dog.

"Boris! Here, Boris!"

The dog didn't obey. He kept on sniffing the ground, the weeds he knew only too well, the gate. He ventured on tentatively, and they, arm in arm, and shining their flashlight in front of them, followed along the sidewalk. They called him from time to time but not urgently, shaking his chain as an admonition when they saw him getting ready to cross the street. He stopped next to the acanthus plants. Jumping around, he began to bark hysterically, in higher and higher tones, pointing with his nose at something that he saw under the plants: a moon-colored couple. The woman, with long spectral hair, stretched with the slowness of fairy-tale characters who finally wake up after centuries of enchanted sleep and sat up on the grass. The beam from the flashlight assaulted the eyes of the man and the woman, who yawned amid vegetation that had been transformed by the light from ornament into something dangerous and primeval. They weren't beggars, a logical enough fear at this time of night, so they wouldn't attack. Since no defense was necessary against them the man called the dog: "Boris! That's enough!"

"Enough!" ordered the woman, scrutinizing the couple's faces from behind her flashlight.

"What are you doing here at two o'clock in the morning?" said the man threateningly. "Don't you know there's a curfew? Do you want me to call the patrol?"

Neither of the two figures answered. They were slowly getting to their feet, helping each other up, as if having slept for so many centuries in a bed that hard had crippled them. When he saw them get up, white against the black leaves, the dog redoubled his barking without paying any attention to his master, who shouted at him to shut up. The man took a step toward Mañungo, demanding, "Come on. Identify yourself."

Mañungo frowned. "Why should I identify myself to you?"

The blonde kept Mañungo's face captive in the beam of light, evidently her assigned role in circumstances like these. The man put his hand in his pocket and took out a device with a small red light at one end. He spoke into it: "Central."

"Central," replied the device.

"Urgent. Patrol six-six-one."

"Roger," answered the device.

"Farías here."

The blonde, tugging at his sleeve, whispered, "Listen, Ricardo . . ."

"Shut up!" Farías shouted at her and then at the dog, who continued to snarl at the two figures arm in arm in the vegetation, "You shut up too, asshole!"

"Ricardo . . ."

"Reading you. Farías here, on Las Hortensias . . ."

"Don't you think he looks like . . . ?" She kept Mañungo prisoner with her flashlight.

"Who, Liliana?"

"This man."

"Central. I need a patrol right away. . . . Cut it out, honey. Who does he look like?"

"That singer."

The man let a second pass while he examined the character in front of him and then passed sentence: "You're nuts, baby. There's no resemblance. My daughters told me he's in exile and lives in Paris. What would he be doing here on Las Hortensias at two in the morning?"

Farías, Ricardo: finally her revenge had acquired a face and a name, besides a nasal voice. His voice. Or *was* it his voice? Nasal voices are imprecise, cottony, wintry; you take them in as if they were hot caresses over your stomach. This voice, on the other hand, was a military voice, and even if he'd had a cold, like Medina with his damned summer cough, it could never have the same character as the voice that had excused her years ago. But Ricardo Farías's voice was nasal. And she found it tempting that her revenge have a name and a face with a mustache, and a house and family, and an address. And would he also have a soft hand, moist from timidity? Judit was buttoning her dress where Mañungo had been caressing her, but she left her hem buttons open—just in case. This disquieted night with its fragrance seemed about to reveal the content of its omens. Judit bent over to pick up her bag.

Before she could complete the movement, the woman shouted: "Halt!"

Judit straightened up.

"What are you doing?"

"Picking up my bag. May I?"

"Go ahead."

She opened it. She took out her comb and as she passed it through her hair she kept her bag open to look at herself in the mirror inside. When she finished combing her hair, she'd put the comb back in, take out the pistol and kill him. Because he was the one, and the moment for revenge had come. There could be no other revenge but killing him. She, Senta, Ada Luz, Beatriz, Aury, Domitila. The blonde, moving the light back and forth in the eyes of the couple, spoke to Judit while she was focused on Mañungo.

"Who is this guy?"

"His name is Mañungo Vera," answered Judit, showing her contempt.

"Mañungo Vera?" exclaimed Farías, turning off his walkie-talkie, into which he'd been fruitlessly repeating the word "central . . . central . . . central."

"It can't be," said the blonde in triumph. "What can Mañungo Vera be doing stretched out on Las Hortensias at two in the morning?"

"We were at a party and lost track of time," explained Judit, realizing, when she saw both the blonde and Farías smile, that they'd gone for the bait.

The smile that broke the ice on the platinum blonde's face was the smile of someone who has just begun to understand the language spoken by two fugitives from another planet. Farías slipped the leash on Boris, giving it a good yank so the dog would stop barking—they were all friends now.

"Mañungo Vera on the town!" laughed Farías. "Who'd ever believe it? Rolling around in the grass at two in the morning! When I tell this one to the guys on duty tomorrow they just won't believe me!"

Judit shivered.

"Cold, honey?" asked the blonde.

"The grass was wet."

"And Mañungo here probably wouldn't let you keep covered! Why don't you offer her a little drink, Ricardo?"

Farías took a small flask out of his back pocket. He shook it next to his ear, but it was empty. He turned to the blonde: "You drank all my Chivas, babe!"

"Me? Sure I did! Why not? Unless your little flask's got a leak. Why don't you invite them in? You've got enough Chivas there for a regiment."

"Why don't you come in for a drink? Then I'll call a patrol to drop you off so you don't freeze to death. Or maybe you've got a car? No, you don't. Otherwise you wouldn't be fooling around here on the grass."

"Mañungo Vera!" exclaimed the woman, taking him by the arm, Farías pulling the dog along by his leash. "Who'd ever imagine? Weren't you living in Miami?"

"In Paris," answered Mañungo. "I just got back today at six. I mean yesterday."

"Is this your wife?"

"No, just a good friend."

Liliana's face curved into a malicious smile. "Good friends ready the minute you get off the plane? But you can't beat the girls from Chile, right, Mañungo?"

"These show people," commented Farías, "always get the best women."

"Why thanks," said Judit, taking his words as a compliment. "And we all know how well soldiers get along with women."

"I'm not a soldier."

"No? What then?" asked Mañungo.

Farías flipped back his lapel to show them an insignia. Mañungo whistled his admiration, but Judit knew what it was even without looking. After closing the gate, Farías let the dog loose. Dragging his leash, he took off at a run and began to scratch at the door of the bungalow, whining all the time.

"He's going to wake the family up," said Judit.

"Nobody's home. You don't know how many years I've had to wait to get him to invite me home when Cristina's away."

"My family's on vacation in Viña," explained Farías.

Winking at Mañungo, the blonde said, "We've got the decks cleared and can be as bad as we like. And when Ricardo's naughty, he's really naughty! Now we're going to celebrate Mañungo Vera's return from Europe and that we won the prize of finding him flat on his back right in front of our house. You'll give us a little song, won't you, Mañungo, just for us?"

"If you behave yourself, Lilianita," said Farías.

"I always behave myself, when gentlemen behave like gentlemen."

On the sofa next to Judit, Liliana confessed that she had a very serious problem. She was best friends with Cristina, Ricardo's wife, and she was just the greatest love in the world. That's why, even though they worked together and saw each other almost every day, Ricardo had said no until this summer, when he had to stay in Santiago because with the curfew they had a lot of work, so he took advantage of the fact that Cristina was away and decided to invite her over tonight. Her own husband—almost always on duty when Ricardo was off duty because they had the same rank—was Ricardo's best friend, and the four of them often went out eating and dancing together. People said Ricardo was a skirt-chaser, but it wasn't true because he adored Cristinita, and his conquests—lots because he was a nice guy and had clout—didn't mean a thing. But she was going to have her way, because when she set her mind on something she could melt rocks. Of course, this was risky business. They'd have to cover things up if they got serious. The bosses wouldn't put up with this kind of hanky-panky in the service because it only led to problems.

"Of course," said Lilianita, putting on lipstick, "things are going to change right now, because I'm going to kill Ricardo with jealousy over Mañungo. I just *love* Mañungo!"

22

◆ *W*ith a second whiskey warming in her hand she listened to the man speaking calmly at the other end of the room, showing off his voice as if it were a rug so she could identify it as he filled his glass next to Mañungo at the bar, decorated with an American print of two horses fleeing over a meadow. She'd been waiting for a revelation that would clarify the universe with a blaze when she would finally hear his voice, and in an act of total certainty that would liberate her she would not hesitate to fire. But Judit could not go beyond shaking the small piece of ice that still floated around the tepid whiskey in her glass.

"Ah, no! Guys as attractive as Mañungo, it's immoral to let 'em walk around loose! I'm going to play around with him even if it's only to flirt a little bit. He's my type!"

Seeing that the blonde, having made this statement, was getting ready to stand up, Judit held her back, saying, "You know? I really like men who are little older, you know, like Ricardo, men with more authority, more experience."

"I can't believe you. You'd rather have a guy like Ricardo Farías than Mañungo Vera? You're nuts."

"I would. He's got something, well, manly, I don't know, something a little rough to him."

"Ricardo Farías, rough? A man who's so afraid of his wife you'd think she knew some dark, dirty secret about him? Don't make me laugh! Ricardo is anything but rough. You've got a bad eye for men, kid."

"But he's got a certain something in his voice I just love, his way of talking especially . . ."

"What's so special about the fact that he talks through his nose? You're weird, kid!"

"I don't know. Ricardo turns me on."

"Let's switch then, just for tonight. Ricardo, honey, put on some music so we can dance, okay?"

Ricardo followed orders and put on a cassette, then went back to his stool behind the bar to continue his chat with Mañungo. He was showing Mañungo his Doberman, pulling back the dog's dewlaps so that Mañungo could see his teeth, spreading his toes so he could brag about the daintiness and strength of his paws. Liliana stood up and went to the bar to stand next to Mañungo, her back to Judit. From where she sat, in the half-light, Judit saw all three of them framed by the rectangle of light around the bar, stage front occupied by two dark backs and, beyond them, Ricardo showing off his dog.

Was this woman an accomplice? What did she know? Did she know that his soft hand perspired when he placed it on the knee of a woman he felt to be powerful? Did Cristinita, exempted the same way Judit was, enjoy strange privileges in exchange for keeping Ricardo's secret? Liliana didn't know that if her plans for Ricardo worked out, she too was condemned to pardon. The complicity between the two of them was negligible, unimportant, partial, which shouldn't have surprised her, since these were unimportant human beings who only acquired life in the reflected light of cruelty. Was it possible that this man, with his high, falsely noble forehead, vigorous neck, black mustache above loquacious lips, engrossed in a dissertation on Boris, would pay for pardoning her? Was it possible for her to aim the pistol at him and avenge all pardons, including the imprudent Lilianita's? Because from the beginning in Ada Luz's house—and she, and son César, and all the women knew it—this was no seduction but a murder.

The pup was really splendid, said Ricardo. He'd won prizes at every show his daughter Cristy had entered him in. They were rare, these miniature Dobermans, as ferocious as the regular kind and much easier to train, even if at the beginning you had to punish them so they'd see the difference between what they could and couldn't do. Farías had punished her with the worst punishment imaginable. No, he hadn't punished her. He'd condemned her, because ever since her return from Caracas, with the remains of her ideology in rags after so much time and distance, she could not focus on anything but finding the man responsible for the rapes.

When she'd returned, she'd reestablished her network of accomplices from her underground days and sought their knowledge of the urban night—don César, with his contacts and pals and his knowledge

of jokes, bars, and wine, and Aury with her beauty-parlor chatter, and
Darío's father and Darío himself, with the kids in his slums, and Ada
Luz—enlisting their help in her plan to destroy the past and begin
again at zero. But every lead until now had turned into a dead end,
and she and the others always came back empty-handed. It was never
the right man.

Finally, a year after Judit had returned from Caracas, they managed
to pick up the trail of Medina, the man who had given her the passport
so she could leave. He'd been discovered to be a leftist infiltrator in
the passports section, had disappeared, and was assumed dead. His
widow, mending her sons' T-shirts, sitting in a chair at the door of
her little house in the Lourdes district, did not even raise her head
from her work when Judit tried to recruit her for the revenge project.
She said she knew nothing and didn't want to have anything to do
with anything. She didn't want to talk or to be talked to: Medina was
erased by the terror, gone forever for his wife and children. But in a
certain sense less gone for Judit, since she would take vengeance for
him as well when she eliminated the man with the nasal voice who
had condemned them all to lives with no meaning more complex than
the simplifications wrought by obsession. She put her hand in her
bag: the shot would pass right through the two necks in front of her
and hit the forehead of the guilty man, who was holding up Boris's
snout and his stub of a tail, showing off the champion's unbeatable
lines.

"He's skinny," commented Farías.

Skinny. My skinny. Nasal, yes, but it wasn't the same voice. Even
so, doubts and all, she would have to kill him. Because what right did
this man have to pardon her? From what improvised source did the
legality of his power emanate, so that he could murder or pardon?
That's why he would have to die. Judit took the pistol out of her bag.
She clicked off the safety.

She raised her arm in the half-light, aiming first, tentatively, at the
back of Mañungo's neck. Death. That's what she wished for them in
that instant. The consummation she'd never been capable of achiev-
ing. Except with that impotent shadow in the cell, who made her lie
about pleasure and pain to save her. But it was no lie. It was the savage
surprise of the orgasm devoid of sex—physiological, sad, solitary—
which a torturer with a nasal voice and moist hands had been capable
of giving her. That's why he had to be eliminated.

At the end of her extended arm, the pistol began to weigh heavy, pointing all the while at the square of light at the other end of the room where the three figures stood watching the dog. They released the animal. Judit hid the pistol because she had no time to squeeze the trigger. Mañungo and the blonde began to dance, quite closely. Boris bounced on his hind legs following Ricardo, who had no other partner but his dog: she was his partner, his bitch. Boris was only a puppy, he explained while they both twisted and swayed and shook to the music of The Police, but Dobermans were a privileged breed, very special, artificially developed by the German army during World War II to chase down Jews who got away from concentration camps.

Panting, Farías sat down next to Judit on the sofa, where the dog promptly jumped into his lap and curled up.

"Don't they use Dobermans for the same thing here?"

"There are no concentration camps here."

"No detention centers either?"

"No. Those are stories invented by the communists."

"Ah, of course . . ."

The great temptation to believe that nothing like that existed except as a lie made up by fanatical proponents of an ideology that was not your own. The cell where she had waited for hours and hours did not exist; neither did the barking, or the echoes of her friends's screams. Or the moment of guilt when she felt something that might have been pleasure.

Boris caught up to Ricardo as he went back to the bar, his muscular little body dancing, sensitive, eager to show his affection despite punishment, or perhaps because of it: Mañungo and Liliana joined in the puppy's hopping dance in the middle of the room. Mañungo, Judit noted, was laughing. Should she kill him for being happy about the banal luck of the evening? Had her story not touched his heart after all? Pleasure made him forget Matilde, his son, Chiloé, Schumann driven mad by something worse than tinnitus, this exhausting night shared with her, just so he could enjoy the cheap pleasure of rubbing up against this bleached blonde's jeans, jeans that merely accentuated her advancing age and the fact that she'd probably had several children. Judit hated Mañungo so much for being able to experience pleasure that she swore if the man with the moist hand ever touched her knee again, she would kill him right then and there.

She smiled at Ricardo. He smiled back and put his hand on her knee in the way one does something out of good manners, doing what was minimally expected from a gentleman in these circumstances. It was *his* hand: a bit tremulous, warm, wet. Judit's emotions rose up to meet that hand, but they couldn't reach it because the hand's intention was not what it had been that other time, and sensations cannot be duplicated. But Mañungo and people like him knew how to duplicate sensations. He was dancing in a tight embrace with the blonde, who seemed to get older with each step, with each hug, as if every squeeze deflated her a little. They both tumbled onto the sofa, kissing, while Ricardo, sitting next to Judit, watched them with pleasure as if it were a great honor for the house and took his hand off Judit's knee. Was Mañungo in that instant listening to the tinnitus inside his broken inner ear? Was he listening to the voice of the old woman coming to him from the beaches of Cucao? The host was so overjoyed with his kissing guests that he forgot her.

"Mañungo," Judit heard Liliana's amorous voice plead from the sofa, "sing us a song now."

"What would you like him to sing?" asked Ricardo.

"Something pretty."

Mañungo began dancing with the puppy, holding his drink over his head. Liliana, spread out on the sofa, her face sleepy, tried to get up, slapping her tangled chemical hair into place.

"Judit," said Mañungo, putting his glass down, "I think we ought to be going."

"What, are you leaving?" asked Liliana. "Don't be a drag! Party poopers!"

"I have to go see my son."

"What son?"

"I brought my seven-year-old son from Paris. He's waiting for me in the hotel. I promised him I'd be back early. This curfew thing scares him. They say the police shoot at you."

"Communist bullshit."

"He's scared anyway."

"Oh no you don't!" shouted the blonde, suddenly de-eroticized, trying to smooth her tangled mane with a red comb. "Nobody leaves this house. We invited you, we served you Chivas Regal and everything, and we didn't throw you in jail for screwing on the street at two in the morning. So, buddy, you've got to pay us back for our hospitality by singing us a couple of songs that I'm going to record with your dedication so there's proof you were here and so you don't go around later saying that people in the service don't respect human rights."

"I can't record anything unless my agent authorizes it."

The blonde jumped up with the halo of her bleached hairdo swirling around, an animal ready to attack, wielding the comb bathed in blood like a weapon that has already claimed many victims.

"Not even for us?"

"And just who is 'us'?"

"Don't try to play dumb, asshole."

When Judit tried to walk toward the door to be next to Mañungo, the barking puppy cut her off while Liliana continued her diatribe: "And skinny here can stay right where she is while Mañungo Vera sings. Why, even the stones around here know he's a commie! How'd they ever let him come back?"

"I was never exiled," protested Mañungo.

"So why didn't you come back sooner? Are you yellow?"

"You've got no right to say things like that to me."

"Lilianita has the right to say anything she likes in my house," intervened Ricardo Farías.

"Thanks. See how we stick up for each other in the service, sonny?"

"They say you really lived it up over there."

"I left before the coup."

"So what? Ricardo, this guy's starting to piss me off! What coup are you talking about, you fucker? The word is 'intervention,' just so you don't make the same mistake again. You've been bad-mouthing this country ever since you ran out, so you'd better start learning."

The blonde managed to tame her enormous head of hair, ordering the brittle metallic fibers into a bell shape. Ricardo, straddling the arm of the sofa and with a whiskey in his hand, expected some interesting reactions from his companion's arrogant speech.

"Let's go, Judit," said Mañungo, calculating that things were just about ready to explode and that what you can't see you can't hit.

"Got a guitar, Ricardo?" asked Liliana.

"The girls have one, I think. But they probably took it with them to Viña. Let me take a look—I suddenly feel like hearing the famous Mañungo Vera sing, especially if he's playing hard to get."

"No, I'll go. You keep an eye on them, 'cause we're going to have some fun with this pair of lovebirds. The night is young and we've got plenty of time to make them sing. Later we'll hand them over to the patrol and have them dropped off wherever we like—after all, we *are* in a state of siege."

The blonde disappeared into the bungalow. Judit, her hand in her bag, moved next to Mañungo. When he realized what she was going to do, he warned her:

"Careful."

Judit didn't take her hand out of her bag because Ricardo had gotten up from his place on the sofa and was chasing them awkwardly around the room with movements that were more complicated than the simple feints that Judit and Mañungo were making. Little by little, they edged toward the front door. Boris, barking and jumping to nip at his master's trousers, couldn't understand what was happening, if it was a game, a dance, or if he should attack. Ricardo tripped over the sofa and collapsed on top of it. Mañungo and Judit opened the door and went out. Then Judit took out the pistol.

"Don't do it," warned Mañungo.

"I have to," she said. "He's the one."

Through the front windows, they saw the blonde, who had returned with the guitar, standing in front of Ricardo and bawling him out for having let them escape. He gave the dog a kick to make it stop barking, which left it whimpering under a table. Liliana's shouts and gestures grew more and more violent until Farías took a swing at her and missed.

Judit had to kill her torturer, whose name, she finally knew, was Ricardo Farías. Everything else, the makeup, the hairdo, the silk dress, was the masquerade of a seduction, but she, and Ada Luz, and don César, and Aury knew that even though she had always stayed out of direct action, she was the only one capable of taking revenge. How could she not, when the hand on her knee tonight was the same hand as that other time? There was no such thing as revenge through seduction. The only acceptable revenge was the pistol that had begun to warm in her hand.

Judit raised the pistol until she was aiming through the front window into the living room, at that high forehead that was only useful as a target. But the negation of the pleasure that had always eluded her, except once, guided her hand and, instead of stopping it at his eyebrows, raised it higher and higher. She fired at the skylights on the sloping roof. With the owner of the house frozen in surprise, with Boris's barking and the blonde's screams silenced, Mañungo and Judit ran to the street before glass had stopped falling.

23

◆*T*he only means of communication between the western shore of the large island and the outer world was the launch that once, sometimes twice a week, crossed Lake Huillinco, which connected to Lake Cucao to form a figure-eight that at the far extreme touched the Pacific shore. The land route was blocked by miles and miles of cold evergreen forest and a curtain of fog and rain that covered the shores of both lakes. When travelers got off the broken-down bus that went from Castro to Huillinco, they found a crowd of people boarding the launch that seemed too fragile to hold all the passengers who had waited bunched up inside since early morning.

As rain was more or less constant in this zone, few of those waiting to leave had taken special precautions against it—at the most a knitted cap, the usual dark-brown ponchos, handkerchiefs tied tightly around the heads of the women with flattened, Polynesian features, huge plaid shawls. Men and women jumped from the end of the wooden pier onto the launch, which was ready to sink, and made themselves comfortable inside with their packages of purchases, because the village of Huillinco at the easterly end of the lake was the supply center for Cucao. Almost without turning her Chinese eyes toward him, a short, fat lady, her breasts cinched in, her complexion yellow, made space on the crowded bench for the boy who ran from the bus to reach the launch.

The boat left the dock covered with the stench of diesel fuel. A rain squall hid the village, but soon passed. Fog settled in for a while, and then the rain came back more forcefully. Conversation was limited to the usual themes: the lame horse that finally healed, the letter that arrived from the son living in Río Gallegos, how expensive sugar was this year, tea as well, it looked as if they were going to open the new highway. The prow, thick with passengers huddled under the rain, cut through the mist. Flashes of sunlight suggested the profile of a person in the group, the pompom on a cap, mustache, a hand cupped against the wind to light a cigarette. The boy sitting next to the fat woman took advantage of a break in the rain to light a Viceroy in the hollow of his hand, just as the pilot on the prow was doing. He offered the package to the lady, who accepted without looking. Later, the boy leaned over the carefully wrapped guitar he held on his knees. Absorbed, her eyes tearing, the lady, putting a perforated shoe box filled with chicks on her lap, said nothing for a long while, as if she were listening, and then murmured, "The voice of the old woman. It's going to clear up."

Ten minutes later the sky began to clear. Before noon, passing through the strait between Lake Huillinco and Lake Cucao, under a gentle blue sky, the boy took off his wool cap, letting his black hair hang down to his shoulders. Then the fat lady asked him, "Are you Mañungo Vera?"

"I wish I were," replied the young man with the guitar, laughing as he offered her another cigarette, which she accepted, saying, "He's probably older than you. But he looks just like you."

"Was he from around here?"

"No. From Dalcahue. Or from Curaco de Vélez. I can't remember now."

Doña Petronila Quenchi did not speak again to the false Mañungo Vera for the rest of the trip, which was long. Even though they'd left Huillinco at midday they would not reach Cucao until the sun began to weaken. Doña Petronila saved what was left of her energy after sleeping in the open air once she had sold all her kelp to the Japanese. She had to save it, since she'd have a four-hour walk along the beach, south to her hut in the dunes facing the surf.

When they docked in Cucao, those who disembarked before her, along with the boy, who stayed aboard because he was going to the other shore, helped her unload her gear. She panted as she settled her load on her back or tied a string of packages to her arm, but the other passengers let her load up alone among the keels on the shore because doña Petronila was a feared artist. The group began to walk toward the hamlet, dissolving in the sand of the barely demarcated streets, where ten or fifteen frame houses whitened by the salt from the breakers rose in no apparent order.

Doña Petronila started on her way. She was tired, yes, but loaded with everything she'd planned to buy. It was the sixth trip she owed the owner of the launch, a man named Barrientos (but from a different Barrientos family, not the ones from around here), to whom she said that when she'd made ten trips, the youngest of her sons—"They're not my sons, but they're more than sons"—would pay him back by loading and unloading. An insidious little wind had come up, the dragging kind that gets under the skirts of sexually hungry women and makes them pregnant. Doña Petronila bent over to meet the wind. On the streets, all the doors and windows were closed. Not a soul was to be seen. Of course: how could there be with this wind, and with this tide that pushed the planet so high that it was as if the Pacific were rising up to the curve of the immense horizon to join with the sky, which began high above.

"Shitty wind," murmured doña Petronila.

As she walked around a wooden house, made of boards that had been broken by the wind and never fixed or replaced, she found herself face to face with a woman in black. They greeted each other. Doña Petronila took her to one side to seek refuge against a wall.

"Listen, Ulda," said the artist. "I wanted to ask you something."

Ulda knew that running into doña Petronila on an empty street like this was a bad omen. She hesitated a second before following her and helped her unload so they could chat. Doña Petronila put the box filled with chicks on her lap, and the two women sat down on the sand. After searching through several layers of clothing, doña Petronila offered Ulda a cigarette, which the other refused.

"Listen, Ulda," repeated the witch once they were comfortable and she had her cigarette lit. "Was Mañungo Vera from Dalcahue or Curaco de Vélez?"

Ulda restrained her smile. Her mature black eyes were too heavily shaded with lashes, too attentive in her white, fresh face. Her thick brows furrowed as she asked, "So you can do something bad to him, is that why you want to know?"

"No. So I can call him back. I think he was from Dalcahue."

"No. I was never a teacher in Dalcahue. Mañungo was from Curaco de Vélez, born and raised there until he went to Concepción and Santiago, and Paris when the government changed and they sent me here for being a suspicious character . . ."

"Curaco de Vélez? I don't know Curaco de Vélez. It must be so far away!"

"What about Dalcahue?"

"Don't know it either. People say you made Mañungo go to Santiago and that you won't let him come back."

"I don't have powers like you. Who says that?"

"People talking on the launch," lied doña Petronila, who, like all artists, had the gift of turning her lies into the truth, and who, people said, had sailed on the *Caleuche* when she was young. Which is where she had learned her arts.

"Why were they talking about Mañungo?"

"Because there was a boy on board who looked just like him."

Next to doña Petronila's lumpy body and pudgy Asiatic face, Ulda Ramírez looked as sharply drawn as a face in a steel engraving, pure line, pure control. But as she listened to the old woman's words, a smile escaped from her fine mouth and refreshed the contours of her face.

"How do you know he looks just like Mañungo when you don't know him?"

"Do you think you're the only one who knows Mañungo Vera just because you were his teacher? And more than his teacher, if you listen to gossip. Why shouldn't I know what he looks like when my kids have one of his posters nailed to the kitchen door? And a record with his picture on it, a record they bought with the money they got the last time they panned for gold. Even the boy's voice sounded like Mañungo's. Well, child, I have to be going."

She threw her cigarette away and stood up, helped by Ulda, and once again shouldered her load. Ulda begged her to send her kids to school even if they were grown up. The old lady said no: this year the storms would bring down a lot of gold for panning. She was too old to take on so much work, and she was afraid her kids would go north and never come back, like Mañungo. Ulda's expression never changed, but what femininity was left in doña Petronila perceived so much longing in Ulda's white mask that she decided to make up her most powerful charm that very night to call Mañungo back from the north to see poor Ulda, who had loved him since she taught him to play the guitar at age fourteen. And more than the guitar, doña Petronila confirmed in the depth of Ulda's transparent heart. Cinnamon. A cod. Honey from an *ulmo* tree. Hair from a *pudú* deer. Excrement from a *choroy* parakeet. And a toenail from her eldest son, which she'd cut off tonight while he slept, when, without knowing what was happening, the boy would be hard with visions of the naked women dancing on the *Caleuche*.

Saying goodbye to Ulda with a nod of her head, doña Petronila headed for the beach. Ulda went to her little house on the marshes. Before the distance between them was so great that she'd have to shout, doña Petronila turned and, without unloading her burdens, called to Ulda. "Listen, Ulda . . ."

Ulda stopped and looked at the old lady. "What?"

"I'll bet that one of these days Mañungo's going to turn up right here in flesh and blood, not as his ghost, which is what I saw on the boat."

"What's that to me?"

"All right, no need to get angry. I was just saying . . ."

The mist swirled up by the waves, settled like a quilt over the sand. First it erased the feet, then the legs of the women who walked off in opposite directions. They floated over the fog for an instant and then disappeared.

24

*A*ll traffic had disappeared from the streets in the upper part of town. The leaves on the plane trees and the dew on the grass were as still as in a photograph. Mañungo felt that only things beyond human perception—an insect's call the human ear could not detect, the secret shine of small eyes staring out from under the dirt, the movement of snails marking the tender underside of leaves with their corrosive trail—prolonged life until dawn. Meanwhile, they were being held prisoner within the hours that impeded them from fleeing to Judit's house.

Not because they were being chased: Ricardo Farías hadn't been shot. He'd only leaned out the window, shouting insults because he couldn't see where they were going, as if shouting at the immensity of the night were enough to stop them. The couple fled toward Avenida Lyon because it was so straight and wide that they could see anyone coming from a distance, and have time to take refuge in the doorway of a building or in an open garden or under bushes.

The shot was not sufficient cause to call in the police. To bring them in would only draw attention to the irregular conduct of two members of the service. Ricardo Farías had time for second thoughts before shouting into his walkie-talkie with the red light to have them chased down by a patrol, and he turned it off before saying, "Central." Fortunately, nothing of any importance had happened. He'd have the glass in the skylight replaced, as a precaution against Cristina's foolish questions when she came back from vacation. It would be much easier to trap Mañungo Vera in some other way, he assured Liliana, who had already quieted down, trap him from above to punish him for real, arrange to have the authorities send out people they could count on to bushwhack him over the next few days, since that way he'd be a surer catch than in a simple night raid.

At the slightest noise, the slightest rustle of leaves or movement of a shadow or twinkling of a light, Mañungo and Judit would hug a wall or hide behind a bush or column. How could they get to Judit's house in Bellavista? How could they walk these streets and cross Avenida Providencia, Avenida Once de Septiembre, the park, and the bridges to get to the other side of the river without being discovered? The only thing Mañungo's body wanted was sleep, days and days wrapped up in Judit as if she were a blanket, and she wanted the same thing so she could weep and weep in Mañungo's arms. It was three-thirty in the morning. They had in fact spent the night together.

"I've had it," murmured Judit, stopping in a shadow-filled hollow. "We have to make it."

"I can't. Let's stretch out here for a while."

And she threw herself down under a bush in a grassy plot next to the entrance of a building, a vantage point from which they could see north and south, up and down the avenue, a smooth blue surface like a frozen river. But it was Mañungo who instantly dove into a sleep as unfathomable as his southern ocean, contemplating the woman dressed in black who approached from afar along a beach whose surf shook the ground as if it were a huge heart made of invisible helicopters that kept the night alive. The woman in black silently bent over him, and secretly cutting off one of his toenails without taking off his shoe, she called him without a voice. But he refused to follow her because he couldn't see her face, and her pulse and sex were not beating, which left him covered by the thickness of sleep. He only heard the voice of the old woman, the persistent tinnitus that from the ocean announced change.

Judit could not rest. She sat next to her friend sleeping under the bush. She clasped her knees with her arms, her bag hanging off her hand. Should she go home instantly to show Mañungo she was capable of giving herself to him out of pure pleasure, and not merely to prove a point—even if that were a contradiction? She looked at Mañungo's sleeping face. How invulnerable he was, with his mythological history inherited from a strange antiquity to which she could never belong. To return to Chiloé or not didn't really matter—he could just as easily go back to Paris and find the thing he thought was held prisoner by the island spirits!—because Mañungo was one of those beings who only get lost for a short while, so he could easily exclude her from his future mythologies.

There was a salvation, nevertheless: those mythologies might not turn into realities. She took out the pistol. She smelled the barrel. The safety was off. She put the pistol to Mañungo's forehead. May he never wake up from his absurd native dream. But that wouldn't resolve anything. Just as killing Ricardo and the cheap blonde wouldn't resolve anything. Pointing the gun at her own temple, she thought that, again, nothing would be resolved if she eliminated herself, because her guilt would go on living in her women bereft of vengeance, in the barks of Czar in other ears, in the moist hand defeated by yet another knee. Czar! Czar! Czar was a giant Boris, designed by the German army to track down murderers in the Santiago night, as was the ridiculous miniature that Ricardo exhibited on his bar. Czar's nocturnal footfalls echoed on the grand avenue, so quiet under its double row of plane trees. A stray dog crossed the street, his padded feet breaking the silence with the steadiness of a heartbeat. That dog could walk around the streets after curfew and do as he pleased with no fear of punishment. But, as usual, translating the most modest personal detail into the new-mystique of politics, Judit could only note that she and Mañungo lacked the freedom to go home and sleep in each other's arms, in a bed, because the law prohibited it.

She stood up to take a look at things from behind the bush. It wasn't just one dog walking around over there. Four, no eight, ten, twelve, fifteen dogs swept in from the side streets, all following a small white bitch that was the first to cross the street, strutting along. Then she waited, shivering, for the other dogs: fifteen, twenty mutts of heterogeneous species and genealogies, of all colors, predatory, growling, their eyes shining, foaming at the mouth, their paws filthy. Yapping, they crowded around the fragile white bitch with a smooth coat, a face that looked powdered and shadowed under her eyes.

On the grass next to the sidewalk, just opposite the bush where Judit was watching her, the little dog delicately squatted and urinated with an expression of modesty, as if she wanted to dissimulate what she was doing because she knew that it drove the beasts crazy. They didn't believe in her modesty. They sniffed her, whining frantically, maddened by her smell. A light brown dog who seemed to be the leader of the pack awkwardly pushed her down with a paw, another lifted her up by the rear with his pointy snout; they tried to mount her, to lick her, to bite her, they bit each other, excited and malignant, enormous dogs, woolly dogs, fat dogs, spotted dogs, golden, yellow, black, driven by the simple biological fact that the little white bitch, almost hairless, whose face was pinched and whose eyes had blue circles under them, was in heat.

There was no love involved. They followed the orders of nature because she was female and the power of her scent brought these beasts together from blocks around. A tan bulldog pushed his way through the crowd with a killer's presumption. Growling ferociously, he grasped the little dog in his clumsy paws. She let herself be used, although she did not cooperate, certain that the pretensions of this dog would come to nothing. What if this killer were to impregnate her? What if he made her pregnant with his gross sperm, producing in her puppies in his image so that when they were delivered out of that womb not made for giving birth to such large dogs, her delicate reproductive organs would burst? It was not piety but indignation that made Judit come out from her hiding place, throw herself into the circle of turbulent dogs that materialized from places concealed in the vegetation, with their instincts ready. From what fetid corners did they come? What fences did they jump, what hedges did they destroy, what holes did they dig and doors did they knock down to follow the call of the effluvia of this little dog with blue shadows under her eyes and her face powdered as if she were a performer in a cheap dive, and seemed to smile to herself at provoking this lascivious tumult?

The dogs, surprised by Judit's sudden appearance, fled but did not scatter. They let themselves be pulled by the undulating gait of the bitch, not one of them willing to exempt her. Dogs don't know how to pardon. She heard their barks, their whining, their quarreling, their implacable growling, but none of them was nasal. The entire pack was going to rape and devour the bitch, and she knew it and wanted it, evasively skirting the routine destiny of her heat merely as coquettish play within the tyranny of her cycle. Judit crossed the street after the bitch, not caring whether she was seen from north or south or from the windows of a building, or from the post of a hidden guard. She didn't care if someone told the authorities that a madwoman was chasing a pack of dogs.

"Judit!"

Mañungo ran out from behind the bush. What was she doing? he shouted. Was she trying to get caught? Didn't she realize the danger she was in with the patrol probably on the alert, sirens ready, walkie-talkies, whistles? Judit shouted at him to go away, that he understood nothing, that she never wanted to speak to him again, that she never wanted to see him again, because he was incapable of understanding anything. She had to save the white bitch from the rapists. The dogs fled, knowing how to disappear in the bushes along these streets. When Mañungo reached Judit, he embraced her, and they walked away, her blond hair falling over his shoulder.

At a corner, they saw the pack of dogs on the opposite side of the street. The enormous, maddened dog, and underneath him, between his paws, with her fur sticking to her nakedness, the little white bitch waited, licking her chops, while the beast satisfied his trivial impulse. The other dogs formed a querulous and expectant circle around the male, who could not seem to mount the bitch to his satisfaction. As soon as she saw the little white dog, Judit pulled away from Mañungo, crossed the street oblivious of who might see or hear her, and shouted scat, leave her alone, pardon her. But the dogs were unwilling to leave the bitch, whose eyes seemed even more deeply shadowed and decadent, her face more concentrated and pale, accepting that all dogs wanted to possess her.

The males turned their big heads toward Judit, growling, foaming, showing their teeth to defend their right, hatred in their fiery, bloodshot eyes. But Judit, brandishing her handbag, beating their mutilated ears and frothy bodies, managed to open a path through them even though they tore her dress to keep her from entering their circle. The big dog, vibrating in his haunches which strained with the effort, his gigantic pink tongue lolling out of his mouth, desperately searched for the bitch's sex with his. She was willing, but his eagerness made him fail.

Mañungo, just outside the circle, shouted to Judit to get away, to let the disgusting dogs do what they wanted. The dogs jumped around Judit, tearing her sleeves, her skirt, her blouse, staining her with their saliva, with their semen, their blood, ready to rape her. The smaller dogs frenetically clung to her naked legs and masturbated. Mañungo jumped into this sexual bonfire, first centered on the bitch and now on Judit as well. Phosphorescent jaws had torn her handbag away, ripping it apart and fighting over it amid the clamor of their barks, as if it were a piece of Judit's body.

The handbag opened and the pistol fell out; she was able to bend over and pick it up. She aimed at the dogs. There were so many. All the same. All of them deserved to die, undifferentiated males sticking to her and sullying her. In the middle of the pack was the little white bitch, unique, delicate, ironic, poised as if all this were taking place in a salon, revealing the effect of this fury unleashed by her situation only in her melancholy smile, as if she knew that while she couldn't escape her destiny, she could at least play. Judit did not reach the bitch because the dogs were biting her streaming legs. She was a yard away from her. Between them the seething mob heaved. It seemed the little white dog was not upset, because from between the paws of the tan dog in the center of the infernal circle, tender, clean, tired, she smiled at Judit, her accomplice, her savior, her sister, who aimed the pistol and shot her in the head. The body twitched and the bitch fell dead.

The dog that was raping her relaxed his taut haunches, dropping the vestige between his paws. He sniffed her once, and then began to smell and chew some grass. The other dogs also smelled her, disinterestedly. Some licked her little pool of blood before disappearing. One approached the body and, as a final homage, briefly licked her sex, as if to be sure that it was no longer useful, then went to poke into some black plastic garbage bags, scratching at them to rip them open before wandering away.

"Idiot!" shouted Mañungo, tearing the gun out of Judit's hands.

"Leave me alone!" answered Judit when she felt him taking her by the wrist to drag her away.

Then Mañungo reached back and hurled the pistol over the nearest laurel hedge and into a garden where no one would find it until late the next day, when everybody would be at Matilde's funeral. He took Judit firmly by the hand to look for a place to hide, but felt her resist him. The dogs had dispersed. The cadaver lay all alone on the sidewalk. Judit went to it. Sitting on the curb, she put it in her lap, petting it and whispering to it.

The howling patrol flew along one of the avenues—perhaps Avenida Lyon, which they couldn't see from this side street on which they were lost. With the little dog obstinately in her arms as if it were a doll she'd won in some sideshow, they huddled next to a hedge for protection. They remained silent awhile. Why didn't the *Caleuche* cut through the darkness, illuminating everything with its white sails and golden masts, sailing majestically along the street, so they could climb aboard and sink into eternity?

"Let's go," he said.

"Where?"

"I don't know."

"To hide."

"Where?"

Then Judit said, yes, let's go, I know where. And she started off with the dog in her arms. He begged her to leave it on the street. Was there anything more absurd than wandering the early-morning streets of Santiago under curfew with the dead body of a dog in her arms, not knowing where to go because it was illegal for them to be walking around at this hour? Judit stopped on a corner. She looked up and down the street. Then, with the sureness of a sailor who has sniffed the breeze and knows how the wind is blowing, she said, "This way."

Off in the distance, toward the west now, sirens wailed and slowly faded.

*I*n the fog drawn in by the coming dawn, the idyllic garden—pyramid-shaped thuyas, boxwood shrubs cut into balls, black yews, laurel obelisks, all so overgrown that it was difficult to guess the forms into which the bushes had originally been cut—began to take on life as they turned into the ragged figures who came to meet them. Darío's father spoke first, while the others gathered behind him.

"We heard shots."

"More than one?" asked Mañungo.

"Yes, one from the east and a little to the south."

"What a sense of direction you have!"

"Just lots of practice."

"That one was over on Las Hortensias. We went to Las Hortensias after all."

"Did you kill him, ma'am?"

"No."

"And the other shot was close to here, just now."

"That was for the dog."

They sat down to talk, their legs hanging into the ruined pool. In the high, dark building behind them, a light went on, and after a few minutes in which they stopped talking to look, it went out again. Darío's father told Judit that if she had listened to him instead of don César, they wouldn't have had to face that idiot Ricardo Farías, who in fact was in the center for political prisoners when she and her friends were there, but who could not have condemned them because he was in charge of the men's sector. The information he'd given her, said Darío's father, was better because it was about the man in charge of the women's sector at that time. The two members of the same service had spent most of the night celebrating the summer absence of their good wives, and then they left, one in the blue Mercedes, toward Las Hortensias, the other in the green Volvo, toward Lota.

One of the bushes listening to the story of the two shots said to Judit, "Give me the little dog, miss, so we can bury it."

"No."

"Before it starts to smell," insisted a laurel standing behind them.

"With this cold it won't rot."

While Mañungo finished his version of the two shots, Judit leaned on his shoulder. She was very tired and wanted to sleep. Before he finished speaking, she told him so.

"I'm tired."

"Me too," sighed Mañungo.

"You'll have to sleep here tonight. It's impossible to cross the city with all the patrols out," said a boxwood obelisk.

"That's why I came here."

"You have a good sense of direction, ma'am."

"When I was a kid I lived in this neighborhood. But almost none of the houses from those days is left. It's all different. They used to bring me to this garden to play. It was very pretty."

They got up. A shadow or an untidy yew held out its arms to receive the remains of the dog when it saw that Judit was ready to rest next to a bush that would protect her sleep. The fog was growing thicker. It was just before dawn. The sirens were singing their mortal song out in the distance, and what was left of the night seemed to explode again with the pulsating, invisible helicopters. Judit refused to give up the body; the small, powdered face slept, bored with it all, in her arms. She was stretching out on the ground without letting go of the dog. Mañungo lay down beside her.

"Do you want something to cover yourself with?" asked Darío's father.

"No," she answered, rejecting the probable grime of his blankets.

"Thanks," said Mañungo.

They lay down next to each other. He begged her to give the body to one of the acolytes. But Judit hugged the little dog against her stomach as she put her head on the ground. Did she want something to put underneath her, as a pillow? they offered. No. She had slept too many times with nothing to rest on, and didn't answer, closing her eyes to reject everything around her, and to try to sleep. Mañungo thanked them. He stretched out behind her, his arms around her, copying the fetal curve of her body with his own, snuggling against her. He put one arm under her neck, the other over her waist, and drew her to him, in the same posture in which Judit hugged the body of the little white dog. Wrapped in the mist, the false bushes walked away, they too to sleep before day broke and curfew would be lifted. That way they would be the first scavengers on the street in the morning.

"Ju?" whispered Mañungo.

She didn't answer.

"Come and live with me in Paris."

She interrupted her regular breathing to answer him in a low voice: "Don't try to redeem me."

"Why not?"

"I don't want to be redeemed."

"Don't you love me?"

She took such a long time to answer that Mañungo feared she might have gone back to sleep and that they'd never again speak about anything.

"I don't know," answered Judit, a while later.

Their breathing grew quite regular before she woke up to rearrange the dog, now very stiff, next to her body. She asked Mañungo, who had also awakened, "And you?" He knew what she was asking, so he immediately answered, "I think I don't."

"But you want to make love, isn't that so?"

"Yes, but get rid of the dog first."

"No."

"So then what?"

"As soon as it's light, we'll have her buried and go to my house. Okay? By then it won't matter if we don't love each other, right?"

"It doesn't matter now either."

"No, it doesn't."

He fell back asleep. And when Judit felt his breathing to be that of sleep, she was finally able to hug the little dog as she wanted and go to sleep herself.

·III·
MORNING

26

*T*hey woke up cramped because of the lumpy ground, the sun burning into their eyes. Mañungo's first impulse on waking up was to check his watch. But his watch was not on his wrist.

"They stole my Rolex!"

Going through his clothes, he confirmed that during the night his money had disappeared, along with his leather satchel and the shreds of Judit's bag. All he had left was a small roll of warm bills in the hip pocket of his jeans, where, because of the position he was sleeping in, the thief's hands did not venture.

"And my papers?" exclaimed Mañungo, alarmed, as he shook out his clothes. His alarm was brief, because he found his papers thrown near where they'd been sleeping, right next to Judit's.

"They stole our money," she said, sitting up on the ground and shaking the dry grass and twigs out of her hair, near the discarded body of the little white dog, now as stiff as a toy carved from a single block of wood. "But they left us our papers."

They were alone in the vacant lot, which had been transformed by the morning light into a dump filled with cans, papers, and rags; the soil was stained by the charred remains of small fires where the scavengers warmed food, burning some of the dried weeds. On a balcony, a woman in a bathrobe was watering her plants, and on another, a second woman was polishing a brass planter that glistened in the first light at the top of the tower. Judit told Mañungo not to worry: the Rolex, well, that was a shame, but he still had his papers, which was the most important thing. She had nothing of value in the bag the dogs had torn open. Sitting on the ground, combing her hair with her fingers, she turned her back on the little white dog. When she stood up, she did not even reach toward Mañungo for help, and that

indifference chilled him; when she later tried to hug and kiss him, he
could only react in a conventional way. Here was a woman he didn't
know promising him the happiness she could never give him, begging
him to go home with her and stay with her.

"What about my kid? What do I do with him?"

"Call him from my place."

"Let's go."

What a pain Jean-Paul's crying fits were, especially when he had to
deal with Judit—another problem—before facing them! The boy would
make him pay dearly for this escapade, probably with months of pout-
ing, settling the score by making all kinds of demands.

But things were going to change with Jean-Paul. It was a good idea
for him to get used to another life-style, without so many compen-
sations for his parents' mistakes, because in underdeveloped countries
parents have more rights, including the right of not needing to justify
themselves, and children must put up with situations just as they come.
In this case, for example, the boy had no reason to complain, because
even if his father had not returned at the appointed hour, he had
seen to it that he had a good Chilean baby-sitter to take care of him
in the Holiday Inn, so Jean-Paul should not ruin his marvelous first
night in Santiago with recriminations. But had last night really been
marvelous? And weren't the concrete results, seen from this morning's
perspective, cadaverous and sinister? Could he and Judit love each
other? When you come right down to it, that was the issue between
them this morning.

It seemed to him too early for these kinds of deliberations. Although
the sky at dawn had the golden skin of an apricot, the light would
soon peel away that fine cuticle, and by the time for the funeral the
sun would be beating down from an implacable blue sky. They took
a taxi on Providencia, where traffic was still thin. They went to Bellavista: he would drop her off at home before going to the hotel. What
exactly was his commitment to her? There wasn't any. He could just
drop her off, say so long, and that would be that. Toward the north,
San Cristóbal hill was just shedding its shadow. The taxi was identical
to the one he'd taken yesterday afternoon: was it possible that all these
things had taken place in less than twelve hours? The dogs and the
helicopters, and Farías and the wake, and Judit telling her story under
the honeysuckle and their entwined bodies under the acanthus, a
whole world, a whole life, two lives, because her life counted too, and
Paris and Chiloé: could all of it fit into that handful of hours? Could
it be that Matilde hadn't been dead yet for twenty-four hours, and

that in six more she would be buried? The taxi entered Bellavista, prosaic at this time of morning, with children walking to school and women with bags going to market. The taxi stopped. They pooled the few pesos the thieves had left them, and after paying they went upstairs, arms around each other's waists, rubbing the other hand along the banister that shone like a chestnut where earlier generations of hands had polished it. At Judit's door, they were surprised by the smell of fried eggs. They knocked.

"Who . . . ?" Judit managed to ask before Lopito opened.

Of course. They had to accept it with dismay: Lopito. Who else but Lopito would be there to screw up her plans and blur the image of herself in Mañungo's arms? Lopito received them freshly bathed, his hair combed, perfumed, the most affable housekeeper, dressed in Judit's blue Viyella robe. She shut the door, staring at him in shock. He walked over to the stereo, begging them to make themselves at home, and changed the cassette.

"*The Two Grenadiers*," Mañungo recognized.

"Elementary, my dear Watson," assented Lopito. "Sung by Fischer-Dieskau, who, I don't mind telling you, I really don't . . ."

"What the hell are you doing here?" shouted Judit, passing rapidly from surprise to anger—because she remembered all too well, when it was too late to take back the question, exactly what Lopito was doing there. Because, of course, it was not really Judit's style to arrive home first thing in the morning trailing an amorous adventure, so it never occurred to her that this absurd obstacle was going to keep her from passing days and days in Mañungo's arms as a remedy for all her problems. The presence of the immortal Lopito, nicely bathed and well rested, intruding into her private life and acting like an understanding husband in his own house, was, at this hour of the day, psychologically unmanageable for her.

"I'm actually bored with Fischer-Dieskau," said Lopito to Mañungo, not paying Judit any attention. "So monotonous! He leaves you no choices because he's recorded the entire musical literature for male voice. You can't escape from his ubiquity. Disgusting! It means Schumann sounds just like Ravel and Fauré the same as *Adelaïde*. Musical dictatorship is what I call it. He's nothing but a cheap tradesman. He is! He owns Deutsche Grammophon, so he can record his farts if he wants to! Of course, they're the best records in the world, that's a fact. I wonder what's going to happen to Deutsche Grammophon now with compact discs? Have you heard them? They are so real . . ."

"What the hell are you doing here, Lopito?" Judit shouted again.

She knew what he was doing, but she thought she could blow off some steam by repeating herself. "I need my private life."

Lopito turned to face her.

"You do, do you? Don't you remember, my darling Virginia Woolf chilensis? You lent me your key so I could sleep here last night, provided I take a bath. Well I did it, and I'll tell you something, bathing really isn't a disagreeable experience. Let me enjoy this oasis just a little while longer before I go back to the horrifying world of reality, for which your house is such a civilized antidote. Don't blush because Uncle Lopito has caught you after a night's dissipation. I assure you I'm a perfect pander. Shall I turn down your bed? Or shall I draw your bath or run the shower? What would you like? Shall I make you some scrambled eggs so you have enough protein to enjoy a morning of love before the funeral? Oh yes, I have an urgent message for you, Ju. Celedonio wants you to call him. And Ada Luz too. Both seem to want to tell you something about Matilde's funeral, and they're both wild. They say Lisboa's furious about something. Look, look, listen to how marvelous Schumann is when he suddenly slips and falls into the total madness of the *Kreisleriana* and can't put himself together again . . . listen . . . that guy's the absolute truth!"

What made Mañungo angriest was the fact that Lopito had put on Judit's blue Viyella robe, as if using it were a permanent part of a routine and he were showing off an almost marital intimacy. In fact, he thought, the logical thing would be for him to go, leave the apartment to Lopito. What circumstances united these two, circumstances he knew nothing about because of his twelve-year absence? Underground life, death, brutal changes, hunger, cold, mutual betrayal, mutual forgiveness, consolation . . . ? And after all, wasn't the accumulation of all these acts what people usually called love?

First it was hope, then disappointment with all ideologies. Afterward, they were left alone together, in the extreme situations to which the authorities pushed them. They read the same novels at the same time, were both suffering a passing bout of Schumann fever, and quoting the same poems to illustrate similar circumstances. They'd shared evenings without light because they didn't even have candles, and the only blanket, and the last apple, belonging to the same landscape, united, with or without love, for so many years lost to Mañungo.

He wore the blue Viyella robe because it was the "husband's" prerogative. Nadja could never share old Viyella robes with anyone. With her, everything was either yours or mine. Had Lopito and Judit ever made love after that first time so long ago? He couldn't stand the idea!

But beneath the intimacy of these two, Mañungo guessed that Judit wanted to give herself to him so he would help her explore her confusion, resolve her perplexities by making love urgently, right away. He had to get rid of Lopito and capture the blue Viyella robe. How could Judit go to bed with someone as disgusting as Lopito? The answer was that she too was disgusting. His need to throw Lopito out and throw Judit onto the bed to ask her everything was now intolerable.

She must be in the kitchen making coffee and trying to figure out how to get rid of Lopito, who was amusing himself by discrediting the idea that Schumann had thrown himself into the Rhine using his night table as an anchor. It was a surrealist story invented by don Celedonio! It wasn't a bad idea. Too bad today's night tables were not useful for these purposes. They were so light that they floated because they were only bamboo, not solid structures made of carved mahogany, all drawers and bronze pulls. It would be necessary to warn night-table manufacturers if they didn't want to lose their clientele. Of course, the night-table incident was not when Schumann killed himself. That was only an attempt, as unimportant as attempts made by sensitive people like him, he reflected, although it was no longer fashionable to tie oneself to a night table to do it. And of course, the Mapocho was not the Rhine. Raw sewage flowed into the Mapocho, so its image was rather tarnished. On the other hand, the Rhine ennobled everything, Lopito declared, coughing as he hummed the most dangerous moments of the *Kreisleriana*. He answered the telephone when it rang.

"You've reached the residence of don Juan López."

"Stop fooling around, Lopito!" shouted Judit from the kitchen. "Who is it?"

"It's Freddy, my love!" Lopito was saying, making obscene gestures. "What a great pleasure! But didn't you know that Judit and I have been living together for years? Yes, you have three handsome nephews named López Torre—dappled, unfortunately, because Judit is so white and I'm so black. Too bad they didn't turn out café-au-lait, it would have been so exotic. But they're fine boys and get good marks for conduct and speak French like Jean-Paul. Who cares who Jean-Paul is? Why does Ju love me? Easy: her *amour pour la boue*, as respectable as your fondness for pacifiers, although I understand that's just a long-forgotten phase in your sexual evolution. After all, love is pure fantasy, as everyone knows, and Pyramus is worth as much as the donkey's head . . ."

And what if Lopito's horrible joke was true? Suppose three mulatto dwarfs with Judit's jaw and Lopito's green teeth were to walk in? thought Mañungo, who couldn't take his alarmed eyes off the front door. Judit leaned on Mañungo. He withdrew his body from hers discreetly, unwilling to accept any intimacy without clearing things up first. She, choking back her laughter, finally took the telephone away from Lopito.

"No, Freddy, I am not going to explain why Lopito is in my house, and undressed, at eight o'clock in the morning. Yes, he slept here. I'm not answering any more questions because I won't put up with your playing the role of elder cousin watching out for the good conduct of his female relatives."

Lopito threw himself onto the rug, suffering cramps from laughing so much. Mañungo went to the kitchen and filled a glass with water, which he did not drink. He stayed on the threshold listening to the comedy.

"Well, that's enough. What do you want, Freddy? You know very well I don't have anything to say to a son of a bitch like you. It can't be that urgent. Nothing in this world is that urgent now that Matilde is dead. Why today, the day of the funeral, when there's so much to do? I've arranged to meet with Celedonio and Fausta at Matilde's house and I can't be late. Before, with you? No, I don't want you to come here. So that you can go around saying, 'To think how Judit's parents used to live, to say nothing of our grandparents, and look how the poor thing lives now'? No. You're perfectly right: company like yours would dirty me. What's your hurry, Freddy? No, I don't want to go to your office either. Why can't you wait until tomorrow or the day after?"

She listened to him carefully, seriously, for a few minutes. Mañungo, in the kitchen, poured two cups of coffee. He had no idea to whom he would give the second. He should have brought three, but he couldn't carry all of them. The second cup could be for Judit or Lopito. He lowered the volume of the music so he could decipher what Judit was saying, because suddenly she was paying close attention to her cousin. Then he heard her say:

"Okay, in twenty minutes." She hung up without saying goodbye, murmured, "I'll barely have time to take a shower."

"Where are you going?" asked Mañungo, two steaming cups of coffee in his hands.

"That idiot Freddy wants to speak to me urgently about some 'high-level matter,' as the newspapers say. I can't imagine what it is. Lopito, while I'm getting dressed, do me a favor and call Celedonio. Tell him I'll be at Matilde's within an hour. That we'll meet there. And that it's very possible Freddy Fox will be there too. Fausta should warn the kids so no one gets out of hand."

"Those bums will get out of hand anyway!" observed Lopito, projecting his own attitude.

Ten minutes later, Judit was ready to leave, fresh and with her hair still wet. She kissed both of her friends on the cheek—two identical kisses, as Mañungo could not fail to notice, two kisses that nullified the night they'd just shared and that he'd been naive enough to believe would link them, at least for a time. Taking the cup out of Mañungo's hand, she drank a sip before handing it to Lopito. Whose was the other cup, the one he'd prepared in an effort to define a couple? When Judit had closed the door behind her, Lopito began to sip the coffee, later giving the cup back to Mañungo, who went to the kitchen to wash it. The dishwasher was stuffed with Lopito's dirty dishes. How did he manage to use so many dishes by himself?

"Look at the mess you've made, asshole!" he murmured in a low voice so as not to offend his friend.

"What's your hurry? Where can you go today in this city except the cemetery? See? This city only gives us funerals, nothing for the living. We inhabit the 'Island of Lost Souls.' "

"I'm going to see my son."

"Jean-Paul?" The sinister little tone appeared with its touch of mockery: intolerable, like the fact that he'd not even bothered to take off Judit's blue Viyella robe.

"Yes, Jean-Paul."

"When are you going to introduce me to this monster?"

"He's no monster."

"So sorry," said Lopito, with a courtly bow. "I forgot you VIPs usually lose your sense of humor, completely and absolutely."

Mañungo felt confused, ashamed, entangled, not knowing how to go on or how to get out, nor in what tone he might pick up what was left of a possible dialogue with Lopito. He couldn't keep from making one last effort.

"Okay, Lopito. Would you like to forget everything and begin again, *da capo*? Let me start, and see if you can follow. It isn't hard not to be odious. I'll introduce you to my son, Jean-Paul, at the cemetery."

"Terrific. I'm going to bring Moira so they can meet and become friends, since it seems hard for us to do it."

"Who is Moira?"

"Moira López, my six-year-old daughter, known as Lopita when I have to take care of her because Flora is working, and I drag her along to some bar to pass the time because if I don't I die of depression in the house. Don't laugh: I admit that Moira is a pretty fancy name for her. And since everybody calls her Lopita, they've screwed her the way they screwed me."

Mañungo, next to the open door, could not keep back the laugh of his petty revenge: *"Moira!* Shit, man, you've got to be schizo to give a poor innocent kid a name like that . . . and if she looks like you . . . !"

"She does. She's ugly. But she doesn't know she's ugly because I tell her she's pretty and she believes everything I tell her. But the poor thing is ugly."

"A chip off the old block."

"Lay off, Mañungo, unless you want me to sock you one!"

"You sock me? Don't make me laugh! Your hands are shaking and you breathe like a broken percolator . . ." As he closed the door, he said to Lopito, "Bring Moira to the funeral, if you've got the guts."

"Mañungo . . ." Lopito's voice was hoarse.

"Now what?"

"Don't be that way."

"What way?"

"When you and Jean-Paul meet her, don't laugh at her. Please. Promise?"

Mañungo closed the door when he said yes, with a wave of digust and compassion he could not stand because Lopito was tearing him to pieces, and only when he got to the corner could he take out his handkerchief and blow his nose.

27

♦*H*e decided that the doorman's
wide grin as he entered the hotel was not for the illustrious Mañungo
Vera, recently returned to his native land, but an authentic greeting.
He was shocked by the general friendliness, the almost excessive pas-
sivity of waiters and taxi drivers expressed in their gentleness, a luxury
now virtually extinct in Europe. Doormen smile there, but they do it
professionally, which was not the case of the bellboy who was tidying
up the morning disorder of the lobby, and who in passing said good
morning with a cordiality that came from below that skin of courtesy—
which in his world, in his slums, would surely be discarded when the
time came to ventilate his rage. Did this bellboy belong to the same
species as last night's nomadic silhouettes whose hands brandished
knives and who'd robbed him of his beloved Rolex? Perhaps. Maybe
it was the necessary flip side of Lopito's anger, which was always just
below the surface. In any case, it wouldn't be a bad idea for Juan
Pablo, reared with the rigidity of Nadja's French obligations and the
pitiless competitiveness of the schools and kids over there, to experience this gentleness.

"Sir . . ." said the desk clerk. "Good morning . . ."

"Good morning. Room nine-seven-eight."

"The boy is down here."

"Playing?"

"No. Sleeping. Here in the office," and he opened the door so Mañungo could come in.

"What happened to him?"

Juan Pablo, covered up in plaid blankets, slept on the imitation-
leather couch.

"Why is he here?" Mañungo became upset. And, kissing the boy to
wake him up, he said, "Jean-Paul . . ."

"We had to give him a sedative to calm him down."

With no transition, the boy passed from sleep to crying in his father's arms, with a scream that was not of recognition but of fear: *"Tu es en retard. Tu m'as dit que tu allais rentrer bientôt. Papa, Papa! Rentrons chez nous, je ne veux pas être ici . . ."*

And while Jean-Paul sobbed, the desk clerk and other employees gathered around the father with his hysterical son and recounted exactly what had happened. Last night there'd been an earthquake, not very strong in comparison with the kind they usually have in Chile. It scared Jean-Paul, and he started to cry and scream because, of course, a room on the ninth floor sways quite a bit with any tremor. Besides, the electricity had been cut off, so the boy—and the rest of the hotel—was in the dark until the generators had started up. The foreigners had all been upset, so much so that a group of Canadian botanists on tour changed their schedule and left today even though they had reservations for four days. They just weren't going to go through another scare like the one they'd had last night. It wasn't a strong tremor compared with the real ones—the desk clerk talked about points on the Richter Scale with the pride of a champion—but a child like Jean-Paul, poor thing, who'd never experienced anything like it, was naturally scared out of his wits. He didn't want to stay in his room upstairs. Not even if the baby-sitter stayed with him to explain these curious natural phenomena. He sobbed, insisting that he wanted to walk on solid ground, downstairs, and even went out in the garden, refusing to understand that it was much more dangerous because if the ground shook again a cornice could break off and fall, while inside the whole hotel was made of reinforced concrete, the highest-quality American construction. The boy screamed so much for his father to come and take him back him to Rue Servandoni that they finally brought him down to the office to sleep.

Mañungo hadn't felt the tremor. He picked Jean-Paul up in his arms to carry him to their room, trying to calm him down as they went up in the elevator. It was his fault, Papa's, he who was from this damned continent filled with cataclysms, funerals, and revolutions! Jean-Paul wanted to leave. Why couldn't they leave right away?

Mañungo ran the bath water. He undressed Jean-Paul and put him in the hot tub, first washing his tear-stained face. He asked for breakfast to be sent up in fifteen minutes. The soaping and the bath calmed the boy down a bit, finally extracting him from the world of catastrophes that pointed to a fate he saw as totally hostile, and about which

no one had told him a thing. How could Mañungo explain to him
that the snow-covered mountain chain and the breaking up of the
islands he'd see on his trip south, the channels the *Caleuche* plied with
its sails puffed out by the wind were the result of ancient catastrophes
not so different from this one, only larger?

He could not help remembering that you could almost touch the
disturbing presence of the geology here. The Cenozoic period, which
in other places was nothing more than a beautiful word, was here a
reality prior to men and languages. As you went down the hill that
led to Dalcahue on a clear day, you could see the various straits, the
tender green islands like geologic ruins that took refuge in the mar-
supial pouch of Castro Bay spread out in the transparent atmosphere.
And the spinal cord of the great cordillera was the background, dazzling with its snowy vertebrae.

Yes, that sensation of a transcendental dialogue with time was what
Mañungo remembered, and perhaps, although he did not always present it to himself that way, missed. After the tidal wave that eliminated
the coastal life of his family and decimated the survivors, his father
took him for protection to his land in Curaco de Vélez, which at least
supplied money enough to keep him in high school, and later, precariously, at the University of Concepción. At Curaco de Vélez, everything was dairy farming, potatoes, fish, produced and consumed at
home, and the tone of life was that of a hard apprenticeship for
standing up to the infinitely prolonged and infinitely destructive storms.
At the town high school, Ulda taught him to play the guitar and charm
the darkness of the isolated afternoons, because Ulda came from lands
farther north where music was happy and the people expansive.

It was as if she were the female of an animal wiser than man. After
giving him two years of music and love, she banished him. Get going,
she said, you're too intelligent, if you stay around here you're going
to suffocate and die of starvation, it doesn't matter that you leave me
dying of love, I'll always find someone who can substitute for you, at
least physically, and I'll have to get used to that, but I'm no longer
young and I have little to hope for, and in a year you'll be looking at
other women, younger than I, with the eyes I opened for you, so get
going, what matters is that you save yourself. Would Ulda have changed
much in fifteen years? Would her black hair that smelled of wood fires
be gray? Last night, sleeping with Judit in the vacant lot, he'd felt that
smell from the past circling around him.

He woke up angry, with the sensation that from the island, for the first time in all these years, Ulda was mobilizing unknown powers to summon him. He hugged Judit and the little white dog, clinging to them so he would not let himself be dragged to the southern fog, against which Ulda herself in another era had warned him, but to which she, now, was calling him back. He could learn little in Europe about what was happening on the island because don Manuel sent him scanty reports, more than anything about his stock or his crops that year. For the illiterate old man, each letter had to correspond to even greater necessities, because each one required a trip to Castro to find a scribe he could trust, one who would not betray the austere secrets he shared twice a year with his son.

Jean-Paul, on the other hand, naked and still wet, wrapped in a thick bath towel that seemed to give a certain degree of comforting pleasure to his senses, knew not only how to write, but read, in French and English. Walking by his side down Rue de Seine under Sartre's canonized windows, the boy once commented that when he was older he wanted to study electronics to be able to make the machines that produced music. He made that kind of confidential remark only rarely, because the boy never seemed to outgrow the childishness of "Au clair de la lune mon ami Pierrot."

How would it be to walk down from his father's shingled house to the cove, leave their clothes in a pile under a blood-red wild fuchsia, dive in, as much for pleasure as for cleanliness, and in that diaphanous stream soap the child's belly, white and palpitating as a frog's in the cloud the soap made? That current, thick with mackerels and jurels, sometimes brought seals to the nearby shore, which would stay there for hours or days or weeks bellowing cavernously among the rocks. That current carried everything along to the Guaitecas Islands and the Isthmus of Ofqui farther south, in the zone of the storms and whales, where erosion constantly changes the topography and herds of *guanacos* gallop on nameless mountains, while generations of marine birds enrich the cliffs with centuries and centuries of excrement.

The boy was already dressed in his jeans and shirt, miniatures of his father's outfit, enjoying a breakfast above reproach. In any case, despite the tenderness with which Mañungo spoke to him and consoled him, Jean-Paul remained severe with his father, interrogating him about where and with whom he'd spent the night, accusing him, requiring from him—as had Nadja after his escapades, when her "Slavic soul" tortured her with suspicions all too often well-founded—direct answers, names, times, dates.

Mañungo explained to the boy that it was his first night back in his country, and he had gotten involved with a dear lady friend of his. Now he was waiting for her call, which would come any minute, so they could all go to the funeral of Matilde Neruda—that "queen," did he remember?—who had just died. It was not only a personal matter but a public and historical matter, one he could tell to his grandchildren, probably the last time that anything similar would happen in this country, because his unfortunate nation was being held prisoner in a "state of siege" where they threw people in jail for nothing and the newspapers lied because the government owned the newspapers and they only published what the government wanted, and there was fear and curfew . . .

"*Couvre-feu . . . ?*" asked Juan Pablo, suddenly delighted. "*Comme dans* Vinqt ans après?*"

"*Comme dans* Vinqt ans après. *Mais ici c'est douze ans après, et pire qu'au debut.*"

"*De quelle heure à quelle heure, le couvre-feu?*"

"*Minuit jusqu'à cinq heures du matin.*"

"*Tu as donc été avec cette femme de minuit jusqu'à cinq heures du matin!*"

"*Cette dame, Jean-Paul, pas cette femme.*"

"*Tu vas donc l'épouser et nous resterons ici?*"

He felt the impulse to slap Jean-Paul for that impertinence. But how had he been impertinent? Mañungo relaxed his tightened hand, and caressed the boy's golden, moist head without answering, without answering himself, because, of course, it was a possibility. Would Judit be capable of caressing his son this way, his poor son who needed it so much and who he himself only rarely, when he felt really guilty, ever caressed? Perhaps that was the insult he glimpsed in the marriage idea his son suggested. The boy was pure antenna, pure sensibility. But Mañungo only knew how to love women devoid of tenderness, like Judit. Like Nadja. But Nadja's coldness was gratuitous, an aesthetic, an experiment with her own limits and the limits of others, while in Judit it was a vertiginous destiny that someone else, or perhaps history, had established.

Her rebellion was fixed by her social class. Judit would thus be a backward companion, underdeveloped, in fact, because she allowed herself to be defined by something so insignificant that it shouldn't count either way. He felt anger at seeing her broken up by her obsession with paying idiotic class debts that left her without energy for pleasure, in which tenderness was a principal ingredient. Was it that lack that kept her vivid in his senses: her wet silk dress, molding itself around her haunches under his hands, his senses invaded by the vegetable freshness of her breasts contaminated by the green cleanliness of the grass and the acanthus?

Jean-Paul's question had wounded him. Yes. Why not marry Judit? Why not get married if it was true that he was attracted by women imprisoned by their ghosts? Juan Pablo went on with his interrogation.

"Dis-moi la vérité. Il y aura la révolution cet après-midi? J'ai très peur. J'ai vu des choses comme ça à la télé. Et on mange même les enfants quand il y a la famine."

"On ne mange pas les enfants au Chili. Nous sommes civilisés."

"Çe n'est pas vrai. J'ai vu des uniformes à la télé, ils sont très beaux, comme dans Tin-Tin, pleins d'or. Et que me dis-tu de ces tremblements de terre? Est-ce qu'on peut dire qu'un pays est civilisé quand il tremble comme ça? Et les révolutions . . . Non, n'est-ce pas? Partons, Papa . . . allons chez nous. Laisse cette femme ici et partons . . ."

"Je t'ai dit de ne pas l'appeller femme. Dame, merde, alors."

"Dame."

Mañungo tried to calm him after that outburst. They would go out after they finished breakfast, take a walk through a pretty park that was near the hotel before going to the funeral. They had time. The boy refused to go out, refused to go to the funeral, refused to do anything. Mañungo had to drag and push the bawling child out of the hotel. To pacify him, he let him carry his splendid camera. If he behaved himself, he would be allowed to take photos, something Jean-Paul, who had exposed a roll of film and broken a button once, was not usually allowed to do. The weight of the camera around his neck consoled him.

In the park, the German Fountain was at the apogee of its optimistic grandiloquence. Water shone on bronze drapery and metallic breasts, false cannons, seals, garlands, and rocks. The haze made by the arches of water flowing from the muzzles of the mythological beasts turned transparent. The water, falling in cascades and rivulets, delighted Juan Pablo, who opined that the fountain resembled some monuments in Paris. Mañungo decided not to ask him which monuments because the boy could detect all too easily any note of irony in his voice. He tried to take photographs of the fountain with his father's camera. Seeing him try to manipulate the camera, Mañungo corrected him, irritatingly, uselessly, because Juan Pablo was born knowing how to do everything with any machine and hated to be corrected. They ended up having a fight, the camera once again hung around his father's neck, and they went back to the hotel without speaking to take a rest before going to the funeral. Back in the room, Mañungo began to leaf through the newspaper as he stretched out on his bed, trying not to pay any attention to Juan Pablo, who was looking out the window, just as he had back in Paris.

28

◆ *A*nyone who hasn't studied for exams or discussed politics and art and life under the plane trees in Forestal Park, or read Neruda's *Twenty Love Poems* in the shade of its bushes while holding hands with a shy girlfriend, does not know the dazzling novelty of being finally adult and free, thrown in with the rest of the population of the big city as a university student. The sunken lawns flood with sunlight, the embankments and slopes, a modest monument from the *belle époque*, the refuge of pigeons and weeds, bearded students setting the world aright, have been the constant decoration of this park that lies like a narrow green sheath next to the rusty slice of river that cuts through the city: an urban park despite its heavy vegetation, a refuge, despite the noise of the cars that run along both flanks of its narrow, saberlike shape, transparent at night to the lights and eyes of the police who patrol it.

The bureaucrats treat Forestal Park well because it is the most presentable face of this leaden city—the little "green lung," as people call it nowadays, of the downtown area; a frontispiece worthy of being exhibited as a proof of our so-called traditions. This park has for generations been a country within a country, strong because it has been able to keep its identity despite atrocities and transformations. Freddy Fox had lived its various incarnations as if they were his own. He had identified with the park, from the time his nanny took him out for an airing in his carriage sucking on his first necklace of pacifiers until his strolls as a myopic student diligently studying both his law books and any girl who happened to get within reach. Later on, it was Freddy Fox who had organized the raids against the marijuana smokers who flooded out of the slums during the Popular Unity period to disfigure neighboring buildings and the river embankment itself with obscene graffiti. The present moment brought the submission and withdrawal of the citizenry, willing at last to let itself be guided in matters in which it had no expertise, an obligatory maturation in which Freddy had no small role. Waiting for Judit on the bench in front of the museum, he could say with satisfaction that the present and the future of "his" park were now under the protection of his authority and his taste, since the decorative policies most esteemed by those who understood these matters emanated from his person, or at least had to receive his blessing at some point in the process.

To a certain degree, and setting aside all *criollo* pride, Freddy Fox thought the Fine Arts Museum better proportioned and less pompous than the Petit Palais, on which it was modeled. The building had been the nucleus of the park ever since it was built, with money from the new mining fortunes made at the turn of the century, when it was inaugurated with a huge ball of which he possessed a curious series of photographs. His paternal grandmother, one of the great beauties of the day, had actually danced at the ball. A trivial fact, no doubt, but one of the many that made him feel he was deeply rooted in the country's history and reinforced his disdain for the parvenus who tried to seize any crumb of power other than the ones he threw them.

That Neruda collected holograph texts and manuscripts was all well and good. Neruda was a genius, a mutant, but in the last analysis Neruda should have been collecting for him, for Freddy Fox, whose grandmother, decked out in white crepe and carrying a feathered fan, had danced a mazurka with President Pedro Montt to inaugurate this museum in 1910. Everything in Chile was ultimately related to politics, from Grandma's feathered fans to holograph collections, and anyone who did not act with the authorities, or who opposed them, was left out of the flow of history—which was rough and as filthy as the little urban river that wound its way between stone embankments.

Before he identified as Judit the woman who crossed the bridge at Calle Purísima and came toward him under the trees, a small voice whispered to his fickle fat man's heart that the careful construction and splendid movement of the woman approaching him satisfied the aesthetic desires of his own outsized body . . . yes, that hypothetical partner had powers that would assuage his need to acquire more and more and more without being satisfied by anything. It was only after that shock that he recognized Judit—I must be getting nearsighted, he thought, cleaning his glasses with the end of his thin tie, which fell to one side of his prominent stomach—and rose to meet the silhouette that crossed the sunken lawns, which in another age had been a pond filled with swans and rowboats.

As Judit and Freddy shared the grandmother of the feathered fan and the mazurka, his sitting next to her on this bench at one end of the former pond, where the light in the chestnut trees imitated the shimmer of the watery past, was something of a family reunion. Like the perfunctory kiss on the cheek. He knew this rebellious, taciturn traitor hated him, but he also knew she possessed a power over him, a power incarnated in her excessive beauty. He wanted to tear her to pieces with his huge, doughy hands, to penetrate her with his phallus, if that awkward object could indeed be called a phallus. But he held that violent fantasy in check because the victory he really coveted was of another sort: he longed to destroy her moral right to judge him, longed to force her to confess her crimes in public and remain silent about his. In an act as trivial as lighting her own cigarette—which negated the possibility of his practicing traditional masculine good manners—Freddy saw her negation of his very being. Judit accused him of being old-fashioned, pre-Freudian, pre-Marxist, and pre-feminist, of thinking he could dictate cultural policy simply because he'd been born into a class traditionally familiar with culture. This in itself, she commented, pointed to his lack of complexity, his unsuitability for the job.

"Here I am," said Judit in lieu of a greeting.

"A pleasure to see you! How are you?"

"Let's cut the chitchat, Freddy. I have twenty minutes. Start talking."

"You're always running somewhere."

"What do you want me to say? Shall I tell you how Lopito, my current lover, is doing?"

"Don't tell me that you're with that scummy swine again."

"No, Freddy. It was only a joke."

"In bad taste."

"If you'd ever slept with Lopito, you'd know just how bad the taste is. Like everything I do."

"A lie. Judit, your taste is as impeccable as mine. How are you?"

"As you see. I've turned into an old crone."

Freddy wiped the sweat from his cheeks, and Judit realized that he wasn't perspiring merely because it was a hot morning.

"Now you're just fishing for compliments," he answered. "You look splendid."

"Thanks, but . . ."

"There are people who in different phases of their lives enter into and leave beams of light that illuminate them, as if during a brief period they find their definitive face. Your beauty is, in my opinion, in one of those high points."

Pretty speech, thought Judit. And nice observation. Although the glow to which he alluded was the ironic effect of having stayed up all night. In any case, what Freddy was saying was too contrived. Perhaps the speech would have moved her or at least pleased her if someone else had pronounced it, in other circumstances and in a different style, with shorter sentences and fewer interpolated clauses . . . and also less simple. And because she realized that Freddy really was simple, she decided to say nothing.

"How are you?" repeated Freddy, who seemed to be in rapt contemplation, not of Judit but of his own speech.

"From what point of view would you like to know? Politically speaking, as you see, I am alive and not in jail for my supposed subversive activities, which is saying a lot for a dissident in this shitty country. And erotically . . ."

"*Emotionally* is what nice people say, Ju," corrected Freddy, and both of them smiled.

"Emotionally . . ." But in her hesitation before describing her feelings, Judit realized she was getting ready to lie. After the intrusion of her walk last night, the truth of her answer would have to be exactly the opposite of what she usually said, because she now discovered she was full of Mañungo, and her heart leaped in surprise. Despite that, she decided to give her usual answer: "Emotionally . . . zero. And economically, just barely surviving, like almost everyone in Santiago except gangsters like you."

"What do you call surviving? There are many kinds of survival . . ."

"Well, let's say that I'd be happier if I could survive in a category a little higher than the one I'm in."

"And what things do you do to survive?"

"What a sordid question, Freddy, for God's sake! I can assure you I'm not a secret agent and that I'm not embarked on dark projects that will change the life of the country."

"Would you like to change?"

She realized she'd been trapped in the plot her cousin had woven in asking her to the park. He wanted to buy her, because for him there was nothing or no one not for sale, above all objects and wounded people, and her being wounded was no secret. To give herself time to react, she bent over to pick up a shiny horse chestnut.

The instant of silence her gesture created gave Freddy a chance to feign a change of subject: "How is Celedonio? He didn't look well yesterday."

"He's depressed because of Matilde's death."

"Well, I'm a bit worried about him. And about the fate of the Pablo Neruda Foundation. Do you think he's up to the job, Ju? It's taken so much time to approve the foundation. And what if Celedonio dies on us?"

"Remember, for the regime the foundation is part of a murky communist plot."

"Maybe you're right. It's so hard to tell. In any case, for one reason or another this thing is getting bogged down—the papers that authorize the foundation are lost somewhere in a mountain of documents, I suppose somewhere in the court system or in some other public office, so that the thing may never be resolved. It would be a great loss to the country if the foundation did not become a reality. But last night I was thinking and an idea came to me that was not half bad, just in case the government, as you correctly suggest, or whoever it is, stops the matter for too long a time."

"You have? What an angel you are, Freddy, to lose sleep over an idea that, if it comes from you, must certainly be for the good of humanity."

"How tedious you are!"

"And how crude you are! Anybody could figure where you're going with this."

"Maybe. But it may also be that you're not as sharp as you think. Shall I go on? As I was saying, this morning it occurred to me that if the authorization gets blocked, perhaps it would not be too difficult to find some legal accommodation to arrange things so that the heirs to the estate can hold a public auction of Neruda's belongings. Then, with the funds from that sale, they could make a generous donation, to the university, let's say, that no one could criticize or reject. That's what's been on my mind and that's why I wanted to talk to you."

"This was the urgent matter you dragged me down here for?"

"Yes, before the funeral."

"I don't understand why."

"Before the communists dominate Celedonio and Fausta and have things done the way they want. I saw that they were in a rebellious mood last night in Bellavista, and if we're not careful, that rabble could destroy everything. If the foundation doesn't come into existence soon, those hordes are going to send everything to Moscow, unless they burn it first."

Judit could not hold back a loud guffaw. Freddy stood up in front of her, his nervous hands in the pockets of his trousers, which rose disturbingly high above his paunch; his open jacket revealed the catches of his suspenders.

"What's wrong with you?" asked Freddy, aware that her laughter was pure sarcasm.

"I just can't believe a word you're saying."

"Why?"

"That a man of your intelligence could repeat those paranoic, ridiculous commonplaces!"

"And what about the commonplaces you communists repeat—Yankee imperialism supplying weapons to machine-gun the people during the curfew, the CIA everywhere. How do those commonplaces strike you?"

"I don't see why you put me in the Party. I was a member for only six months when I was at the university, and I hated it. Later I was in the Revolutionary Left Movement, but I walked out a long time ago. As you well know."

"That's not true. You belonged to the Party until they declared armed struggle two years ago, when you quit—and I congratulate you for doing so. We also know that you don't belong to the RLM, but that you are part of a group we haven't yet been able to identify. An independent group, it seems, and violent, although we can't understand what you're doing in it since you proved your nonviolence when you left the Party at the exact moment they opted for violence and joined this group which doesn't seem defined by anything . . ."

"By rage."

"Worse and worse. I knew we'd end up fighting!"

"So what was the big emergency then?"

"I need you."

"Oh, no, Freddy, I'm not going to be your agent in any of your slimy maneuvers."

Then, standing before her, Freddy said simply, "Understand this: if you're free it's only because we want to find out what you're involved with, and with whom, and who they are and how many."

He sat down next to her. In another tone, imploring now, he took her hands, which Judit freed from his while he spoke to her with a redoubling of his sticky intimacy.

"Listen. Don't be a fool. Didn't you say you wanted to survive in nicer style? Well, help me then. I'm your cousin. I don't understand why you oppose me and favor a bunch of slobs you don't even know. Listen to me: the only thing I'm asking is that you advise Fausta and Celedonio to hold an auction, which frankly would be the best thing, even better than this dumb foundation. Oh yes, Judit, my dear, I forgot to tell you: this morning before I left the house I sent you a gift, because I know you like music, a fabulous stereo system. A company of mine imported them before it went bankrupt . . ."

Judit jumped to her feet and stood in front of Freddy, who had his arms stretched out on the back of the bench. Her indignation was so great that Freddy was afraid she was going to strike him with her handbag; he remained on guard to duck in case of attack. But as the volume and the sordidness of his cousin's recriminations increased, and as she mixed in filthy memories of childhood with invectives that made him responsible for the humiliations the nation was currently suffering, Freddy's own anger began to grow. Judit's obscurantism, her stupidity covered over by a mask of good intentions, her false naiveté (false because she had not an iota of naiveté in her), her social rage built on lies, were all slightly subtler forms of terrorism and betrayal, but terrorism and betrayal nonetheless, and they had to be destroyed. Judit should just give up all that nonsense. She was dangerous to society with those airs of purity and vindication, and soon she'd get involved with something that would reveal she had illegally left the country and returned. And then the justice system would land on her and perhaps on her strange group, which the police weren't after yet only because they didn't know what they were up to, but soon orders would come to hunt them down. No, Judit did not have the right to insult him or throw his sins in his face, because everybody, *everybody*, knew she was a whore who slept with the entire Party, and who was an inch away from disappearing, which would not be such a bad idea . . .

"Why? So you could get everything at the auction?"

"Wouldn't that be better than seeing it exported to Russia, or Cuba? Just imagine . . . Or, hypothetically speaking, what if the foundation were to become a reality: to see those marvelous things sullied by students and poetasters with filthy hands and bad breath? I would take good care of everything . . ."

"Frankly, I would rather see the rats eat Pablo's last manuscript and wait for the authorization of the foundation than see even one page in your sweaty paws."

Sweaty hands. Soft, terrified, hands, that hid their terror by disguising it as something else. Warm hands, trembling slightly: yesterday his, now theirs, the All-forgiving, who were the same people. These unmerciful hands exempted her for the moment, in part because Judit was his cousin and in part because he wanted to follow the trail of a group it would be necessary to dissolve today. Freddy's hands were sweaty and decadent, but very different from the ones that had pardoned her, even though those hands had also been, at another time, fearful of her female body.

In that moment of silence, Judit thought she'd won her victory. But Freddy said, "I'm sorry to tell you that who gets to touch those papers or not is all going to depend exclusively on me."

"What do you mean?"

"The documents that authorize the foundation are on my desk waiting for my signature."

"You've stalled things?"

"I have. For the moment. Later we'll see what happens."

"I don't understand what you gain by doing something so . . ."

"It isn't as perverse as it seems. Very simply, I want to take at least a slice of the collection for myself. In my hands it will be better off than anywhere else, because I'm the only person in the country who really appreciates its value. In a foundation, which will be strictly in Chilean style, that is, a joke—I think we can take that for granted—the papers will be badly catalogued and badly kept, and little by little they'll disappear, stolen, allowed to rot, or simply lost through carelessness, like everything else in this land of savages. And I'm sure that neither you nor I want any part of this treasure to go to Moscow, because it belongs to us, to all Chileans. I think, certainly, that it would be a good idea to advise Celedonio not to have a grand-scale international auction, with Sotheby's, for example, because if he does they'll print superb catalogues to bring it to the attention of the press in Paris, London, and New York. And the innocent bourgeois desire that the great Pablo Neruda had to be a grand collector might draw unfavorable commentaries about the authenticity of the sentiments motivating this poet of the people . . ."

"What you mean is that if there *is* an auction, Sotheby's shouldn't handle it, so that millionaire collectors from all over the world won't come and raise the prices, and you can get it all cheap . . ."

"Frankly, that is my idea, my dear. Oh yes, I wanted to ask you something. Is it true that there exists an important correspondence with Trotsky in Neruda's papers? I'm afraid, for example, that such a collection might compromise Neruda's Communist-Stalinist position, and that the leading commissars in Chile, to keep Pablo's image pure, might burn them and they'd be lost. He always denied the existence of those letters, but . . ."

Judit, taken aback by Freddy's heat and his ravenous vehemence, answered that she knew nothing because those things had never interested her. Certainly, she had seen the various collections from time to time, and like any well-educated person she couldn't help but be moved at having in her hands the letters of Isabelle Rimbaud, in which she described to her mother the sordid, syphilitic death of the poet in a Marseille hospital, and how the mother had abandoned him even though she knew he was dying because she thought it more important to supervise the potato crop in her poor cold lands in Charleville. And *Leaves of Grass*, annotated by Walt Whitman himself. And so many other items that made certain things in her own culture all the more moving and immediate. But it wasn't the papers in themselves.

She actually felt repugnance, she said, for collections of any kind, and for collectors in general, as if for them it was impossible to admire or love something they couldn't acquire for themselves, and that possessive mania brought out certain gluttonous traits that disgusted her. When she stated these ideas to an attentive but unmoved Freddy, Judit saw with shocking clarity, in which she recognized a slight touch of rather vulgar romanticism that she would later try to eradicate, that if at this moment she did love Mañungo, and her mind was struggling with the strange idea of marrying him or going away with him, it was in part because Mañungo possessed absolutely nothing. Nothing but his music, his cassettes, his guitar, his lined paper, yes, a free romantic vision, a night in a friend's house, another in the house of a protective couple after a party, or with a woman in whose arms he'd slept for a week and then gone his way. An old hippy, she thought, laughing affectionately at the pathetic cliché of so many people who never made a go of it and took refuge in that disguise. In any case, no books. No clothes. No objects that would be a burden. In Paris, Judit knew, Mañungo had a beautiful apartment, well located but utilitarian, that he took care of himself so that no one would get in his way. The pleasure of possessing things was not his; *he'd* never had a necklace of pacifiers. Trotsky? No, Judit knew nothing about that. Although she seemed to remember that once she'd heard Celedonio say something about Trotsky. She told her cousin that she would transmit no messages.

Freddy scraped his shoe around in the golden sand of the path as he listened to her talk, and a light coating of dust settled on his patent-leather toe. When Judit finished explaining her repulsion, Freddy again sat down next to her and, becoming sweet again, explained, "I don't blame you for not understanding these things. I do blame you, however, for condemning people who derive pleasure in ways that are not yours. I know you tell everyone who cares to listen that you get no pleasure from anything and that it's my fault. But it simply isn't true. Your problems, my dear, predate my small intervention in your childhood and are independent of it. Don't oversimplify, like all Freudians, although Freud and Marx don't seem to me to blend too well, even if both are dogmatic. Does it bother you that I have my little 'hang-up,' as the Americans call it, with Trotsky? It's really quite simple. Trotsky was Stalin's enemy, a fine and perceptive intellectual you can't help but admire. It's an admiration we share, cousin dear, don't deny it now, because it seems that you're heading for 'permanent revolution,' if not for pure nihilism. . . . Anyway, we can talk about that some other time. I'm sure that Trotsky would have made a real revolution triumph, above all if it's true, as the Stalinists claimed, that Trotsky was financed by William Randolph Hearst, which is not improbable because that *gringo* was a real genius. If Stalin hadn't had Trotsky killed, we wouldn't be seeing the chaos we're living in now. Perhaps an even worse chaos, but not this chaos. Neruda met Trotsky. At least that's what people say, and Celedonio knows it. All the communists living in Mexico met him. They say that cretin Siqueiros killed him and was paid by the Kremlin. He was such a bad painter that I wouldn't put it past him. There also exists a rumor, widely contradicted, I must add, that Neruda, friend of the whole mob of communists in Mexico then, was implicated in the assassination and that the Kremlin covered it up—I mean covered up for Siqueiros—for services rendered. I have several documents that allude to the Siqueiros-Neruda-Trotsky connection, but unfortunately they clarify nothing. What's missing is a series of letters it seems Trotsky wrote to Neruda. Don't tell me the correspondence of someone who could have changed world history, like Trotsky, isn't fascinating! You, as an anti-Stalinist in the RLM, would certainly recognize that fact more than anyone . . ."

Judit closed her eyes tightly until she saw stars bursting in the morning light. She shook her head to exorcise and banish her cousin's voice, the words of that man who now, standing in front of her, speaking to her with a certain degree of repulsive seduction, was sinking his hands into his trouser pockets. Even there his hands were fidgeting, as if he were masturbating. His penis was flaccid, white, long, she remembered it as a viscous reptile, just opposite her mouth, very close, so she could bite it off. Make him howl with pain and not go on listening.

"No, no, no . . . !" shouted Judit, standing up.

"No what?"

"What are you going to do with Trotsky's papers if they do exist?"

Freddy stopped playing with his sex and, softly laying his hands on Judit's shoulders, his blue Fox eyes dissolved in the blue gaze of his cousin Fox, he said, "If they let me have the Trotsky papers now, immediately, before they make up the inventory of the Neruda collection—only the Trotsky papers, because I'm sure that in them I'll find proof that not only Trotsky but many of the big bosses of the time were paid by Hearst and the American government—I promise official authorization for the Pablo Neruda Foundation will go through, and that it will be protected from anyone who might question or fight it. I think I can say with some confidence that the foundation would be firmly established within, let's say, ten or twelve days. Tell Celedonio that . . ."

Judit angrily and brutally snapped her knee up into Freddy's crotch.

"You animal!" he shrieked.

"I learned that trick in the RLM training camps, just so you know," she said. Then she turned away and walked very rapidly toward the lawns from which she'd come, toward the Purísima bridge, which was submerged in the underwater light of an already mature morning. She never looked back. Striding along, she crossed the grass without feeling anything but a blind hatred for Freddy, disgust for his world, his tricks, his friends, the way he used people, corrupted them, manipulated them and influenced them, his voracious acquisitions and earnings. It was late. Freddy had taken longer than he'd promised to pour out his shit, and she had to meet Fausta at Matilde's house, above all now, so she could warn Ada Luz and the other women who were in danger because they were being watched. Above all she had to hurry to forget, forget that sordid character, to carry out with some dignity the final, solemn rites of tenderness for Matilde. After a while she heard Freddy trotting behind her, shouting:

"Ju! Ju!"

Judit stopped and turned to face him. He was sweaty, as if he were wearing makeup made from the ocher dust he'd raised by running and which had stuck to his greasy skin. His blue shirt was soaked, his head bent forward as if ready to hear his sentence, which would have no appeal.

Judit said to him, "As soon as the funeral is taken care of, I'll return your stereo. Never forget that you and I are enemies." And she turned to keep walking.

"Yes, I know we're enemies, my dear, but not because of me. Want me to go with you?"

"Where?"

"Matilde's house."

"Why?"

"Frankly, because unless I'm with you they probably won't let me in, and I want to talk to Celedonio."

"Stop fucking around and get lost."

She began to walk without looking at Freddy, who was right at her heels. Her cousin was still following her when they crossed the bridge, and to the other side of Avenida Bellavista, and entered the tangled streets of the neighborhood. Half a man, his hat theatrically covering his eyes, seemed to be waiting for her with his back against a wall, his hand out, begging for money. She made a minute gesture to tell him to flee, and as soon as they'd left him behind, Judit heard with relief the sound of don César's skateboard rolling in the opposite direction, until its noise blended with the other noises of the city.

29

◆ Ada Luz could not speak with Judit because Judit walked in with don Federico Fox, who frightened her; she didn't dare say a word. Judit was in a bad mood because of some unnamed misfortune she must have suffered during her nocturnal adventure. By a certain familiar dejection in her attitude, Ada Luz guessed that once again nothing had happened to the poor thing beyond the usual trivialities that took place in her hunts, which never ended with a kill because the game only existed in her imagination and was "just in her head," conjectured Ada Luz.

Nevertheless, she realized, something different from the other times did seem to have happened, although not as part of the plan. Judit was downcast, yes, but more beautiful than ever, victim of a torment that Ada Luz had never seen in her. It was as if Carlitos's roar, piercing the yellow canvas awning over the patio, did not rise from the beast's throat but secretly and mysteriously from within Judit, like so many things in her that kept the other women at a distance. Carlitos's roar seemed to break the poor animal's heart with the pain of farewell. Besides, an ear attuned to sounds like Judit's perceived that this apparently silent morning was filled with animal voices. Weakened by their passage through the trees on the mountainside, they seemed to be rustling leaves rather than the squawks of parrots and monkeys, the barks of unfortunate dogs inexplicably caged up, the brays of mules and the snorts of camels who in this way expressed a final homage to their illustrious neighbor.

Hoping to talk to her, Ada Luz followed Judit to the bar in the dining room, where she saw her dial a telephone number. A wrong number . . . or no answer. She hung up. Impatient, clumsy, she dialed again, while Ada Luz noted her disquiet. It was not only because she'd lost the pistol, as she had insinuated, telling bits and pieces of the

story while she misdialed once again, recounting trivial details. Her
newest problem, which curiously enough enhanced her beauty, was
the space that Judit kept the other five from entering; and when Ada
Luz sensed that Judit's defense mechanisms about her private life were
going up, a kind of instinct, like the motions of a mollusk, closed her
up too, making her withdraw from her impulse to consult Judit about
Lisboa's visit last night and about the new directions the matter of
Miss Matilde's mass had taken because of it. Judit misdialed every
time. Today she was equal to Ada Luz, to all of them, no longer
superior.

"We have to talk right away. It's very important," Judit said, while
she waited for someone to answer the telephone.

"About what happened last night?"

"Partly. And about us, all of you, and don César . . . I'm probably
going to have to go to France . . . don't say a word, I don't know for
sure yet . . . but maybe, we're being watched . . ."

"With Mañungo," guessed Ada Luz.

But before she could contradict Ada Luz, Judit took out her anger
at being so easily unmasked on her daughter, who finally answered:
she would not let her miss the funeral, even if a funeral was the most
boring idea in the world for a summer day during vacation. Not every
kid has the privilege of participating in the funeral of a person as
important as Matilde, who had inspired our hope of recovering our
lost rights—a hope that, with her death, which was like the second
death of Pablo, might disappear forever.

Her admiration for Judit shook Ada Luz as she listened. How she
understood things, and how she made others understand them! How
precise her seductive friend's ideas were! She was incomplete, certainly, but capable of using words to lift an ordinary event like the
death of this woman to a higher dimension, and make her listener,
Ada Luz, who was pure immediacy, understand that everyone can be
the incarnation, if he or she dares, of history. Yes: she would ask Judit
for advice. Tell her how that shameless Lisboa had appeared at her
house last night after Aury had gone, threatening that he would never
make love to her again if she dared tell anyone the story about Matilde's confession and her request for a graveside mass. Only when
she tearfully swore to Lisboa that she wouldn't tell anyone did he
agree to spend the night with her. Judit would certainly understand
her perplexity and tell her what to do. At the same time it was getting
late, and with each passing minute it would be more and more difficult

to carry out Matilde's last wishes. In a little while there would be no time to tell anyone anything, and the procession would have to leave. The responsibility to use these few remaining minutes properly was a maddening burden that wouldn't allow her to think. She wanted to grab Judit and make her tell her what to do.

Drop everything, Judit was ordering her daughter over the telephone, girlfriends, movies, TV, games, whatever, and go to the cemetery. But for the love of God, asked the grandmother, who was going to bring the child? She was too old for that sort of thing. She had to take care of her husband, afflicted with Parkinson's disease, shivering as if it were snowing on his poor body, sitting as he had been for years at a window that faced onto a patio bound by tanks of paraffin and a chicken coop. The grandmother insisted that a young girl like Marilú could not go by herself to a huge funeral where there would probably be incidents of the kind Judit, they, and the girl knew only too well, unfortunately, only too well. Ada Luz agreed, despite Judit's protest that if Luz was old enough to go dancing, she was old enough to take a bus and look for her mother at the cemetery.

On the other side of the marble-topped bistro table, where Judit was leaning on her elbow and smoking as she argued with her daughter, Ada Luz noticed that Judit's security was synonymous with her hardness, and suddenly, turning away, she decided not to tell her anything. She would tell her secret about the mass to the person she chose, or to no one. The people who would attend the rites would be arriving in half an hour, time enough for her—owner of a talisman that made her powerful, aware that her decision to speak out or not could change the course of history—to get the truth out of Judit about what had happened last night. Because Judit always refused to share with them: no matter what she said, she considered them her inferiors. Ada Luz, nevertheless, armed with the talisman of the secret about the mass, was no longer inferior.

Judit, furious, hung up. "That kid's a little bitch!"

"If you like, I'll go get her and bring her to the cemetery in a taxi," offered Ada Luz.

Judit walked out of the dining room, taken aback by the yellow of the huge awning that covered the stifling patio and dazzled her, almost causing her eyes to hurt when she closed them. Standing just outside the door of the dining room, where Ada Luz made coffee while the hyperkinetic kids from the Communist Youth took down the wreaths and piled them up in huge mounds of fragrant putrefaction next to the stairway, Judit opened her bag. She took out her comb and ran it through her hair. Her conversation with Ada Luz had made her so frantic that while she was trying to explain the dangers of Freddy's traps and the need to dissolve the group, she'd started to braid her hair. The result was that her hair was a tangle, and that Ada Luz did not understand anything beyond the fact that she should be careful. And that was not the point. It was much more serious: it was a matter of life and death, justice and injustice, executioners and victims. What drove Judit madder than Ada Luz's incomprehension was her baby talk that rendered everything absurd.

At the other end of the patio, setting his traps for Celedonio, was Freddy Fox, probably using the language elegantly. Judit's first impulse was to join that other conversation, to free herself from her friend's infantilisms and reach a haven of good speech. Pablo and Matilde, she remembered, spoke in a curious way, consciously mixing peasant expressions which they'd retained from their youth with the most cultivated, most polished language imaginable, seasoning the blend with delightful neologisms they devised at home. When they'd first met her, the Nerudas had laughed at her, asking if she thought their too-precise diction was vulgar compared to the shapeless blur of her upper-class speech. Ultimately, Judit had modified her own speech because of her contact with the poet and his wife, with Fausta and Celedonio and their circle, even imitating Neruda's slightly singsong cadence, with which he infected all his friends. She put away her comb and closed her bag.

"Judit!"

Lisboa, carrying an enormous wreath of white chrysanthemums with a hammer and sickle in red carnations, had stopped to say hello, and fell into an involuntary caricature by laying the funerary offering at her feet—the feet of a renegade. It was the principal wreath in the funeral, and carried by someone like him, would have a significant place among the other wreaths. To find that place was his mission, because—just like Ada Luz, thought Judit, again annoyed by the memory of her friend—Lisboa was only interested in the value of Matilde's death, not in the simple, devastating human fact; they both wanted to capitalize on it. Ada Luz use Matilde? How? Why? How was poor Ada Luz going to use Matilde? No, not Ada Luz, unless Lisboa dragged her into it. He would lay the wreath in a prominent place, transforming the ancient rite of death into a cheap power struggle.

"Yes, Lisboa?"

"Where's Adita?"

"She's making coffee in the dining room."

"Did she tell you . . . ?"

Staring at him, certain, very certain that he was setting a trap, Judit let a second pass. "Tell me what?"

"Weren't you talking in there?"

"Were you spying on us? What would we be talking about all alone?"

"About Miss Matilde's last wishes."

"No. I had no idea she had any. Why would she tell them to Ada Luz instead of to Fausta or to me? I'll ask her."

Lisboa grabbed her arm, with more force than necessary, and lying, explained, without Judit's believing a word, "I think she wanted something to be sung when her remains left this house. Adita and I thought that you might say something to Mañungo Vera . . ."

Judit blushed violently, then, irritated by what she'd done, answered, "I don't even know if Mañungo is going to come this morning. And I'm not close enough to him to ask for something like that."

She'd said Mañungo. Not Mañungo Vera, the way Lisboa did, the way the public, the morning papers—to which Mañungo Vera belonged—did. They were a couple, the two of them, the chosen ones. Anyone even modestly inspired would link them, these two, these individuals who did not feel the need to bow to the directives of political parties or social conventions to achieve heroic stature. All they needed was talent, beauty, arrogance, gratuitous gifts, like Mañungo's solitary air. They blazed their own trails, invented their own laws, Mañungo with his famous voice, Judit with her martyrdom, known to everyone, to the point of having made her a legend, a kind of lay saint of the left. No one had seen the horrible scars on her thighs. People said that to keep them hidden she had no male friends. Hadn't there been enough collective grief? Wasn't it time to head for Paris, far from danger?

"If Mañungo hasn't called this morning, I don't think he'll come. Probably he'll wait for the procession at the cemetery," said Judit.

Mañungo. His name echoed freely in the patio as Lisboa walked away. But she remained with the uncomfortable sensation of having answered the unasked question that he wanted to force her to answer, without knowing what the question was or what her answer told him.

30

. . . *A*nd I'll tell you something else, Freddy, he was a wizard with poetry who turned out to be a wizard with finance as well. Imagine, his widow is leaving a much larger fortune than you'll probably leave, with all your manipulations and shady deals. I don't even want to think about what people are going to say about this millionaire communist poet when they find out! It's simply going to destroy the right wing's preconceived notions. In any case, they always hated him and never understood him. And I think the lesson this poet's going to teach you bankers, economists, and entrepreneurs destroyed by your own debt-ridden system, while the widow of this Stalinist writer dies with an estate worth millions earned honestly from royalties, all for singing to conger-eel soup and onion salad with tomatoes, is just plain delightful. It's enough to make you die laughing, don't you think?

"And that money is just what he had in the bank, not including his property and his collections, his rare books for instance, whose value has gone up a hundredfold since he began to collect, unlike those stinking stocks and bonds of yours that fall and then aren't worth a cent. Comic, isn't it? I get a certain pleasure in imagining the expressions on the faces of the upright bourgeoisie when they hear this news. I wonder what this regime, which is in a shameful state of bankruptcy, will try to do to get its hands on the property of this barefoot boy from Temuco, who managed to reconcile his communism with the greatest honors a poet can receive as well as millions of dollars. It's hysterical—but of course, Pablo was an expert in shows like this, which only he understood and only worked when he put them on.

"When the authorities allow the Pablo Neruda Foundation to become a reality, we shall set it up here, just as Matilde stipulated in her will, in this house named after her. There will be a magazine to keep up, I suppose, and an imprint for poetry, giving lectures and inviting illustrious foreign authors to illuminate us, and giving scholarships to young writers, all with this house as a center, an international cultural institution. The star, of course, will be the library, with its incredible number of extremely rare editions.

"Holographs? No. Not many, I think. Pablo wasn't really interested in them, or in manuscripts either. He didn't even save many letters of his own, not even from important people. Not like me. I save mine because if I didn't I wouldn't be sure I exist. Yes, of course I have three or four letters from Trotsky. I told you last night. But I've changed my mind and I don't want to sell them because I don't plan to die just yet. My letters are from when Pablo had just reached Mexico and asked me to write in his name to Trotsky, to get in touch with him and possibly serve as a bridge between him and the Stalinists, who were going crazy.

"But his ecumenical spirit didn't last, I'll tell you, because right in the Hotel Montejo where he was staying, there was a meeting of the Stalinist Mexican writers and painters who hated Trotsky more than anything else in this world because they considered him counter-revolutionary and reactionary, an enemy of the first great country to become socialist: the sacred Soviet Union.

"These artists were all friends of Pablo's because they'd all fought in the Spanish Civil War, which brought so many to the New World. Well, it didn't take them long to pull him into the tidal wave of anti-Trotsky hatred. Before the month was out, Pablo asked me to stop writing to him. The whole problem came about because the Mexican Stalinists were angry with President Lázaro Cárdenas for having offered Trotsky asylum in Mexico and for giving police protection to the house in Coyoacán where he lived, which belonged to Diego Rivera and Frida Khalo, who were Trotskyists then. How could the Mexicans not hate Trotsky, Stalin's archenemy, when Stalin had helped the Republicans during the Civil War, a cause with which the Mexicans identified profoundly?

"They would swear that it was Trotsky, supported by Yankee money provided by the Hearst syndicate, who organized the uprising in Barcelona of the Trotskyists in the Workers Party for Marxist Unification. The uprising left five thousand dead, aside from diverting a force of thirty thousand men who should have been fighting General Franco to a useless confrontation. They declared that it was because of that debilitating lack of troops that the Ebro front collapsed, giving Catalonia and Spain itself to Franco. The Mexican Stalinists interpreted the defeat of the Republic as the direct consequence of Trotsky's intervention and Hearst's support of him from Mexico. So, they thought, Mexico was to blame for the defeat, because the Mexican government aided and protected the guilty party: it was a stain on the national honor some crazy Mexicans felt they were obliged to wash out by murdering Trotsky.

"Now don't go saying that Pablo was mixed up in that, Freddy, don't be a fool. I was there with him, and I know it just isn't true! He was friendly with some of the people who took part in the assassination, the ones who hung around the Hotel Montejo, but that's it. That much is clear in the letters of all the people who were there at the time. Now I remember: one day Siqueiros sent Pablo a present, the correspondence between Trotsky, Frida Khalo, and Diego Rivera, letters that directly linked Diego and Frida to the WPMU business in Barcelona. I haven't seen those letters for years and I don't even know where they are. No, he didn't buy them. Siqueiros gave them to Pablo, I already told you, intentionally too, because he hated Frida and Diego, for being Trotskyists and for other, dirtier reasons.

"People gave Pablo lots of things like that, things he kept only if he thought they were important, like the famous letters from Isabelle Rimbaud that Eluard gave him. How could you ever imagine I'd sell anything when it all belongs to the foundation! Are you mad? Last night I said I would? I doubt it. I don't remember. In any case, we old folks have a right to bad memory, to contradicting ourselves, and to changing our minds, so today I'm not selling them.

"Just to show how little Pablo cared for manuscripts, I'll tell you that once I went with him to a bookseller on Rue des Saints-Pères, a hole in the wall, tiny and dark, but the owner was one of the most important booksellers in Paris. Pablo had just read Mérimée's *Lokis*, and was very excited about that strange story of a werewolf that had fired the imagination of all the Romantics. Pablo's personal taste and pleasure was to read his favorite authors in exquisite editions—not luxurious editions, but authentic ones—and he asked the bookseller if he had a *Lokis*. The man answered that unfortunately a week ago he'd sold his *Lokis*, after having it collect dust in his shop for a decade without anyone's looking at it. Pablo wanted to know which edition it was, to which the bookseller, piqued in his professional pride, answered that what he had was no edition but the manuscript—the original, *bien sûr*—of *Lokis*. When Pablo, a bit disappointed, told him he wasn't interested in manuscripts, the bookseller went berserk, saying that an ignoramus like him, incapable of appreciating a Mérimée original, should not be in his store. Of course, if it had been a first edition, Pablo would have done anything to track it down and buy it on the spot! I don't mean on the spot, because he never carried much money. What he did was put a deposit on whatever interested him. It's a way of buying things that is greatly respected in France, I'll tell you, well, at least in my time it was. And later, when he had money he'd pay off the balance and take his books.

"I remember that in 1965 we—Pablo, Matilde, and I—were in their hotel room in Paris when he received a cable informing him that the money from the Viareggio Prize, seven thousand dollars, I think, had arrived at the bank. He instantly put the cable in his pocket, and Matilde and I watched from the window as he left the hotel with his characteristic shuffle to go to the bank to get his money. He was gone for an hour. He returned with his arms loaded with first editions that he'd put deposits on in different bookstores all over Paris, and that now the Viareggio Prize enabled him to pay off. Freddy, you can be sure that the quality of his library is really astonishing.

"I agree with you that here in Chile, since we have nothing, we think that all the attributions, the 'school of' stuff, the drawings from someone's worst period, are great, and that since we don't have anything else to inflate, as the kids say nowadays, we push everything local, from our tennis players and soccer stars to our earthquakes and revolutions—to say nothing of our poets and writers. Everything is inflated here, imitations, falsifications, but what can we do when there never was anything here? People don't even suspect the value of Pablo's library. Of course they also deflate things out of pure envy, or to try to get them cheaply if there's an auction. And there will be no auction, Freddy, let's get that straight.

"Me, inflate myself? Or someone else inflate me? Who, when no one remembers me? Even Fausta sometimes forgets I exist. And they're right to forget, because the final truth is that I haven't written anything that stands and I accept it. What does it matter? What are a pair of centuries or millennia of memory, when we think of the full extent of time? When I was young, I thought I was the Chilean Lautréamont. Why not, after all, when I loved his poetry so much that I accepted not having my own face? And later Mallarmé . . . and Saint-John Perse. I loved those literary masks I appropriated to the point of madness, just so I could feel I was alive. Poetry is eternal and will not disappear with the ages. I love it so much that at times I think loving it is a greater gift than writing it. When I really enjoy something, Quevedo, for example, I think that perhaps it's not so terrible not to be a great writer, but that it would be really horrible not to be able to love the melancholy and worm-eaten Quevedo, who after all says, 'Dying alive is the final sanity.' It must be terrible to be like you, poor Freddy, who only knows how much things cost, for whom that's their only value. How much does a sonnet by Quevedo cost, or an ode by Keats? Nothing: the superiority of literature is that it costs nothing. Poor Freddy! And how is your mother? She died? When? You don't say. And how lovely she was . . ."

31

*I*t was just ten and the funeral procession was to leave at eleven, the hottest hour of the day. More people came to say hello to don Celedonio, who was sitting under the yellow awning with his cigar in his mouth and his hands resting on the head of his cane. Later, everyone went upstairs to stand next to the coffin awhile before it was brought down. Under Lisboa's direction, the Communist Youth organized this operation, which involved some difficulties. They moved about in small murmuring groups, some at the top of the stairs, some in the kitchen, some in the patio, some in the street on the lookout for the hearse, some carrying red carnations in their hands as if they were extras in a Spanish operetta waiting for their cue to go onstage.

The ivy covering the rocks at the edge of the patio, the glossy bushes, the very ground, was moist, as if during the night the elves had watered everything so that it would be fresh for the last day of life in this house, which had begun to fill with journalists, disciples, polemicists, comrades in political and literary battles, quondam muses, and others who aspired to be muses for bards of the future. But despite the nocturnal misting, the patio was suffocating; a huge cyclone of flies spun madly at its center. Don Celedonio had always said to Pablo: Pablito, there are lots of flies around here, maybe the same ones that visit the monstrous red backsides of the mandrills in the zoo.

Pablo would tell how one night those extravagantly derrièred beasts escaped from their cages—a keeper had gotten drunk and left the doors unlocked—and invaded Bellavista, terrorizing kids out playing at nightfall by dropping onto their backs from trees and scaring the wits out of housewives by poking their horrible, sarcastic masks through the windows. The authorities finally cornered them in the woods up on the mountainside, where they had multiplied as if in their natural habitat. Some say they're preparing a second, more brutal, attack against Bellavista, which could not stand up to them and would finally submit to monkey rule. This fantasy was certainly nothing more than one of the inventions by which Pablo transfigured the world, although he would swear to the skeptics that at dawn he would wake up to the chattering of the descendants of those runaways who had "chosen freedom," using the cliché of the Yankee newspapers to describe Soviet dissidents who refused to go back to the Soviet Union.

Since don Celedonio was in for a long day, Fausta acted the part of the hostess, leaving the worthy poet resting in the care of Freddy and Judit so he could save what strength he had. Fausta was wearing a long dress that draped over her in tiers of such deep mourning it was almost operatic. Her congenital lack of sobriety, her theatrical arms, and her clanking jewelry all combined to make her look rather like a figure in an illustration ripped from a deluxe nineteenth-century edition of *Salammbô*. Judit could not help feeling some nostalgia for Fausta's exuberant vocation, while Freddy commented in her ear: "There is nothing more vulgar than a vulgar woman dressed in black."

But Freddy's understanding was limited by his good taste, and he was incapable of taking that perhaps fatal leap of the imagination. To Judit, however, on this ritual occasion to which she was rather alien, Fausta's costume seemed strangely appropriate, although her hem did raise a dust cloud as it dragged along the ground. Hadn't the essence of Celedonio's wisdom always been not only to tolerate everything Fausta did, but actually to celebrate her caprices without attempting to control them?

She said to Freddy, "Pablo was often criticized for the same thing. You reactionaries are the worst. It's as if you felt that with his intelligent lack of sectarianism, he was supporting you in your little games, although he was criticized for the same reason by the other extreme, the Party. They, of course, understood Pablo least of all, because the world of ideology is an essentially puritan world. For ideologues, there's no place in life for pleasure, art, poetry, not even in emotions or sensitivity—unless it is a *certain* emotion or a *certain* sensitivity—because for them artists shouldn't play or doubt, or contradict themselves, or be themselves, but should simply accommodate themselves to a given 'truth.' Everything is obligation, utility, pure *thanatos* and no *eros*.

"It's true that poor Pablo is leaving us an immense cultural legacy with his poetry, which may be immortal because it contains joy and play. But he also left other things, lesser, more mysterious things: the objects he collected, for example, with which he liked to surround himself to exercise some infantile part of him, something related to the greed all children have. He searched for those objects in every corner of the world. His talismans, his fetishes, symbols with obscure meanings, were the toys of the poor child who could only buy them when he was rich and older. In that act of possession, he realized his enjoyment of material things, of the gratuitous, the superfluous, of play, which has barely any place in the puritanical schemes of the ideologues, who have to justify everything rationally within one of their damned systems.

"One of Pablo's main traits was his antipuritanism. He was criticized so much for not being 'communist enough'! They just didn't understand the main point, that his sense of the banquet was something very ancient, a complex, extremely intelligent ritual, full of cultural echoes that went way beyond his 'elemental odes,' which were interpreted to be merely 'elementary' and folkloric. They are, in fact, a celebration that has nothing to do with the crass simplicity of the earthly man, the costume the left has tried to dress Pablo in to transform him into a wooden saint, in order to simplify his mischievous contradictions and his jokes. Do you remember when he bought a house with a beautiful old tile roof that everyone admired, and the first thing he did was remove the tiles and put on a zinc roof, to the horror of all the local aesthetes, who were concerned with 'our heritage,' and how he explained it by saying he liked to listen to the sound of rain on a tin roof . . . ?"

The three of them were still laughing as they recalled that incident, when Ada Luz came up to don Celedonio to offer him coffee, which, thought Judit, she's going to call "a nice little cup of coffee."

"Yes, thank you, Ada Luz," he answered.

"Would you like me to bring it here?"

Judit said that she and Freddy would also like some coffee, but that Ada Luz should not bring it to them in the patio because then all the guests would want some. They followed Ada Luz into the dining room. Lisboa opened the door, first letting in Fausta, who came as soon as she smelled the coffee, while Ada Luz went into the kitchen to put out some cups on a tray. A "nice little cup" for her too? she thought. No. It wasn't her place. She shouldn't even sit down at the other end of the long dining-room table. A little cup for Lisboa? What right did he have to come in here and sit down with "us"? To humiliate her, making her serve him as if she were his maid?

Lisboa felt superior to her, not because he'd made love to her last night—an acceptable enough reason, in fact—but because his disgustingly bullyish behavior had forced her to obey him and not communicate Miss Matilde's last wish to anyone: I'll kill you if you tell anyone, get me? Last night he'd spoken intimately to her in bed, his accent thickened by a dozen foreign languages, his body metallic with a desire devoid of tenderness: I'll kill you, Ada Luz, I'll never see you again, you'll be left alone forever thinking about me because you're too old to get another man, and you won't ever be able to see Daniel or your grandson unless I help you.

The coffee was boiling furiously and aromatically in the percolator. Ada Luz gave everyone cups, trembling because she anticipated that in the hour remaining before the procession departed something terrible was going to happen. She took Lisboa's cup off the tray. What right did he have? He'd made her swear she wouldn't say a word to anyone, not even to don Celedonio or doña Fausta or Judit. Why not to don Federico, for example, whose name Lisboa did not mention in his rage, and who was now pensively stirring the cup she'd put in front of him? How long ago was it—a week—since Miss Matilde had whispered her dying wish that a revolutionary priest say a graveside mass? And she, the fool, had said nothing to anyone because she hadn't thought it important until last night, when she'd told Lisboa on the stairs. Stupid, for confiding in him.

How was she supposed to see so many political sides to a remark made by a dying woman? It could drive you nuts! But it was also true that last night on the same stairs Lisboa had taught her that no remark made by the widow of Pablo Neruda, the Nobel laureate and winner of the Stalin Prize, was a mere remark. She'd felt the force of the hurricane that was dragging her into an intrigue so much greater than her modest stature that she couldn't hope to understand it, control it, or defend herself from it. Lisboa could, Judit could, but she couldn't. She put a glass of water in front of Lisboa, the way he liked it with his coffee, because he'd lived in Europe, and then brought coffee to the other end of the table, where don Federico was spouting off about the foundation. He was saying that he had no idea if there was any way to speed up the judicial process to authorize the foundation, but that he was offering his influence, his millions, his power, his good offices to free the papers from the sordid bureaucratic trap into which they'd fallen. It would be difficult, given the political situation, but he would do whatever it was in his power to do.

"How much will you charge to bring it off, Freddy?" asked Judit.

"I'm not doing it for money. I'm doing it as an homage to Pablo and Matilde."

"Don't make me laugh."

"Now, Judit," said don Celedonio placatingly. "What do you know about all this? Freddy might save us. Sit down and be quiet, Judit. Now, Freddy . . ."

Judit sat down, angrily explaining to Fausta and don Celedonio that not only could Freddy help with the processing of the papers for the foundation, but that whether things moved forward or not depended entirely on him; that this venal reactionary, this thug of the regime, had the power to destroy the Nerudas' marvelous dream, which was something intellectually sound and on another plane from the one where the low, provincial, mean-spirited, neocolonial projects to which they were accustomed in Chile took place. That was why Freddy's attitude pained her.

"What attitude, Judit?" demanded Fausta.

In this country, she answered, everything was done through influence and the old-boy system, so everyone felt close to power, felt he had the right and obligation to exercise it. Freddy had the papers for the Neruda Foundation stopped in order to invalidate Pablo's project, not only because of an obscure, idiosyncratic species of envy, but because it involved a project that came from the people they called communists and who were nothing more than the critics of this regime. Freddy stopped the project, said Judit, out of pure hatred . . .

"How well you understand me, dear cousin! And so you should, after all, we share the same blood! But don't be so definitive. Remember that this morning I told you I was willing to look the other way and help if . . ."

"I don't understand you, Freddy," said Fausta.

"It's simple," explained Judit, crackling with indignation and sitting down again. "On the one hand we have his ideas: it's not good for him or the regime if the Neruda Foundation goes forward, because it will have continental significance and bring prestige to the Communist Party. What I'm trying to tell you is, this morning Freddy called to tell me that he would be willing to betray what we might call his political ideals just a bit if it was worth his while. In other words, a bribe. A vulgar bribe."

"What do you want more money for, Freddy?" asked don Celedonio.

"He doesn't want money. He wants Trotsky's letters."

"You can have mine as long as you speed up the approval."

"No," said Freddy. "I don't want yours—which doesn't mean I'm not interested in them. Someday they'll be mine. If you can include them in the deal, so much the better. But the ones I want, which I've been after for years, are the letters from Trotsky to Diego Rivera and Frida Khalo, in which he incriminates half of Mexico and maybe half of Latin America in the massacre of the anarchists in the WPMU in Barcelona."

"They belong to the foundation."

"You said that the inventory was still incomplete and that no one has seen them."

"Are you suggesting we steal those letters and give them to you, in exchange for your intervention with the government?" asked Fausta, stupefied.

Someone knocked on the glass door. Lisboa, who had been listening attentively to the conversation, stood up and let in a boy from the Communist Youth, who came to announce the arrival of ex-Senator Gualterio Larrañaga, who was extremely old and who had just returned from exile. The boy suggested to all present that it would be polite to invite him to have coffee with them.

"No," said Ada Luz from her corner, putting her knitting down on a chair.

"Why not?"

"Because it's ten-fifteen and the procession has to leave here at eleven. There's no time."

Lisboa started to leave the dining room, intending to greet the old leader with the respect due a man whose importance these frivolous creatures, all arguing about a pile of moth-eaten papers, were incapable of understanding. Picking up his empty cup, Ada Luz brushed Lisboa with the tray as he was angrily stalking out; the tray fell and the cups and crystal sugar bowl smashed to pieces on the floor. Lisboa did not deign to look back as he ground the sugar and the bits of glass with his heavy shoes; nor did he pay any attention to Ada Luz's anguish as she crouched down, sniveling, to pick up the pieces.

"What's that matter with you?" asked Judit, coming over to help.

"Nothing."

"Lisboa . . . ?"

The name made Ada Luz stand up abruptly so she wouldn't hear it, sobbing now, her face streaming with tears. And blowing her nose, she addressed don Celedonio, Fausta, and Freddy while Judit went to the kitchen to get a broom.

"I'm sorry . . . I'm sorry!" implored Ada Luz, whimpering as if she were standing before a judge about to pass sentence.

"But it's nothing, dear! Why get so upset?" said Fausta magnanimously, as she took her last sip of coffee and looked at her watch. "It's ten-twenty. The hearse should be getting here any minute. Ada Luz, dearest, please tell them to bring the coffin down now. What's wrong, child, for God's sake? Why cry over such a silly thing?"

Ada Luz's outburst was so strangely tempestuous that it canceled all other concerns. Judit left her broom and went to comfort her at the corner window. She wasn't crying about the sugar bowl, she stammered, but because she was sorry she'd kept quiet until now and told that awful Lisboa. He'd made her keep quiet. If it hadn't been for the threats of that communist, she would have told everything days ago, she lied, and she lied to herself as a consolation.

"See how the communists are involved in everything?" said Freddy, amused with the spectacle, which was turning into *marivaudage*, replete with serving girls in love and stolen documents—all the conventions of the genre.

"Shut up, Freddy! Tell us what, Ada Luz?" asked Fausta, impatient with all this intrigue that did not promise a very interesting denouement because the characters were so seedy.

Collapsing into a chair, hanging her head, and twisting her green knitting in her hands, Ada Luz told the whole story, punctuated with whines and hiccups: extreme unction in Texas and the desire Matilde had expressed near the end, that a priest, one of the ones living in the slums, say a graveside mass.

"Why did she tell Ada Luz and not me?" blurted out Fausta, showing her outrageously wounded pride.

Don Celedonio stood up and paced back and forth in the dining room, leaning on his cane and limping painfully, as he always did when he was upset. The sound of sugar crushed under his shoes made Ada Luz raise her head, but when she heard don Celedonio declare that what they'd just heard was something of the greatest seriousness, something that could have enormous significance in the political history of the nation, she buried her face in her knitting. The old man asserted that the matter was doubly important at this instant because they had about half an hour to carry out Matilde's wish and no one was doing anything . . .

Someone said it was already too late.

The minor poet insisted that perhaps it was still possible to do something. If the procession left at eleven as planned they would have

an hour, the hour it would take to get to the cemetery on foot behind
the hearse, an hour during which they, her intimate friends, could
get organized to have a mass said there in the chapel at the cemetery,
with the whole crowd taking part. It would be marvelous! The authorities would be shocked out of their wits! The opposition united
in a political action under the sign of the cross!

Fausta interrogated Ada Luz about the details of what Matilde had
said to her, without bothering to hide her unbearable jealousy of the
modest recipient of such a magnificent confidence, given perhaps
because of debilitation to someone who wasn't able to appreciate its
true worth. Out of ignorance, Ada Luz would not only have wasted
Matilde's intentions but a whole range of political implications that
could point the way to consolidation and moderation. Judit, not as
comforting as she'd been a moment before, shook Ada Luz by the
shoulders, asking her what right she thought she had to keep silent.

"Lisboa. He threatened me."

Instead of answering, Ada Luz threw herself into Judit's arms, repeating Lisboa's name again and again disconnectedly. She was in
love, poor thing. How stupid! What follies we commit for love! Would
Judit be capable of undoing herself like that for Mañungo? She trembled as she answered no. In any case, not even Ramón, when it had
been all comradeship and enthusiasm, the cause and martyrdom, with
the appropriately desolate tears. Not even then had love disordered
her thinking to such an extent. It was so . . . so glandular that it was
profoundly repulsive. And, who was Ada Luz, anyway? Why had she
suddenly turned into an important figure in Pablo's house, when he'd
never even known her? She was an intruder, a hysteric.

This was the same conclusion reached by everyone in the room—
none of whom was completely free of envy. Fausta was whispering to
Freddy that Ada Luz was not old enough to understand things like
this, when she saw Celedonio make a sign that she indeed understood.
After looking through her address book, she called a priest who was
a friend of hers, one who lived in a slum, the kind who ends up shot
by "person or persons unknown," and whose death leaves a bullet
hole surrounded by a commemorative, anonymous chalk circle on the
wall. "The plague of the Church," murmured Freddy, "priests who
only spread confusion, since everything would be so clearly black or
white without their interference!" He pressed his index finger on the
table to pick up the bits of sugar spilled there, and then sucked his
finger. Fausta hung up.

"He's out," she said.

"There's no time left," noted Freddy.

"Call another priest, Fausta," urged don Celedonio.

Just when Fausta had begun to dial, Freddy stood up. He walked over and softly took the telephone out of her hands; she, shocked, gave it up without resisting. He stood coiling and uncoiling the cord as he spoke.

"Don't call," Freddy said, in the tone of someone advising a very dear friend.

"Don't listen to him!" exclaimed Judit.

"Call, call," shrieked Ada Luz from her chair, raising her streaming face. "For God's sake, call so that poor Miss Matilde's soul can be saved. She's going to hell and it's my fault and I want God's forgiveness!"

"Don't call," commanded Freddy, holding back Fausta's hand by force as she was starting to dial another number. "I know this matter of the mass is important. Since the communists as yet do not have the Pope's permission to say mass, although the way things are going I'm sure they will, you can see that they plan to turn Matilde's funeral into one of their carnivals. Which might be good for my side, since these spontaneous carnivals always end up a disaster for the people who organize them. What we have to avoid is Matilde's being turned into a flag for the united opposition, because nothing should unite the opposition. That would be worse than any carnival. Perhaps Ada Luz's discretion has saved us. Don't call anyone, Fausta."

"On the contrary. After what you've just said, I'm even more willing to do it. Let go of my hand, Freddy! Let me go, unless you want me to have you thrown out of here!"

"So that the newspapers can say the distinguished financier Federico Fox was vilely thrown out of our Nobel laureate's house by extremists? No. You're not going to throw me out. It doesn't suit your purposes," he said, laughing, and he released her wrist, although he still played with the cord.

"It's twenty minutes to eleven," said Fausta, dialing another number. "No time for your schemes, Freddy."

After releasing her, Freddy sat down on the end of the dining-room table to watch while Fausta dialed numbers and got no answers. The table groaned under his weight. He was nervous, and as he talked, he unwound the black telephone cord which was wrapped around the table leg. He spoke so serenely that Fausta stopped dialing to listen to him, even though she never took her finger off the dial.

"Don't call, Fausta. This is my last proposition. I'm telling you this is my last offer, and if you don't take it, well, the next step is open war. This is it: if you don't call your priest to say the mass, I swear by my sainted mother that I'll go straight from here to my office and within a half hour I'll have signed the documents that authorize the Pablo Neruda Foundation, papers that at this very minute are—and for a long time now have been—on my desk waiting for my decision. These people, as you no doubt understand, are quite primitive and don't understand much about these matters, so they turn them over to me. As soon as I sign the papers, I name myself administrator of the foundation, and under my guidance things will proceed smoothly. In exchange for that, you, the so-called moderates, the most dangerous people, must not organize a graveside mass, but instead let the communists run the show and, if they so choose, create a minor disturbance."

"What's your price?" asked Judit. "That we should rob the Trotsky letters from Neruda's estate to pay you off?"

Freddy laughed. As he spoke he tied a complicated noose with the black telephone cord without watching what his nervous hands were doing. He said, "Bascially, and despite the terrible things you've been through, you really are simple, Judit. The Trotsky letters and all the other things we've been talking about here only have a secondary importance compared to something else—which is my keeping power, defending it, not letting it go for any reason or any price. I'm resigned to losing the Trotsky letters . . . for the time being. They must be marvelous, and I hope, Celedonio, that someday you can show them to me. I'm very sorry you don't want to sell them to me, or . . . cede them to me. But I'm happy because this time I've made a good purchase: I've bought your silence, for which I give you your little foundation."

They didn't have to think it over. Freddy's cynicism was suffocating. No doubt the part about the mass—in the hypothetical case that it could be organized, which, as time went by, became more and more doubtful—would be eye-catching, but a bit, let's say, ephemeral. It would vanish in a day of effusive enthusiasm and then, like everything else in this country, even crimes, be hushed up, forgotten with the perpetration of an even greater crime. The foundation, on the other hand, was something solid, real, a beacon for the generations that would be able to enjoy and learn in this very house, where everything, thanks to Pablo's legacy, would become coherent and positive. Were they selling out by opting for silence with regard to the mass that was Matilde's last wish—at least according to that unidentifiable character Ada Luz and no one else? It was worth selling out at that price.

Once they'd decided the matter among themselves—without consulting Ada Luz, who had fallen asleep like a drug addict on her nest of green wool—don Celedonio asked Freddy, "Are we all scum, then? Do all of us have our price?"

"If you don't know it yet at your age and with all you've lived through, you'll never know it, Celedonio. In any case, let's not get melodramatic . . ."

"I agree. If you do what you promised, I'll give you my own Trotsky letters as a consolation prize. My poor four letters are nothing compared to the Frida and Diego letters, but they're better than nothing."

Don Celedonio was not so old that he couldn't see the irony in Freddy's eyes as he thanked him for his gift. He decided that the first thing he'd do when he got home would be to burn his Trotsky letters, because they didn't even have the modest value he attributed to them since they moved Freddy to laughter and were nothing but a placebo for him. He was, after all, a man who only dealt with grand-scale items. Nevertheless, the financier said to him, "I'll get them from you at the appropriate time."

Through the door they saw that in the last few minutes a multitude had congregated in the patio as the time approached for the procession of people to depart. Judit went over to wake up Ada Luz to go pick up Marilú and bring her to the cemetery.

"Lisboa," called Fausta, as she looked at her watch.

"Yes?"

"It's a quarter to eleven. They should bring the coffin down now."

"Who's going to bring it down?"

They all looked at each other, hating each other.

"The kids from the Communist Youth," decided don Celedonio, and Lisboa went to give the order.

"Good," said Freddy.

"Good," agreed don Celedonio.

"But what assurance do I have," asked Freddy suddenly, still sitting on the table, "that as soon as I turn my back you won't call one of your communist priests?"

"Freddy, for God's sake!"

"How could you think such a thing?"

"Of course I could think of such a thing. Nowadays business is just not done by two gentlemen shaking hands. It's all opportunism, scheming. Anything can happen," said Freddy, and, giving a savage pull on the telephone wire he'd been playing with, he yanked it right out of the wall, pulling out a chunk of plaster with it. He explained, "To avoid temptation."

Fausta's shout of surprise and her sobs were instantaneous, and with her face covered with tears of terror she went running up the staircase, the blazing sun beating down on her. Her sobs were audible from below.

She moved her lips a bit automatically, as if blending her memory of an almost-forgotten prayer with the prayers of the women upstairs who were reciting the traditional litanies of grief around the coffin.

Judit stayed downstairs, watching how they awkwardly carried that melancholy box. She thought about the stiffness of last night's little white dog, which she'd abandoned as if it were a wooden toy, and about Matilde's body, also stiff by now, which for the last time would be knocking about inside the coffin, in the silken white cocoon of death.

32

◆As Mañungo left the elevator, leading Jean-Paul by the hand, he saw Lopito leaning on the check-in counter, asking the desk clerk something. His first impulse was to protect himself from Lopito, turn around to avoid him or ask if there was another way out of the hotel so he wouldn't have to face his friend. His second impulse, parallel to realizing that it was absurd to be afraid of Lopito, because he'd probably forgotten the little scene at Judit's house, was to protect Jean-Paul from his friend's resentment, which had doubtless been building since Mañungo had returned to Chile. When had he returned? Sixteen, eighteen hours ago? Incredible! Everything had taken place in the small space of eighteen hours! Even his fantastic intention to get married, concocted by his son while he was alone, but whose doubtful aspects were now troubling Mañungo.

He walked toward Lopito, who did not see him. To go to Matilde's funeral with him was not the most attractive idea; nor was it the most solemn idea for an occasion that demanded solemnity. Lopito would no doubt take charge of him, administer him, tell him which persons to greet, which not to greet, which women were willing and which only looked that way: in sum, monopolize him, and above all, keep him from any spontaneous contact with the old friends he'd probably run into after so long, all of whom would be delighted to share in his rediscovery of the city.

Just before he tapped Lopito on the shoulder and put a benign smile of welcome on his lips, he was taken by a desire he had to repress: to flee with his son directly to Chiloé to hear the rain pattering on the roof and to relearn, alongside the elders next to the fire, the endless, eternal stories, polished like stones that have been rolled and rolled, and not to face this sad day in the company of Lopito, to attend this funeral which a sordid political struggle was going to empty of genuine emotion.

"Lopito . . . !"

Lopito spun around as if he were being attacked, as if his whole life were summed up in that poor gesture of defense. As soon as he recognized his friend, he lowered his implicit guard and greeted him affectionately. Mañungo had Jean-Paul next to him, clinging to his hand. The boy looked at Lopito with the awe of someone confronted with a natural phenomenon that might turn out to be dangerous.

"Is this Juan Pablo?" asked Lopito.

"Juan Pablo, this is my good friend Lopito."

"Bonjour, monsieur."

Juan Pablo. Not the sarcastic, ill-pronounced Jean-Paul: the olive branch offered as a morning pledge of his good intentions, repentance, contrition. Things might not work out so badly if he maintained this attitude. It was clear that he intended to erase the scene at Judit's house and begin over. He had arrived scrupulously clean, his hair recently moistened and parted in the middle, like a boy going to school, before the fights of the day alter that neatness: tie, polished shoes, everything about him announced good intentions. His little eyes, whose ends sagged toward his temples, did not shine as they usually did because his pupils, two opaque fish scales, hid guiltily beneath his thick eyelids. Juan Pablo continued to scrutinize him as if he were an animal in the zoo, noting what was different about him.

Yes, explained Lopito, he'd come to get them because Santiago had grown a lot over the last few years, and they'd never get to the cemetery on their own. Didn't they think it was utterly charming of him to take such care of them? Lopito wheezed a lot as he spoke, but Mañungo remembered that he'd always wheezed, and besides, he'd just lit another cigarette.

"Guess who I've brought," he demanded triumphantly.

For a terrible second, Mañungo feared that Lopito, who took pleasure in creating difficult situations for his friends, had managed to bring Judit along. Aside from his own discomfort at facing her in the company of others for the first time since last night without first clearing up their relationship, it would mean having to explain the presence of his enemy to Jean-Paul. He would find a way to make the day unbearable, when in the best of circumstances it was not going to be the easiest day in his life.

"Who?"

"Moira."

At first Mañungo didn't recognize the name. Lopito realized it and cleared things up: "Moira López."

Of course. How could he have forgotten that pretentious name, suitable only for a prima ballerina from Havana and New York? Of course she had another, more picturesque name, appropriate for a risqué cabaret singer: Lopita. He tried to react positively at this news, but he was sure her presence would make the morning even more unbearable, and Jean-Paul even more difficult, especially if Lopita was as ugly as he imagined. Lopito was bright red, like a fiancé bringing his provincial girlfriend to meet his high-toned parents. Lopito added that he'd brought her not only so she could be a part of Matilde's funeral, but so she could meet Juan Pablo and play with him.

"Where is she?" asked Mañungo.

"Right over there," answered Lopito in a low voice, as if he didn't want to disturb anyone, pointing to a far-off corner of the lobby. "She's watching television. She loves it, and we don't have one."

Mañungo and Jean-Paul (who still clung to his father's hand) turned their heads simultaneously. Sitting in a dark corner of the room, as calm as a doll on an enormous satin ottoman, watching television with her back to them, was a little girl dressed in red muslin, with two stiff, thin tresses tied with white ribbons hanging down her back. Ecstatic, she seemed to hold her breath in order not to miss anything happening on the screen. Mañungo told Jean-Paul to go say hello to her and bring her over, because he wanted to meet Moira López.

When he saw the boy about to follow his father's order, Lopito immediately took the boy by the hand. Lopito's expression had changed: he smiled with such real sweetness that the boy couldn't help smiling back. Then, still holding Jean-Paul's hand, Lopito bent down in front of him, asking him softly, "You won't laugh at her if you think she's ugly, will you? No, because you're enough of a man not to make her suffer. Besides, she might amuse you by doing pirouettes, which she already knows how to do, because she wants to be a ballerina when she's big. I won't deny that the poor thing looks a bit ridiculous doing entrechats, but I think they could give her comic or scary parts. Go on, Juan Pablo. You're intelligent and understand what I'm asking. Well, she's smart too and understands everything. More than she should for her age, poor kid. But don't laugh at her, because I've convinced her she's beautiful. Understand? Good, I wanted to tell you so you would, even though I know you only understand French. Go on . . ."

Mañungo gave his hand to Lopito to help him get up, because he seemed crippled and old, and told him at the same time he shouldn't talk that way to children. Fortunately Juan Pablo didn't understand Spanish, so he couldn't understood any of the silly things Lopito had said about Lopita. The best thing was to let the kid act naturally, because if an adult told him something he'd go right out and do the opposite. Besides, Jean-Paul was sufficiently civilized to behave himself with a little girl he'd just met. He told Jean-Paul, pointing to Moira López, who still hadn't seen them:

"Vas-y, donc. Elle s'appelle Moira."

They stood there watching him, the desk clerk included. Juan Pablo walked quickly away from them, dodging around an ottoman, an armchair, a little table, but as soon as he came closer to the girl, his steps slowed until he was right behind her, standing there while she continued to stare at the television screen. Then he touched her shoulder. The little girl turned around. Mañungo couldn't see her from where he stood, so he could not evaluate the accuracy of Lopito's description. He could see, on the other hand, that sitting there, wrapped in layers of muslin on the ottoman, the girl was talking to Juan Pablo, moving her little hands for emphasis, touching him gently, explaining, and Juan Pablo stared at her and listened, astonished and attentive.

Still speaking, she got up from the ottoman. She rapidly spun around so that her tresses and skirts would stand straight out as she turned. Then she bowed to her new friend and sat back down, making room for Juan Pablo to sit next to her. Which he did instantly. The two fathers stayed where they were and didn't call them over, even though time was passing and they might be late for the funeral. They were absorbed in watching the silhouettes of their children framed by the television screen. Sitting with her back to them on the ottoman, Moira López went on talking, as if she were explaining what was happening on the screen, gesturing so charmingly with her caressing little hands that Jean-Paul laughed out loud.

"The first time since we reached Chile," said Mañungo.

"A good sign," agreed Lopito.

Mañungo was worried that his son had laughed at Moira López, which was just what he shouldn't do. Her father sensed Mañungo's discomfort and told him not to worry, because he was an expert in the kinds of laughter his daughter produced—whether people were laughing with her or at her—and that laugh, he assured Mañungo, meant that Jean-Paul was laughing with her, which was beautiful. The children got off the ottoman—Juan Pablo taking Moira López by the hand, for which she thanked him with a curtsy—turned off the television, and came toward their fathers.

"The vulgar things her mother teaches her, that dumb Flora, so she can be in some bullshit mime show in the neighborhood," explained Lopito.

"She's charming!" lied Mañungo.

"How do you do?" she said. "You're Jean-Paul's daddy?"

She pronounced the boy's French name carefully, as if she'd just learned it, and, being a good student, had spent the morning practicing it.

"Yes. And you must be Moira López."

"Yes. It's a ballerina's name. Isn't that so, Jean-Paul?"

"Yes," he answered, in Spanish.

Lopita was in fact exceptionally ugly. The Asiatic antiquity of her face, as long and dark as her father's, made her head seem a superfluous excrescence attached to her delicate trunk and skinny seven-year-old's legs. Her gums were prominent and red like her father's, and her nose rough and long. The oriental slits of her eyes were so narrow that at first Mañungo could not see her soul in them. But when Lopita smiled, explaining the movie about kings and queens they'd been watching on TV, the light of meanings hidden in appearances shone through, and intelligence transformed her ugly little girl's face into a glorious grotesque mask.

Mañungo and Juan Pablo had seen masks like hers on Gothic cornices and peeking out from shadowy corners in Italian gardens, and it was easy to recognize in her the prospect of style and admire her for it. Besides, she was dressed with such care, so immaculate, her hair perfectly arranged with not a lock out of place, moist and redolent of cologne. Her ugliness incarnated an abstract perfection not very far from beauty. Her smile, as she took her father's hand, was so trusting that it seemed she wanted to calm with her joy the insecurity that plagued Lopito: it was she, not Lopito, who had learned to live with insecurity.

Jean-Paul spoke first: *"Son papa dit qu'elle est moche, mais ce n'est pas vrai. Elle n'est pas moche du tout. Elle est étrange, comme un personnage de fabliau, plutôt mignonne, comme un gnome. Ou une gnomesse. Gnomesse est le féminin de gnome, papa? Elle est rigolette. Je comprends tout ce qu'elle dit . . ."*

"We've got a wedding on our hands," said Mañungo, laughing, more than a little concerned.

"You'd like me to be your son's father-in-law?"

"*Allons-y, papa?*"

"*Où ça?*"

"*Au cimetière.*"

"*Je croyais que tu ne voulais pas y aller.*"

"*Je veux voir la révolution dont Moira parle.*"

"My kid's very politicized."

"*Et le couvre-feu,*" added Juan Pablo enthusiastically.

"*And it will fall . . . and it will fall,*" Lopita began to sing and clap. "Shall we be on our way to the revolution, Jean-Paul?"

"*Je peux aller avec Lopita, papa?*"

"*Elle s'appelle Moira.*"

"*Elle m'a dit de l'appeler Lopita si je veux.*"

"*Bon.*"

"Shall we go?" invited Lopito.

And they walked toward the front door, the two children holding hands and skipping in front of their fathers, who followed behind, pleased.

33

*T*he gray cars with opaque windows had to be the last word in sophistication. They'd probably existed before, but it was only recently that people began to notice them, parked here and there next to ordinary vehicles, hidden among them. Their windows were not completely opaque, only the upper part, in order to hide the faces of those inside, whose job was even more ominous than their cars. Rumor had it that they were in radio contact with a data base that could instantly tell them everything about the people flocking to the cemetery this morning. The black windows only masked the faces of the passengers, revealing their headless, mannequin bodies sitting with their muscular arms folded over their chests, waiting for the signal to do something to the crowds that filled the side streets leading to Avenida Recoleta, going to Matilde Neruda's funeral, crowds that passed the gray cars without daring to mention them.

They were not afraid to comment on the big green trucks standing on the streets near the cemetery, bristling with helmeted silhouettes carrying automatic weapons, nor on the uniformed men standing guard on the corners. People would stop to buy ice cream, a fuchsia balloon for a child, a bag of peanuts, a package of popcorn, juices, pink and yellow marzipan, nougat, the corn-and-peach drink called *mote con huesillos*—all being hawked—and stare unblinkingly at the feared agents, although these were not as feared as the ones with their faces hidden behind car windows. What were they going to do, what was their specific job on a day like this?

People had been seeing lots of gray cars in different parts of the city, waiting for something, observing, ready to give secret alarms and contact each other with instruments as mysterious as butterfly antennae. Only rarely did they enter the slums, where night after night barricades made of old tires burned and made noxious fumes, and where the walls of some tin or wooden shacks could boast bullet holes surrounded by the famous chalk circle that marked the bullet guilty of an unsolved, unforgiven murder. They took up stations around the houses of important leaders on days when there would be protests or strikes, in the tranquil middle-class neighborhoods, hidden under trees at intersections, or patrolling a corner where someone was abandoned by kidnappers, or near the place where a nonexistent bomb was supposed to go off.

Hidden eyes watched the amputee get off the Matadero-Palma bus. After the passengers got off at the corner of the cemetery, the amputee, joking with the driver, lowered himself with his long, simian arms onto the bottom step and then, placing his skateboard on the street, lowered his trunk onto it. Happily waving goodbye to the driver—someone hidden behind the gray windows wrote down the number of the bus— he pushed off with the palms of his hands. Skirting the insane traffic jam, he melted into the crowds on the sidewalk.

The taxi had left Mañungo, Lopito, and the children several blocks away from the cemetery. They preferred it that way because the traffic on the other side was getting heavy. Since they were a bit early, Lopito suggested they walk along the extremely *criollo* avenue so that Mañungo could Chileanize himself again. He doubted the value of this process, given the country's situation: our only destiny, nowadays, seems to be to disappear, bound, gagged, persecuted, and enslaved, Lopito said. The only thing left was to become a nihilist and renounce any ideology that promised solutions. What good was it to look for peaceful solutions when all the answers came from machine guns? What possibilities did Mañungo see in this passive, submissive crowd around them? Didn't he realize that their misery had reached the point where the regime had them completely under control, that it would be easy to conquer them, not to say seduce or buy them, with a glass of *mote con huesillos* or with the perverse aroma of blood sausages roasting over charcoal on the sidewalk, or with a joke that ridiculed a government minister? These innocents sweeping them along in their stinking tide of sweaty clothes—as if the heat didn't make Lopito smell—led lives saturated with politics, which acted like an acid and was devouring them. In love, art, business, even in death, as they were seeing right now, it was impossible to avoid politics, although it was also impossible to take part in politics, because the regime had a monopoly on it. And so, without the chance to be exercised, political ideas and passions wasted away and became impoverished in a kind of prolonged verbal masturbation.

"For example," Lopito continued, "let's start talking right now about any subject you like. About our friend Schumann, for instance, who —leaving aside all this bullshit—means more to you and me than this goddam social justice thing. Okay, how many minutes do you think our conversation would last without turning to politics?"

Lopito's hair, until now held in place by his morning ablutions, was sticking up again. From time to time, he would speed up, breathing with difficulty, fearful that the children running ahead would get lost. He stopped at a stand to offer a glass of *mote con huesillos* to Mañungo, who didn't dare accept, although he paid for the *mote*, along with Coca-Colas for himself and Jean-Paul, while Lopita hesitated at the prospect of the seductively cool bottle of imported stuff. But when she saw the pleasure with which her father was drinking his *mote*, she opted for the local product.

"Like to try some, Juan Pablo?" offered Lopito.

"I don't think so," intervened Mañungo. "We were told to watch out for salmonella."

"Right, salmonella," murmured Lopito, holding himself back with an almost visible effort from rushing headlong toward the sarcasm this theme invited. "Is your *mote* good, sweetheart?"

"Delicious."

On the corners, the crowd buying flowers carefully divided into two streams to go around policemen carrying automatic rifles, and then joined together again once they'd passed them. Bam, bam, bam! his guitar/machine gun/sex would fire from the stage. But his shots never got anyone except for a few pretty little lovebirds that flew too low . . . until both he and those lovebirds became skeptical of his bullets. These automatic rifles, on the other hand, were for real and killed without having to justify a single shot. Would they attack today, with or without reason? wondered Mañungo in horror, asking himself if the same thought wasn't going through the heads of all the thousands of people who'd come to Matilde's funeral.

Three flashily dressed gypsy women pushed their way against the flow of the thick crowd, indifferent to the event that congregated this river of people who belonged to a cultural sector with martyrs and saints different from theirs. No one was interested in having his fortune told, because today everyone had other business, so babbling away in their sticky Central European dialect, whirling beads and skirts, they faded into the crowd, which paid them no attention. Near the entrance to the cemetery, Lopito began to see friends: bar poets, nightcrawlers who had turned out for the occasion, neighborhood muses, drunks, perpetual students, militants in ephemeral political parties to which Lopito had briefly belonged, a few kids with red T-shirts on or carrying some red emblem, even if it was nothing more than a carnation.

Lopito went along shouting out that in his opinion, the most odious part of all this was optimism: "Look here, Mañungo, this bit about carrying red flowers—where do they get off doing that? The next thing is for them to start singing 'Little Red Carnations'! They think they can convince people that everything is going to be okay, and every time the regime has a setback, they start it with 'See? They're on the way out.' But they're not on the way out, even though stadiums full of people chant 'It's going to fall' during soccer matches. Every horror and scandal just gets forgotten and everything stays the same, wrapped up and monolithic, despite the cracks that lead to the monotonous replacement of one politician by another who's exactly the same."

We all have shorter index fingers now, Lopito was saying, like those Spanish Republicans who pounded their fingers against the table for forty years saying "This year Franco's going to fall . . . this year Franco's going to fall," and the useless wear they caused by banging on the table made their index fingers shorter. And Franco didn't fall, and the poor pinkos were left with their hopes rotting inside them while their leaders died or changed passions and ideas. Which is just what was happening to the Chileans who stubbornly refused to lose hope, the very thing they *had* to lose to begin over from zero, to bear the burden of despair that manifested itself in sporadic outbursts of senseless violence which the regime's repression pushed them to.

Mañungo was very tall, rare for a native of Chiloé, the only man in the crowd whose hair hung to his shoulders, a solitary silhouette in a crowd of pygmies. A group of silly high school girls followed him, giggling. They too stopped at the food stands across from the coffin shops near the Catholic Cemetery, and the girls surrounded Mañungo asking him if he really was who he seemed to be. The idol, smiling his contagious bunny smile, a bit timidly, as he knew they liked it, said he was. They crossed toward the General Cemetery, skirting the enraged buses that almost tipped over on their screeching tires as they went around the corner, with a tail of girls who, when they reached the other sidewalk, among the kiosks overflowing with verbenas, carnations, and gladioli, besieged him waving notebooks and paper to get his autograph. They called more and more and more kids over. Then the curious and not-so-young began to recognize him when they heard his name, and they began to cheer. Boys with red T-shirts on tried to break up the crowds of fans waving paper and pushing their way to the idol, who now refused to sign because there were too many people asking.

The best thing, said the Communist Youth boys, would be for them to carry him out on their shoulders. No thanks, said Mañungo: he preferred to make his way on his own. The horde of kids still followed him, touching him softly at first, in the way people touch the robes on a sacred image, throwing flowers at him, although amid the flowers there was a dirtball that fortunately missed. The crowd called him by name, putting flowers in his hair, in his clothes, pulling his hair, his clothes, tearing them, more flowers, more pats on the back, an occasional slap, an occasional stone, shoves that were more and more violent from the compact mass of admirers against whom he could not defend himself because it was impossible to know what they wanted from him. Sweaty and tousled, he tripped and fell to the ground, where he was promptly trampled.

Two policemen carrying automatic rifles opened their way through the crowd, the black muzzles of their rifles like the noses of bloodhounds. The furious multitude around Mañungo calmed down when they saw them, parting so they could get through. The men in uniform helped him up while the spectators shouted, who knows for what reason, *Ma-ñun-go . . . Ma-ñun-go*. The police smiled at the fallen idol, helping him clean off his clothes, asking him if he wanted to press charges against anyone for the assaults. He answered, "No."

One of the policemen went ahead to make sure people were entering the cemetery in orderly fashion. The one who remained extended his hand to Mañungo and said, "A pleasure to serve you, Mr. Vera."

"Thanks."

"See you later."

"Bye."

Inside the cemetery, three or four steps inside a group, Lopito had gotten together with some of his cronies, and with an expression of joy on his face gulped red wine from a bottle until his friends ripped it out of his hands. Lopita and Jean-Paul, both clinging to Mañungo's belt so they wouldn't get lost, were crying about what had just hap-

CURFEW   ◆ 249

pened, trying to get the victim away from the policeman, who realized
that the children were reacting negatively to him. What lies had these
Marxist-Leninists told their children about them, when all they were
doing was their duty? The policeman was very dark, his cheeks rough
with scars from the acne he'd had during the adolescence he'd only
recently left behind. His eyebrows formed a mass that hid his eyes,
delegating all the life of his face to his African mouth, which was as
soft and orange as a mollusk, and to his polite smile.

Mañungo watched the white helmet march off and join another
white helmet on the corner; and both, following orders, blended in
with those whose heads had no protection against the sun and who
were blocking the entrance to the cemetery. Lopito was shaking his
head in a reproving way about Mañungo's relationship with the authorities. With the children still clinging to his belt, Mañungo tried to
join Lopito and his noisy chums. They slapped him on the back and
hugged him while he tried to exhume their identities from a distant
common past lost in the more recent collapse of their features. Lopito
was again drinking from the bottle. His daughter tugged on his shirt.
Without looking at her, he flicked off her hand with a negligent gesture, as if he were scaring off a fly. Lopita began to cry very softly,
biting her nails, her stiff tresses disordered and lifeless. Jean-Paul tried
to console her.

Standing in a group that included more than one underground
Party leader who'd come out of hiding for this event, Lisboa shouted
at Lopito and his friends to please move away from the entrance
because the procession would arrive in five minutes. Lopito laughed
in his face, refusing to move from where he was. This jerk Lisboa, he
was saying, ever since the Party had announced the armed struggle
against the regime, he thought he was a general without stars and
Matilde's funeral was nothing but an act of solidarity with the Communist Party. And now his juvenile true believers were trying to follow
his orders to clear the entrance! Because of the repulsion Lisboa caused
him, Lopito asked for the bottle again and, throwing his head back,
let the red wine flow to refresh his throat, which was sore from dust
and unsolved problems. Mañungo and Juan Pablo could not console
Lopita: she wept without letting go of her father's belt, both to keep
from getting lost and because she knew that soon she'd have to help
him.

The sun was at its zenith and left nothing but a tiny circle of shade
at the bottom of each cypress. Mañungo noticed that the dust raised

by the thousands of feet did not make the light sweeter—as it had in Paris, the day before yesterday, when it drizzled and everything seemed bevelled and silvery. In Paris, the rain blurred distances but did not produce the specters of witchcraft as it did in Chiloé. But in Chiloé the rain lubricated his vocal cords and the sweetness of the air dissolved the hardness of his nostrils, which were bothering him here. In this dryness, it would be impossible to sing even one note. Should he leave to look for something else? Here, he'd be mute forever. Without being able to control the air in his lungs, wheezing, coughing like Lopito, a voice only useful to shout harsh sayings like the ones popping up around him: *And it will fall . . . and it will fall . . .* And just beyond, someone chanted, *He's here! He's here!* . . . But the claws of the plush lion stuck into his throat wouldn't let him sing a single note, not a single word. Bits of news flashed through the crowd, dividing it: there would be a mass for Matilde . . .there would be no mass for Matilde . . . Federico Fox was going to speak at the grave because the authorities would stop the whole event unless he spoke. How? How could they stop a funeral? Of course they couldn't stop it, but they had the cemetery surrounded by machine guns, police, trucks, cars ready to close it off the moment Matilde's remains entered. Then they'd enter themselves and exterminate the left which had gathered there, an exemplary slaughter in the cemetery where today, right at this moment, the turbulent heart of Santiago was beating.

The mob milled around, coagulating in groups that tried to organize themselves into lines on both sides of the proposed entranceway, lines that promptly dissolved because the procession had not yet arrived. Darío, wearing sneakers he'd pulled out of the garbage, was ready with the juvenile commandos to flee or retaliate if the police attacked. He was arguing with a leader of the Communist Youth about having representatives from the Manuel Rodríquez Liberation Front help carry the coffin. Yes, they should help too, he said, because today, for the first time, the front showed itself publicly as a unified body. No. The procession was late. It hadn't come yet. It's being delayed, Aury heard the man next to her say, and pushing through with her breasts, she made her way to where it seemed the first row would be, next to ex-Senator Larrañaga, yellow, wrinkled by the climates of exile, who took up a position in the shadow of the pine that perhaps would be shading him forever. After all, that's why he'd come back.

34

*B*ecause he wiped his mouth on it after every swig, Lopito's shirt cuff was red with wine. He passed the bottle to Mañungo, who pretended to drink so that the others would think he was drunk and let him join in their carousing. He did no more than pretend, realizing that this event would be an opportunity for him to watch and understand. The fumes of wine would keep him from evaluating his abilities in this tremendous present in which he found himself entangled.

Entangled? Was it valid to think of himself as entangled when he was only simulating euphoria, while the others were awash in it? No. But this was his style: to be present and yet not present; able and not able to observe himself; condemned to see everything from the shore, immersed only in this painful outcome of his conflicts.

It wasn't so that he could retain the kind of clarity with which he created his "Mañungo Vera" character on stage, but another kind of clarity: the painful lucidity that he'd need to destroy his preoccupation with himself. On this stage, so different, so vast—the raw present of this multitudinous funeral, the burning breath of the demanding, shouting mob, the dusty confusion of sweaty faces, each one declaring the special validity of his poster or slogan, hoarse from hollering, their foreheads sunburned under newspaper hats or handkerchiefs knotted at all four corners—he saw clearly that it was in relation to all this that he had to judge himself, because he hadn't come back to his country to rehabilitate the sweet vernacular of old songs. That project was too simple for him. Unfortunately, he was no longer simple.

Neither was Judit. That was the parallel the clairvoyant Juan Pablo had perceived before he did, and that's why he'd linked the two of them, not because he sensed love, but because of a sinister tie that was legally binding. "You're going to marry that woman, and we'll

have to stay in this country of funerals, revolutions, and earthquakes,"
Jean-Paul had said in lapidary fashion. But they were not going to
stay.

Amid this crowd, in which he felt so strange and where he saw Judit
appear and head toward him, the only thing he could desire was to
return to Rue Servandoni, this time with her, the woman he did not
love (he warned himself), but whom he recognized as his partner—
irreplaceable, at least for the moment. They say children are clairvoyant about their parents, a concept he didn't accept because he
found children selfish and possessive; but it was a faculty that at this
moment he was forced to recognize in Juan Pablo.

She made her way to him, pulling along the three children, exasperated by having to keep them under control. Ada Luz was able to
dominate the little flock without wasting the energy Judit had to ex-
pend just getting them to Mañungo and Lopito. Judit's cool eyes,
whose irises were so clear that the light erased them as it would on a
marble statue, gave him infinite pleasure, especially when he compared them—smiling and fixed—to the crowd's excessive gestures.
Bending over to kiss Marilú's forehead, he thought that the girl looked
like an escapee from another universe, even though she was Judit's
child: sullen (as her transitory, revolutionary father must have been),
her face a mask of makeup that distorted the well-sculpted features
her mother's genes had supplied, her wrists and her neck tinkling
with cheap jewelry ill suited to the daughter of Judit Torre. Mañungo
told her he was happy to meet her, that he was a good friend of her
mother's.

"I didn't know. How could I know that my mother had any friends
worth meeting?"

She didn't know. His past with Judit hadn't added a grain of nostalgic sediment: she hadn't even bragged to Marilú about her youthful
relationship with Mañungo Vera. Was the present in which they were
soon to take part—perhaps tomorrow, in any case before the week
was out—also destined to get lost in obscure geological strata, un-
reachable even by memory? Was it worthwhile to give of himself when
she didn't know how to reciprocate? Was it worth asking her to allow
him to touch and caress her, as she hadn't under the acanthus plants
on Las Hortensias, leaving an aseptic vertigo as the only thing that
linked them?

"Don't say silly things like that, Luz," said Judit, kissing Lopita's still
tear-stained cheek, preparing herself to be effusive with Juan Pablo,

whom she saw ready to flee at any hint of an advance on her part. "I told you to wash your face. You're too young to be walking around made up like that."

Marilú either paid no attention to her mother or else didn't hear her. She went on playing admiringly with Juan Pablo's blond hair, while Ada Luz combed Lopita's hair and rearranged the white ribbons the child's hands, made nervous by her father's excesses, had undone. Marilú took the blond child by the hand, with the intention of leading him away from this group of old people and that ugly little girl. When she grew up, she was going to be a cosmetician—in her neighborhood she already made up her homely friends and turned them into princesses. Juan Pablo was reluctant to go with her, because he had to hear what his father was saying to Marilú's mother. They weren't fooling him, they'd spent the night together, and because of her they'd have to stay in this funeral country, with these people who only knew how to shout and push.

The crowd kept swelling and shaking all around them, bodies pushed together, rude howling, the ground slippery with crushed flowers, faces expectant about what would happen when the coffin arrived: the procession should have left already, the hearse was coming, get the signs up and start singing. But Matilde made them wait. Lopito drank. Lopita, pulling on his belt, wept, begging him not to drink any more wine, to remember what always happened to him, and that it was so bad for his poor heart.

"Did your mother give you my pills?"

"Yes. Here they are." And she took a little knotted handkerchief out of her pocket and untied it.

"To hell with my medicine!" shouted Lopito, giggling and wheezing, slapping at the handkerchief and sending the pills flying while Lopita cowered.

Mañungo swept Lopita off the ground and set her on his shoulders, as if she were an organ grinder's monkey with red skirts. Little by little, her tearful grimace turned back into a smile. When Mañungo began to wade through the crowd with Lopita perched on him, people recognized him because the news of his presence had spread. They cheered him again: sing, Mañungo, sing a song of protest so that the police have to enter the cemetery by force and break up this demonstration with bombs and leave us bleeding.

Now, yes, the procession was coming, it was only a block away. Behind Lopito—who was swigging out of the bottle again, shouting

greetings and obscenities, stumbling and elbowing his way through—
came the rest of the group, trying its best to cross the overflowing
street, surrounding Mañungo, who carried Lopita on his shoulders.
People cheered as they passed and Lopita waved greetings left and
right from on high, calm as a trapeze artist acknowledging the audience's ovations after executing a masterful trick, while Marilú, tugging
Mañungo's shirt, shouted, "My turn now! My turn, Uncle Mañungo!"

Mañungo paid her no attention. Lopita was the one marked by an
ill-starred destiny, the one to whom it was necessary to give this one
instant of glory because she'd probably never know another. On the
other side of the street, in the shade of a pine, they joined Fausta and
don Celedonio, who recounted what had happened an hour earlier
in Matilde's house, while Ada Luz moved off a bit and watched over
the children. Lisboa had blocked the execution of Matilde's last wishes,
and Freddy Fox, in exchange for the mass, would speed up the authorization of the foundation.

Where was that stinker Freddy Fox, so he could kill him, so he could
castrate him if he wasn't already castrated? shouted Lopito. His friends
begged him to shut up. Didn't he see that, mixed in with the crowd,
there were vigilant eyes behind sunglasses, alert ears that heard everything, that recorded every word, memorizing attitudes, faces, and
groups? Lopito's anger flicked like a whip to his friends for giving in
to Freddy Fox's hoax. Yes a hoax, they should realize it because that's
what it was, he wanted to declare it here and now within the unthinking
mob that surrounded them so that anyone with ears might hear it,
yes, he wanted to state that he, Juan López, considered that this entire
murky affair of the foundation was nothing but a pile of Neruda's
senile and narcissistic shit, and the circus he'd left would do nothing
more than feed the hungry vultures that always waited to pick up the
remains of the left. The mass, on the other hand, which they had
stupidly given up, if said by a revolutionary priest, one of those who
seemed as meek as a lamb, would have provoked an immediate storm,
erasing the power of these crazy Manuel Rodríguez people, although
he was not anxious to attack them, because, after all, the oppressive
brutality of the regime was the only reason these extremist groups
came into being. Typical! Theirs were typical bourgeois mentalities:
the mandarins, the arrogant chosen and anointed few, to think up
elegant long-term solutions like the foundation and sacrifice fulmi-
nating remedies, shock treatment, that in a situation like this were the
only ones that would work!

"We're bourgeois and you're the perfect proletarian who specializes in Schumann and Duchamp, is that it?" Fausta interrupted him, irritated by the heat, the pushing, the horseflies. "When are you going to stop contradicting yourself, Lopito, and figure out who you are once and for all?"

"The only luxury I can afford," answered Lopito, "is never to figure myself out. But just calm down, Fausta. For now, I'm not going to answer you—but later on I will. In any case, I'm nonviolent. I'm a bit sorry I am, because it may only be for physiological reasons: I'm more than ten years older than when Judit and I got our kicks making bombs in a friend's garage. Remember, Virginia Woolf?"

A hatred of all for all had arisen in the group, each one disagreeing with the other, each of them enemies, scorning each other, challenging each other, each one's defects so magnified that reconciliation was impossible, since it would be washed away by storms of irrationality. It was impossible to understand how they could have been friends until just a few minutes before, how they could have believed they were on the same side. Mañungo pronounced a few calming words. He had now become the "good guy" of the movies, Lopito said to himself disdainfully, disgusted by the complete balance that seemed to guide his friend in everything; since he was no longer Mañungo's friend, the senseless excess that had given them courage in the past was eliminated. How was he going to sing like this? Could one postulate Judit as his salvation? Because over the course of these last hours, a link had formed between those two, a certain arrogant symmetry you could see despite their clothes, although they themselves might not be capable of recognizing it yet or naming it. And despite her sensible side, Judit was the first to dive headlong into whatever whirlpool appeared in her path. Perhaps she would succeed in bringing Mañungo to destruction, and through destruction to restoration.

The rumor that the hearse was arriving distracted them. In the rear of the procession, at the gates to the cemetery, the boys wearing red T-shirts, absolute masters of the situation, lowered the coffin containing the late lamented from the hearse, decked it out with flowers, and raised it up on their shoulders. The shouting ceased, the vendors stopped their hawking, and for a second everything was silent, very still, even the dust that danced in the light, although some said they heard something like the rustle of angelic wings. Then, spontaneously, a group began to chant:

"Matilde—Neruda: The People Salute You.
"Matilde—Neruda: The People Salute You.

"Matilde—Neruda: The People Salute You.
"Matilde—Neruda: The People Salute You."

Another group joined in, then more groups, and the wave of noise grew until it washed away everything else. The armed forces had resolutely remained outside the cemetery. It had become a free zone where, for the first time, the people could gather without sanctions and shout whatever they wanted; a space of liberty, perhaps the last until the definitive asphyxia; Matilde's final gift to the people.

The Young Communist groups from various neighborhoods raised signs and shouted, *The People United Can Never Be Defeated*, shocking the less enterprising groups, who had brought no signs. They slowly mobilized behind the coffin as it began to move forward, dragging with it the crowd and some members of the recently revived Revolutionary Left Movement, who attended the funeral with their faces hidden. A left-wing priest lost in the throng, the one who should have officiated at the mass, but who didn't because no one got in touch with him, stated that it was improper for the left to criticize the Communists for shouting their slogans, and that they only criticized them because they were too scared to shout their own. They should shout! Here was their long-awaited opportunity to demonstrate! Why didn't the Radicals, why didn't the Christian Democrats raise their cowardly voices? Why were all of them except the communists weak, with flimsy identities, fragmented, fearful of taking action?

Like a wave, "The International," spontaneous and out of tune, broke over the crowd, recovering its long-lost right to be heard in Chile, and fading toward the entrance, where the procession had just begun to move. The priest had wanted to balance "The International" by singing the "Hymn to Joy," but no one picked it up because they were all waiting to chant the most daring slogan of all: "He's Here! He's Here! You Know Allende's Here!" At the same time, another group began to chant, "The People United Can Never Be Defeated," amid the party ovations screamed by the sweaty boys walking forward in the dust with the coffin on their shoulders under a rain of red carnations. From on top of the few trees, from the side paths, from the roofs of chapels and mausolea, from miniature ziggurats and doll-house Parthenons embellished with ancient names crumbling off their archways, people shouted out their salutes to the passing coffin: Matilde belonged to them; Neruda belonged to them, even if they'd never read a word he wrote; and this moment, above all, belonged to them because they would save the country, since "The People United Can Never Be Defeated," and they and Pablo and Matilde were the people, or at least that's what it seemed at the moment of glory when the coffin passed before their eyes.

And Mañungo also belonged to them. They dragged him to the group that surrounded the coffin covered with carnations, he with Lopita on his shoulders, she still waving because this was her party. One boy wanted to surrender his place at a corner of the coffin, but seeing that Lisboa was cutting through the mob with a red handkerchief in his hand, Mañungo walked away, resolutely saying, "No."

He knew he was wrong in letting them take charge of the coffin—but what could he do alone, how could he act, and in whose name could he justify his action?—and make their emblems the centerpiece of the funeral. It was already acquiring the meaning they feared it would. But he was in no mood to get into a fight when his own position was so fragmented, so rickety. Besides, he knew them all so well, these well-intentioned young "reds," for so long a time, from his university days, or indignantly waving newspapers with news from Chile in exile cafés . . .

And yet . . . nevertheless . . . yes: sometimes, their voices drowned by certainties they strove to maintain despite everything, they yet seemed to offer a better approach to the change desired by so many. But he refused to share it, precisely because of what was happening right now before his eyes, because of this shoving and exacerbation, and trampling and dogmatism, and the demand of bland fealty in everything and by everyone. They were decidedly not "everything," although of course they were a part of the thing, and it would be criminal not to include them in the dialogue. But their demands, their totalization, seemed just as noxious to him as any system that promised heaven in exchange for servitude. How could he drape himself in red, then? How could he join his voice to theirs, to their naiveté, to their power, when he was neither the one thing nor the other?

The coffin made its way toward the interior of the cemetery on the shoulders of the boys, robbing Mañungo and Lopita of their ephemeral stardom. Mañungo finally deposited the girl on her father's back, where she was besieged by questions and praised by Marilú, who had earlier made fun of her.

Mañungo let his friends move ahead of him in the flowing multitude. He wanted to be alone at this funeral, to hear the waves pounding on Isla Negra with the emotional power of the throat of the plush lion, who broke the terrible barrier of his tinnitus, roaring like Carlitos's ancestors, as in chorus they cried in Cucao for the loss of Matilde, preserved now like an idol within the green amber swirl of memory.

Up ahead, far away, at the head of the procession, Fausta and Celedonio led the mourners, in front of a cohort of notables. Two blocks behind, the turbulent atmosphere of the political funeral dissolved, taking on the unwilling, seedy tone of a poor country fair— the vendors selling popsicles, the sellers of brightly colored pinwheels offering their festive merchandise, the children escaping the watchful eyes of their parents to race paper boats in the stream. When someone shouted, "Anyone who doesn't jump is Pinochet," those present, seized by an absurd Saint Vitus's dance, began—to Mañungo's surprise and chagrin—to jump around with a smile of idiotic discomfort and celebration on their faces. The personalities from the worlds of politics and art who had no defined role at the gravesite also remained behind, dissolved among the mob, their jackets folded over their arms, sweating, their suspenders on display, their shirts sticking to their backs and their ties undone, also licking ices or fanning themselves with the morning paper, which was at least useful for that purpose. They chatted calmly in hushed tones about subjects more related to politics or to their summer vacations than to Matilde.

Up ahead, the procession finally stopped, and, with a shudder, even the rearguard, where Mañungo found himself, also came to a halt. In the distance, he could just make out the figure of a woman, solemn and emotionally shaken, standing next to the coffin and the flowers. Fausta Manquileo stood up on a dais and for a long time read the stuff she'd written down. Mañungo was too far away to hear the words. All he could see was the noble gestures of her arms as she waved the veils and silver bracelets of her legendary status. Hers was the first funerary oration to be given in this contest among official geniuses. How many would he have to endure?

"Mañungo."

Judit, who had just touched his shoulder, smiled at him.

"You can't hear a thing from here."

"Luckily."

They stood next to each other, motionless. After Fausta, other lofty figures gesticulated inaudible litanies from the dais, next to the grave where Matilde would soon be placed. Was it necessary to witness all this horror? Wasn't it the most banal ending of any life, so banal that it seemed superfluous to show emotion when it all was more a legal procedure than a rite? Why attend such a dehumanized ceremony? Mañungo asked Judit. She answered, "It's hot."

"Let's go over there in the shade," and he led her to a frail willow next to the stream.

When Judit had leaned against the trunk, under the shower of branches that camouflaged the two of them, Mañungo told her he was going to leave Santiago.

"For Chiloé?"

"Just for a couple of days to see my father. From there directly to Paris with a three-hour layover in Santiago."

"When?"

"Tomorrow," Mañungo improvised.

Judit stuttered as she said, "It's a shame. We've been together such a short time."

It wasn't true: of the eighteen hours Mañungo had been in Santiago, they'd shared thirteen. As he answered her, above all because he realized she would have wanted to be with him longer, it was his turn to stutter: "Why don't you come with me to Paris?"

Judit laughed. "Mañungo! I'm shocked! Should I interpret that as an ardent declaration of love?"

"I don't know if it's love. Anyway, it's the second time I've asked you."

"Are you in love with me?"

"No. I told you last night I wasn't, and I haven't changed. It seems that things like that just don't happen to me, or I don't know how to recognize them or name them when they do. But I know that I want to make love with you, nights and weeks and months without being interrupted, without curfews. And I also think I'd like to live with you . . . I liked your apartment and your blue Viyella robe . . . and I like walking with you. I don't think I'll forget last night's stroll so quickly. I don't know if it'll last forever. But right now I do want you to come, for now. For as long as it lasts, it's what I want most in the world. Don't you think it would be great if we lived together in Paris for a while, Ju?"

"Until when?"

"Is it the end you're afraid of?"

"The end of what, if there isn't going to be any love between us to end? How will we know when . . . when something has ended if there never was anything?"

"Frankly, I don't know, Ju. I don't want to think about it. But, please, come with me and stop thinking about it."

"I'm not Lilianita," she warned him.

"Who?"

As he bent over to kiss her, Mañungo stopped and remembered: "Speaking of Lilianita, isn't that Ricardo Farías over there in the tan gabardine suit, the one with sunglasses on, mixed in with the people in the procession? He's looking for us."

"There are so many people he'd be looking for here!"

Mañungo peered through the willow branches, inviting her to look too. But no: the man Mañungo pointed out in the crowd, among so many male *criollo* heads and muffled faces, was not last night's man; but he was the same, and also the same as the man in her story, and perhaps the same as all men.

She imagined his eyes, bloodshot from partying, moving behind the Polaroid lenses, looking for her. She didn't want to be here. Yes, yes! Let's go, Mañungo, far away from my persecutors, far from Lopito's polemics, far from this shred that remains of Matilde, this shred I cannot be moved by! Let's leave tomorrow for Chiloé, Mañungo, I won't say goodbye to anyone, then to Paris, where no one knows me, to live everything through to see if it's love, and if love's worth the trouble, or if it's only the physiological spasm I felt that time when the man with the Polaroid lenses moving ahead in the crowd put his hand on my knee and ordered me to scream with pleasure in an act that never took place. What a stupid word: "love"! Only people like Ada Luz should ever use it.

What she wanted was very different, not that confusion. How could things be put in order?

Despite the lucidity with which she'd told her story to Mañungo last night under the frowning glow of the bougainvillea, she hadn't told him everything, not even the essential part. Where could she begin? Where did her story begin and where would it end? She had never succeeded in letting herself be touched, loved, not only because of the fetid muddiness of the idea, but because of the main reason why reasonable people resist falling in love: so that they don't have to tell their own story again from the beginning and realize that they've lost the beginning, and that they don't know where it is or where it should be. With the fearful fatigue of these repetitions in perspective, her enthusiasm for following Mañungo to Paris suddenly faded, because if she did it she'd have to look for the beginning of her story and establish a thread, and characters and realistic dates for her heart. She made an effort to banish the negative avalanche of the confused history that was falling on her, and that would keep her from running away with Mañungo. She had to nullify that avalanche, be brave, and leave without her own story and without love. That way she would postpone—with new confusions, for which she was eager—being persecuted by the enemies who pursued her in the morning light of the park, would leave it all to turn into inert junk, along with the senile babbling of Celedonio and Fausta about masses and foundations, along with these impassioned shouts ringing out around her.

"So we go to Paris, then?"

Judit laughed. "Don't rush it. We have to talk it over."

Everything had to be talked over. And as soon as she'd put that condition on their trip, her eyes filled with tears, which she held back and expunged, because she realized that she had begun to get entangled in the repetition of her own story.

"Are we going to stay until it's over?"

"They never shut up and you can't hear anything. Let's go."

"Where?"

And Judit answered, "I want to show you the family tomb."

35

♦ *A*fter jumping the stream behind
the willow and abandoning the funeral and its pantomime speeches,
they entered an area filled with crosses barely marked with a name
or "Unknown/1973" or nothing at all, although some, despite this
anonymity, bore wreaths of rotten flowers or a circle of the faded
petals of disconsolation. From the edge of the ossuary, they could
make out the beginnings of the mausoleum city under the miserable
cypresses covered with wooden fruit. Walking through the field of
crosses was like getting lost in the preamble to a dream where the
tautology of death, expressed in the uniformity of the crosses, was so
monotonous that it seemed to them, even though they were walking,
that they were getting nowhere. From a distance came fragments of
voices worn out from wandering so long without finding an ear in
which to take refuge.

This, said Judit, was not what she had wanted to show him, because
the field they were sinking into was nothing more than a nightmare
filled with beings of ephemeral identity, extant only as far as some
personal memory maintained them. Later that identity would be lost,
after the time for which the plot had been rented had passed, and
the remains would be condemned to the disgraceful ocean of the
common grave. That really frightened Judit—irrationally, childishly,
as she herself recognized—because her adolescent nightmares were
about sarabands of faceless souls whose dance, pale and heatless like
the deathly flames of burning alcohol, licked the walls of a ditch overflowing with bones. This was not for her. She invoked her origins,
about which she rarely thought, in order to be able to leave for Paris
tomorrow with Mañungo, bearing with her the security of the family's
pious stone mausolea, which time had polished, making the callig-
raphy of their inscriptions all the more discreet.

Now they had reached the avenues of cedars that protected the small Gothic chapel and Aztec or Roman mini-temples, all nestled under the breeze that intoned short prayers among the branches for the salvation of the souls fluttering above. This was a dream devoid of fear, she laughingly explained to Mañungo, a ceremonious lethargy, because when families acquired sepulchers of this category, they also purchased the privilege of establishing an eternal contract for their eternal sleep.

Instead of going out toward the Recoleta gate, through which they had entered as they followed the procession, they now headed for Avenida de la Paz, along the old road of cypresses, perpendicular to the one which had led them to Matilde's modest niche in the brick wall of identical niches and which no one would use to return because it was the long way out. On the path, which had the curious air of an unhurried time for contemplation and strolling, they occasionally ran into somber groups of people surrounding a coffin pushed on a little cart—not carried on the glorious shoulders of spirited youth—funerary honors that were not symbolic, personal grief for someone whose death didn't "mean" anything despite the mourners who wept because for them this was the only significant death in the world. Everything else was the scent of the pines and discreet figures disappearing down paths, as if they were walking on tiptoe in order not to bother anyone.

"Come on, I think it's this way," said Judit as they caught sight of a small Romanesque sanctuary, pompous in the whiteness of its marble even if the outline of its bas-relief was covered with dust.

They penetrated into the avenue through a mix of decrepit family chapels and monuments erected to the memory of notables wearing pocket watches on long chains and standing on plinths, and a stack of little temples and miniature pyramids under whispering pines. Jumping from illegible headstone to illegible headstone, knocking over a vase of dried flowers, and trampling names covered over by moss, they tried to find the Torre mausoleum. The sun, still merciless, ricocheted off the architraves and bounced off the peristyles, burning Judit's delicate skin.

"I must be as red as Miss Hughes after playing field hockey."

"Who's Miss Hughes?"

"She's buried in the mausoleum. She was odious."

They hopped from semiburied stones to broken stones, among unrecognizable rubble, which made it difficult to get into the aisles of vaults and closed chapels until they came into an open space between the portico of a Gothic structure and a greenish granite pyramid. In the dappled light under the pines, they saw a stone slab as soft as a bed of moss and a water faucet that dripped to form a small stream in the shadow of the modest chapel with its high rose window. They drank from the faucet. They cooled their faces and explored the paths among the buildings. They realized that the labyrinth came to a dead end from which they would have to retrace their steps. This, said Judit, is not the site of my origins. How stupid to have gotten lost here! This place had nothing whatsoever to do with her childhood and All Souls' Day visits, all dressed up to bring flowers more expensive than her cousins' to her grandparents' grave.

Judit stretched out on the warm slab, where the moss had definitively eliminated the identity of the bones resting under her body. But the lassitude with which her anatomy took over the stone, as if it were a cushion beneath her repose, was inviting—and, Mañungo noted, animal-like for the first time.

He stretched out facedown next to Judit on the same stone, as if they were sunbathing on a beach and had nothing important to discuss. He turned to kiss her on the mouth. But he chose instead to lightly caress her lips with his, as frisky as lizards playing on the warm stone they were using as a nuptial bed. Where they going to make love here, finally? It wasn't the best idea. If they took a taxi, they'd be at her house in twenty minutes. But no matter, it was clear that she wanted him right now; her eyes were charged with Mañungo. They had to project this relationship beyond the point where it was stalled, just like that solid citizen on that marble plinth, incapable of taking a single step. They wanted to advance, to go on, in order to see, as Judit said, as Mañungo said, what their smells would be like mixed together, and what words would season the lexicon of their intimacy, and thus understand what existed for them beyond the point where everything had stopped that morning at her house, before she'd gone out to meet Freddy. She didn't know. Here, hidden among these stones, she felt the urge to begin to know. From under the stone on which they lay, her legs and Mañungo's wound together, there rose a vision of something like age-old bones that composed a pirate flag. This calcareous sensation made her nostalgic for skin sliding over skin, Mañungo's chest on her naked breast. She opened her blouse to show him. A cluster of cypress fruit suddenly fell through the silence of the branches when he caressed her. Judit bolted up, frightened, and closed her blouse. Facedown on the stone again, Mañungo dedicated himself to the modest paleographic pastime of cleaning out the letters with a twig and said:

"It wasn't anyone. Come back."

"Let's go. I'm hungry."

"Look at this."

"What does it say?"

"It looks like . . . *Policarpo Campodónico*."

"Or maybe *Campocarpo Polidónico*."

"Could be. What does it matter?"

"You're right, I guess."

While they were laughing about the possible variations of the tongue-twisting name, they forgot the touch of their so recently eager mouths and the skin cooled by dried perspiration. What was his father like? Judit asked, lying beside him. What was his house like? Its smells, its cooking? Surrounded by the hideouts of tumbled-down stones that weren't hers, and yet at the same time were, she wanted to know about the cemetery where his mother slept. Was it like this one? No, said Mañungo. Nothing there was precise or neatly cut in the dry air as it was here. It was all reverberations dissolved in dreams or in the past. Everything was silvery and hairy and wet with rain and fog, the angles all bearded with lichens, edges cancerous with mushrooms, and in the ephemeral wooden cemeteries next to the canals, the tides came right up to the shingled sheds that covered the tombs, and when the tides were very high or the wind was howling, these little houses for the dead were washed away just like the houses for the living. Sometimes you'd see them floating along the green estuaries, a funerary village sailing along on the tide along the inlets until they came to the sea . . . the cemeteries would be all washed away and the people would have to build new ones.

Was his mother still in the place where he'd left her? He heard the herons shriek to announce the rain that poured down on the crops and saw the cows defend themselves from it by closing their big, sad eyes. The houses of the dead rocked back and forth with the wind, the clapboard siding flew up in the air, the shingles leapt up, the crosses and the desolate souls went out to roam the pastures and wander over the water in the canals. He didn't know if the most recent storms had washed away his mother's grave. He didn't know if he'd find her. He didn't even know if he'd look for her. Why should he, when those souls without houses were everywhere, feeding the air and the plants that lived on earth?

While Mañungo remained on the stone reciting his ancestral tale, Judit got up and explored the neighboring paths. She was studying the chaotic assortment of architectural styles. Here the lingering dead were not dissolved in Mañungo's green nature. They remained sealed up in marble boxes, which in turn were sealed inside the walls of mausolea so that their relatives could live with the simple illusion that neither time nor rain would touch the eternity they'd bought. The vaults and chapels faced away from the secret corner where Judit and Mañungo were hiding.

They were afraid they wouldn't be able to leave the spot, because if they tried they might fall into the hands of the crowd and have to shout to be saved. Either that or spend the night sleeping on the stone and not in Judit's house, as they wished, because satisfying the urgent demands of the body was a necessary prelude to the marvelous ceremonies love led to. Then, naked, lying side by side in complete darkness as they smoked, each one would slowly recite parts of his own story, whispering it as if it were the first time they were being told. Mañungo would still talk about the south and the rain, but as if for himself, almost chanting.

Judit admired the high rose window in the Gothic chapel with its small rear made of pink stone. The space between the cypresses and the stone was already in a shadow. "Very Böklin, with all these cypresses," Judit noted. "What's Böklin?" asked Mañungo. "Nothing," but she began to fear what Lopito would have said about Böklin. The shifting light on the portico made the stained-glass window glow.

"Why does the light do that?" asked Judit.

"Elementary, Watson . . ."

"Please don't say 'Elementary, Watson' to me. I'm sick and tired of hearing Lopito say it."

"It's easy to explain. Look, this is the back end of the chapel. The sun enters through the front door and pierces the stained-glass window, producing in the shadow that combination of lighthouse and kaleidoscope . . . you're standing exactly where the red, green, blue, and yellow lights are falling. You've become a legendary heroine. I'm going to kiss you . . ."

She allowed herself to be kissed without sharing in it. She was disguised in the transitory mantle of those storybook colors and did not want the light to change or the colors to fade, turning her back into what she was tired of being. She would undergo a metamorphosis with Mañungo and set sail, not in Böklin's skiff but in the *Caleuche*, embarking on the extraordinary itinerary that he promised her. Paris. Anyplace where she would not be enslaved to the screams that had torn Matilde away from her, far from Freddy, from the traps set by the man in the tan gabardine suit who wouldn't leave her alone, and the nocturnal scavengers.

"Help me up," she said.

"What are you going to do?"

"Take hold of my legs and push me up."

"Why?"

"I want to see something."

The sinister undertone had all but disappeared from her voice, leaving her a playful, amused adolescent. He took her by the legs. She told him to lift her up so she could see the stained-glass panes close up, so that the colors would shine with their greatest intensity right on her face. What was inside that chapel? What did it look like on the other side, its facade, to which they couldn't find the way? Mañungo would have preferred to have lunch, just as she herself had suggested before the sound of wings from the other world had interrupted that all-too-normal inclination, so they could then take refuge in her apartment and finally make love. He wanted to wear the coveted blue Viyella robe, which belonged to that ceremony of intimacy.

Judit, in the meantime, was absorbed in her mischief. She'd kicked off her shoes and, propped up by Mañungo, had begun to climb on top of the chapel.

"You're only going to see the reverse of the stained glass," warned Mañungo. "And besides, it must be filthy."

"I don't care. I want to see."

With her eyes at the same level as the window, Mañungo holding her up precariously, she discovered that the rose window was so dirty she couldn't see through it. And since the sun had moved in its path from this mausoleum to go on to the next, the window was transformed into a sampling of opaque colors. Judit began to clean off the panes with her hand and brush away the pine needles and seeds. She pushed too hard on a blue pane and it smashed. A rush of cold, stale air hit her face.

"You broke it."

"I didn't mean to!"

"Well, now you'll have a better view."

"It was 'The Temptation of Saint Anthony,' I think . . ."

"How do you know?"

"I don't know. The temptations would be good for you, though . . ."

Judit stood there examining the inside through the hole.

"What do you see?"

It was a cavernous chapel made of white marble, but all in shadows because the sun that had illuminated it just a second before had retreated through the iron gate, and was now playing on the grass outside. Judit, studying the interior, reviewed the names and dates. Then she shouted:

"My dad . . . !"

"Who?"

"And my poor mother . . . ! And my Uncle Carlos and my Grandmother Emilia. Mañungo, Mañungo, this is it, this is the mausoleum I wanted to show you, but we haven't been able to reach the facade and I can't figure out why. Why don't we work our way around to the front?"

"Should I lower you?"

"Don't let go! I want to see because I'll never be able to see it again in my life. My grandfather Agustín. Oh, Mañungo, this is where I begin! How hard it is to change and go to Paris with you, when you start out with something as solid as this! Stone from Pelequén. Pink. Do you realize what that means? The Chilean equivalent of Carrara marble. Do you realize how secure and solid all this is?"

She continued looking in silence for another instant. She read aloud, *"Judit Torre Fox 1952–* No! I don't want to see it! I'm not dead! Get me down! We've got to leave here! Get me down! I don't want to be locked in a marble box! Let's get out of here, please, Mañungo, I'm suffocating!"

She was weeping when Mañungo took her in his arms. She told him that her father had announced to her one day, "Daughter, you may lack many things in life, but you'll always have a place to throw your poor bones when you've finished your foolishness." Weeping with the terror of death before death, she feared she'd fall apart instantly if she stayed in the shadow of this pink chapel any longer. Mañungo should take her away! Now! She didn't belong here. This was neither her origin nor her ending. Her origin was high school and university, political struggle, Matilde and Lopito and Ramón and Fausta, and so many others, and Ada Luz and her weaver-women, not these frozen names or these dates that meant nothing because they belonged to another history. Mañungo should never allow her to be locked in this niche with her name on it which had always been there waiting with open jaws to swallow her! The cold that had blown into her face from the inside of the mausoleum froze her so she couldn't live, because it was bad to live, and she sobbed, making him promise that he would save her from all this. Mañungo, Mañungo, help me put on my shoes to run away. Then, with her shoes on, she slipped out of Mañungo's arms and began to run through the labyrinth of chapels and monuments and broken stones until she got lost several times in dead ends and came back and looked and couldn't find anything in this confusion of the dead. Until Mañungo led her easily to the way out, holding her around the waist so she wouldn't trip on the broken headstones. Judit stopped crying. Mañungo gave her a handkerchief to wipe her face. She opened her bag and looked at herself in the mirror.

"What a mess I am."

Under the cedars, she stopped to comb her hair.

"Shall we go, Judit?"

"Forever."

"And leave tombs, children, and the struggle behind? Everything?"

"Everything. Promise me you'll never let me come back."

Never: a short word that was still too long. Like *always*. The word Mañungo hated most. But Judit was in no mood for disquisitions. She wanted to go home to pack her bags and leave tomorrow. Wouldn't they leave tomorrow, Mañungo, please, for Chiloé? She didn't want him to be away from her even for a second. She didn't want to spend another day here, Freddy and Ricardo Farías and don César all hounding her, harping on the same subject, just like Lisboa, that she wasn't alone, that she belonged to a historical moment and a struggle, and life was only truly personal when one defined oneself according to which angle of history was one's personal struggle. She didn't want to hear anything more about those demands. Maybe later . . . "When I grow up," as Fausta so amusingly said when someone would try to get her to define her decoratively vague positions. Everyone would laugh when they heard her and there was no need then for a concrete answer. Mañungo should take her to Chiloé to see coffins floating in the channels until they were lost at sea. Didn't he want her to meet his father? And the archipelago drowned in the arms of the estuaries? Yes: let's go. Tomorrow. They'd have to hurry if they didn't want their enemies to catch them. Besides, she told Mañungo, she was ravenous, and she didn't care anymore if anyone saw them eating together in the fanciest restaurant in Santiago. Good, let them start talking just before they disappeared together, it would be amusing, especially if it reached Freddy's ears.

36

*H*olding hands, they walked along
the avenue of cypresses toward the cemetery's main entrance, which
was protected by the dome that rose behind the trees. Things had
begun to fall into place for them; nothing was horrifying, everything
was free and easy now. At least as far as they cared to look into the
future, which for the last quarter of an hour seemed benign because
of their tacit agreement about not being committed to anything—not
even those terrible things like eternal love or extraordinary happiness—except leaving together for Chiloé tomorrow morning, which
perhaps was crazy. But if it was crazy it was also sensible, because by
running away, Judit would momentarily alleviate her panic about being
tracked down.

As they walked, they saw people walking in the same direction who
would pause to evoke personal matters next to an ogive or the fragment of a gargoyle; people who, because of a certain disdain in their
manner, revealed they were coming not from one of those funerals
where grief took the concrete form of a black suit but from the turbulent funeral of Matilde, and who, for the same aesthetic reasons
Judit and Mañungo had done it, were taking the long way out, leaving
Matilde abandoned in the depth of a remote Santiago cemetery.

Even more remote after tomorrow, after Chiloé, and later, after
Paris, forever. When would she see her again? She'd never considered
how painful this separation would be; she'd never imagined it. Now
it was impossible to analyze in any other way her grief at not being
able to bring her flowers from time to time, or take care of her niche
so that ignorant hands didn't deprive it of its stylized poverty, or simply
to visit her, to be close to what had been her body, to stand awhile at
her grave. Someone passing said hello to Judit. Didn't she want a ride
at least partway downtown? No, no thanks, and she didn't take the

offer because it was evident that the person who made it was in even more of a hurry than they to have lunch.

At the cemetery entrance and in the street, they avoided being absorbed by different contrite groups that awaited the arrival of bodies to be buried. On the other side of the street, in the palm-lined little square where the taxis parked, they saw their friends: Ada Luz and Lopito arguing, the children running on the grass, don Celedonio and Fausta totally worn out, sitting on a bench and absentmindedly fending off the beggars who pestered them with offers of water for the nonexistent flowers they'd brought their dead, trying to explain to them that the ceremonies for Matilde's death were over. Mañungo and Judit crossed over, dropping their hands so that no one would ask them about their disconcerting new relationship.

Lopita crowed with joy when she saw Mañungo, joyfully ran to him with her arms outstretched and her tresses flying, and hugged him around the knees, sinking her face into his legs. Marilú and Jean-Paul imitated her. Everyone, even the indolent policeman with his semi-automatic rifle, who should have been patrolling the plaza with his partner, but who was leaning on the hood of the gray car to listen to music, laughed at the spontaneity of the scene.

On the other sidewalk, the other officer, the more polite of the two, was taking orders from someone who was in the back of a truck with a handful of men whose rifles were clearly visible. Surrounded, muttered Mañungo. Why? What for? Why didn't they leave now that everything was over and Matilde, inert, had turned into an inoffensive thing? Surrounded. Along Recoleta, around here, everywhere, surrounded to keep the threat present in everyone's mind, although nothing had happened today and everyone could go home for lunch, after a mass, a funeral, shopping, or a soccer match out on the vacant lot. The door of the gray car was open and its occupants—Judit thought she recognized a leg in coffee-colored gabardine trousers, but she couldn't be sure because the face was hidden by the upper part of the windshield—had the radio on full-blast to listen to a popular singer said to hail from this miserable neighborhood.

She didn't look back because, as she walked across the plaza, she'd spotted the half-body leaning against a column in the arcade, his hat pulled down low, his hand uselessly begging because everyone had gone home to eat. He was her connection with the network of hatred in the people who had not dared leave their shacks for the burial because the police were sure to be on the lookout.

Judit sat down next to Fausta and Celedonio to ask what they were going to do now. They had invited the children and Ada Luz to eat at Burger King and promised Jean-Paul they'd then bring him to Chile in Miniature so he could get to know his country. The plan was not very enticing. They were so tired they would probably end up giving money to Ada Luz so that she would take them. Or would Judit rather do it?

"I'd rather die."

"Did you hear me speak at the funeral?" Fausta asked. "I hope you saw I took advantage of the opportunity to pour out a few drops of venom on the regime, so no one can say I'm reactionary. What's the matter, Ju?"

Why didn't she tell her the truth? Fausta had had grand passions, and at that primary level would be the person who would understand her best. Judit could simply say: I fell in love with Mañungo Vera last night and I'm going to live with him in Paris, the way they did in the old-time novels. How Fausta would celebrate Judit's capitulation to that romantic word to which Fausta was so addicted! But this midday torpor was too stifling for her to go into ironic explanations and put up with Fausta's overreacting, above all now that a kind of lethargy was making the hangers-on clumsy as they evacuated the plaza, where nothing more was happening except the incredible indifference of the pigeons to the blinding sun. Why tell all now instead of waiting until tonight, when, with her bags already packed, she'd call Fausta up to say a sober and affectionate goodbye, on her own terms?

"Let's go," she said to Marilú.

"I don't want to go."

"Why?"

"I want to stay with Jean-Paul."

"With Jean-Paul and not with Lopita?"

"Not her. She's ugly. With Jean-Paul. She should go."

"Everyone's going to leave at the same time, so just keep quiet."

Lopita was the center of everyone's attention because of the mysterious seduction of her ugliness, part of the terrible subsoil which very few touch because it teems with suffering and humiliation. Laughing the macabre laugh of a funerary idol that had been badly restored and attracted by the music, she dragged Mañungo toward the grey car where the policeman with the mollusklike mouth and acne-pocked cheeks was leaning. They recognized each other, but the policeman preferred not to acknowledge the brief exchange they'd had earlier at the entrance to the cemetery, as if that fact might compromise him with regard to the men whose faces were masked by the opaque windshield. Everyone, including the cripple who came a bit closer on his skateboard and then posed with his hand outstretched, was staring fixedly at Lopita, as if she were something fantastic or dangerous; puzzling at her power to incite hate, love, laughter, respect, fear, and aggression; freeing their fettered imaginations, to study the darkness that is never only what it seems to be. Lopito, smiling but uncomfortable, followed by Judit, tried to get closer to Lopita, but just when Mañungo was about to say a cordial hello to the policeman, Lopita asked Mañungo:

"Want me to dance for you, Uncle?"

"Sure, dance for me."

"No, no, Moira," Lopito begged. He was on the point of stopping her when Judit intercepted him. "Not here in the street, sweetie . . . let's go, come on, please."

"Why not? Let her dance. Don't repress her."

Because it's too hot. No, because she's going to look ridiculous, Lopito wanted to say, but he was afraid of hurting her, and since he couldn't say anything, he turned around. He walked toward the bench where Ada Luz was ruminating Lisboa's definitive goodbye, which he'd pronounced amid slogans shouted out in the cemetery. This relegated her grief to the periphery of the circle that surrounded Lopita. At the center of the circle—in the car, someone had maliciously raised the volume of the music, as if to trap those who were listening— the little girl clapped her hands, spun around like a drunken top, and, holding up her skirts, began to do a Spanish dance, showing the palms of her open hands and moving them in cadence with her horrible little head.

Lopito closed his eyes. He asked Ada Luz for the bottle and tipped it back. He didn't want to see anything but the colored stars that burst behind his tightly closed eyelids. He didn't want to see that his daughter's seduction was so painfully grotesque that in another minute it would cause those fucking cowards to burst into peals of laughter. They would use her to get themselves promoted to the rank of executioner. How could he save her? For the moment, the warm wine was the only thing that soothed the trivial wounds of love.

"What wounds, Lopito?" asked Ada Luz.

Why bother to answer this woman who lacked the sensitivity to understand? Didn't she see his daughter playing the fool by dancing in front of everyone as if she were doing something spectacular? Didn't she see her pudgy little body, her heavy feet, her inability to keep the beat, her inability to hear the melody? In a minute of flamenco, she revealed the drama of someone not gifted in precisely what she announces as her vocation. Lopita was a little monster with leaden feet, an insistent, troublesome little girl, who opened herself to general mockery because she was ugly, clumsy, and ridiculous! How he would have wanted to have an invulnerably beautiful child! One nobody could wound or touch! What a relief, what security he'd have then! How impossible this laughter was, the laughter of these stupid men, laughter that was growing around her, these men who were shouting obscenities at her, urging her on!

Still, he had to accept the humiliating fact that this misshapen dwarf totally possessed his love. The policeman leaning on the hood of the car was laughing: an ignorant brute from whom Lopito had to protect her. He'd kill him when that restrained little laugh turned into a giggle! He clenched his fists and then put them in his pockets as if he were looking for a knife. Lopita, in the center of the music and spurred on by the spectators, was totally absorbed in her ungainly dancing. The helmet of the man in uniform was pushed back on his head, revealing the mollusk of his ignoble orange mouth. What a shame it was to hate him now! Why didn't he protect Moira, use his authority to order her to stop dancing, cut off the mistreatment of all those eyes? She was ugly! ugly! awkward! ridiculous! Why not a different vocation—seamstress, teacher, nun? But the poor thing felt this call for fun and dancing, an irrepressible vocation to which her body did not respond. Then she stumbled over her own feet. The grimace that passed over her big, greenish face when it occurred, and the insecurity of her fat little body and her leaden feet and her short legs transformed the earlier sympathetic laughter into guffaws. Especially the policeman, who was holding his stomach with laughter. Lopito clenched his fists, making a huge mental effort to hold himself back. After all, why wouldn't this poor boy laugh, when his very uniform obliged him to act as an executioner? He, the child's father, was no one, and could therefore not demand the respect for his children that Mañungo could if Lopita were his child.

But of course, the children Mañungo and Judit would have would be very different, ethereal and graceful, destined to dance and be happy, the way he would have wanted his own to be. He had to hate her even though he loved her, with a hatred that would last as long as her ridiculous dance to the music whose loudness had been redoubled by the men in the car, and whose beat Lopita could not follow. Why not? Why not, for God's sake, when every kid in the world could follow a simple beat? Why couldn't his daughter? In what way was she inferior? The spectators were laughing. He had to answer this affront because only he could protect her. The policeman, doubled up with laughter on the hood of the car, was laughing at her, not with her, and Lopito's heart became inflamed at the insult. Pushing his way through the small group, he walked up to the policeman and asked him, "So what are you laughing at?"

The policeman's attitude changed; he straightened up and became tense. Mañungo tried to hold Lopito back, but he wriggled free. Lopita ran to hold on to her father, pulling on his belt, placing herself between him and the men in uniform. The door of the gray car closed and the music stopped. Then the car disappeared, as if its status was much too elevated to a stop a street brawl.

"No, Daddy . . . !"

"Let go of me, you little bitch!"

And moving toward the policemen with a violent shake—while four men with rifles got out of the other vehicle to arrest the drunk for disturbing the peace on a day like this—Lopito freed himself from his daughter, throwing her into Ada Luz's arms, from where she rebounded to join the fray again.

"No, Daddy . . ."

Without even getting free of her, as if the child were merely an outgrowth of his own body, Lopito squared off threateningly in front of the still-smiling policeman and shouted into his face, "Well, what are you laughing at, assholes?"

"Let's show some respect for authority, buddy," warned one of the men in uniform.

"What authority are you talking about, murderer?"

"Shut up, Lopito!" Fausta and Judit were screaming, horrified to see that it was too late. "Don't say something you'll be sorry for."

"He already did," murmured Mañungo.

And Lopito, crazed, went on waving his arms and making frantic gestures. "Why shouldn't I say whatever I like? I *want* to say something I'll be sorry for. Murderers, fucking murderers!"

The police jumped on Lopito, while Mañungo tried to keep him from swinging at the authorities with his soft drunkard's fists. In the scuffle, kicking, elbowing, biting, doing whatever he could, Lopito screamed, wheezing as if his heart were going to jump out of his chest: "Fucking murderers . . . torturers . . . thieves . . . stinking cops . . . it was you who killed Matilde . . . you killed all of them . . . crooks . . . torturers . . ." His voice was drowned out by the fight, his face deformed by repeated blows and blood, his clothing torn and sweaty, tears impinging on his curses and finally transforming them into sobs.

Fausta, Ada Luz, and Judit tried to take the terrified children away. From across the street, don César signaled to Judit to tell her that it would be better in a situation like this to disappear, because this petty incident might have serious consequences. They were all covered with blood and drunken vomit when they finally managed to get the handcuffs on Lopito, who was about to faint but was still sobbing and murmuring: "Murderers . . . ignorant savages . . . one of these days we're going to cut all your heads off . . . assholes . . . torturers. . . ." Through the legs of the police, who didn't see her crawl through, Lopita managed to get to her father and make him shut up. With his two hands manacled, Lopito still managed to swing at his daughter and miss, shouting at her, "Leave me alone, you little shit-ass! Can't you see it's your ugliness that got me into this?"

"No, Daddy, don't cry. It wasn't because I was ugly. Mister, tell him it isn't because I'm ugly, so my poor daddy doesn't cry . . ."

"It's true, kid. I never saw any hootchy-kootchy dancer as ugly as you. You look just like your commie old man."

"Me a communist? Why not? Go fuck yourself! Anarchist, extremist, violent, a nihilist with a bomb in his hand to blow up the world, beginning with all of you sold-out cops . . ."

"That's enough. Put him in the wagon."

Kicking and punching him, the police dragged him to the van, while his friends begged them to excuse Lopito's inexcusable behavior. The police, their teeth flashing fury, warned them that now they'd get what they deserved, that if all of them were creating a commotion at Mrs. Neruda's funeral with those crazy communists and the Manuel Rodríguez people, it must mean that the prisoner was also a communist, and unless they all wanted to get in trouble they should get out of here right now. As for the drunk here, well, he was going to get it but good.

Lopita, meanwhile, was distraught. She still hung on to her father's shirt. Either no one could pry her loose or no one bothered because she was so small she wasn't worth bothering about. Please, please let him go! Lopita's cries were lost amid the arguments don Celedonio was having with the authorities, combined with Fausta's allegations and Mañungo's barely controlled rage. They threw Lopito into the van and drove off.

When they returned to the bench in the plaza, they were all crying. A few steps away from the group, no longer begging, don César was observing them. Don Celedonio and Fausta dropped onto the bench, too exhausted to try to understand what had just happened. Why, why, why . . . ? But everything in this country would be reduced to why, why. To stop the children's tears, they decided to go directly to Chile in Miniature and eat some hot dogs with Ada Luz, who announced that she couldn't go because she had to meet Lisboa to talk over an important subject.

Judit took her aside: "What subject?"

"That's my business."

"You're joining the Party?"

"What if I am?" And she boarded the Pila-Cementerio bus that stopped near them.

Lopita was left with Mañungo and Judit, because Fausta and don Celedonio just could not handle her. Their advice was to go directly to the police station to see what could be done. When they'd gone, don César, who had taken cover behind some columns in the arcade just in case something might happen, came out of the shadows. Scattering the pigeons, he came up to Judit.

"This is serious business."

"I know."

"The cops don't let anyone say things like that."

"I'm going down to the station house to see what I can do."

"Better not."

"Why?"

"Because your name's probably on one of their lists, and now with these modern machines, they can find out about you in a few seconds. No one can hide anymore . . ."

"But I just can't leave Lopito like that."

"If they get you, they get all of us."

"How can I get out of Chile in that case?"

"You can't. There must be someplace you can hide out."

"I have to leave. Tomorrow. They're looking for me. Ricardo Farías was at Matilde's funeral and never took his eyes off me, and he's going to track all of you down, and the women too . . . tell them all, please. And Ada Luz seems to be acting strange about this Lisboa stuff."

"He won't love her anymore, he said, unless she joins the Party."

"What did she say?"

"That's where she was going."

Judit covered her ears and closed her eyes.

"I don't want to know anything more. I want to get out."

"With Mañungo?"

"Yes, with me," Mañungo said.

"She won't be able to leave."

"I want to get out, I'm telling you, don César! I can't stand it anymore! If you'd seen that tomb . . ."

"What tomb?"

"It doesn't matter."

"And what's going to happen to your women? They'll die of hunger. With no work and no one to advise them, no support, or mixed up with those Hindu groups who smoke that crap . . . I just don't know . . ."

"I just don't care anymore. I can't stay."

Don César took off his hat. He was bald. It was the first time in all these years that Judit had ever seen him hatless. Sighing, the amputee said, "Okay. People like you always have ways of landing on your feet. Talk to your cousin, don Freddy Fox. He's been protecting you all these years . . ."

"How do you know . . . ?"

". . . so it won't be any problem for him to get you out of the country so you can marry a rich guy like don Mañungo Vera . . ."

Don Mañungo Vera. Not plain Mañungo. Not Mañungo Vera. And she, protected by Freddy Fox. A couple protected by all kinds of privileges. Don. Don Mañungo: it was a condemnation. People like them, in some way or another, always manage to find tricks to escape from the definitive terror, and everything became a deal between equals who were experts in twisting the truth. She, if that's what she wanted, could do it by some well-timed praise or with a minor sin— begging Freddy, who wouldn't think her marriage to Mañungo would be such a bad idea (even if he was from Chiloé), because he was famous, rich, good-looking, spoke English and French and German correctly: a gentleman, if he could be taught to change his shirt every day. He should play tricks with the truth, abolish his origins, erase his past and begin over again. Yes, she'd swear to Freddy that she'd start all over again if he'd intercede to let her leave Chile, go far away from the frozen genealogical tomb and the hoarse party harangues and the weaving women who drowned her in guilt. Would Freddy then be the ultimate, the supreme All-forgiving?

"Go with Mañungo, Ju," said don César.

"What?"

"Go with Mañungo. Are you two going to get married?"

Why did everyone insist on asking the same question? Was it written on her forehead? Did her feminine body have a smell borrowed from the man's body? Did her hard, blue, mirroring eyes reflect the outline of a guitar, and was her voice the counterpoint to a brutal baritone? No. Of course not. Ridiculous! Sounds like Fausta! Why should they get married if she didn't love him (as she'd just said), and he felt the same way toward her, and they only wanted to explore what would happen to them if they lived together the time a bonfire lasts, until they got tired of feeding it? Get married?

"Never. I'd rather die."

But when she said it, she felt her heart—which she thought immune to such things—breaking with pain for tearing Mañungo out of the land that nurtured him. She told don César she was going with Mañungo to the police. The singer would have to play the part of the hero this time. They had to save Lopito. Maybe Mañungo's fame would help, the way it had last night. Yes, a name like that ought to be good for something.

The taxi brought them to the Santos Dumont station house, standing among empty lots on the north slope of San Cristóbal hill, where the streets began to disappear and there were very few houses. Judit said she was not going near the station house, because for years she'd been leading a shadowy life—not exactly underground but certainly covered up—and she didn't want to draw attention to her having left the country illegally or to the activities of her weavers.

"I have to be so careful . . ."

"You can't say you were very careful last night."

"Last night was different."

"Was it really?"

"Don't start making fun of me."

"Do you swear you'll straighten things out so you can come with me?"

"It makes me sick to my stomach, but I'll do it."

He kissed her until the tears flooded her eyes as she thought about what she'd have to say to Freddy. Mañungo reminded her, "Do you realize we haven't even been able to make love, for God's sake?"

"What do you mean, for God's sake? What's God got to do with it?"
She laughed and they both laughed and hugged because the taxi was
getting to the station. When they got out, Judit said, "It's better that
you talk to them. I'll wait around the corner over there behind the
station house so they don't see me. As soon as you can, come and tell
me how Lopito is."

Mañungo went into the station, and Judit hid. She sat down in the
shade to wait on the stairs of a very modest house that had only these
stairs, the front door, and one window. It seemed to be one-dimen-
sional, a string of rooms and tiny patios where on Sundays the anguishing process of a happy lunch would be enacted, with children
and grandmothers and the smells of frying and onions, and the em-
panadas. All of which she detested but accepted as an annoying festive
ritual.

On the corner of the main street, a taxi stopped. The amputee put
down his skateboard and lowered his body onto it. Judit waved to him.
Don César came over, saying that he too was on their lists and would
also have to hide out. Besides, what influence could a poor man like
him have . . . ? But Mañungo certainly was the hope for getting Lopito
out of their claws, especially because it was well known that the people
in the regime had a weakness for anyone who appeared wearing a
tinsel crown in fan magazines. He had to declare that Lopito was
drunk, that it was Sunday, that more than once Lopito had been to a
sanatorium to dry out.

Then don César got off his skateboard and put it under his arm.
Bouncing along on his hands, he led Judit along the side street that
slowly climbed the hill behind the station. Half a block later, the street
disappeared, replaced by the arid countryside, turning into a mountain covered with thistles and brambles white with dust.

Don César ascended with great difficulty, his skateboard still under
his arm, swinging along on his powerful hands over the stones that
cut his palms. They walked along a chicken-wire fence that ran along
an almost-dry stream and a basketball court that had been laid out
on the lot behind the station. The court was littered with manure,
because the mounted police exercised their horses there. On the other
side of the fence, next to the stream, the underbrush had recently
been cut down, and don César explained that the young recruits were
usually forced to do idiotic things like paint tree trunks and stones
white so they'd learn what discipline was. The weeds had been cleared,
and the hemlock and fennel perfumed the hot afternoon air. Judit

and don César were motionless, staring through the wire, their fingers holding it tightly, contemplating the station house decorated with green pediments and white stones arranged in some incomprehensible order.

"Let's wait," said don César in a low voice.

"For what?"

"For something to happen."

For something to happen. How long had they been waiting for something to happen? Years and years. As the minutes went by, the memory of so many disappearances and deaths, and the hatred that comes with all recollection, accumulated in the two of them. Many thought that there was no other solution to this hideous situation, to which they had been pushed by despair, except violence.

It was for this reason, because she hated violence, and had shown again last night she was incapable of it, that Judit had to run away. Not weapons, not organization, not power, not money: only stones, homemade bombs, a stolen pistol. What did all that mean? Was it violence, a way of giving oneself naive satisfaction in the face of the powerful imported weapons that decimated the poor, childish Manuel Rodríguez people? Don César tried to convince her and bring her back to her old road, when she was underground, at night, in houses without electricity, under grape arbors or behind a tangle of bushes, where they would assemble "infernal machines" that actually killed no one. Run away. Flee. That's what Mañungo was there for—to get her out of the bland footsteps of Ricardo Farías, which were tracing concentric circles around her. And around Mañungo too?

"It was all Lopito's fault," said don César, hanging on to the wire.

"No."

"What are you talking about? Didn't you hear him?"

"Sure. But I know Lopito. It was something else."

"What?"

Judit hesitated. Then she said something she realized was the most absolutely irreparable thing she could have said: "Something . . . you wouldn't understand."

Fortunately don César wasn't paying close attention. His only reply was: "Whose fault is it, then? People have to take responsibility for their actions in a revolution, and what Lopito did, which was so useless, only helped put the cops on alert. Do you think the ones in the gray car didn't identify you and don Mañungo?"

"They might have."

Did don César ever feel guilty, about his thefts for example? About
what he'd stolen last night? About how he'd mistreated Darío? About
forcing his younger daughter into prostitution? Yes, but he shared
that guilt with all of society. She, on the other hand, was alone and
couldn't share her guilt with anyone, because she wasn't one of the
women. Go. Go away. No more questions. Mañungo was immediate:
he should take her away. Except that Lopito was locked up in this
notorious place, whose back entrance she was watching through the
wire her hands clutched.

*I*nside the station, it was as if nothing had happened. Everything was orderly, as it should be; everything was clean and calm and painted white and disinfected. Behind a railing, sitting at a mahogany desk, the corporal of the guard was writing in an enormous book. At another table, another policeman was dialing a number he couldn't seem to reach. From the corridor came a wave of foul air that smelled of chlorine, and from time to time a man in uniform would pass carrying office papers. Four boys were walking around and discussing the fluorescent green shorts they were carrying in their hands. Behind a door, Mañungo heard a voice he at first confused with Lopito's. But he realized it wasn't Lopito because it was speaking with too much emphasis, and just now Lopito must be extremely short of emphasis. He decided that another, begging voice that barely answered the first was his friend's voice, but he couldn't be sure because of the door between them. What the hell had Lopito gotten himself into? What had he gotten them all into? He was filled with uncertainty and hatred—hatred for these mannequins who did not understand Lopito's despair, because they only understood carrying out orders and arresting him for cursing them and, characteristically, not thinking about the consequences of his acts, leaving it to others to be responsible for getting him out.

Mañungo walked up to the corporal writing in the ledger to ask if it would be possible to speak with the commanding officer. Yes, of course, you can speak with him if you don't mind waiting until the interrogation is over, he said. Mañungo explained that the police had just arrested his friend, don Juan López, for a misdemeanor, and that if it was necessary to bail him out he would be happy to do so. The policeman stood up and closed his book, leaving a pencil as a bookmark, and said he'd call the captain. Mañungo should take a seat in the hall. He disappeared through the door through which Lopito's voice could be heard, and it was as if that room, suddenly transparent, had come closer to him with its figures and noises; as if he were seeing it through a zoom lens. He heard the racket of a typewriter, urgent telephone calls, the clamor of people making allegations, moving, calling, answering, but the old door interposed its wood, only letting meaningless sounds pass through. Questioningly, Mañungo's eyes tried to make contact with the eyes of a policeman who was so absorbed in his paperwork that he didn't perceive the anxiety in Mañungo's stare. When the captain appeared, Mañungo immediately offered to pay Lopito's bail.

"There is no bail in this case."

"Why not? He's just another Sunday-afternoon drunk, that's all."

"Is today Sunday? I forgot. But don't try to soft-soap me. There was disrespect for the government, profanity, irreverence, extremist, subversive ideas . . . and besides, the officers feel insulted. That's the worst part. We don't have time to worry about drunks who get violent and political. There are too many of them, and there are too many serious things going on in this country for us to waste our energy on stupid things like this. Criminals like López have to be punished like bad children so they learn their lesson, because in the meantime we have to defend ourselves against real dangers. In the slums they kill us like flies and no one says a word on our behalf. They hate us without realizing that we only want to defend the country against Soviet agents. Yes, they persecute us, they swear to take revenge on us, and this scarecrow, as drunk as a lord, who seems to pride himself on being an intellectual, comes along and insults us. So many protests against the government . . . and he, what does he do? Write poems?"

"Who hasn't protested against the government when he's drunk? It's a Chilean custom, a tradition . . ."

"This case is different. Sit down over there, please, and wait."

Mañungo's voice trembled as he asked, "What are you going to do to him?"

It was the terrible thing, the nightmare that everyone knew would come: the unthinkable poured over Mañungo through the person of Lopito. Torture? Perhaps not. Perhaps only the disgrace of a beating, days in jail on bread and water, delirium tremens filling the cell with monstrous lizards and insects, while the police kept him locked up with his poor demented face stuck to the window as he howled. Perhaps only that. But it justified the fear that began to make the city boil. What were these brutes going to do to that brute Lopito? Would they torture him with their hideous devices, as they did with dissidents, who always came out crippled or brain-damaged, or so full of hatred that only going back to violence satisfied them? It was true that Lopito was disgusting, and violent with the authorities over nothing at all, he had to admit it. But how could you not be violent?

And besides, had Lopito really overreacted? Was Lopita nothing? When the policeman laughed, her father's hypersensitive flesh had retracted painfully, like a clam under the proverbial drop of lemon juice that kills it. That the policeman with bad skin had laughed at Lopita was much more painful than if he'd laughed at Lopito himself, because it was as if he'd mocked his impossible dream of grace. That's why Lopito's shameful tenderness, which he'd hidden under the shell of the *maudit* who bristled with poisoned barbs, exploded.

The fact that Lopito's fury over a purely private, human, and individual thing—which is what the offense committed against his child was—turned into a dangerous political row; that things had no other release except violence and political protest; that all personal pain had to have at least a political subtext, was *something*. Waiting for he didn't know what on the corridor bench, Mañungo—dazed at the realization that he represented so many people, and that so many people represented him—had to accept it the way one accepts the winner's knock-out punch: private life ceased to exist. He was not willing to submit to this condemnation. He would get out immediately, right away, as soon as this mess was cleared up. With Judit. Yes, Judit was necessary because she had an old blue Viyella robe that he hoped to share.

Mañungo felt his time was flying by like a comet that won't return for another millennium, and that he couldn't tie himself to its tail. The only reality was this corridor, where there was nothing for him to do but wait until Lopito's time on the other side of the door, where his voice was no longer audible, was used up. He stood and again walked over to the officer behind the huge open book. The corporal looked up at him. Why didn't he recognize him, now, when he urgently needed to be recognized and admired? These thugs were brutes, as Lopito said; so ignorant, so much a pair of a different, lower level of culture than the one to which Mañungo's music belonged, so much lower that they couldn't admire his music, so that he was no star in their insignificant firmaments.

It was curious that they didn't recognize him. The other one, the one with the acne scars, had recognized him instantly. Why wouldn't this corporal do the same, so that he could follow Judit's advice and use his glittering name as an influence? But he *did* recognize Mañungo. His feigned ignorance was the result of an order given by those in command. It only made the whole thing more daunting.

Lopito's voice behind the door was monotonous and discouraged as he answered questions that someone was writing down. From his desk, the corporal of the guard stared at Mañungo without blinking, without recognizing him because the order was not to recognize him. But how could he hope to have Mañungo believe he didn't recognize him, since, thanks to the infinite transparency everything had acquired, he saw that in a boat in Chiloé an illiterate old lady who sold kelp and lived in the desolate Cucao dunes came toward him and said, "You are Mañungo Vera." Although his identity was assured by that statement, the corporal's disagreeable stare undermined it.

Mañungo wasn't surprised by that vision of the old lady he'd never seen, or by that of the beach and the waves he hadn't evoked in so many years, or by the fact that they were pounding like a maddening tinnitus in the station-house corridor—unless he'd seen it all last night, when that woman, wrapped in shawls, had cut his toenail. But now, as it had last night, transparent time made him recognize as present or past things he'd never actually experienced, but that were taking place simultaneously somewhere else, far or very near, behind the captain's door, or with the huge gates of the landscape open wide. The old kelp seller had recognized him last night. When she pronounced his name, she circumscribed him within a magic ring of letters that told him who he was.

This policeman, on the other hand, refused to recognize him, like the four young cops who trotted by, now wearing their new shorts. One of them—and he malignantly looked away from Mañungo—was the mollusk-mouthed officer who'd spoken to him at the entrance to the cemetery, and later provoked Lopito's outburst. No one wanted to recognize him; perhaps because of the *Caleuche* he'd been turned into something else. If he called this officer, who no doubt knew who he was, so he could corroborate his importance and his glory, the man would say, No, I don't know you, I don't know who you are.

And suppose he were to call Freddy Fox? Hadn't Judit told him to do it?—but only if the situation was really out of hand, because she wasn't willing to suffer any more of Freddy's humiliations, not even to save a life. Wasn't the situation out of hand? No one knew anything yet, everything was happening in secret, in that room, without reasons or explanations, so that later it would be easy to deny, refute, and erase everything. Judit explained without boasting that her cousin Freddy Fox's name was gilded with the gold he'd stolen, and that he controlled the key people in the regime. Mañungo politely asked the officer if he might use the telephone to call don Federico Fox. The corporal, without raising his head from his paperwork, told him it was against orders to let the public use the telephone: this was neither a theater nor a hotel. If he wanted to call his friend—this jerk hadn't even heard of Federico Fox, whose name was on the front pages of all the newspapers!—he should do it from somewhere else. When Mañungo sat down again, the officer said, "Sometimes the ice-cream parlor on the corner lets people use the phone."

Mañungo answered, "It's closed. It's lunchtime. Won't they ever finish in there?"

"I don't know."

He couldn't leave Lopito alone, even for a minute. Lopito was like an invalid child. He'd always been that way, with the effervescence of his enthusiasms that flared up and then died away, leaving only his frailness shivering out there in the cold of the world. What messes would the fool get himself into if Mañungo left him alone? He had to be taken care of. The way the waiters in the café took care of him, tired of seeing him get drunk. The way his friends took care of him, he and Judit. Judit was nothing more than Lopito's friend. In any case, this damned problem was standing between the solution of his problem with Judit and his own future. What to do? Shouldn't he be in a bed with her, wrapped in her long (perhaps too long) and polished arms, making plans for the future which should begin tomorrow with the trip to Chiloé? What was he doing here, in this hallway, freezing despite the heat outside, dark despite the sun, all because of that imbecile Lopito?

He'd been sitting on his wooden bench for half an hour when another door opened—not the one behind which the supposed interrogation was taking place—and three officers came out, leading the prisoner: handcuffed, shirtless, shivering as if he too were cold, followed by an officer and an unkempt old man with rheumy eyes. It wasn't they who captured Mañungo's attention, but the repulsively soft, almost infantile whiteness of his friend's body in comparison with his dark face. Mañungo could not hold back his disgust at seeing not white but discolored flesh: a badly cared-for, unloved, unrespected body; a poor body abandoned like a shred of flesh left for dead, out of indolence or hatred or laziness; a body for which one would feel anger because it hadn't achieved the revelations its owner dreamed of. If he, Mañungo, loved anything, it was his own body, because unlike Lopito's it was the only thing that he could still count on to give him pleasure. As they came toward him around the bend in the hall, he stood up. Lopito didn't look at him. Or rather, he didn't see him, as if his eyes were incapable of focusing on anything that might suggest salvation. He knew he was damned. Damned only because he had always been damned. But as he passed next to Mañungo without looking at him, Lopito stopped.

"Lopito!"

Lopito didn't answer or look at him.

"Where are you taking him?"

"He's being held."

"I know. But where are you taking him now?"

"To work. Come on, let's go."

Lopito didn't move. His features seemed blurred, reddened, like raw meatballs on a plate. Clouds covered his eyes, and a terrible panting came from his concave chest.

"How do you feel?"

Lopito answered with a moan in which Mañungo thought he heard the word "bad," and he turned to the guards.

"Can't you see he's not well?"

The old man with the worn-out suit wiped a drop of scum off his bulging eye with a gray finger and said, "There's nothing wrong with this man."

"But he's on medication."

"Where is it?"

"Where did you leave your medicine, Lopito?"

"Moira threw it away," the other gasped.

Then, raising his handcuffed hands, as if to protect himself, he rested them on his prominent sternum, which precariously supported a rib cage on the verge of collapse.

"See?" said the old man.

"See what?"

"See, he has no medicine, and if he has no medicine it means there's nothing wrong with him. I just took his blood pressure. A little high, but that's it. Mine is much worse, and it doesn't keep me from getting up early in the morning to go to work."

"Let's get going," said the captain to Lopito, who didn't budge. "Get moving."

And he gave him a shove that put Lopito's flaccid frailty into the slowest motion.

"Don't hurt him!" shouted Mañungo.

The sticky-eyed old man looked at him threateningly. "Look, young fellow, I'm the doctor here. I'm the one who says what's wrong with people. I've been in practice for fifty years, so I know enough to tell that there's nothing wrong with this prisoner, just that he's full of the shit the Marxists have pumped into him. It's not the first time I've come across one like this. So get out of the way."

"But don't you see he can barely move? And that difficulty he has in breathing? He could die . . ."

"If he dies, he dies: tough. There's nothing we can do about it."

They pushed Lopito again, and little by little they all moved down the hall. Then the four boys in shorts came in through the other end. One of them had a ball under his arm: that was the one, the one who recognized him, the one with the acne, now that he needed him so desperately to declare his eminence and in that way to get better treatment for Lopito! The boy didn't look at him. Instead he went to the officer and saluted.

"Sir."

"Speak."

"The field is rough and full of horse droppings because the mounted unit exercised there this morning."

"You can't practice?"

"No, sir. Can we . . ."

"No, no. You're off duty. But since we have nothing better to do, we're going out there right now," he said, shoving the prisoner.

This is torture and I'm witnessing it and I can't do a thing, which is another kind of torture: the acting out of those horrifying rumors, those tales told by the exiles at café tables in remote countries, talk that built a chamber of horrors so awful that it took over all corners of memory—torture, beatings, tricks, pain, chains, handcuffs, cells, electricity . . . dogs. Through the walls of the station house, Mañungo could hear barking, as he had last night, and shouts: *Boris! Czar!* How would it be to kiss the scars left by the cattle prod or some other instrument on Judit's thighs? What acrid or sweet taste, what novel texture would that tender, martyred flesh have for his tongue and lips? And all of him, in that brief instant, loved at least that fragment of Judit, her probable scars, completing his love of before with a love like that of Lopita, and his love for his friend being led to infamy.

In a dark cell they'd probably seal his eyes and mouth for committing the simple, subversive act of trying to defend his daughter—and more, he knew, and worse, much worse; but he wanted it to be only that— and they covered his head with a denigrating black hood, which is how these things were done according to what people involved said. But why torture Lopito? What information could he give them? None. Because there was no doubt that Lopito would come apart completely, abjectly, with the first touch of the cattle prod. He wasn't brave. Maybe that was his strength, but like all negative things, in him it was transformed into a sort of luminous pilgrimage to other regions of the mind. Nevertheless, aware of that—of his ability to cry and beg forgiveness and retract and even, under pressure, to betray, although it was horrible to think it—for the first time since he'd returned, Mañungo could feel respect for Lopito, for this ability of his to collapse. He'd give in at the first shock. With no shame, he would break down in tears.

Mañungo saw him disappear at the end of the hall, surrounded by the silent torturers disguised as basketball players and by the doctor and the captain. He couldn't let them proceed with their macabre plan. This was the real danger, the extreme point that Judit had spoken about when she'd mentioned calling Federico Fox for help. He ran out looking for a telephone, because suddenly it seemed the most intolerable thing in the world that Lopito should double up in pain in front of some basketball players.

38

*T*he early-nineteenth-century illustrations of the valley of Santiago del Nuevo Extremo show bald mountains, poor native palm trees isolated within their own shadows, and a village of tiles, patios, and clay. The grays of the steel engraving give a good idea of the rigor of the dusty fields under the blazing sun and blue sky. Very little of that city remains today, and not very much of the countryside that surrounded it then, because nowadays it is camouflaged by exuberant, acclimated European species. The topography in those illustrations seems polished and bare without the caress of willows, poplars, and vineyards, a pure bone structure under a thin skin of soil in which little grows; the conical mountains are a part of a space that prefigures the great desert isolation.

Toward the north of the capital, which faces in the direction of the distant desert, above the square plan of the houses that survived the earthquakes, among the crumbling cement buildings, there seems to settle something like an ancient dust raised by the hooves of the herd that the nostalgia of our elders evokes when they link this zone with their memories of country life.

Even the lunar mountains of Lampa, Batuco, Colina, and Quilicura that appear in the distance above the tile roofs conserve the strict geometry of stark landscape forms seen by our great-grandfathers, now buried in the great neighborhood cemeteries. Everything has changed and yet everything remains overwhelmingly the same in this inert, crumbling zone behind San Cristóbal hill. Urbanism takes the shape of four-sided ruined churches with adobe cloisters, hospitals, schools, and madhouses, convents where nuns embroider sheets for brides who no longer stain them. The edges of this zone fade because of carelessness and misery, and the brambles entangle just beyond the new housing developments, on the flanks of hills made narrow by the sun, where black circles under the thorns gather the animals during the heat.

This old, violated city with its northerly vocation belongs to an infertile country gray with dust, in contrast to the land of rain, grass, and lakes that Mañungo remembered down south. But its austerity moved Judit, who often went out to stroll along these godforsaken streets. They were the opposite of coquettish Bellavista, even though in terms of urban planning they were its consequence. They were Bellavista's opposite, because no Neruda had adopted them and they were untouched by fashion. Which meant that the town fathers did not deem them worthy of their caresses and had forgotten about them. At nightfall, back in her apartment after her long, solitary walks— unless she went to see Ada Luz—Judit would leaf through an album of Rugendas's prints, thinking that perhaps when she was "grown up," as Fausta would say, and in different historical circumstances, she would love to publish an illustrated book comparing these places, then and now, looking for the traces that ruined or ennobled a given view, more and more unrecognizable—that is, until some genius bestowed its eternal face upon it. But it was impossible. There was no time now. The pressures were too great.

With their fingers clutching the wire, their anxious noses pressed to it, hoping that Lopito or Mañungo would emerge from the back of the station house, Judit and don César could see the configuration of the bald mountains that surrounded the city of squares and tiles and sometimes the green refuge of an uncontrollable fig tree. Behind them, the parched, bramble-covered hill slowly but surely grew steeper until it reached, much higher up, beyond the forests, the monumental Virgin who, with her generous, ironic gesture, went on blessing the city, even though she knew it was damned.

But her blessing was not for this sector of the city, to which she turned her back. Through the fence, Judit and don César disconsolately scrutinized the station through hemlock and fennel. It was a fragment of a modest nineteenth-century villa, with its rear patio in the form of a U and a glass-enclosed gallery, and a zinc roof, with a wooden pediment that dissimulated it. A modest, classical house with a moral horizon different from the palaces downtown, the kind of house Judit would have wanted to use in her projected book, a house she imagined with bantam roosters scratching around in the sunbaked yard, and at the edge of a quince grove, worn-out, faded wicker armchairs with cushions made by an invalid sister. Reduced and transformed now, militarized, painted by the police, only part of the original structure's U remained open toward the dry patch in the back, which must have been part of the small orchard. Here they'd set up a basketball court.

Everything's calm, thought Judit. Nothing's happened here, nothing will ever happen, because despite the stones the police had incomprehensibly painted white, the amiable specters of the ancient inhabitants of this place prevailed, a family now scattered, which left no trace in the annals. Tomorrow, when she left for Paris with Mañungo, she wouldn't even bother to tell her sisters: she would disappear. Her niche in the Gothic mausoleum, behind the rose window, would remain unoccupied because that was the destiny of that insignificant space to which they wanted to reduce her. Love Mañungo? Why not? The hard part was the word: desire, yes; love, no. Pleasure was something purely physiological, like urinating or defecating. In the cell, the timid hand that belonged to a brutal person touched her knee, and in the other cells the women were screaming while the dogs with bloody muzzles howled. The laughter of the men was the most brutal part of all. That man had followed her to the cemetery. Last night, she hadn't been able to shoot. And she would run away from her women, who someday would discover her lie and kill her with the cold-bloodedness of classical heroines. Mañungo would take her away. Mañungo, who was going to save Lopito and then perhaps take him away, too, from all this horror. But no. She alone and he alone. Without witnesses to keep track of their lives.

"I'm tired."

"Let's wait."

"For what?"

"For something to happen."

Twice before they'd had this same dialogue, clinging to this same fence, staring at the same basketball court. How long had they been waiting? As the minutes passed and Judit's sweat turned her hair into a sticky mess, the need for violence began to build in them, violence of any kind, even the most humble and immediate, like knocking down the fence, shouting insults, or starting a brush fire. Don César said he needed her help, even though she insisted she was against armed extremism. But what about last night? How could she explain last night? Wasn't that shot in the air an attempt at violence? How could she justify it? So many people were on the verge of carrying out a direct attack, unstructured and without direction. They were doing a job in a very discreet garage in the La Reina district. She and Lopito had made bombs when they were university students. The Manuel Rodríguez Front had bigger bombs, but to join up with them would mean submitting herself to a hierarchy it was necessary to reject.

Making bombs and nothing else and planting them anywhere and scaring the police, the regime, and the people. It was necessary to do that at least because the situation was intolerable, and one of these nights the harmless scavengers would not just carry boxes on their carts, but instead, under the protection of darkness, would sneak into the privileged neighborhoods with bombs under their papers and with people willing to do anything, to attack because it was impossible to go on like this.

What Lopito had done was not stupid; within the confusion of those conspiring against the regime the folly of his despair was legitimate. Coordinated efforts accomplished nothing. It was useless to work in hope of anything now—even the mere hope of surviving in peace was absurd, let alone Lopita's pathetic dream. Only revenge was left. De-stabilize them, make the lives of these sons of bitches impossible. Judit hated don César because he represented the logic of terror. Respon-sibility, action, injustice, vengeance; no subtlety, no shades of meaning, no other sides, no humanity, no personal stories that turned into cases like Lopito, who didn't know what else to do except transform his scream of pain for his daughter into a discharge of political invective.

"Look," she said to don César, as if he hadn't been looking at the same thing she'd been seeing all the time he'd been speaking, clinging to the fence.

Down at the station, the door opened and a group of people came out, among them the four boys in shorts and Lopito, handcuffed and dragging his feet. They seemed to be making fun of him, because their laughter was emphatic and hostile, but Judit couldn't be sure because the scene was developing at such a distance. As they passed out of the shadow of the house into the sun of the court, it was as if they were in a movie, because suddenly their faces whitened and they all looked identical. After a few seconds, however, the differences reappeared. That one was Lopito. They'd taken off his shirt. Judit felt a chill. How could she not recognize, even at a distance, the sick grain of his discolored skin? How could she forget the compassionate re-pugnance of that slippery contact of so many years ago?

They surrounded him, interrogating him, shouting at him. But Lopito, as if one of his cervical vertebrae were broken, did not raise his head at the jokes being made about him. The policemen screamed at him and shoved him, but Judit and don César were too far away to hear what they were saying or to discern anything except the captain's indignation at some negative response from Lopito, while the boys in fluorescent shorts began to practice on the dung-spattered court. The captain made them all quiet down, and asked the prisoner a decisive question. He didn't answer, and all of them, except the basketball players, who had begun to shoot baskets, stood stock-still at the brutality of Lopito's negation. Don César, holding on to the wire, increasingly tense, muttered, "They're going to do something to him."

And Judit was afraid.

"What?"

Don César looked at her without answering and instantly turned back to watch. The captain gave his detail an order, which they obeyed by going into a shed while he himself took Lopito's handcuffs off.

"Are they going to shoot him?" Judit asked.

"No."

"Torture him?"

"They don't torture out of doors."

The three men in uniform reappeared, dragging a huge cement roller they used to flatten the court. The basketball players were shouting and jumping happily because one of them had just scored. The captain ordered them off the court, and they left the ball in the crotch of a quince tree so it wouldn't roll down the hill. He gave another order. They turned the roller over to Lopito.

"No!" shouted Judit in a stricken voice.

And immediately afterward, heedless of the consequences, both of them grabbed the fence and began to shout at the top of their lungs, "Murderers! He's sick! Lopito! He didn't do anything! Lopito!"

But the action was taking place too far away, and in the open space their words dissolved while the first afternoon breeze carried their indignation up the hill without anyone's hearing a thing. Judit cried. Through her tears, through the hemlock and the wire, she saw her friend trying to push and then pull the roller to flatten the court. He could barely move it. The others stood back in the shadow of the station house. They seemed to be laughing or at least to be in a festive mood, these indifferent functionaries, as they perhaps answered Lopito's insults of half an hour ago at the cemetery entrance, insults that still annoyed them. Drunk, extremist, they shouted, urging him on as if he were a draft animal. But they never mentioned Lopita and her ugliness; they didn't realize the meaning of her tiny figure and they'd forgotten her, even as an object of ridicule. Work! That's it, work on this court and leave it nice and smooth while they think about what to do with him for shooting his mouth off! Lopito, dazed by all that was happening, laid his back, which was shining with sweat, on the roller. Judit trembled, imagining his wheezing increased by the effort he was making. When Lopito suddenly stopped to catch his breath, Judit heard the spectators scream at the top of their lungs, "Come on! Back to work, asshole!"

"You were pretty brave before, what's the matter now?"

"These guys ought to get in shape."

"Who told you to stop?"

As he gestured to wipe the sweat off his brow with his wrist, he paused briefly, and his legs gave out. He slowly doubled over while the spectators stopped talking for a second to watch him. He collapsed in a heap. The players stopped their game. They all gathered around the wreck, burning with rage or fear, not to see what had happened to him but to accuse him of laziness and make him get up. But they couldn't do it. The heat seemed to have dissolved his ligaments definitively. One of the spectators took a stethoscope out of his bulging jacket pocket and, bending down, pressed it to Lopito's chest.

"What happened to him?" whispered Judit.

"Why don't they give him a pill?"

"He threw them away. I saw it."

The policemen went back and forth from the station to the place where the body was lying in the sun without anyone's deciding to move the nuisance. They gave him water which he couldn't drink; they patted his hand, they spoke to him, they fanned him with their caps. But the time for breathing was over. After a while, the doctor made a negative gesture, which was both definitive and totally clear.

"Is he dying?" asked Judit, out of false hope.

"No. He must have died already."

Judit relaxed the fingers she had clenched around the fence, and her arms fell to her sides. She let herself drop to a sitting position in the fennel: without realizing it, she was now at don César's height. He was still clinging to the fence, and he too was crying. Not because Lopito was his friend, but because of his and everyone's impotence in this and a thousand other situations. Judit hugged the amputee so she could cry with him, because there was nothing left on the basketball court now but the cement roller on one side and, in a corner, the ball, like a marvelous, unique, and empty fruit in the quince tree with silvery leaves. Judit cried, telling don César that she should have called Freddy Fox, who could have fixed everything—in this case, perhaps even death itself.

But it was all too unforeseen for her to act. Because who would ever have imagined that Lopito was going to die? She shouldn't cry, don César consoled her, it wasn't her fault. She did not enjoy the privileges of omnipotence or having everything be her fault. She shouldn't cry, he said, because Lopito, like all those who dream and who leave their dreams to others, as Lopito left his daughter her impossible dream of grace, is damned. It was not her fault he'd died.

Judit, after cleaning herself up a bit, said it would be better to get Freddy Fox. Don César was against the idea. Why now, when Lopito was dead? Now the only thing that mattered was getting even, hiding out so they could come out of the slums at night and take their revenge on these criminals. Because this, it went without saying, had been a murder. The doctor, along with those in command in the station house, had to have realized that Lopito's physical condition, leaving aside his being drunk, was terrible. Had they done what they did just out of pure unthinking cruelty, to have fun? In the hole of silence opened by death, Judit head the buses rolling along the avenue in the distance and the bells of Recoleta Domínica and La Estampa, where her nanny had secretly taken her to worship Brother Andresito—a plebeian saint her mother would never have approved.

"Let's go," said Judit, already standing, her face stained with tears and dirt.

"Where?"

"To talk with the cops," she answered, starting to run. Don César, hopping onto his skateboard—and not without some pleasure at the idea of rolling down the steep hill, like a macabre child—followed her at top speed, holding on to his hat so it wouldn't blow away. He quickly passed her and then expertly braked at the intersection.

They found Mañungo, who was running back from the ice-cream parlor. They signaled him to hide with them on the side street so the police wouldn't see them together. Judit threw herself into his arms, crying. She described the scene they'd just witnessed on the basketball court while the players were taking their shots. Mañungo knew nothing about the accident. When he heard, he did not collapse. He stiffened at the absurdity of the event, and, hard and cold, pushed Judit aside, saying that this was not the time for sobbing if they were still not sure of what had happened or even if Lopito was dead. Perhaps he'd only fainted. She should calm down. But don César, who knew more, without saying a word moved his head from side to side, giving a verdict Mañungo could not accept. Twisting away from Judit, who had clutched at him with her entire body, he ran to the station house.

Inside, panting with heat and fury, he asked again for don Juan López, and once again the corporal told him to wait. Mañungo asked again in a harsh, rough tone. The corporal politely explained that the captain was about to leave and would see him quite soon.

"How soon?"

"Depends."

"On what?"

"Well, on the work the captain has to finish."

"Suppose he's dead?"

"Who?"

"My friend, Juan López?"

"Nobody's died around here."

"Tell your captain that Mañungo Vera wants to talk to him."

The policeman raised his eyes and lowered them again. He did know. It was a plot. Lopito was dead.

"Wait there, please."

Mañungo sat down again on the same bench where he'd been before telephoning Freddy Fox in Judit's name. He was waiting, but he didn't know what for or why: for the officer to appear, he supposed, or for them to show him Lopito, or for someone to explain something, or for the arrival of Freddy Fox—who'd said he was most honored to speak with a person like him and assured him he'd be there in fifteen minutes, twenty at the most. He could telephone an order, true enough, but nothing was more certain than the imposing physical presence of a VIP like him. Besides, he'd be delighted to meet him personally because he admired him so much.

Behind the doors that opened onto the corridor, he could hear exactly the same voices he'd heard before Lopito's death, as if he were having a friendly chat with the officers. Now those same voices were not as loud, and Mañungo felt a chill at that minute change of tone. Lopito dead? It couldn't be. It wasn't true. It was Judit's mistake, don César's malevolence. Lopito, of "Ich grolle nicht," of the blue Viyella robe, had fallen into the madness of the *Kreisleriana* and now couldn't— or didn't want to—save himself. Because this whole business had not been so different, after all, from tying a night table around his neck and throwing himself into the Rhine. In any case this was the bottom line. Time to add things up. Or subtract them. Or just get the remainder: the unruly Lopito's destiny had been carried out abjectly, as perhaps his own should be carried out, and Judit's, and everyone else's, simply bcause one fine day it becomes impossible to stand things any longer and you shout a bit more than you should.

Mañungo felt the bite of grief when he realized that he did not want to go on living even one minute more in a country capable of killing that idiot Lopito. Nothing meant anything, not Paris and walking at night under Sartre's sacred windows toward the Seine hand in hand with Judit, not a visit to Cortázar's tombstone in the Montparnasse cemetery, a pious act to which he felt he had a right because he'd met Cortázar once. They'd both laughed fraternally because both of them were taller and more awkward than the others at the concert, their beards blacker and their hair longer.

Taking advantage of the corporal's brief absence, Mañungo walked over to the door that muffled the voices. He opened it. The doctor with the rheumy eyes was in shirtsleeves, sitting on the stretcher, and smoking under a sign that said NO SMOKING, chatting with the captain in a low voice as they told dirty stories. They both stood up when he entered.

"What are you doing here?"

"Who let you in?"

"I want to know what happened to don Juan López."

"Show some respect, mister."

"And do you respect anybody?"

"Who are you to ask me questions?"

"Mañungo Vera."

"And who is Mañungo Vera?"

How do I answer him, simply, that *I* am? What the hell! He should just ask his younger subordinates, the ones who were playing basketball, the one who had recognized him right away at the entrance to the cemetery on Recoleta. This captain and this sordid quack with red eyelids and shaking fingers that were lead-colored at the knuckles, and a suit that time had turned a sort of vanilla color, these two were too old to recognize him with the proper enthusiasm, because they belonged to a generation that didn't know him. The famous little captain here could just wait for don Federico Fox to arrive. He would identify Mañungo Vera for them!

The officer took advantage of Mañungo's fleeting perplexity at their perversely refusing to recognize him: "Please get out."

"I'm not leaving until you tell me what you did with Lopito."

"Why would we have done anything to him?"

"You killed him."

"Get out unless you want me to call the guard."

"Go fuck yourself, you stinking cop! You killed Lopito and God knows how many others!"

The doctor had opened the door and was calling the guard. Three men in uniform seized Mañungo, who went on shouting, "Murderers! Criminals! The doctor refused to give Lopito his medicine. You'll pay for this!"

The captain laughed and then became very solemn:

"These are serious accusations. Maybe *you'll* be the one who does the paying."

"What you did isn't serious?"

"We're not to blame if this Mr. López had a heart attack here in the station."

"Sure! He had an attack because you made him do hard labor and he was sick."

"Sick! That's what they call it when they're intellectuals! *Drunk* is what he was! I'm not here to explain things to you or anyone else. I wrote the death certificate."

"Take him away. Take down his statement, and while he waits for the official report on his buddy, lock him up in cell number two," ordered the captain.

Mañungo had been locked up for ten minutes when Judit, who could no longer stand the wait, dared to enter the station to inquire, even though don César begged her not to. The policemen told her that unfortunately Mr. López was incommunicado for the time being. No one could talk to him. And the captain was involved in a questioning, so he couldn't see her either.

Judit asked, "Who's he questioning?"

"A Mr. Vera."

"And you don't know who Mañungo Vera is?"

"There must be lots of Mañungo Veras."

"And lots of Juan Lópezes."

"Right."

"How is Juan López?"

The corporal didn't answer. And without daring to reveal her possibly incriminated identity, Judit walked out of the station, slamming the door behind her to rejoin don César at the intersection. When he heard that Mañungo was being held, don César said, "But Ju . . ."

"What?"

"You have to spread the word."

"To whom?"

"To the newspapers, the television, magazines. The news they're holding Mañungo Vera will go all over the world in fifteen minutes, and the place'll fill up with journalists. The anti-regime propaganda will be tremendous."

Did everything have to be used, then? Wasn't even a drop of pain allowed to go to waste? Was it necessary for the person who took advantage of it first and in the most useful way to metabolize Matilde's poor remains, Lopito's death, Lopita's broken dream, Mañungo's grief over his friend? And was it Judit who had to do this, when her dream, because of all this, now seemed as impossible as any other dream in this country? What might the jailing of Mañungo lead to if she didn't use it before the vultures arrived? Without thinking it over another second, Judit ran to the ice-cream shop to use the telephone.

In ten minutes, journalists eager for exclusives were there, taking statements from the captain, who was cornered and didn't know what to do or say, and from the corporal, who was basking in the notoriety. Voices and more voices demanding that Mañungo make a statement, that he tell his version of the facts, which, of course, would be the version everyone would believe, because Mañungo Vera was Mañungo Vera and he had a juicy baritone voice and a rabbit smile and little eyeglasses with gold frames that had started a fashion.

But unfortunately, insisted the officer, Mañungo Vera was incommunicado until orders came down from his superiors. No one outside the chain of command could change that status. When Freddy Fox finally showed up, sweating and licking his lips, Judit and don César stopped him before he entered the station. Freddy laughed and told them not to worry and to follow him, that he would have Mañungo Vera released. He added that Mañungo could make whatever statements he'd care to make. The news had been spread all over, and the foreign correspondents in Chile waiting for "something to happen" were gathered in the corridor, notebooks, lights, a mass of cables all at the ready, waiting for the release of the star whose mysterious incognito return to Chile was in itself front-page news, to say nothing of his being imprisoned by the regime's police in a station house in the middle of nowhere.

In the corridor, Freddy confronted the officer surrounded by the throng of curious people from the neighborhood through which word of the extraordinary event had run just as it had run through the multitude of reporters. In front of everyone he berated the officer, who was an ignorant hick, a fool for having laid hands on a public figure who was essentially apolitical—and it was of the utmost importance that he remain that way, apolitical, because you can never trust these artists—even if he'd called all of them murderers.

The captain, taciturn now after being so verbose before the arrival of the unforeseen VIP, closeted himself with Freddy in the infirmary to explain the incident of Juan López and his daughter—foolishness, actually, which through no fault of his had turned out badly. He invited his illustrious visitor to please step into the barracks where the uniformed police slept, but before they went, Freddy asked him if he would be so kind as to call in Judit to accompany them: "She's my cousin, who was nice enough to accompany me. I think she knew the deceased . . ." When she came in, she allowed her cousin to kiss her forehead.

In the barracks, the officer lifted the corner of one of the olive-green blankets that covered all the beds, and Lopito's profile in the half-light, his features relaxed by the discreet hand of death, cut off Judit's breathing with the tremendous surprise of the expected. Still, she would not allow herself to cry. She had already cried too much. And she was getting ready to cry even more when they finished interrogating her, to cry not only because of Lopito, but because she saw herself lost, without knowing what would become of her, who she would be, what her face would be, what her heart would be like, because this had changed things so much, nor when hating would not be the only form of existence.

What was Lopito's wife's name? Where did she live? Where did she work? Those questions asked by Freddy and the officer, which she had to answer, were nothing more than a caesura in the implacable rhythm of grief, facts to fill in the sordid forms of any death. What was the name of the modest school where Flora taught sewing, the name of which Lopito hid from almost everyone out of shame? But contemplating that rejuvenated face below the blanket the captain's hand kept raised, Judit realized that since she—and Lopito—had defined themselves through hatred, their lives gave them intolerable pain because of this sad mutilation history had imposed upon them. Lopito's lips moved to whisper to her: Don't go to Paris with Mañungo to extirpate your hatred, because if you do, you'll cease to exist. You can't escape, that's only a sentimental dream belonging to a world that doesn't exist for us. Peace is nothing but a good-natured abstraction in the face of so much blood and death. And with a kind of hunger, Judit recalled the old times of constant danger and the underground life that fleetingly gave her life a pattern. Then the officer dropped the corner of the blanket on Lopito's face.

They left the barracks. In the captain's office, Freddy dialed the minister's private number. After a brief exchange, in which they agreed that the matter of Juan López had been resolved before Freddy reached the station house, the VIP passed the phone to the captain. Holding the phone at some distance from his ear, he heard the minister demand that he free Mañungo Vera immediately and that he not bother him anymore with the other matter; he had no time for nonsense.

A few minutes later, Mañungo walked out of the jail and was instantly besieged by journalists, who asked him how long he'd been held, and why, in a station house in Recoleta, and if his arrest had anything to do with Matilde Neruda's funeral. No, he told them. He was there because of the death of his friend Juan López. And he told them Lopito's old familiar story: misery, alcoholism, the infinite promise that life cheated him of and of which he cheated life, his weak and simultaneously rebellious personality, his defense of his daughter, the abuse committed by the captain who made him push the roller in the hot sun, when Lopito was so obviously ill. Freddy listened to him with a beatific smile on his face, explaining into Judit's ear that a telephone call would be sufficient to alter all those press articles, or eliminate them completely. After all, they didn't control the press for nothing: reality could take the form they chose. The photographers wanted to shoot photos of Lopito and his best friend, the singer perhaps bent over his body as if to identify him, but Mañungo refused.

"Why did you come back to Chile at this particular time?" the reporters asked.

"To stay here."

"For how long?"

"Forever."

"Didn't you say last night in Neruda's house that your visit would be short because you didn't understand the situation your country was in?"

"Now I understand it." He thought for an instant and then went on. "I've changed my plans. In any case, after twenty hours in my country, I can assure you that I have never been clearer on any subject than I am on this matter of staying."

"In order to define your political action?"

"Could be."

"Armed struggle?"

"No, except in self-defense or to defend someone else."

"Songs?"

"I'd like that. But who knows if bombs won't turn out to be the only alternative? It's their fault. Because what can we do when they force us into violence by taking away all our hope? I am not justifying bombs, but I do understand them."

No one was interested in Lopito, because the Juan López affair had become the much more interesting Mañungo Vera affair. The police paperwork was taken care of quickly, thanks to Freddy's intervention, and Judit and Mañungo walked out arm in arm in a few minutes. They hadn't walked more than a few steps when they were joined by don César. In the receding heat, wide bands of shade streaked down from the houses in front of them. Mañungo said he had promised to meet his son at Chile in Miniature, where the boy might perhaps be missing him.

"I don't like your being in a hotel," Judit told him. "It's too easy for people to spy on you. It's . . . well, almost as if you hadn't arrived, or as if . . ."

"As if I weren't going to stay?"

"Come and live in my apartment. Your son can sleep in the room where Lopito slept. It isn't as luxurious as your Paris apartment, but . . ."

". . . but the place comes equipped with a blue Viyella robe . . ."

"What's that got to do with it?"

"Let's go get Jean-Paul."

"What will you say to him?"

"I'll think about it in the taxi."

At that moment they realized that don César had abandoned them, perhaps out of discretion, perhaps because he realized that in one way or another their hatred and his could combine at any moment. They heard his skateboard rolling down the street on the next block. Judit put her arm around Mañungo's waist, and a moment later he put his arm around hers.

"But don't lie to Jean-Paul," Judit begged him. "Don't you dare tell him you're staying because you're in love with me."

Mañungo stopped to look at her, stained with tears, her hair in a mess, in the bright sun.

"But I'm not staying because I'm in love with you. And you know it."

"Why are you staying, then?"

"Didn't you see what happened this afternoon?"

"Of course."

"Then you know why."

Mañungo hailed a cab.

"Shall we go?" he invited Judit, opening the door.

She covered her face with her hands, finally sobbing.

"What's the matter?"

"It's that . . . it's that . . ." she stuttered, ". . . it's that I can deal with anything . . . but not with Lopita . . ."

And she got out, running away as fast as she could.

It was a beautiful toy country: the trees and lakes, the snow-capped mountains made of papier-mâché, the delicacy of the historical buildings reproduced with hyperbolic, invented luxury, the slow coastal channels, the golden beaches, the pampa, the little human dolls and the indolent animals grazing on fields that descended to gorgeous bays with tiny colored boats anchored at the beach. Everything cute and neatly painted in this ideal country: cute but not beautiful, lacking the seed of the terrible, the comic, and the tragic that would give it character.

This picture of perfection was a naive—or not so naive; probably totally intentional—paean to a supposed although clearly weak national progress. LAN CHILE, PROVIDA, COPEC, AMBROSOLI: distinguished companies whose miniature billboards, next to the play highways, demonstrated the nation's power, its order, its cleanliness, the indefatigable industry of its free citizens who lived in peace next to snow-capped volcanoes, perpetually green forests, and eternally blue lakes. This paradisiacal vision was crisscrossed by roads walked by a public astonished to recognize its own portrait in this small magic mirror that allowed them to ask themselves excitedly: Are we really like this?

But perhaps, if it weren't for the fences that separated the miniature landscapes from the persons of normal size and of flesh and blood, the visitors might have destroyed it, trampling its meadows and forests or stealing something, perhaps a toy tree, to take it away as a souvenir, until there would be none left, or destroying for the simple human pleasure of doing evil.

Of course the reality of the entire country couldn't fit into the plot of land the city fathers had assigned for this park. So the imaginative architects were forced to blend fantasy with sound judgment, cutting

or eliminating this or that, abbreviating distances and changing relationships, even erasing whole areas that were either totally uninteresting or monotonous or so poor or difficult to idealize that it was
better to exclude them altogether. It had to be: after all, not everything
can fit into a miniature, and unpleasant things should be left out.

So at the extreme southern tip of this long and narrow country, in
the part where there is no industry to finance the advertising displayed
in the small buildings and perfectly reproduced road signs—DON'T
RUN! AMBROSOLI IS EVERYWHERE!—along the highways, the country
is suddenly cut off by a mass of papier-mâché ice, eliminating by sleight
of hand an entire region. Which made Lopita and Marilú laugh their
heads off at Juan Pablo, because no matter how hard the grief-stricken
child looked along the complicated meanders of the footpath, he could
not find Chiloé, which did not exist, or the girls had convinced him
didn't exist because they had in fact found it, hidden and insignificant,
at the end of a twisted little road next to the water, the entrance to
which they managed to conceal from Jean-Paul. Where, where was
Chiloé? Did it really exist? Or had his father invented it to solve his
problem of not knowing who he was or where he was from, so he
could lie to him that he wasn't from Paris or Chile but from a nonexistent place called Chiloé? Lopita and Marilú, arm in arm behind
him and making fun of him, followed Juan Pablo, who was desperate
as he traced the twists and turns and got nowhere, deciphering sign
after sign without finding Chiloé and with the sensation that he, unlike
Marilú or Lopita, who were self-satisfied and killing themselves to
admire everything just to see how Jean-Paul would react, was from
no place. His blue eyes were full of tears that still weren't falling; his
lips were stuttering, soft, and tremulous.

A little later, when Fausta and Celedonio announced that it was
getting late and that they were tired, the children protested, and don
Celedonio said that if they were going to stay longer he was going to
find a place to sit down. They watched him shuffle off, head bent and
worn out because too many things had happened, limping with his
gold-headed cane until he fell fast asleep under a small willow. Fausta,
who had separated from the children, suddenly stopped at the end
of a path, and, reading the sign, began to call them over, waving her
arms wildly so they would come quickly. The children ran over, and
there, next to the blue channels, on the sweet green shores of one of
the islands hidden in the coves, they saw the sign: CHILOÉ: HOUSES
OVER THE WATER. There were strange wooden buildings on storklike

legs standing in the places where the tides were low, and reflected in
the calm waters of the archipelago was none other than Chiloé. Juan
Pablo smiled triumphantly at the girls, who were charmed by the tiny
houses, so odd, so different from the others.

Fausta was showing the children the islands—especially Jean-Paul,
whom she kept close to her so the heat of her body would alleviate
his homesickness. Lopita, on the other hand, could not keep still because her vital, perpetually renewed happiness would not allow her
to remain calm. Marilú was restless because she was beginning to get
bored.

"*Mais où est le grand bateau?*"

"What ship?"

"Can't you see there's no ship here?" said Lopita.

"*Le bateau magique dont mon père parlait.*"

"Wait . . . wait: you'll see it in a minute, as soon as it gets a little
darker and the fog thickens. Over there!" exclaimed Fausta, pointing
to an island covered with tall trees above which birds were chirping
and a silver cloud gathered, out of which blew a wind that ruffled the
waves in the channels. "Look carefully. You've got to learn to look
carefully, to learn to distinguish the gray of a storm cloud from the
gray which is almost a caress. Being able to tell shades of difference
is an important part of being intelligent. Look beyond the rocky pe-
ninsula where the seal who dared to come so close is bellowing: that's
where the ship of art appears. Wait until there's more fog and the air
fills with sparkles, getting ready for night or rain. Don't you hear the
far-off sound of a groan, the deep bronze bell that rings and rings,
and warns the other boats anchored in the channels that the ship of
art is coming and that they should get out of the way? Pay attention,
Jean-Paul, because if you want to know these things you have to
concentrate on every detail and see all the differences and understand
everything the winds tell you. Don't you hear the music? Tell me what
it is. You should know. Guitars or zithers or mandolins? Listen, they're
playing a saraband, which they say is the devil's dance. Or is it an
habanera? Ah, the slow, slow habaneras I've danced aboard the ship
of art, and what applause I received from Pablo and Matilde and
Celedonio and the others! If we dare go aboard when the ship comes
to this shore at dawn, we can turn into anything we like, the way your
father has changed. But if we stay on land, we'll always be the same,
prisoners of this lying miniature, because lies are always miniatures.
Would you like to go aboard? Do you hear the sailors singing, the

dizziness of the rigadoons, the laughter and the mandolins, the bronze bell ringing in the fog? Look, look, over there. Finally, our ship of art is coming . . . look how the eyes of its lights get bigger in the fog, how its bells sing, filling the air. And do you know why they sing? Because anyone who boards the ship of art and joins in its dances and eats at its banquet is transported to the south, beyond this papier-mâché ice, to a land where the trees give breadfruit and the air is warm and the birds have colored ruffles on their necks, and there's a golden city there that glitters like the sails on the ship, and anyone who dares embark on the ship of art lives forever, and will never know the insult of death."

Fausta thought she ought to write all that down, those things she'd repeated and heard so many times, but that no one knew how to tell properly. She hadn't published anything for so long that perhaps this might be the right moment to renew her own ticket on the ship of art, so that her right to it wouldn't be forgotten! In any case, she'd talk it over with don Celedonio, she thought, as she went on spinning this legend for naive ears that were perhaps not so naive . . . the songs, the sirens, the good wizards, the medicine trees, the classic interventions of supernatural beings.

The ecstatic children listened to her, along with other people, who had come to see Chile in Miniature to participate in the fantasy of a prosperous but even more nonexistent country than the one being described by this bard in a long black gown, who appeared to be in a state of rapture. They were enchanted listening to the woman—soon it was revealed that she was a very famous writer, a bit of a witch—who was improvising for her grandchildren. Yes, they had to be her grandchildren, they whispered, the perfect family in the perfect country. Just look at the tenderness with which she hugs the boy with blond hair—perhaps a bit too long; with what security the ugly little girl dressed in red holds on to her matriarchal thighs; and the wonder with which the slightly older girl, who has sinfully made herself up, contemplates her grandmother! Many visitors had already heard the legend of the ship that plowed the somber channels and submerged in them to rise again renewed from their waters, but never so well told, nor so delicately expressed as by the slightly hoarse voice of this mysterious lady in mythological clothing, who raised her arms thickly hung with primitive jewelry like a phantom worthy of being in the crew of the ship she spoke of.

Fausta was so enchanted by her own story that it took her an instant to realize that the children had slipped out of her embrace and were running, shouting with joy, toward the entrance of Chile in Miniature. Lopita led the pack, singing:

DON'T RUN! AMBROSOLI IS EVERYWHERE!

She was in front of the other two because she was the first to see the person who first pulled her and then the others out of the world of legend. But as soon as she saw them run, Fausta too began to run, impeded by her high heels and her voluminous skirts, because she didn't want to lose sight of them and because she didn't understand or see (because she was so short-sighted) what had started the stampede. A bit farther ahead she realized when she heard Lopita, who was running at full speed with open arms, screaming:

"Uncle Mañungo! Uncle Mañungo!"

And behind Marilú was shouting:

"Uncle! Uncle! Now it's my turn!"

And Jean-Paul, trying to push through, shouted:

"*Papa, papa!*" He was happy to see him return alone. "*Papa. Où étais-tu?*"

The three children clung to Mañungo's long legs. But despite the demands of his son and Marilú's insisting that now it was her turn, now it was her turn, it was Lopita he lifted into his arms and set on his shoulders. She began to wave to everyone as Mañungo carried her toward Fausta, who saw that his face had been painfully changed by a wicked wizard. She did not have to ask him what had happened.

CASTRO (CHILOÉ), JANUARY 1985—SANTIAGO DE CHILE, FEBRUARY 1986

ABOUT THE AUTHOR

JOSÉ DONOSO was born in 1924 in Santiago, Chile. After three years at the Instituto Pedagógico of the University of Chile, he was awarded a Doherty Foundation Scholarship for two years' study at Princeton, where he received his B.A. in 1951. He has taught English language and literature at the Instituto Pedagógico of the Catholic University of Santiago and held an appointment in the School of Journalism at the University of Chile. In 1956 he received Santiago's Municipal Prize for short stories, and later the Chile-Italia Prize for journalism. In 1962 he received the William Faulkner Foundation Prize for *Coronation*, the first of his novels to be published in the United States. José Donoso was visiting lecturer at the Writers' Workshop at the University of Iowa from 1965 to 1967. His other books include *The Obscene Bird of Night* (1973), *Sacred Families* (1977), and *A House in the Country* (1983), which was awarded the Critics' Prize in Spain. He lived in Europe for fifteen years, but now makes his home in Chile with his wife and married daughter.